THE LOVES OF CATRIN

Iris Gower

CORGI BOOKS

THE LOVES OF CATRIN
A CORGI BOOK 0 552 13631 X

First published in Great Britain by Robert Hale & Company as two separate titles: *The Copper Cloud* (1976) and *Return to Tip Row* (1977).

This omnibus edition first published in Great Britain by Century Hutchinson Ltd.

PRINTING HISTORY
Century Hutchinson edition published 1986
Century Hutchinson edition reprinted 1986
Century Hutchinson edition reissued 1987
Corgi edition published 1990
Corgi edition reprinted 1990
Corgi edition reprinted 1992
Corgi edition reprinted 1993
Corgi edition reprinted 1995

This book is set in 10/12pt Plantin by
County Typesetters, Margate, Kent.

Corgi Books are published by Transworld Publishers Ltd,
61–63 Uxbridge Road, Ealing, London W5 5SA,
in Australia by Transworld Publishers (Australia) Pty Ltd,
15–25 Helles Avenue, Moorebank, NSW 2170,
and in New Zealand by Transworld Publishers (NZ) Ltd,
3 William Pickering Drive, Albany, Auckland.

Printed and bound in Great Britain by
Cox & Wyman Ltd, Reading, Berkshire

To my children
Susan, Angela, Tudor and Paul,
with love.

Part One

THE COPPER CLOUD

ONE

It was cool on the Town Hill with a soft breeze blowing in from the sea. Above me stood the gaunt walls of the Jews' burying ground and I shivered a little, thrusting my breasts forward against the tightness of my bodice, knowing that Dylan was watching me.

'You are like a witch, there, girl,' he said quietly, 'with your hair hanging loose to your waist, for shame, Catrin.'

Smiling, I turned my back on him, looking across the valley to where the smoke rolled heavenward in great bursts from the forest of chimneys above the copper works. A shower of sparks lit up the night sky and a change of wind brought to me the unmistakable smell of sulphur.

'Poor dad is down there.' I sank down on to my knees beside Dylan, slipping my hand into his. 'He's on the night watch so God help us, come morning, between coughing and shouting he'll shake the whole house to bits before he goes to bed.'

Dylan's arm encircled me, holding me close.

'It's a good thing your dad is working, you wouldn't have dared come up here with me otherwise.'

His fingers strayed towards my breast and I let them stay there, sweet and warm while I turned my face towards him waiting for his kiss. We clung together and inside me was a shooting of flames more spectacular than anything the copper works could offer.

Dylan moved closer, he was breathing hard, he pressed his leg between mine and I could not breathe for the feeling that flamed through me.

Suddenly, I pushed him away and started to run down the hill full pelt.

'Wait, Catrin, damn you!' He was between anger and laughter. 'Watch you don't trip over your petticoats, girl.'

He threw himself upon me and together we rolled over the rough, stunted grass that snapped drily under our weight.

'You are wild, a vixen!' Dylan's voice was husky and his lips were warm on my neck. He was heavy, hard against me and mingled with my excitement was a strange, nameless fear.

'Let me up,' I said, very quiet. 'I want to go home.' He moved away from me, his eyes gleaming. 'I'm warning you, girl, you'll tease me once too often.'

I smoothed down my skirts, suddenly shy which was foolish because I'd known Dylan Morgan ever since we were no bigger than penny chickens.

Nervously, I brushed the hair away from my face, 'I'm going back to Tip Row,' I said, 'are you coming?'

He took my hand. 'You are just a little girl really,' he said, 'you look so womanly that I forget you are no more than sixteen years old.'

We made our way in silence over the rough ground of the hill and down into the valley. We were under the smoke now, it rose above us into the night sky, incandescent like specks of gold that diminished even the moon's light.

We stopped on the corner of the row and Dylan drew me close, his lips briefly touching mine.

'See you tomorrow, girl.' He was casual now, a different person to the one he'd been up on the hill. I clung to him

10

for a moment trying to recapture the thrill I'd felt earlier but it was gone.

'Good night, Catrin,' he said, and then he was striding away whistling into the darkness.

Mam had a pot on the fire, she glanced up her face like a red cheeked apple from the heat.

'So you've come home at last, have you?' she said, sharp as a needle. 'It's a sad thing for a woman when her only daughter runs wild. A good name you'll make for yourself Catrin Owen and be thankful your dad's not here.'

Even as she grumbled, she was busy spooning up some rabbit stew for my supper and the smell made my mouth water.

She stood watching me eat for a moment, her arms folded over her ample breasts and there was a small frown between her eyes.

'Your father is asking down the works for a job for you, it's time enough, Catrin, spoiled you silly we have.'

I looked at her in dismay, 'What, me work in the copper, mam, shall I be pushing barrow loads of ore for a living?'

Mam turned away, 'Don't make a fuss now, most girls of your age have been working for donkey's years.'

I pushed the bowl of stew away from me, there was a heaviness in the pit of my stomach as I looked at mam in askance. She sat beside me.

'I know you've always wanted to be a scholar, Catrin, and I'm proud that you read and write so good. Well, you were a pupil at Mrs Vivian's school and that's honour enough for anyone.' She touched my shoulder, 'But the money is needed, good girl.'

She rose and went to her rocking chair near the fire, her face turned away from me.

'In any case, you'll only be taking the water round to the

men in the tew gangs and you'll be earning five shillings a week remember.'

I brightened up a bit at the thought of being paid, I'd have to give some of it to mam but the rest of my money would be mine to do as I pleased with.

'When am I to start?' I asked, still a bit apprehensive and mam looked into the fire.

'Your father changes shifts on Monday,' she said. 'You are to go in with him so you won't feel strange among all the men.'

In the silence came the sudden patter of feet on the wooden stairs and my brother poked his head round the door, a wicked gleam in his eyes.

'I'm hungry, mam,' he said, lisping a little and mam tried to look angry.

'Hungry? You don't know what hungry is until your stomach sticks to your backbone.' She softened and held out her arms. 'Oh, all right then, come and have a bite of stew.'

He sat next to me, his cold feet finding some warmth against my legs.

He dipped some bread into the stew mam placed before him and sucked on it with greedy delight.

Mam went to the door swinging it open to look down the row, the glare from the works illumined her face, big boned and somehow noble.

'I wonder where that eldest boy has got to now,' she fretted, 'I hope to God he isn't in another brawl down at the beer house.'

'Sit down, mam,' I was a bit impatient, 'our Huw is a man and if he can't look after himself now he never will.'

I suppose I was jealous, Huw was mam's first born and she had a soft spot for him that she did not bother to conceal.

She returned to her seat. 'Come on, Iorwerth, boy,' she said, 'bed.'

He stood by the fire staring into the glow, his black curls gleaming almost red from the flames. 'Tuck me in, Catrin?' he asked and I caught his hand laughing.

The door opened with startling suddenness and Huw swung into the room bringing the feel of the cold night air with him. He moved lithely like a cat with a cat's contained power and when he was in the room no-one could ignore him.

'What do you think, mam?' He said quickly, pausing for effect. Mam got to her feet, her dark eyes alive with interest.

'Don't keep me in suspense, boyo,' she said, her hand over her heart, 'I'm always afraid of news, it's usually bad.'

Huw stood beside me and the blue of his eyes shone red in the firelight.

'There is going to be a trial against the Vivians, have you ever heard the like of it?'

Mam shook her head in bewilderment, a lock of her black hair escaping from its pins, hanging down to her shoulder, giving her a youthful look.

'A trial, what are you talking about, Huw, no-one can do that to the Vivians can they?'

Huw nodded. 'It seems someone can, the trial will be held in Carmarthen and the men are talking about getting up a crowd of workers to walk down there.' He laughed. 'Me and dad will be among the first to find out what's going on.'

Mam was at a loss, not fully understanding the situation but fearing that it boded ill for us.

Huw, well pleased with the effect of his words, seated himself on a stool and faced mam.

'They are saying that Mr Vivian has spoiled the Hafod with the smoke from the copper works. One man claims that his wife got the lung disease from it.'

Mam clucked her tongue, 'To bring Mr Vivian to trial, what is the world coming to?' A new thought struck her. 'Huw! What if they close the works?' There was something almost like panic in her eyes and Huw was quick to reassure her.

'Don't be soft, mam, it won't come to that, the men won't stand for it and nor will Mr Vivian.'

Mam was not easily comforted. 'I do not want any of you going into the mines. I always said no man of mine would go into the black hell under ground, not after the way my own father died coughing up his lungs until there was nothing left of them.'

Huw put his arm around her and she was gentled like a beast in a thunder storm, her eyes soft as they looked at him.

'Don't worry, mam, Mr Vivian is sure to have the best of lawyers to speak for him and if you don't smile I'll be sorry I told you.'

Mam smiled and went to the hob and picking up the big black kettle, 'Let's have a cup of tea, is it?' She stirred up the fire and the warmth spilled out over me as I stood still holding Iorwerth's hand.

'*Duw*, people don't realize when they're well off,' Mam would not leave the subject alone, now. I knew she would worry at it like a dog with a bone. 'The copper workers live better than anyone in the town of Swansea.'

Huw leaned forward, tense on the edge of his seat. 'Have you never wondered why they pay us so well to work the copper, mam?'

Huw's big hands twisted together. 'Haven't you heard

dad coughing of a morning? And think how you complain of the pain in your joints when the smoke is down over us like a dirty old blanket.'

'Well, boy, we have to put up with things like that. Money doesn't come for nothing and we Owens have always been hard workers.' Mam's voice was sharp. 'There is food to put in our bellies now and no fear of you or dad being crushed under a fall like those poor dabs in the coal measures.'

'The smoke is bad, mam,' Huw said obstinately. 'It isn't natural for folk to live under a cloud of stinking fumes that brings sickness to the stomach.'

Mam's eyes were bright as she warmed to the challenge. 'But the smoke drives away the ague, you know that's true enough.'

Huw shrugged his big shoulders, 'Maybe, mam, but if it is so harmless why will nothing grow around here? Kilvey hill is stripped of all its grass and even the few flowers that are left have all the colour bleached out of them.'

Mam had no answer to that. 'Well, give me the copper before the coal any day,' she said and closed her lips tightly.

Huw sighed, 'Mam you haven't seen the sheds where me and dad have to work, it's a living hell with the heat enough to take the skin off your nose and a glare that would melt the eyes in your head if you looked at it for too long.'

I frowned and shook my head and Huw stopped talking as mam sniffed, touching her eye with the corner of her apron. She knew how to behave when she was beaten in an argument. Huw winked at me and changed the subject.

'*Duw*, Catrin, you should see my new girl friend. I've been going out with her for three nights in a row and she's

15

still saying "no," to me, there's resistance for you,' he chuckled, 'but I'll have her before many more nights have passed.'

Mam tutted furiously, 'Don't talk like that, Huw, your father waited for me until we were all respectable and married, never laid a finger on me he didn't.'

Huw made a face behind her back and I put my hand across my mouth to stop myself from laughing out loud.

'Ah well, mam,' Huw said sounding as serious as a chapel deacon, 'Times have changed since you were young.'

I smiled at him, 'Well you've tried out every girl in the Hafod so where is this one from?'

'She's a farmer's daughter from up the valley a bit. A well built girl is Rhian with fine legs on her and a pair of tits that would make any man's mouth water.' He laughed wickedly, 'I'll have my work cut out laying that one down in the hay!'

Mam slapped Huw across the head, 'That's not proper talk, Huw Owen, and I won't have the like of it in my kitchen. You treat young girls with respect or I'll have dad to take his belt off to you, big as you are.'

Huw ducked out of her way. 'My guess is that dad sowed all his wild oats before he met you, mam, but he picked a good woman in the end, I'll give him that.'

I could see that behind her anger mam was pleased, her dark eyes gleamed and she stood up straighter, tall and imposing not small like me.

'Well, I'm going to bed now,' she scooped Iorwerth up in her arms and his head dropped tiredly against her shoulder. 'Don't you two stop down here all night talking, do you hear?'

There was silence in the kitchen as we heard the creaking of the boards above us. Huw sat in mam's

16

rocking chair, his long legs stretched out towards the fire. A big boned family we Owens are but something went missing when I was conceived and I was cast from a different mould to the others. I used to resent my smallness but now that I was becoming a woman I realized that there was something about me made men want to protect me and it was a heady feeling.

Huw grinned at me, 'Bed for you, isn't it? You are only a baby still in spite of the fact that your dress is getting too tight on you.'

I felt the colour hot in my cheeks. 'Anyone can tell you've been to the beer shop,' I said. 'The fine words come easy then, how was it your Rhian was able to resist you?'

'She went off in a huff,' Huw said, 'just because I tore her bodice a little.' He laughed his devil's laugh. 'Just wait until she knows what I can offer her, she won't be able to leave me alone then.'

There was a great deal of truth in his words, I'd known girls to wait outside the copper works by the hour for a chance to talk to him. Thinking of work reminded me.

'Oh, Huw,' I said quickly, 'mam says I must come to work in the copper next week, taking water to the men.' I sat on the floor and tucked my bare feet up under my skirt. 'What is it really like, Huw?'

His eyes were sombre, more black than blue as he stared down at me.

'As hot as hell itself,' he said, 'when the smoke is down and blowing into the sheds you think you are going to die of suffocation.'

He stared at me for a long moment in silence, 'Go to bed, little sister,' he ruffled my hair, 'if you start me off again I'll never stop and I'm in for an early shift in the morning.'

I rose from the floor and kissed Huw goodnight, his hair was dark and springy under my hand. 'Sleep well,' I said softly and made my way to the narrow slope at the back of the house where I slept alone. I stared through the cracked window at the searing light from the works but at last my eyelids began to droop and sleep came softly over me.

A little while later, I was disturbed by a noise from the kitchen, there was a bump and then a retching so violent it turned my stomach.

I pulled a shawl over my shift and slipped soundlessly from the slope, mam was crouching over a bowl, her face white and beaded with sweat and her big hands were shaking.

A sudden fear tore at me, I hurried to her side. 'Mam what it is?' I said in a whisper, 'have you caught the ague?'

She shook her head splashing water over her face and her eyes were weary.

'There is nothing for you to worry about, Catrin, girl,' she said rubbing her hair from her forehead, 'it is just that your father has filled me up once more with child.'

TWO

'I hope you are ready for work, now, Catrin.' Mam shouted to me from inside the privy and I shook out my clean, stiff apron so that the folds crackled.

'Yes, I'm as ready as I'll ever be, mam.' I pulled the ribbons tight around my waist so that they pinched me in smaller and I pushed out my breasts, making myself appear as tall and womanly as possible, all the men in the sheds would be giving me a good looking over, no doubt.

Dad came in from the yard, his face morning fresh from the cold water. He pulled on his shirt and tucked the tail into his trousers.

'You look as neat as a pin,' he said, his eyes twinkling, 'I'll be proud as billyo to show off my daughter down at the works.'

I leaned against my father feeling suddenly sick with fright. 'I will be all right won't I dad? I don't want to go making a fool of myself in front of all those men.'

He looked down at me from his great height, he was a big man, broad of shoulder and tanned on the face and neck by the heat of the furnace and the blast of the copper. Like all copper men he had come to be almost the same colour as the metal he worked.

'You'll be all right girl, you're my daughter aren't you?'

He patted my head, 'Now, no more nonsense or we'll both be late. Where's Huw?'

'He's gone on ahead, dad.' My mouth was dry, I pulled

19

on my shawl. I wanted to bawl like a baby.

Mam came in from the privy and washed herself in the bowl of cold water near the door. Her eyes were red and though she was smiling, her mouth wobbled a bit as she looked at me.

'Take care, Catrin,' she said, not touching me. 'And Will, look out for her, mind, I won't have the men speaking vulgarities in her hearing.'

Dad winked at me. 'I'll see that Mr Vivian himself is civil to our Catrin, don't you worry.'

Mam allowed a smile to creep into her eyes, 'Go on with you Will,' she reached up and pulled his head down to kiss him and then she turned to me.

'Careful how you behave yourself with those men, do you hear me?'

I heard the break in her voice and hugged her quickly. 'I'll be as right as a rooster, don't you worry, mam.'

Out in the row I glanced back for a moment to see mam waving and I felt as if I was leaving her for ever.

Above the houses was the black face of the tip and in the early morning light, mists rose from it like the silver lines left by snails.

'You can't learn about the world if you don't live in it girl,' dad said.

We walked the rest of the way in silence but his presence was a warm solid comfort and I felt closer to him than I'd ever been before.

Nothing in my life had prepared me for the noise and the blasting, searing heat of the copper sheds. I stood for a moment on the threshold, shivering with fright. Dad's hand was on my arm then, drawing me gently forward. Beads of perspiration rose at once over my face and it was as if the breath had left my body.

'Roll up your sleeves, Catrin,' dad said gently, 'and

don't worry, you'll soon get used to things here, the fountain where you get the water is right alongside the works so you are lucky. I've heard that in Port Tennant the girls have to walk a mile or more with casks of water tied to the back of a donkey, there's a heavy job if you like.'

He hesitated, not knowing how to leave me.

'Go on to your work, dad,' I said quickly, 'I'll be all right, and what I don't know I can ask.'

'All right then girl, I'm off but remember to come round to the gangs every two hours without fail, the heat is killing without a draught of water to settle the dust.'

As he strode from me into the deeper heat of the sheds I almost called him back. I wanted to run home and to take dad and Huw away from the hell of this terrible place. But I knew that I would do no such thing.

The heat seemed to wrap itself around me like a blanket and I dipped my hand into the cask and scooped some of the water into my mouth. It was delicious as it trickled over my tongue and down the back of my throat that had become dry already.

'Hey, girlie, how about bringing some of that water to us!' I spun round startled, splashing water on to my clean apron.

'Oh, it's you, Mr Morgan,' I said in relief. 'I didn't recognize you for a minute.'

He rubbed a hand over his sweat grimed face and laughed.

'No, I don't suppose you did, Catrin, it's a devil of a job to know anyone once the dust gets over them. You'll be as dirty as the rest of us before your shift is over.' He took a jug of water from my hand and downed it in one mightly gulp. I heard it run, gurgling down his throat and I watched in fascination.

'So you and our Dylan are courting now, is that right?' Mr Morgan winked his eye at me, 'A fine boy but he needs a bit of restraint, like a young animal, see.'

I knew my colour was rising but Mr Morgan had remembered his job.

'*Duw*, bring the casks over here, girlie, my gang are as dry as a dog's old bone!'

I followed him quickly, nervous as I drew nearer to the roar of the furnace.

'Give it another pole, Dai!' Mr Morgan shouted and one of the men thrust a slim tree trunk into the glare. It disappeared as if being fed to some unearthly creature and I shuddered in spite of the heat.

I heard Huw's voice then, calling me, 'What about your brother, doesn't he deserve a drink?'

He pulled off his shirt and was wringing it out. 'See that Catrin?' he said with pride, 'good honest sweat.' He turned to look at me. 'All right?'

I nodded, unable to tell him it was like the devil's hell to me, I'd never get used to it.

By the end of the shift, I felt I had taken more than I could bear, I almost fell out into the street, glad of the sweet soft rain that was soothing to my burnt hands and face. Mam met me at the door, her face anxious.

'Come inside, Catrin. Are you very tired, girl?' she put her arms around my shoulders and drew me to a chair.

'It wasn't too bad mam,' I lied, 'but it's nice to be home again.' I leaned back thankfully, drinking in the familiar sights and smells of my home, loving it all more than I'd ever thought possible, Iorwerth came and sat beside me, catching my hand in his.

'Where have you been?' he said, 'I was looking for you all day.'

Tears misted my eyes as I rubbed my hand over his

springy curls. He stared up at me in open curiosity. 'You're all dirty Catrin, look at her mam, isn't she dirty?'

Mam smiled, 'Yes she is. Take your clothes off Catrin, I'll wash you down before you have something to eat.'

I stripped off my clothes and stood naked near the fire and mam folded an old piece of flannel and washed me just as she'd done when I was a baby.

'You'll feel better once you've eaten,' she said. 'Here, put on your clean petticoat.'

When mam put a dish of chicken and potato pie before me I realized how hungry I'd been and I tackled it with relish. Mam sat watching me, I could see how tired she was, there were dark circles under her eyes.

'How are you feeling today, mam?' I asked, between mouthfuls and she tucked up a piece of stray hair and puffed out her lips in a sigh.

'A bit sick now and then but that's only to be expected in my condition.

'I've missed you, *cariad*.' Mam stared at me over the bundle of sewing on her lap. 'It hasn't been like home without you.'

I couldn't speak. If I did I would blurt out the truth that I hated every minute of the time I had spent in the sheds. I would beg mam to let me stay at home but I couldn't, not now with the new baby on the way.

I managed to smile, 'It's quite exciting being a working girl and just wait until I get paid, I'll be rich.'

I don't think I fooled mam for one moment but she went back to her sewing with renewed concentration as if every stitch she put into the cloth was of the utmost importance.

Dad and Huw came in together, their shift was three hours longer than mine and I wondered how they stood it, day after day with no hope of ever getting out of the works.

23

Dad picked me up off the chair swinging me around in his strong arms and I could smell the copper and see the tiny, glinting specks on his hair.

'She's the best water girl in the whole of the Hafod works!' He rubbed his coarse face against me and I winced pulling away from him but enjoying the bit of nonsense.

Huw was already at the table and as soon as he cleared his plate he went out into the yard to wash himself down. I knew he was eager to be off into the valleys to meet his girl.

He returned to the kitchen, bright drops of water like a halo on his hair. He was handsome all right, no wonder the girls chased him.

'Are you going out to meet Dylan Morgan tonight, Catrin?' he said, shrugging his shoulders into his coat. 'Go on it will do you the world of good, a bit of courting is just what you need to brighten you up after a hard day's work.' He winked at me and suddenly I felt more cheerful. It would be good to tell Dylan all about the sheds.

Mam looked up at me anxiously. 'Are you sure you want to go out? You look as if bed might be the best place for you.'

'Oh, leave her go out mam,' Huw said, 'we'll go together.'

As soon as we were out of the house, Huw put his arm on my shoulder.

'Not all a bed of roses in the sheds is it love? But you'll get used to it, we all do, more fool us!'

'I'll never get used to it,' I said bluntly, 'not if I live to be a hundred and one.'

Dylan was waiting for me on the corner of the row and my heart dipped when I saw his thin frame, relaxed and loose limbed as he lounged against the wall.

Huw dug me in the ribs, 'Watch what you are at, now, Catrin, no funny business.'

'Look who's talking!' I slapped his hand and then he strode away into the gathering dusk, whistling cheerfully.

'Good thing he's your brother,' Dylan slipped his arm around my waist, 'otherwise I'd be tempted to punch his face in.'

I laughed, 'You'd be lucky, Huw is twice as big as you are.' I glanced up at him, teasing him, 'See how broad his shoulders are compared to yours. Still, I think you are handsome too, in a skinny sort of way.'

I laughed and flew down the street, my tiredness forgotten and Dylan was pounding behind me calling my name. When he caught up with me, we walked arm in arm, calm now, up the small hill that led to the Cwmbwrla stream. I sat down on a flat stone and Dylan sat beside me.

'How did you like working down at the Hafod, then?' he said, 'Did you meet any boys who were half as good looking as me?'

I shook my head, 'I couldn't tell, they were all sweating like horses and covered in dust. I didn't even recognize your father at first.'

Dylan sighed and picked some small stones out of the stream. 'You wouldn't catch me working there! Not even for the extra money, I'm quite happy on the barge with Dai the Quay and the old horse for company.'

'I hate it!' I said fiercely, 'But how can I tell mam how bad it is when she needs the extra money?'

Dylan cupped my face in his hands, 'It won't be for long, Catrin,' he said softly. 'I'll marry you as soon as you are old enough.'

'Who says so?' Some devil inside me made me contrary,

'I've never said I'll be your wife have I?'

He pulled me close to him, 'If you don't marry me, you'll never marry anyone else that's for sure. I'd kill you first and him alongside of you.'

I reached up and drew his head down to mine, catching his hand and placing it over my breast. I heard his quick intake of breath with pleasure, it was good to feel power over a man.

'You she-devil, I'm not made of stone.' He lay against me, his body hard with desire.

'I could force you so easily,' he said softly, 'you are so small under my hands, so weak.'

His mouth was eager, his tongue searching and a flame leapt inside me so that I pulled away from him in fright and clutched my stomach.

'Catrin,' the way he said my name turned my blood to water, 'I won't hurt you I promise I won't.'

I stared at him in the gloom trying to read the expression in his eyes. I wanted him, I wanted to feel his body pierce mine. For a moment I wavered like a leaf in the wind and then I thought of mam, with another baby in her belly and common sense returned.

I stood up and brushed the dry stalks of grass from my skirt.

'I'd better go home,' I stared down at Dylan lying tortured on the ground and I felt older than him and wiser. 'I love you, Dylan,' I said, 'but what if we had a child?'

He got to his feet, 'Women are all alike!' he said bitterly, 'they lead you on to expect wonderful things then they leave you with nothing but their fears.'

Angrily I slapped his face, 'What do you know of other women you devil, is it usual for you to be rolling in the grass with anyone you fancy?'

His eyes seemed to burn. 'There are some who like what

I have to offer them,' he said, 'and no pretence of being good, either.'

I stared at him, cut to the quick. 'I'm not making any pretence boyo and you should be down on your knees thanking God that my father can't hear you, he'd have the skin off your back and no mistake.'

'Oh, get to hell out of here!' Dylan pushed me roughly and I slipped losing my balance so that I fell, scraping my arm as I went.

He turned on his heel and strode away without a backward glance and I longed to cry out and bring him back. Instead I pulled myself to my feet.

'I hate you, you mongrel dog!' I shouted and he turned in mid stride and came back to where I stood.

'You sound like a fish wife!' He slapped me hard across my face and the tears poured down my cheeks as if I was a baby. He took me in his arms then, cradling me, kissing me and I could feel his heart beating as if it were in my own breast. He kissed my hair and wiped away my tears with his fingers.

'Come on, I'll take you home,' he said very quiet, 'It's been a long and hard day and I'm sorry I lost my temper.'

Arm in arm, walking slowly like an old couple, we made our way down the valley towards Tip Row.

THREE

'It's not fair, mam,' I said in anger, 'why should all the men go down to Carmarthen and leave us womenfolk behind?'

Mam shook her head, her eyes fixed on her sewing.

I paced around the kitchen, my hands on my hips biting my lip in concentration. There had to be a way that I could go with the men.

'I've got it mam!' I sat down on a chair facing her, 'I could dress up in some of Huw's old clothes, tuck my hair up under a hat and who would know the difference?'

Mam looked up at me, her eyes wide. 'Oh Catrin, girl, I don't think that would be very proper would it?'

'To hell with proper!' I forgot myself in my excitement, 'come on mam, don't tell me you wouldn't have done the same thing at my age.'

She looked thoughtful and I could see the idea intrigued her.

'What could happen to me with dad and Huw along?' I pressed my argument home and mam was convinced.

'I suppose it would be all right,' she said slowly, 'I wonder if I could find an old pair of trousers to fit you.'

She rose from her rocking chair, her eyes dark like my own were filled with excitement. 'I'll go and look.'

She went into the slope and pulled a tin box out from under the bed.

'There's stuff here from years back,' she said, 'there

must be something I could stitch up for you.'

She drew out a pair of trousers big in the waist but the right length and a jacket with a hole in one of the sleeves.

She wagged her finger at me. 'Don't forget, Carmarthen is a long way and the men will no doubt call at every beer house on the way.'

She sank back into her chair. 'I don't know what we're all treating the trial like a Sunday school outing for. If it goes against Mr Vivian we could all be in trouble.'

'Don't worry, mam,' I said, full of confidence, 'the men will not let that happen.'

'It's not up to the men,' mam said, 'it all rests on those clever lawyers that have come down from England.'

'Sir James Scarlett is good, mam, I've heard the men talk about him down at the works, like a preacher he is in his eloquence.'

'I hope so, *cariad*, there's a lot rests on that man's shoulders, I pray to God he knows it.'

It was a cold Thursday morning when the crowd set off from the corner of Tip Row to walk the long miles to the town of Carmarthen.

I turned up my coat collar, glad of the comfort of thick flannel shirt that effectively concealed the shape of my breasts. It was strange to be one of the crowd, unnoticed and free to think my own thoughts in the silence of the early hours.

At first, the men walked in silence but once the sun started creeping up into the sky, voices were raised in song and the lively tune lifted our spirits and gave zest to our footsteps.

I caught sight of Dylan at the front of the crowd and behind him, his father, head sunk on chest as if he was still half asleep.

There was a shout from one of the men, 'The beer house

is open along here, shall we stop for one boys?'

There was a rush towards the low whitewashed building and as the men pushed their way inside, I felt my first qualms of uneasiness.

Once across the sawdust covered floor, I picked for myself a dark corner seat and took out some bread and cheese mam had given me for breakfast. A jug of ale was placed firmly on the table before me and I glanced up nervously to see Huw standing over me.

'Hello there,' he said, 'as you seem to be a stranger, I thought I'd treat you to a drink. Go on, boyo, it's on me.'

The strong taste of the ale made my stomach turn and I put it down and went back to my bread and cheese.

'You are not going to insult me by leaving it, are you?' Huw said, 'Drink it man, if you know what's good for you.' His bunched fist was under my nose and I looked up and saw that his eyes were full of laughter.

'You snake!' I whispered fiercely, 'you knew it was me all the time, didn't you? And you made me drink that vile stuff.'

He sat down beside me. 'Mam was worried. At the last moment she made me promise to look after you so it seems I'm stuck with the job.'

'Does dad know?' I asked fearfully and Huw shook his head.

'Better not let him find out, either or it will be you and me both sent home and good-bye to the trial.'

The men began to trickle back on to the roadway and Huw held me back until we were well behind the rest.

'Look down by here.' He pointed to the ground and as I bent forward he scraped up some dew covered earth and rubbed it over my face.

'It will hide your lack of beard,' he said, laughing, 'that's something you and mam didn't think about.'

He strode out at a good pace to catch up with the others and I hurried after him, wondering at the freedom trousers gave me. It was a new sensation not to have skirts and petticoats wrapping themselves around my legs.

It took several long, weary hours before we reached Carmarthen what with the ale drinking and then the men going behind bushes to relieve themselves.

There was an air of excitement in the town, the streets were crowded with people and the drifting scent of fresh baked bread brought water to my mouth.

I saw Dylan whistle to a huddle of giggling girls, he stopped for a moment beside a big blonde and she simpered at him from under her bonnet, all curls and ribbons. I clenched my fists, the colour high in my cheeks as I passed them.

'Isn't he dainty for a boy, then?' The blonde girl gave me a push, '*Duw* I could pick him up and put him in my pocket!' She made a swipe at my hat and I ducked quickly away from her, my fear of discovery fractionally greater than my desire to scratch out her eyes.

Dad led the men up to the doors of the assize court and held up his hand. A murmur of disappointment rippled through the crowd as dad's booming voice announced that the court was full.

'Listen, boys,' dad said, 'Sir James Scarlett is speaking, be quiet and I'll tell you what he says.'

He bent his great neck, head on one side, straining to hear every word.

'He's talking about 'noxious effluvia,' dad winked, 'it sounds all very serious doesn't it?'

There was laughter among the men as they settled themselves on the grass and dad lifted his hand for silence.

'Oh, this bit is good, Sir James says it was the cholera not the copper that kept visitors away from Swansea last year,' he shook his head, 'Isn't learning a great thing?'

Carefully, I wormed my way through the men, I wanted to hear the great Sir James for myself, I hadn't walked all this way to listen to dad.

Behind my father's back, I slipped on all fours through the half open doors and crouched down behind a seat. Sir James' voice rang out with force and authority, never before had I heard English spoken with such splendour. I listened hard trying to find the sense of the fine words he was using.

'It is a remarkable fact that, although the cholera was in the various works in Glamorgan,' he said grandly, 'it never visited the copper works and all employed in them remained perfectly healthy.'

I stared in awe at the great man, fine and regal he was but he was mistaken in his words because I knew of two young brothers who worked in the copper and both of them had been taken by the cholera.

The gentlemen of the jury were staring up at Sir James as if he were God himself come down from heaven and he had such an air of goodness and truth about him that I didn't blame them.

A timid man with sparse hair seemed to be trying to explain how many years ago his wife and children had been affected by the smoke as they were travelling through Swansea. No one paid him much attention and he soon lapsed into silence.

I yawned, it was stuffy in the courthouse and a slant of sun held me in a pool of honey warmth. With an effort, I crawled out into the freshness of the air, moving around the outskirts of the crowd of men. Many of them were lying back, shading their eyes from the sun, tired after the long walk and cheated of the excitement of actually seeing the great man in person.

I was feeling the effect of the ale I had drunk and I found my way to the back of the building hoping to find a privy. Instead, I came across a thicket of bushes that suited my purpose just as well. I was quick about my business and I was just leaving the shelter of the trees when I saw I wasn't the only one to seek relief in the green dimness.

He was a little older than my brother Huw, I decided. Tall and leaned, dressed well. He nodded when he saw me and calmly continued to unbutton his trousers.

'Hello, lad,' he said in a fine English voice, 'a call of nature must be obeyed whatever great issues are at stake.'

I stood rooted to the spot watching him, I had never seen a grown man exposed in such a way before. The colour flew to my cheeks as I tried to back away.

'Don't be embarrassed, lad,' he said kindly, 'I know this place isn't exactly private but needs must when the devil drives.'

He laughed and before I could move his hand came up and knocked the cap from my head, I don't know which of us was more dismayed as my hair tumbled on to my shoulders. He quickly did up his buttons and the clean pink of his skin was tinged with red.

Suddenly into the silence, I began to laugh and after a moment he joined in with me, flinging back his head so the voice rolled from him as resonant as any Welsh man's.

I snatched up my hat, the silly grin still on my face. 'Quick, help me put up my hair before any one catches us or we'll have a great deal of explaining to do.'

He came closer and I could see that his eyes were a clear, direct blue.

'Is it usual for Welsh girls to dress up as men?' His fingers were deft, tucking up the wisps of hair into my hat.

'Don't be soft!' I said quickly, on the defensive, 'I wanted to come with the men down from Swansea, they wouldn't have let me near if they'd realized I wasn't one of the boys.'

We pushed our way through the trees and I was pleased by the way he held the branches for me to pass.

'What do you hope to learn from the trial?' he asked, and I looked at him in surprise.

'Learn?' I said, 'I don't know anything about that, I just want the copper works to go on as they always have so that dad and my brother will have a job to go to every day.'

He sighed, 'You needn't worry, then, Sir James will win the case, it's a foregone conclusion.'

I looked at him sharply struck by something in his voice.

'Don't you want him to win, then?' He took my arm, his eyes meeting mine squarely.

'Surely you realize what harm the copper smoke is doing?' He shook his head, 'It destroys all your vegetation for a start and causes all sorts of complaints in your live stock. Heaven knows what it is doing to the workers.'

I stared back at him, using mam's arguments. 'All I know is that we are not starving to death nor does my father have to grovel in the dirty blackness of the pit!' In sudden anger I pulled away from him, what could he know of our life, him with his fine English airs?

'I don't know why I'm even bothering to talk to you,' I said petulantly but just the same I stayed where I was. He smiled at me so charmingly that I could not help the corners of my mouth turning up.

'What is your name?' he asked softly and there was an interest I would have been a fool not to have seen.

'Catrin,' I said, suddenly shy, 'Catrin Owen.' I slanted my eyes at him admiring the vigour that surrounded him and the ease with which he slipped his arm around my waist.

'You are a lovely girl, Catrin, even though you are not dressed like one,' he said, 'Do you work for Mr Vivian?'

I nodded, 'Yes, I bring water to the men on the furnaces. They work in the face of the molten copper and the thirst that comes on them is a cruel thing.'

'Poor, Catrin,' he said softly and I stiffened, drawing away from him.

'I do not need pity,' I said a little sharp and he saw his mistake very quickly.

'Of course not, please accept my apologies.' He followed me as I walked a little ahead of him and I glanced back at him, full of curiosity.

'Who are you, then?' The words came out in a rush, more of a challenge than a question but he smiled all the same.

'I'm John Richards, I'm with Sir James Scarlett's retinue.'

'Retinue?' I repeated the word after him, 'he's not royal is he?'

John laughed, throwing back his head in a way that I found very appealing.

'He's not royal but he is one of the finest legal minds in England.'

'Well trust Mr Vivian to have the best.' There was a slight tinge of sarcasm in my voice that was not lost on him.

'You see, Catrin, you do have opinions on the matter after all.'

'Oh, shut up, boyo!' I said, stung to be caught out, 'you are too deep for me. All I know is that without Mr Vivian there would be no work for me except the pits.'

'Let's forget all about Mr Vivian,' John leaned forward,

'this is a lovely day and we are wasting it.' He drew me to him and kissed me full on the lips.

I drew away from him breathlessly, 'Go away with you!' I said and my voice shook. 'A fine silly pair we must look with me dressed like this.'

He smiled wryly. 'You are right, Catrin and I must return to the courthouse though with the deepest regret, I assure you. Perhaps I will see you again when the trial is over?'

He didn't wait for an answer but strode away from me, his long slim legs making short work of the distance to the courthouse.

I was crestfallen now that my adventure was over and there was a strange sense of loss inside me as I remembered John's kiss.

'Where in hell's name have you been?' Huw was scowling down at me as I joined the men on the grassy bank. He gripped my arm tightly and I winced.

'I've been having a *pisio* in the bushes, no harm in that now is there?'

Huw relaxed, shaking his head a little. 'I'm afraid to let you out of my sight, girl, you're nothing but a pest,' he said, but there was laughter in his eyes.

The hot afternoon sun began to move across the sky and a chill wind came with the evening air. The men began to pack their belongings in preparation for the march home. It was sad to leave Carmarthen without knowing the outcome of the trial which was still dragging on behind the closed doors of the courthouse.

One of the farmers went up to dad, putting a friendly hand on his shoulder. 'Don't worry, boys,' he said, 'I'll ride after you as soon as we have any news.'

My legs were stiff as we started to walk in the direction

of Swansea. I edged closer to Huw's towering strength and he dropped back a bit, his arm supporting me.

'It won't be long, girl,' he said encouragingly, 'we'll soon be home.'

FOUR

I awoke to the ringing of church bells and for a moment as I lay dazed in the grey light of the morning, I thought it must be Sunday. There was a sudden booming noise that almost shook me out of bed and I ran from the slope into the kitchen to see what was happening.

There was a hammering at the door and dad clattered down the stairs blinding and cursing until he saw me standing there.

'*Duw*, get some clothes on you, girl,' he said, 'what is happening round here, is it the end of the world?'

Mr Morgan poked his head round the door. 'The case has been won,' he said in his best deacon's voice, 'Mr Vivian has been cleared of all charges.'

The booming noise shook the house again and dad swore.

'What the hell is that, Morgan, boy?' he said, going to the door and looking out.

'The cannons are being fired to let people know the good news.' Mr Morgan was full of importance and dad grunted.

'I didn't know we had any bloody cannons in Swansea,' dad said a bit sharp, 'well Morgan come in or go out, please yourself but for God's sake shut the door.'

Mam tutted, stirring some life into the fire. 'There's no call to swear, Will. Catrin go and call Huw, that boy sleeps like the dead.'

Huw must have heard the commotion, he came down the stairs, his hair ruffled, blinking the sleep from his eyes.

'*Duw*, there's a noise,' he said sitting down at the table, 'did I hear you say the Vivians have won the case, Mr Morgan?'

'That's right boyo, though you don't look wide awake enough to take it all in yet, that's what comes of too many night time activities. Oh I've seen you, boyo, galavanting with the girls,' Mr Morgan was almost dribbling into his scarf at the memory.

Huw grinned, 'Don't you wish you were young again? I bet you'd run the girls into the ground.'

Mr Morgan shook his head mournfully and a drip fell off the end of his long nose.

'Met my Lizzie too soon, I did, she took all the life out of me and then when I was too old to look for anything else she went as cold as a November mist on me,' he sighed. 'The only thing we go to bed for now is to sleep.'

'Outside, you men if that's the sort of talk I'm going to have to hear.'

Mam sounded angry but I could see she was dying to laugh, she had never liked Lizzie Morgan.

There was a knock on the door and mam raised her hands in despair. 'Open it up, Catrin,' she said, 'you might as well let the whole row in here.'

Dylan was leaning against the door frame. 'Dad,' he shouted, winking at me, 'our mam says you'd better get home and have your breakfast before it goes cold.'

Mr Morgan rose to his feet at once, 'I'm coming son, I had to tell the good news didn't I.'

'Don't tell me that, tell mam, she's the one after your blood.'

He made a sign to me to go outside and I pulled the door

shut behind me hoping mam wouldn't notice.

'Did you enjoy the walk down to Carmarthen, then?' I asked in all innocence and Dylan made a face.

'Oh, it was all right, quiet, you know and we didn't see much of the trial.'

'And did you smile at any pretty girls when you were on the road?' I asked and Dylan gave me a quick look.

'Of course not, *cariad*, everyone knows there's none so pretty as Swansea girls.'

I laughed and he stopped walking. 'If that brother of yours has been filling your head with lies I'll give him a black eye!' he said furiously. I put my arm around his neck and rubbed my cheek against his remembering with a feeling of guilt how good the Englishman's lips had felt on mine.

'No, Dylan *bach*, Huw said nothing except that it was a very long walk.'

I grimaced thinking of my blistered feet and aching bones, it had been a longer walk than I'd anticipated.

'Well Mr Vivian has won,' I said and Dylan smiled down at me.

'Don't look so gloomy then, anyone would think it was the end of the world. Shall I see you tonight, after work?' He looked up at the fingers of light stretching across the sky. 'It will be a good day for being on the barge, no rain about and the smoke keeping high.' He sighed deeply. 'I don't know how you can work cooped up all day.'

'Don't rub it in,' I said, 'there's not very much I can do about it is there?'

He bent down and kissed me on the nose oblivious to the men walking behind us. The streets were filling now, everyone wanted to be at the copper works early to talk over the news about the trial.

'So long, girl,' Dylan waved his hand and cut down a

side street towards the canal. I envied him, his life on the smooth flowing water, under the fresh sky and seeing the excitement of the unloading of ore on the docks, his was a good life.

I made my way straight to the sheds and instead of the usual steady movements of the men at work, there were groups of them standing idle before the furnaces, talking on the tops of their voices. 'What's going on here, then, it's like a May day carnival, are these men or a gaggle of cockle women?'

I turned to see a short man with enormous shoulders and bulging arms that showed strongly even through the rough flannel of his shirt.

'Oh, you're new here, aren't you?' I said, 'there's been a trial against the owner of the works but everything is all right now.'

He grinned, 'I'm glad to hear it young lady, I didn't like the thought of working for a place that was in trouble.'

'Oh, Mr Vivian isn't in trouble,' I said, shocked. 'It was about the smoke, see.'

'Smoke, what's wrong with smoke above the furnaces? I've never seen a copper works without smoke.'

I laughed, 'You'd better talk to my dad, he's the leader of the tew gang over there. He'll tell you all about the smoke and anything else you would like to know.'

He chucked me under the chin, his big fist hard in spite of his playfulness.

'I'm Tom Williams, girl, you remember me because I like to drink ale instead of water.'

'Well, I only bring water,' I said flatly, 'no one has ever asked for ale.'

He laughed, 'I'm different, see,' he dipped his hand in his pocket. 'For every pint of ale you bring me I'll give you a penny, how's that for a bargain?'

41

I shrugged, 'All right, so long as dad doesn't mind I'll do it.'

He went over to talk to dad and with a sigh I settled myself down to get on with my work.

By the time I met Dylan that night, I could hardly keep my eyes open. It had been a hard day tired as I was from the long walk to Carmarthen the day before.

Without a word, he took my hand and led me to our favourite spot on the Town Hill and I sank down on to the ground with a sigh of relief.

'*Duw* there's tired I am, my back feels fit to break.' I leaned up on my elbow and looked down into the valley, along the snaking line of the river, topped, as it always was, with wreaths of smoke and copper dust. If I rounded the headland, I would be able to see far out across the pewter waves that brushed the curving coast line.

'I feel free as a bird when the wind is in my face and the smell of the salt comes up strong from the sea.' I lifted my arms up as if to touch the sky and Dylan caught me by the waist, rolling the pair of us over and over on the rough ground.

'Stop it,' I said breathlessly, 'you'll make me tear my petticoats and then mam will be asking what I've been up to.'

Dylan cupped my face in his hands. 'And what will you tell her?' he said, quite serious.

I tried to twist away. 'I don't get up to anything so what's to say?'

His hands were quick and strong over my body and the breath seemed to have left me. I clung to his mouth when it pressed against mine and there were strong longings inside me. I pushed him away abruptly and drew my knees to my chin.

Mam had told me of these feelings, she said it was

42

nature playing tricks on us so that children would be born. But had mam ever known the wild sweet thrill of strong hands exploring her body. I tried to picture them, mam and dad locked in an embrace and suddenly I giggled.

'What's funny?' Dylan was lying on his back staring up at the sky.

'I don't know if I should tell you.' I stared into his dark eyes and he swung himself nearer so that his head rested in my lap.

'Go on,' he coaxed, 'you can tell me what secret thoughts are hiding behind that innocent face.'

'I was trying to imagine mam and dad kissing,' I said, 'do you think they ever do, kiss I mean? Or do they just lay together and make children?'

'*Duw* what things you think of, girl, there are too many thoughts in this head of yours that's the trouble, you should listen to your feelings more.'

'Aye,' I said pushing him away, 'and then I'd be landed with a baby, no doubt.'

Dylan got to his feet, 'You're nothing but a book worm, you should be in my arms begging me to love you but there you sit trying to reason everything out. Why do you have to look inside everyone, why not take them as they are?'

He strode off down the hill and I sat there in the lonely silence wondering what to do next.

'Dylan!' My voice was carried away on the salt tinged breeze and slowly, I began to make my way down the hill.

He was waiting for me at the bottom, staring away from me his face remote and somehow unfamiliar. There in the dimness, he was a man, not the boy I'd known ever since we were children.

Curious, in a frightened sort of way, I took his arm and drew him under the shadow of the trees. He leaned against

43

me and I could feel the hardness of him. Unbidden came the memory of John Richards standing in the bushes revealing himself so carelessly, thinking I was a boy and suddenly I wanted to find out more about Dylan. I moved my hand slowly and he was still, waiting. My hand trembled and I heard Dylan take a ragged breath as I touched him exploringly.

'How strange a man is made,' I said in awe and Dylan was cold, with perspiration on his face like silver beads in the moonlight.

He moved urgently and he was live and pulsating beneath my hand. I knew there was danger in him, some primitive need that could drive him against all reason.

I was away from him before he knew what was happening, running as fast as a hare with a hound after him. Through the valley and across the stream until I was in sight of Tip Row, only then did I slow my pace to a sedate walk.

I let myself into the kitchen and there was the warm, hot smell of cakes, spicy and sweet, bringing water to the mouth.

'Where have you been till this hour, girl?' Mam said in concern, 'you should have gone to bed hours ago, you must be worn to a rag.'

I sat near the fire and I was still trembling and mam's sharp eyes missed nothing.

'You've been up the hill with Dylan,' she said. 'Well be careful, my girl, or you'll end up with a big belly and then what will your dad say?'

'The feelings are so beautiful mam,' I said, 'they pull at me, inside the way the sight of the sea against the mountains makes me want to cry. Are they bad feelings, mam?'

Mam touched my hair. 'No of course they're not bad, it's the most natural thing in the world to feel longing for a man. But there's no pleasure without payment, that's the truth of it.'

I glanced at her stomach swelling under her apron. 'Do you have a baby every time you do it?' I was bold in my ignorance and a smile came to mam's eyes.

'No, not every time otherwise the house would be over run with children. We never know when the seed is going to take root.'

She put a cake out for me. 'It's easier for me to talk than for you to listen but there will be plenty of time for satisfying your curiosity when you are settled upon who you will marry, until then put it out of your mind.'

'Yes mam,' I said knowing there was sense in her words.

I went to my bed in the slope, glad to lay my hot face against the cool pillow with it's faint scent of lavender. In spite of my weariness, I found it hard to settle down to sleep and when eventually I slipped into a fitful doze, I dreamed of John Richards standing before me with his trousers unbuttoned and a smile of invitation on his face.

'Here you are, Mr Williams, I've brought your ale.' I handed him the foaming mug and he winked at me, flexing his big arms.

'See these muscles, little missy? It's not the ladling that does it, it's all the beer I drink, isn't that right boys?'

As he lifted the mug, his arm glinted with sweat and copper dust and I watched him throw back his head and drain the ale in one gulp. He wiped his mouth with the back of his hand but there was still bits of foam nestling in his moustache.

'Beautiful, little missy, that will keep me going for another few hours in this hell hole.'

He went to take his turn, ladling out the shimmering molten copper into the big iron pots. As I watched, he deftly turned the long handle of the ladle so that the copper ran like a smooth glowing river.

'Catrin, bring us water, will you?' Huw was calling me and as I drew near to him he pinched my nose so that the dust flew all over me and I sneezed.

'Behave yourself, Huw,' I gasped, 'you'll have a shin if I kick you.'

He drank thirstily of the clear water to cool the heat of the dust on his throat.

He winked at me. 'I'm taking Rhian up on the hill tonight, I mean to have her if it's the last thing I do.' He grinned. 'Could you say no to a handsome man like me? If I wasn't your brother, that is.'

I gave him a push. 'Oh, go back to your work, chasing after girls is all you ever think about.'

'Well what else is there? Without it there's nothing but bed, to work and up every morning with the cockerels.'

'Come on, Huw,' I said. 'It's not like you to be so grim.' I slipped my hand into my apron pocket and brought out a cake mam had given me. 'Here eat this, it might bring a smile back to your miserable face again.'

I went on my rounds with the water but even as the men joked with me, I was lost in my own thoughts. Huw was right enough, most of his time was spent in the copper, it was eating us up even mam wasn't free of it, the big smouldering tip was outside her doorstep shutting off the sunlight.

Inside me there stirred a desire to be out of it all. If only I could have grown up to be a teacher, dressed in good skirts and fresh smelling blouses with a brooch at my throat and my hair neat on my head.

I brushed my hand over my face, it was time for me to fill up the water casks. For a few minutes, I would be under the sun and away from the noise and dust and terrible draining heat of the sheds.

FIVE

Mam was not well. Her face beneath the heavy coil of black hair, was pinched and drawn and there was a colour about her I did not like to see.

'Catrin, you must stay at home and look after your mam.' Dad sounded angry but there was fear in every line of his face.

Mam pleated the corners of her apron with nervous fingers, frowning up at dad. 'But Will, what if she loses her job?' Her head fell back wearily against the chair and there were shadows like bruises under her eyes.

'Don't worry about that.' Dad tied a piece of leather around his leg, pressing it well down over his boot as a protection from the copper splashes. 'She won't lose her job.' He stood up, his great height almost filling the kitchen. Huw went to the door and looked at dad uncertainly.

'Be off with the two of you,' mam said, flapping her hands at them, 'standing by there won't do anyone any good and do you think I've never carried a child in my womb before?'

Once the door closed behind the men, mam slumped into her chair, all her energy spent.

'There's such a pain inside me, Catrin, girl,' she almost whispered the words. 'Go down to Mrs Lloyd's and get me a remedy, will you?'

Waves of panic took my breath away and I gripped the

smooth edge of the table trying to control my shaking hands.

'Have just a small plate of bread and milk before I go mam,' I coaxed, 'and perhaps a bit of honey over it, would you like that?'

She nodded, 'All right then, girl, I'll try to eat a little bit, it might bring some warmth to me.'

Iorwerth stumbled down the stairs, his eyes still heavy with sleep.

'Can I have some bread and milk, too, Catrin?' He showed me his dimples and I quickly put out another plate for him. He leaned over mam, his silky black hair against her stomach and I saw her wince. Quickly I pulled on my shawl.

'I won't be long, mam.' It was quiet in the row and I made good time down to Mrs Lloyd's cottage. She was sitting at her half open door an old pipe in her mouth and it was sending forth clouds of smoke almost as evil as that from the stacks of the copper works.

Her lined face sat upon her shoulders as if she had no neck but when she smiled, her teeth were as white and strong as those of a girl.

'I want a remedy for mam,' I said and she stared at me with unblinking eyes, not moving a muscle. I put my hand in my pocket and drew out some coins and she took them counting them rapidly and with great skill.

'Better come inside, then,' she said and timidly I followed her into the dimness of her kitchen. 'Your mother's got a child in her belly but her time's not come yet. She doesn't want to slip the young 'un does she?'

I shook my head vigorously, 'No, she has bad pains, can you give her something to ease them?'

She looked at me thoughtfully for a minute, puffing steadily on her pipe.

'Angelica,' she said, 'it is the herb of the sun.' She took a small brown bowl from the shelf, 'Angelica steeped in vinegar, your mam must drink the liquid and smell the roots then she will have comfort and warmth to ease her pains.'

'Thank you, Mrs Lloyd.' I looked round the dark kitchen, the strange scents wafting over me and interest stirred within me. 'I would like to learn about the herbs one day,' I said shyly.

Mam was sitting before the fire her eyes closed and quickly I bent over her.

'Here, mam, drink some of this.' I supported her head as she drank the bitter juice, holding the roots close to her so she could breathe in the scent of them.

'*Duw*, that stuff is as sour as old nick,' mam said rubbing her hand over her mouth. 'I hope it does me some good.'

'Go up to bed for a while, mam,' I said, 'I'll see to things down here.' Reluctantly, she obeyed me, taking the twisting stairs one painful step at a time.

Later, when I went up to see if she was sleeping, I was concerned at the flush in her cheeks and the beads of sweat that shined her forehead. Her eyes were wide as she stared at the cracks in the ceiling.

'Mam,' I said softly, 'do you think you will lose the baby?'

She held out her hand to me, attempting to smile. 'Don't be so soft, girl, it's just that I'm getting too old for this lark.' She moved a little and winced. 'Your dad still has the vigour of a young man, especially on Saturday nights when he's been to the beer shop.'

I took a flannel and bathed mam's face and she smiled her gratitude.

'I'm feeling a bit better now, Catrin, and I want to be up and about again when your father comes home otherwise the old softie will worry himself silly.'

'We'll see,' I said. 'Now how about a nice cup of tea? Do you think you could eat anything?'

She was determined on getting up and nothing I could say would change her mind. She was walking easier and she smiled as I helped her down the stairs.

She was sitting in her chair when dad came in from work and his eyes went straight to her face.

'How are you feeling, *cariad*?' He bent over and kissed her forehead as chastely as if they were merely courting and she smiled up at him radiantly.

'Can't you see how much better I am boyo?' She spoke sternly but her hand crept into his and remained there for a long moment.

'*Duw*,' dad said at last, 'this has been a long day and Tom Williams didn't help to make things any easier.'

'Why, dad?' I asked curiously, 'what did he do?' Dad sat on the stool and began to pull the leathers away from his boots.

'Drinking too much ale, girl, he's a danger to himself and everyone else. Nearly fell over with a ladle full of copper, he did.'

Huw came in from the back drying his face and hands, his dark hair beaded with water so that it shone.

'Telling them about Tom Williams are you dad?' he said rubbing his skin vigorously, 'he's a damn good worker, strong as an ox too.'

'Aye,' dad said heavily, 'but he'll be out on his ass if he doesn't pull himself together.'

'Oh, no, dad,' I said quickly, 'he doesn't mean any harm, I'll try to get him to cut down.'

51

'Another thing,' dad said, 'I don't like you going into Jones' beer shop either, don't trust that man further than I can throw him and that's a fact.'

I avoided dad's eyes, I was afraid to tell him that I hated going into the beer shop, he'd have stopped me for good and all and I'd have lost my extra money picked up by doing the message for Tom Williams.

After supper, I went out into the row, it was a dark night with just a faint moon showing through the clouds. From a little way off I could hear someone singing, the tune was haunting and I felt a deep sadness and a feeling of restlessness that I couldn't explain even to myself.

The smoke was low over the rooftops and I could hear old Mrs Price coughing inside her small cottage and I could picture her sitting alone, huddled over her poor fire.

Suddenly I had the wild desire to run away from the streets and up into the mountains. To lie in Dylan's arms and learn what life was all about. To my surprise, tears were moist on my cheeks, it was a funny old life and no mistake.

SIX

The parlour, bathed in afternoon sunlight was as neat as I'd ever seen it because Huw was bringing his Rhian to tea.

'Don't worry, mam,' I said laughing as she dusted the plates on the dresser once again, 'she isn't going to inspect the place.'

'That's as maybe,' mam said sharply, 'but no girl is going to see my house with so much as a speck of dust in it, no fear.'

Mam was still a bit pale but the remedy Mrs Lloyd had given her was working a treat, the old sparkle had returned to mam's eyes.

'I hope the girl likes a bit of stewed rabbit,' mam folded her hands over her crisp white apron, 'It's all I've got anyway so she must like it or lump it.'

I smiled to myself, mam had been working since early morning to make sure the meal would be hot and tasty, she would be heartily offended if Rhian did not like the rabbit.

'Go easy on the poor girl, mam,' I said, 'she's probably frightened silly coming here to meet you.'

'Frightened of me?' mam looked astonished, 'don't be so soft, girl.' She stood for a moment looking about her. 'I wonder if she means to wed our Huw.'

'Of course she does,' I said bluntly, 'why else would she be coming down here?' I shook back my hair and regarded mam steadily, 'You've got to let him go some time, mam.'

I heard the kitchen door opening. 'Mam!' It was Huw's voice, 'come and meet the prettiest girl in the whole of Swansea.'

Rhian stood in the doorway with the black of the tip behind her and my first impression was of a golden girl. She was big boned with long yellow hair and skin that shone like an apple.

'A glass of wine, Huw,' mam said in a precise voice, 'the old parsnip would be nice.'

We sat in the best room all of us stiff in our chairs sipping our wine as if we were afraid for it to touch our lips.

'Your dad has a farm, is that right?' mam said and Rhian nodded.

'Yes, but it's not very grand, just a small spread, my dad thinks the world of the place.'

'Quite right, too.' Mam inspected her slipper and I could see she was wracking her brains thinking of something else to say.

Just then, dad came in and stood in the doorway of the best room and from the smell of him he had been for quite some time down at the beer shop.

'This is Rhian, dad.' I could hear the pride in Huw's voice as dad took the girl's hand in his own.

'A lovely girl too, boyo,' dad said, 'I'm glad you've learned something from me.'

Mam clucked her tongue in annoyance. 'Out into the kitchen with you men, leave us women to a bit of chatting, is it?'

There was silence for a moment after the men went and mam twisted the wide ring on her finger thoughtfully. 'If you and Huw should get wed, will you all live up on the farm do you think?'

Rhian looked surprised, 'I've never thought so far ahead

Mrs Owen but dad could do with a strong man to help him about the place, it's a good idea.'

'Right,' mam said and there was a pleased smile around her mouth, 'let's go into the kitchen and have our tea.'

I knew then that mam was pleased with Rhian, she is very fussy who she invites into her kitchen.

Rhian was to sleep beside me in the slope and return home to the farm in the early morning. I lay awake long into the night and saw Rhian throw a shawl over her night gown and creep out into the darkness. I heard Huw's deep voice and the clucking of the fowls disturbed from their sleep and I was choked with tears at the romance of it all.

'Lay down in the grass, *cariad*.' Huw's voice was low but very clear and I sat up in bed staring into the darkness.

'Oh, Huw, we shouldn't be here like this.' Rhian's protest was ignored, there was a rustling and then Huw groaned. 'Oh, girl, you've got to let me, I'm mad with love for you, see how I'm trembling?'

There were movements in the grass and a sharp cry from Rhian, 'Oh, Huw,' she said breathlessly, 'you are hurting me boyo.'

'Shall I stop then?' Huw laughed his devil's laugh and Rhian spoke up quickly.

'Oh, no, don't stop now, hold me tight, my love, hold me tight.'

After a while there was silence. I lay with my hot face pressed to the pillow. My breasts were tense and there was a pain in the pit of my stomach. When Rhian came back into the slope, her hair tangled about her face, I closed my eyes and pretended I was asleep.

It was unbearably hot in the sheds, perspiration rolled down my face and between my breasts. I took a sweat cloth out of my pocket and patted my eyes.

'Catrin,' Tom Williams waved a big arm at me, 'Go out for my beer, little missy, I'm fair parched.'

I nodded, at least there would be a few minutes for me out of the stifling sheds.

It was cooler in the streets with a low, damp fog hanging over the houses. Most of the doors were closed against the dust and the dingy windows were scratched by the constant abrasion of the copper particles in the air.

I coughed as I hurried into the beer house and Mr Jones took the opportunity to let his hot hands rest on me for a moment.

'I haven't got time to stand here,' I said briskly, 'Tom Williams is waiting and he can be very impatient. I wouldn't like him to come after me.'

He grunted and fetched the beer from the barrel. Mr Jones in all respects reminded me of a pig from the squashed set of his nose to the way he would always put his hands up any little girls clothes.

I dawdled as long as I dared but at last I returned to the heat of the sheds.

'*Duw*, that's good that is, little missy.' Tom drained the jug. 'I needed that more than ever today, the smoke is down with a vengeance.'

When I reached dad's tew gang, I felt exhausted. My father put his arm around my shoulders. 'Never mind, girl, you'll be getting off home soon, out of this stinking hell. Here, help me with this sleeve.'

His arm was protected from the blasting heat of the copper by a stretch of sailcloth. 'Spread some clay on it, Catrin, that's right, dampen it well.'

I watched for a moment while dad took his turn dipping the ladle into the shimmering, molten copper and then with an expert flick of his wrist depositing it into the mould.

I moved back from the heat and there was a sudden shout behind me. I turned in time to see Tom Williams stagger towards me with a full ladle of copper.

Frozen with fear, I stood still expecting at any moment to feel the terrible heat of the molten copper pour over me. I was lifted clear at the last moment and the spitting as if of a thousand cats filled the air as the copper touched the dampness of the floor. There was a searing pain in my arm and I think I screamed as a few pieces of copper bit into my flesh. I turned to see who was holding me and my startled senses could not register the fact that it was John Richards standing white faced at my side.

Dad tore the sleeve of my dress and I choked on a scream as his knife probed the copper splashes from where they had set in my flesh. He splashed water over the wounds and bound it with the torn sleeve of my dress.

'Huw, take your sister home.' Dad spoke calmly though there were flames in his eyes as he looked at Tom Williams. Before I could move, Tom was standing before me shaking his great head in abject misery.

'May God forgive me for hurting you, little missy,' he said, 'because I will never forgive myself.'

No one spoke for a moment and I realized I was still in the circle of John Richards' arms.

'Perhaps you will allow me to take Catrin home?' he asked, speaking to dad over the top of my head, 'I have a pony and trap outside, she would be most comfortable I assure you.'

Dad stared at him in sudden suspicion, 'Who are you?' he said abruptly, 'I've never seen you around here before.'

'I'm John Richards,' he said bluntly, 'I work for Mr Vivian.'

Dad looked at me and I nodded, 'I'd like to go with him, dad.'

'Go then.' Dad nodded to John. 'Take her back to Tip Row.' He stared at John for a long moment and then added grudgingly, 'And many thanks for your kindness.'

As John led me outside, the men grouped around Tom Williams and dad's voice was loud and angry.

'That was your last mistake here, boyo, any more beer drinking and you are out on your ass, is it understood?'

Tom's answer was too low for me to hear and I hurried away, my face red hoping John had not heard my father swearing.

John lifted me up into the seat of the trap and I shivered a little, my arm felt as if it was on fire and inside me was a strange mixture of feelings. I glanced up at John sitting so tall and proud at my side and somehow it was as if I'd always known I would see him again.

'Our house is alongside the tip.' I pointed with my uninjured arm and John guided the horse towards the doorway.

'You are very pale, Catrin,' he said and I felt a thrill that he remembered my name, 'you will no doubt be suffering from shock for a while.'

'I'll be all right,' I said shakily, 'a nice cup of tea and I'll be as right as a penny chicken.'

Mam's face was a picture when she saw John helping me down from the trap, she bobbed him a curtsey and held the door wide for him to carry me indoors.

'I've just had a little sket from the copper, mam,' I said quickly, 'it's not much so don't go worrying yourself.'

She untied the rough bandage from my arm and winced at the livid mark on my arm.

'I'll have to get something from Mrs Lloyd for that,' she said, 'will you be all right while I run down?'

I nodded and John sat down opposite me. 'I'll look after her, don't worry.' He smiled engagingly at mam and she was quite flustered as she pulled on her shawl.

When the door had closed behind her, John came across to me and cupped my face in his hands. 'I haven't had you out of my mind for one minute since I met you at Carmarthen,' he said gently. 'I was already thinking of leaving Sir James Scarlett and settling down somewhere and Swansea seemed an ideal place because you were here.'

I was disturbed by his nearness and the fresh clean scent of his skin. I tried to move away from him but he held me firmly. His lips touched mine for an infinitely tender moment and then he released me.

'Shall I pour you a glass of wine or will you have tea?' He picked up the enormous black kettle and settled it on the coals, at home instantly in our small kitchen. 'Tea might be more refreshing, I think,' he said making up my mind for me.

Mam was quick to return, she took the cup of tea that John held towards her not altogether approving of the way he had taken command but too grateful to criticize. She spread a herb paste over my arm and the wound was soothed immediately.

'There, it will soon heal,' mam said rubbing her hands on her apron, 'and Mrs Lloyd wants to see you once you feel well enough.' She turned to John, 'Would you like a slice of seed cake?'

It was obvious she was at a loss not knowing how to address him, John smiled.

'That would be very nice and please call me John,' he said winking at me. 'I hope you don't mind me bringing Catrin home but I was there when the accident happened and as I had the trap outside it seemed a better proposition than allowing her to walk.'

'Well,' mam said doubtfully, 'so long as you don't think

you can play fast and loose with our Catrin I suppose it's all right.'

My colour rose and I looked away quickly but John took everything in his stride it seemed.

'I have only honourable intentions,' he said and there was a hint of laughter in his voice. 'Perhaps I may be allowed to visit again some time?'

'Yes, I suppose that would be all right,' mam said doubtfully, 'but why should you want to visit us?'

'I'd like to marry Catrin, if she will have me,' John said and I had no way of knowing if he was serious or not. Suddenly the world seemed to spin around my head. I stared at mam and then at John and promptly burst into tears.

SEVEN

'So I'm not good enough for you now that a fine and dandy gentleman has come calling on you, you're keeping yourself for him, is that it?'

Dylan stared down at me with such a savage look in his eyes that I was frightened though not for anything would I show it.

'Don't be so soft!' I said quickly, 'you don't think I'm taking him seriously do you? His sort don't marry girls like me, I'm quite aware of that.'

'Well, why let him come calling then, him in his fine clothes and bringing you presents it would take me a full week's pay to buy, why not send him about his business?'

'Oh stop treating me in this way!' I said turning from him, 'I haven't done anything wrong and I won't have you bullying me, so just shut up and leave me alone.'

He caught my chin and forced me to look at him. 'Do you love him, Catrin, answer me that?'

'Of course I don't, I hardly know him.' I tried to pull away but he wouldn't release me. He drew me against him, his hand on my breast, warm and tender there.

'You are my woman Catrin,' he said fiercely, 'and you know it, so why fight me.'

I felt tears spring to my eyes. 'It's all right for you to talk like that but what if you got me full with your child wouldn't the shame kill my mam?' I sighed, 'and as for dad, he would skin you alive.'

Dylan pressed me closer, 'I can't think of anything when I'm alone on the hill with you, except how much I want you. You're not like the other girls from the Hafod, you are frail and small and look more like a fine lady than a copper girl.' He brushed back my hair. 'I suppose that is why I'm jealous of your fancy boy friend, he's a scholar like you and I'm afraid that you are going to find out how dull I really am.'

'Dylan, don't!' I said indignantly, 'you are proud and handsome and I love you.'

He drew me down to the ground, 'Prove it to me then, girl,' he said thickly, 'prove it to me now.'

For a moment there was a wild panic inside me, I wanted to run as fast as I could down the hill to Tip Row but then his hands were holding me. I couldn't think any more, just feel. 'You want me, Catrin,' he whispered, 'I know you do.' He pushed aside the bodice of my dress to find my breasts with his strong fingers. I was shaking with a mixture of fear and excitement and then his weight came down upon me and it was too late for decisions.

He encompassed me, he was over and within me, possessing me with a frenzy that filled my being with pain and delight. My arms were on his shoulders, clinging, I was in turn the possessor and the possessed.

A sheet of flame flew from the stacks over the copper works and it seemed as if the same flame was inside me until at last I fell back, spent against the hard ground.

Tears came then, warm and bitter, splashing down on to my hands and my bare legs as I sat crouched like a wounded animal on the ground, hardly able to believe what had happened.

Dylan drew me gently to him. 'It was right for us,' he said with a sureness that I envied. 'You are mine now, and I'll always look after you.'

I was late returning to the row, it had taken me a long time to stop my tears of guilt and fear and now, somehow I had to behave as if nothing had happened.

'Mind you don't bump me in your rush, Catrin, there's a good girl.' I stopped suddenly, surprised to see Mrs Price from next door on her rounds collecting the *pisio* from the houses to take down to the copper works for the pickling sheds. It was even later than I'd thought, she usually waited until most people were in their beds to spare them the unpleasantness. She moved away from me and the contents of the bucket on her head splashed about smelling so strong that I held my nose in disgust. Mrs Price laughed.

'Oh, I know other people's *pisio* makes a terrible stink but it brings in good gin money for me and it's an honest trade.'

'I've got to get home, Mrs Price,' I said quickly, 'mam will be worried about me.'

'I should think so too, get along home with you then, girl this is no time for walking the streets.'

Mam was sitting in her rocking chair agitatedly moving it to and fro and dad standing before the fire, his feet set well apart and an angry frown on his face. I thought at first, the anger was directed against me but then I realized that Huw was sitting at the table a mutinous look on his face.

I crept closer to the fire and sat down on a stool, almost afraid to breathe in case the storm burst around my head. It was Huw who broke the silence.

'I'm sorry it has to be this way, mam,' he said, 'but Rhian is going to have a young 'un and that's all there is to it. I'll marry her as soon as I can.'

'A son of mine,' mam said very low, 'tom catting after women, *Duw* there's shame to bring home to us.'

Dad and Huw exchanged a glance and I could see that my father was proud rather than angry. I shivered, but if ever dad found out about me and Dylan, there would be murder done.

'Well, it could be worse,' dad said, 'at least the boy is going to marry the girl and do right thing by her.'

'I should think so too,' mam said in a small voice and only then I noticed the tears trembling on her lashes. I lay my head against her knee, some deep instinct telling me what she must be feeling. She had brought a son into the world, loved him and watched him grow into a man and now he belonged to another woman.

Her hand rested on my hair and for a moment it was as if our blood intermingled and our thoughts and feelings became one. I took her hand and we sat in silence for a full minute before dad started to cough.

Mam was on her feet at once her arm around him as he struggled to breathe against the spasm that gripped him.

'Sit down, Will, boyo, have a cup of tea.' Dad quietened down and I went to my bed in the slope. I lay with my eyes closed tightly, my body still ached and between my legs was a fire. When everyone was asleep I would have to wash my petticoats so there would be no sign to remind me that tonight was the first time I had lain with a man.

Mam wound her black beads around her neck, smoothing down the silk of her best dress, looking at herself in the cracked mirror over the fireplace. She was tall, almost stately, her thick hair neat and shining upon her head. Dad stood waiting for her patiently, together they were to visit Rhian's father to talk over the details of the wedding. Mam drew her shawl around her shoulders.

'Do I look respectable, Catrin?' she said anxiously and I

knew what she was really asking was if it showed that she was with child.

'You look splendid, mam,' I said and meant it, I was very proud of her. I watched as they went, arm in arm like a courting couple down the row.

I was only inside for a few minutes when a dark shadow fell into the kitchen, I thought it was dad returning because he had forgotten something. I turned and the colour flew into my cheeks. 'John!' I said in amazement, 'what on earth are you doing here?'

'Well that's not a very warm welcome is it?' He laughed and stepped into the kitchen and took my arm. 'Your scars are healing nicely, though I think you will always have a mark there.'

I felt shy of him, as if I had no right to even speak to him now that I'd given myself so completely to Dylan.

I tried to move away but he held my arm firmly, pressing his lips to the scar. A strange sensation took my breath away and then Iorwerth broke the spell that held me.

'I want some soup, Catrin,' he said, pulling at my skirt and John laughed releasing my arm.

'Yes, it smells good perhaps I can have some, too?'

It was strange to sit at the scrubbed table, John with his coat off and sleeves rolled up and Iorwerth full to the brim, almost asleep his head on his arms.

John leaned towards me, his eyes shining. 'This is all I could ask,' he said 'you and I together in a warm kitchen, it could always be like this if you married me.'

I stood up quickly and moved to the fireplace, aware that he had come to stand, very tall, beside me. His hands were gentle then on my shoulders forcing me to face him.

'I am serious, Catrin,' he said firmly, 'I mean every

word I say. I would count myself a singularly lucky man to have you as my wife.'

I avoided his eyes. 'I'm not the woman for you, John. You should marry a lady in fine silks not one like me in Welsh flannel petticoats.'

He held my face so that I was forced to look at him. 'Fine clothes do not make a lady, Catrin.' He drew me close to him and I could hear his heart beating. I felt warm and safe in his arms and yet where was the wild sweet thrill that Dylan's touch awoke in me?

I drew away quickly. 'John, you are asking the impossible our worlds are too far apart. Please, find someone more worthy of you.'

'Worthy?' he said in amusement, 'I am not looking for a saint and make no mistake, Catrin, I mean to marry you however long it may take to convince you I'm right about us.'

'Sit by the fire, now,' I said, a little impatient, 'and leave the subject alone.'

He pulled me to him so suddenly that I was taken by surprise. His lips were not gentle but fierce and demanding and I found my arms closing round him. The whole world was blotted out as we clung together.

'You see?' he said in triumph, 'you could love me, Catrin, there's no use in denying it.'

I was shaken, what sort of woman was I that I could go from one man's arms to another like this?

'There's no use you keeping on,' I said sharply, 'I am promised to someone else.' I couldn't look into his face. 'I am going to marry Dylan Morgan, we have been together on the Town Hill, do you understand?'

His face was red and his eyes burned with pain and anger, I was frightened and sad all at once. He said nothing for a moment but stood with clenched fists watching as I stirred up the fire.

'I'm sorry John,' I said in a whisper, 'more sorry than I can tell you.'

'It makes no difference,' he said at last, 'you are still mine and I'll prove it to you if it takes me all my life.'

'You are a strange man, John,' I said looking up at him, torn between admiration and despair, 'but can't you see it's no use?'

He made no answer, he settled himself in a chair and he was still sitting there when mam and dad returned.

I could see at once that something was wrong, mam's eyes were red and dad was like an angry bull charging about the kitchen.

'What's wrong?' I said, a tight knot of fear inside me. Mam sank into a chair staring ahead of her like someone in a dream and it was dad who answered me.

'There's been a flaming row up at the farm.' He clenched his huge fist and struck at the table. 'Rhian's father took a shotgun to your brother and drove him off the place, Huw hasn't been seen since this morning.' He thumped the table again so hard that blood stood like beads on his grazed knuckles.

'A copper worker isn't good enough to marry his daughter, that's what he said and he wasn't going to have his property pass into the hands of folks like us.'

'What makes him so high and mighty?' I said in anger, 'I don't suppose he smells very sweet after he has been mucking out the pigsty.'

'Shush, Catrin,' mam spoke wearily, she was very white and her eyes were deeply shadowed. 'It's no use talking like that, it won't bring Huw back.'

'Have a cup of tea, mam,' I said in concern, 'I'll put

some honey in it, that will make you feel stronger.'

She took the cup in trembling hands, 'Oh, *Duw*, I'm so worried I can scarcely think straight. What if that madman of a farmer has hurt him? It doesn't bear thinking about.'

Dad put his hand across her shoulders, 'Don't cry, *cariad*.'

She looked up at him, silent in her misery, crouched like a frightened animal, diminished in her grief.

John rose to his feet. 'I'll look for him and if he's anywhere in Swansea, I'll find him.'

He spoke with such conviction that we all accepted his word without question. He went to the door and pulling a shawl over my shoulders, I followed him.

'I'm coming with you,' I said firmly and for a moment I thought he would protest then he shrugged his shoulders.

'All right, come if you must,' he said, 'but remember, if you slow me up I shall go on without you.'

As he strode quickly down the street, I hurried to keep pace with him. There was no doubt in my mind that he would find Huw and I was proud to follow wherever he led me.

EIGHT

I didn't know there were so many beer houses in the town of Swansea, John must have gone into every one asking after my brother until at last the search led us to a seedy lane where I had never been before.

The houses huddled together, tall and narrow along a filthy road. There were lights in some of the windows but others gaped brokenly down at us like evil sightless eyes.

'Wait here, Catrin,' John said, 'I'd better go inside alone.'

I stood for a moment, shivering, smelling the dreadful odour of human filth in the gutters and the overpowering stench of stale beer.

'Hello, girl, waiting for customers, are you?' I looked up startled to see a portly man leaning towards me. His narrow eyes were on my bodice and I moved back a step pulling my shawl closer round me. He reached out and caught my shoulder, his foul breath on my face.

'Leave me alone, you animal!' I cried and my hands were out scratching his face.

'You bitch!' He began to revile me in Welsh, his language not fit even for the gutters where we stood. I hurried away from him into the doorway where John had gone, nothing could be worse than remaining in the street.

The stairs that led upward were covered in dirty sand and the smell was even more unsavoury than the street had been.

I could hear John's voice somewhere in the warren of little rooms and I opened a door hoping to find him. Instead I saw a woman standing against the wall, her soiled skirt lifted high. A man was pressing against her making hideous grunting noises.

Quickly, I slammed the door shut and made for another of the rooms. This time I listened for a few moments until I was sure it was John's voice I could hear inside.

Huw was almost unrecognizable, his hair was matted around his swollen face and he hung almost unconscious in John's arms.

'Help me support him,' John said, and I stepped quickly into the room wrinkling my nose at the disgusting smell.

A woman with yellow hair lay half naked on the floor, eyeing me with hostility. It was obvious what her trade was, she was a prostitute of the lowest kind. Beneath the gaudiness of her painted face, I could see she was not much older than I was.

John threw her some money and she reached out a filthy hand in a lightning gesture, sitting up and crossing her thin legs examining the coins avidly. I felt sorry for her and yet sickened at the same time.

Somehow, we got out of that vile house and into the street. Huw seemed to sober a little in the night air, at least enough for John and me to drag him along at a fairly fast pace. He stopped once or twice vomiting wretchedly into the gutter and I was amazed at the patience John showed towards him. We got home to Tip Row at last and dad who had been waiting at the door rushed to greet us.

'*Darro!*' he said, 'the boy must have been on the beer since this morning, what a mess.' He opened the door into the yard, 'Let's get him out here, John boy and wash him down.'

Between them, they took off Huw's clothes, scrubbing him stark naked as though he was a baby. When they had done, mam wrapped him in a warm blanket and forced a beaten egg down his throat.

'I'm sorry, mam,' he said apologetically, '*Duw* but I'm sorry.' His head lolled against the chair and he began to snore.

'He'll have to sleep it off,' dad said turning to John, 'we might as well put him to bed.'

I helped mam to make the tea, she was happier now that Huw was safe home but I noticed she winced a little as she set out the cups on the table.

Dad and John came back to the kitchen and I smiled to myself to see dad's arm on John's shoulder. The two men were buddies now in spite of differences of age and class.

'This is a good man, here,' dad said to me, 'if you've any sense in your head you'll take him for a husband and thank the good lord for the chance.'

I looked down at my hands, dad was right, John was a good man but some perversity inside me cried out for more than kindness and trust. I wanted the fierce emotion that Dylan raised in me, perhaps I had bad blood in me, little better than the harlot Huw had lain with. At least she was honest asking money for her favours.

I would not have dared to give voice to any of my thoughts, good women were expected to accept their man's attentions from a sense of duty not from a deep, crying longing that tore the world apart.

John rose to his feet. 'I'd better make my way home now, Mr Owen.'

Dad nodded. 'There's a lot we have to thank you for, John, I don't forget in a hurry, believe me.' Dad coughed, 'Well see him to the door, Catrin, girl.'

It was cool outside. John looked up at the tip looming

71

above the street, dominating the cottages and blotting out the silver of the moon except where it melted over the top of the tip like icing on a cake.

I went up on my toes and wound my arms around John's neck, pressing my lips against his for one brief moment and there were tears burning my eyes. His hand was gentle, smoothing back my hair.

'It hasn't been a very pleasant experience for you, has it? I should never have allowed you to come with me.' I smiled then.

'You wouldn't have stopped me, boyo, I don't know how to take "no" for an answer.'

'I'm going now, Catrin,' John disengaged my arms from round his neck, 'and remember, I won't take "no" for an answer either.'

I watched him walk swiftly down the row and there was such a strange mixture of feelings inside me, I wanted to laugh and cry, both together.

In my bed in the slope, I lay awake, staring into the darkness and sleep would not come.

Tom Williams had given up the beer, I wasn't to go to Mr Jones to fetch ale any more and I was heartily thankful for that.

'I'll not touch another drop, little missy, not in working hours anyway.' He put his big hand on my shoulder as gentle as a kitten. 'It's good to see you back, are you quite sure you're better now?'

'Yes, don't worry about me, I'm all right again, see, there's hardly any mark.' I was trying to be cheerful though if the truth be known, the heat in the sheds was beginning to get me down already.

I handed him a jug of water and he took it, a wry smile on his face.

'There's no other woman could put me off the beer, I'll tell you that for nothing, little missy.' He downed the water in one swallow and wiped his mouth with the back of his hand.

I was glad when I'd finished my rounds and it was time for me to go to the spring to fill up the casks again. It was a hot sunny day and for once the stacks seemed to be doing their job of directing the copper smoke away from the works. I walked down to the banks of the river and looked along the winding length of it. It must have been beautiful once, before the copper laid fingers of rust across its wrinkled face.

'Hey, Catrin, out enjoying the sun, are you girl?' Dai the Quay jumped from his barge, sinking a little into the mud of the bank.

'Your young chappie is in the back there, browning himself like a ham and a face as long as a brush handle because he hasn't seen you for a few days. Woa, there, Duke, have some apple.'

He drew the horse to a stop and I looked along the barge to where Dylan lay, half asleep.

'You'll have to kick that one to wake him up!' Dai grinned and pulled off his hat, pushing back his hair with a familiar gesture. I stared at him, fascinated as always by the bright green streak of hair running from the front to the back of his head. Dylan had told me that the green came from the copper ore they carried in the barge.

'Do you want a drink of water, Dai?' I teased knowing quite well what his reaction would be.

'Garn! I never drink the stuff, rots your guts it does girl.' He took a flask from his pocket and tapped it lovingly. 'Gin, that's what keeps me going, a good swig of gin.'

He savoured every drop, rolling it round his blackened

teeth before swallowing it with a gasp of pleasure.

There was a movement from the back of the barge and I saw that Dylan was awake. He neatly balanced along the side of the barge and jumped ashore, sliding his arm around my waist.

'Hello,' I said, and my throat was suddenly dry and I could feel myself trembling. I remembered vividly the love we'd shared under the walls of the Jews' burying ground.

'You look lovely today,' he said softly, his hand sneaking up to where the bodice of my dress was stretched tightly over my breasts. I was angry with him and with myself for making my feelings plain.

'You are too sure of yourself, Dylan Morgan!' I pushed him aside and walked away without a backward glance.

It was hard to return to work and the day seemed to drag by. My feet ached and the heat seemed to drain every bit of energy from me. I was glad when the end of my shift came and I could make my way along the evening coolness of the row towards home.

Huw was sitting slouched in a chair, his eyes bloodshot and as he looked up at me, I was shocked by the pallor of his face.

'Hello, Catrin, girl, I'm sorry I made such a fool of myself, though in truth I don't remember much about what happened.'

Mam bustled in from the back and she looked pinched and drawn. She stood by the fire for a moment, swaying a little and Huw jumped to his feet and helped her to a chair.

'Mam, why didn't you tell me you were ill instead of letting me sit there whining like a sick dog?'

Mam shook her head wearily, 'You know I don't like to be fussed.' She closed her eyes. 'No nonsense from any of you, or you'll have me feeling worse than a worn out shoe.'

I pulled a shawl around my shoulders, 'Shall I run down to Mrs Lloyd's and ask for some Angelica, mam?'

She shook her head, 'Oh, I don't know, girl, the pain seems to be getting worse.'

'Bring her up to bed,' I said crisply to Huw and he lifted her in his arms as if she was a child.

Tucked beneath the sheets, she was small and defenceless, there was a small knot of fear inside me as I looked at her.

She stared at me for a moment and her eyes were those of a frightened animal.

'Catrin,' she said hoarsely, 'I think I'm going to miscarry the child.'

NINE

It was like a bad dream. Mrs Lloyd put on her hat and shawl as soon as she saw my face and gathering up a bag of herbs she walked with me back to the house without speaking a word.

Huw was sitting beside mam, big and awkward, he was, trying to bathe her face with cold water.

'She's feverish,' he said worriedly not yet believing that mam could be really ill. 'She's all right isn't she?'

'Down the stairs with you boyo,' Mrs Lloyd said sharply, 'get the kettle on boiling, make yourself useful.'

I heard Iorwerth cry out in his sleep and I tiptoed into his room, brushing the curls from his forehead.

'There, there, everything's all right.' I covered him over with a blanket and he opened his dark eyes for a moment, still dazed by sleep.

'Mam,' he said fretfully, 'where's mam?'

I knelt beside him, taking his warmth into my arms. 'Mam will come and see you later on, love.' I kissed his soft cheek and his eyes closed again.

'Catrin, come here, girl.' Mrs Lloyd sounded anxious. I hurried to mam's room just in time to see a perfectly formed baby, tiny and waxen lying still on the bed.

Mrs Lloyd folded it in a piece of cloth, her gnarled hands gentle. Mam began to cry, desperate, heartrending sobs, I went to her and put my arms around her thin shoulders.

'There, there, mam,' I soothed. 'It wasn't meant to be, don't grieve.' It was strange to find the roles reversed, that I was comforting mam.

'Here, Catrin,' Mrs Lloyd handed me the pitiful bundle, 'Take it away, girl, the back of the fire is the cleanest.' Her words were hard but there was a tear on her old face.

I went downstairs to Huw. 'The little thing is dead,' I said bluntly. 'It was too small to even draw breath. Mrs Lloyd says we must get rid of it but I say give it a decent burial.'

Huw's face was white but he nodded his agreement, 'Go down the works and bring dad home, Catrin,' he said, 'I will make a coffin as well as I can.'

To my dying day I'll never forget the way we stood in the graveyard, dad still in his working clothes and Huw head bent to hide the tears that flowed unchecked down his cheeks. Then in the moonlight, we made our way silently back to Tip Row.

Mrs Lloyd had been busy steeping herbs. The pot steamed over the fire and the kitchen was filled with fragrance.

'She's sleeping peacefully,' Mrs Lloyd jerked her head in the direction of the bedroom, 'it's the best thing for her.' She looked at dad severely. 'Don't go filling her up with child again, Will Owen, her health won't stand it.'

Head hanging in shame like a scolded child, dad climbed the stairs. I think he just wanted to look at mam to reassure himself that she was really safe.

Mrs Lloyd went to the door. 'You have good hands, Catrin, if you come down to my cottage a few nights every week I'll teach you how to make some of my secret remedies.' She pulled on her shawl that was yellow with age. 'Come, Huw Owen, see an old lady to her door.' She touched my face for a moment, 'Rest you, Catrin you look worn out.'

I stood watching them go down the row and I was just about to close the door when a figure came out of the shadows so suddenly that I almost screamed.

'Sorry, Catrin.' Dylan moved into the light and I breathed a sigh of relief. 'I was worried about you, are you all right?' He put his arm around me and I leaned against him, warmed by his nearness.

'It's mam,' I said almost in a whisper, 'she's bad, lost the little one tonight, she did.'

'*Duw*, there's sorry I am to hear that, girl.' He smoothed my hair back from my forehead, 'Don't fret yourself too much Catrin, perhaps everything is for the best.'

Huw came back along the row and stopped by the doorway, 'Come in now, girl, and get some rest,' he said quietly, 'you can talk to Dylan tomorrow.'

I said a hasty good night and followed Huw into the kitchen. 'Ordering my life now are you?' I said flatly.

'Take my advice and leave Dylan Morgan alone,' he said, 'look at mam up there, she's worn out with work, old before her time, I don't want to see you finish up like that, girl.'

'Things are better these days,' I said gently, 'I know mam hasn't had it easy but my life will be different.'

Huw shook his head, 'Not if you have a few children and Dylan falls sick. Marry John Richards, that's my advice, he's a good man, he would see you all right.' He stood up gazing into the fire. 'Get away from the row, girl, I mean to get out of here before I'm much older.'

I got to my feet wearily, 'I'm going to bed now, I'm so tired I can't think of anything but sleep.'

Once I was in bed, the tears began to flow, I cried for

78

mam and for the lost baby and I think I cried for myself a little too.

'There's no moon out tonight, see how the smoke weaves and rolls in the light of the fire from the stacks?' I leaned against the wall of the house, Dylan silent at my side. He put his arm around my waist, rubbing his face against my hair.

'Come up to the Town Hill with me, Catrin, it's been so long.'

I sighed, 'Yes, it's three weeks now since mam lost the baby, she still grieves about it though.'

Dylan turned my face to his, 'Well you are entitled to live your own life.' His kiss stirred me so that when he took my arm and drew me away from the streets I had no strength to protest.

As soon as we were out of sight of prying eyes he drew me to the ground, his hands warm and familiar on my body. In spite of my immediate response, I was angry with him.

'Don't you ever think of anything else?' I said fiercely, 'I'm not here just to satisfy your needs, you know!'

He drew me back into the warmth of his arms, 'come on, *cariad*, let me help you forget your troubles for a little while.'

His kisses drove my senses away, I had seen the child slip from mam as easily as a leaf falls from a tree in Autumn, I knew it was dangerous to follow the dictates of my body and yet how could I think straight when everything in me cried out to surrender?

'I love you, Catrin,' Dylan whispered and his hand cupped my breast gently, 'the last thing I want to do is hurt you.'

His control served only to increase my desire, 'I want

79

you Dylan,' I said quickly, 'I want you, now.'

He was so tender, so gentle and the way he loved me was in itself a promise that he would cherish me. Later, I lay back in his arms feeling serene and happy.

'Come on,' he said at last, drawing me to my feet, 'I'm going to ask my father to get me a job in the copper sheds, I can earn twice the money there than on the barge and we'll be able to marry all the sooner.'

I put my arms around him, 'No, Dylan, I know how much you love your life out in the open, you would hate the sheds.'

'I'll be all right,' he said, 'It's about time I grew up and did some real work for a change.'

'Please Dylan, you don't know what it's like,' I insisted, 'it can be like hell in there on a stormy day and even at the best of times it's bad.'

He put up his hand gently over my lips and his eyes were full of laughter, 'Shut up, woman,' he ordered, 'I've made up my mind.'

We walked the rest of the way home in silence. I was touched by Dylan's determination to work in the sheds and yet inside me was a strange unease that I couldn't have explained even to myself.

At the corner of the row, I kissed him good night and watched as he ran down the cobbled street like a young animal. He had the energy of three men, but how long would that last once he felt the heat of the copper?

Cautiously, I climbed through my window in the slope hoping no-one had noticed my absence but suddenly my eyes were dazzled by a candle held high.

'Where have you been, Catrin?' Huw came forward and put the light on the box at the side of my bed. 'You've been with Dylan Morgan haven't you?' he said not waiting for my reply.

'It's no use you preaching to me, Huw,' I said quietly, 'what's done is done and you've no room to talk have you?'

He shook his head, 'I just don't understand you, I never will, after all I've tried to tell you, you still go out and throw your future away.'

I sat down, my legs shaking, I half expected Huw to go after Dylan and give him a good hiding but my brother seemed disappointed rather than angry.

'I'm happy with Dylan,' I said pleadingly, 'isn't that more important than anything else?'

He sat on the bed pulling me down beside him, there was a wry smile on his face as he drew my head down on his shoulder. 'Is that what you think? You are a poor fool, Catrin, a poor little fool.'

TEN

There was a terrible scandal along the row and mam spent the days sitting in the kitchen with her apron to her eyes crying because our Huw had run off with Rhian.

'If only he had sent me a proper message instead of that scrappy little note,' she said time and time again but dad was tight lipped and angry.

'Let him show his face here again and he'll get the taste of my belt.'

'Oh, Will!' mam said, 'don't be so unforgiving, the boy cannot help what he feels for the girl.'

'He's mad!' dad's voice rose a little, 'throwing away a good job without a moment's thought, he's more of a fool than I took him for.'

'*Duw*, he's young and strong,' mam said, 'he can always get another job and he's still our son whatever you may say.'

'He's no son of mine,' dad said coldly, 'let him eat the meat he has cooked for himself, he need ask no help of me.'

Iorwerth ended the argument by bursting into tears, his fists screwed into his eyes.

'I don't like everybody shouting,' he said, and dad sat down on the stool drawing Iorwerth near to him.

'Look, you are the man of the house now, after me, so stop crying, son, and watch after your mam when I am in work, will you?'

Iorwerth brightened up nodding his curly head in agreement. 'All right, dad,' he said, gulping.

Dad and I walked to work in silence and I missed Huw who always had a song on the way to keep our spirits up.

Dylan had been true to his word and had come into the sheds. My heart twisted in pain when I saw him, covered in dust with sweat beading his face.

'Well, Catrin, love,' he said grinning wickedly, 'this brings our wedding day a bit nearer.'

'Oh, Dylan, I don't like seeing you in here, you are used to the fresh air, you'll suffocate if you have to stay in the sheds for very long.'

'If you can stick it, Catrin, then so can I. Now don't say another word about it.' His words were stern but the way he looked down at me made me long to fling myself into his arms there and then.

Suddenly, Dylan was looking over my head, '*Darro!* it looks as if your dad and Tom Williams are having some sort of argument,' he said, and I spun round to see dad look down at Tom as if he was a rat.

'Now, Will,' Tom said calmly, 'nobody knows better than you that a good spirit is needed to keep the men going in this hell hole, am I right?'

Dad grunted, his big hands clenched, 'What are you trying to say, then? Spit it out boyo.'

'Right, then all I want to say is this, we all feel sorry about your boy running off but you are putting the miseries on the men with your long mournful face.'

Dad's eyes blazed, 'I've a good mind to lamp you,' he said, his fist raised.

'Lamp away,' Tom said calmly, 'but it won't change the truth of my words will it, boyo?'

Dad dropped his hands at his side and sighed, 'I dare

say you are right, Tom Williams,' he said at last and without another word he returned to his work.

Tom Williams winked as he passed me, 'Your dad is a real man, little missy, it takes a man and a good one to admit he's in the wrong.'

I turned to Dylan and shook my head, 'The lot of you can be more like children than children.' I turned away, 'I'd better get on with my job, I suppose and let's hope that dad will come out of his gloom for good.'

I saw nothing of John for more than a week and in a way I was glad of it. When he was near me, my feelings were in a constant turmoil, I didn't know what I wanted except that it would be good to have a life away from Tip Row.

I thought of it longingly as I constantly wiped my face and arms, drying the perspiration only to be beaded again before I had put the cloth away. It was a particularly bad day in the sheds, the smoke was down and not a breath of air to share between us. The intense heat had all the men on edge and when Tom Williams asked me with pleading eyes to bring him beer instead of water, I did not protest, the prospect of a few minutes outside in the freshness of the day was too inviting.

Tom drank steadily and I lost count of the times I went across the road to the beer house. I was numb with the heat that drained away every ounce of my energy. I stood looking longingly out of the doors when behind me came a mighty sound as if it was the end of the world. There was a roar like a monster screaming in pain and the voices of the men shouting. I was picked up and flung to the ground by a great gust of air and then it was as if I was under the black cloth of the funeral parlour. I tried to move but I could not and it was easier to close my eyes and let the darkness take me.

When I opened my eyes again, dad was bending over me, his face was white and there was an angry graze beneath his eye.

'Thank God you are all right, girl!' He held me gently as I struggled to sit up.

'What's happened, dad?' I asked in a voice I scarcely recognized as my own, 'has the whole place come down?'

'Not likely, girl, it was just a small blow up, hardly anyone hurt.'

There was smoke coming out of the doors of the shed but there was not even a hole in the roof.

'Was it Tom Williams, dad?' I asked guiltily. I had brought him quite a lot of beer and if he was at fault then so was I.

Dad shook his head, 'No one rightly knows, love, Tom and Dylan were nearest to the explosion, either one of them could have caused it.'

'Dylan?' I felt cold all over as I whispered his name and dad steadied me with his arm.

'He's been taken to the infirmary, Catrin, he'll be all right, try not to worry about him.' Dad was avoiding my eyes and fear gave me strength. I forced myself to my feet and stood looking at dad, trembling waiting for him to speak.

'The copper caught him across his back, he's young and strong though, he'll be all right.'

I felt panic rise like a sickness inside me, I stared with hatred at the copper sheds and at the smoke that hung like a pall of doom over everything.

'Go home, girl, wash the blood from your face, you must have cut yourself when you fell. You have broken no bones though, as far as I can see.'

I turned without a word and hurried along the street towards Tip Row. The old people stood in their doorways curious about the explosion at the sheds but too languid to walk down the street to see for themselves.

Mam gave a scream when she saw the state I was in. 'Oh, Catrin girl, what's happened to you and is dad all right?'

'Dad's safe,' I said quickly, 'and I'm only scratched so there's no need for you to worry.' I went into the yard and dipped my hands into the barrel of water.

'Put some clean clothes out for me mam,' I called, 'Dylan's been hurt and I'm going down to the infirmary to see him.' To my surprise I sounded quite calm though my heart was beating so fast I could hardly breathe.

'I'll put them on the bed for you. Is Dylan hurt bad?'

I walked back into the kitchen slowly, drying my face unable to speak for a moment.

'I don't know, mam,' I said at last, 'I think it's pretty bad.' Quickly I pulled off my dust covered skirts and brushed some of the tangles out of my hair. My hands were shaking so much that I couldn't do anything very quickly.

A few minutes later, I hurried down the row. At the bottom of the street Mr Jones from the beer shop was standing, holding one of his horses on a rein.

'I hear Dylan Morgan is hurt pretty bad,' he said, and for once he wasn't leering, 'take a lend of my animal, here, you'll get to the infirmary all the quicker.'

Tears choked my throat as he helped me to mount. 'Thank you, Mr Jones,' I said, 'I won't forget your kindness.' I rode away thinking that there is a little bit of good in everyone, even Mr Jones.

The infirmary was set upon a golden stretch of sand, the sky was hazy but at least here I could breathe the salt air instead of smoke and sulphur.

Lizzie Morgan was sitting beside Dylan, her face

waspish as she looked me up and down. I went nearer to the bed and took Dylan's hand.

'Are you hurt very bad, then?' His face was pale but unmarked by the copper and I thanked God for that much.

'It feels as if my back is on fire, to be truthful Catrin but there's no lasting damage done.'

I gulped trying not to show how near to tears I was. I could imagine Lizzie Morgan's scorn if I should break down. Dylan pressed my hand and winked at me.

'Don't worry,' he whispered, 'I'll soon be well enough to take you up the Town Hill again.'

'What are you two whispering about?' Lizzie Morgan tutted in annoyance, 'I don't know what young people are coming to, in my day we had a proper respect for our elders.' She looked at me disdainfully, 'I really think you should go now, Catrin, the nurse said that Dylan wasn't to be tired.'

I got up obediently and went to the door, 'I'll come to see you again tomorrow Dylan,' I said, and Mrs Morgan looked at me sharply.

'Please to wait for me outside, Catrin Owen,' she said, 'I'd like to talk to you.'

When she came out a few minutes later, she strode right up to me and stared me in the face.

'This is all your fault, you little vixen!' she spoke in a venomous whisper and there was hate in her red rimmed eyes. 'If you hadn't made him go to work in the copper he would have been all right but the money wasn't good enough for you was it miss high and mighty, you didn't want a barge man for a husband did you?'

I turned away unable to speak. Mrs Morgan's words might be cruel but she spoke the truth, it was my fault that Dylan was in the copper works.

Guilt and regret were like twin devils within me. I felt now that I was tied to Dylan and with all the perversity that was in my nature, I longed to be with John.

Mr Jones smiled when I took the horse back to him, he mopped his forehead with a big coloured handkerchief and puffed out his cheeks. 'Is everything all right, girl, you look a bit white around the eyes as if you were upset?'

'Dylan seems all right, Mr Jones,' I said, 'Thank you for being so kind.'

'Tut, think nothing about it,' he said briskly, 'your folks were kind to me when my poor wife passed on.' He looked down at me, his eyes moist and I realized he had feelings too in spite of his dirty way with little girls.

It was good to be back home. I sat on the stool near the fire and mam brought me a cup of wine. 'Here this will bring the colour back into your cheeks,' she said, 'is Dylan bad?'

I nodded, 'Bad enough, but they don't tell you anything down there at the infirmary.'

Dad came to sit beside me, he had a few small burns along his forearm and the graze on his cheek had turned his eye black so that he looked like a bruiser.

'Are you all right, dad?' I leaned against his shoulder and his arms encircled me.

'Yes, good as new except for a bit of a headache. If I have nothing worse than that there will be no cause for complaint.'

I drank my tea. 'I think when Dylan comes home I'll go and help Mrs Morgan to nurse him, if she'll have me that is.'

Mam looked at me in surprise. 'But what do you know about nursing the sick, Catrin love?'

'Old Mrs Lloyd promised to teach me about the herbs, she says they will cure anything.'

Mam frowned, 'Well, I suppose it will be a good thing for you to learn about the herbs cures. Mrs Lloyd knows more than anybody how well they work.'

I stood up meaning to go into the slope but suddenly everything seemed to be melting away from me. I put my hand out to dad and then there was nothing but rushing darkness.

It was a new day when I opened my eyes. Outside the fowls were making their usual early morning noises and I could hear my father whistling as he washed.

I got up and dressed myself for work and dad smiled approvingly when he saw me.

'Sure you feel all right?' He smiled down at me, his hair sparkling with dampness. I nodded and sat down at the table waiting for mam to bring the breakfast.

'It's not going to be a picnic in there today, girl,' dad said, 'if you feel like staying home by the fire, it will be all right.'

'I feel all right, dad, really I do, there's no need for me to stay at home.'

'Good,' he said, 'come on then, hurry up, I want to make an early start, see that the place is running smoothly again. I hope none of the furnaces were damaged in the blow up.'

As we stepped out into the greyness of the row, I felt years older. I made up my mind I was going to make Dylan well again, even if it took the rest of my life.

ELEVEN

It was dim in the scented kitchen and Mrs Lloyd placed a candle on a shelf above the table.

'This is ordinary mint, Catrin,' she held the dried bunch of herbs towards me and I examined the leaves curiously.

'It is the herb of Venus, see girl? If the juice is taken in vinegar it stops wounds from bleeding.'

She looked at me from under her black hat, its tattered white lace making a grubby frame for her elongated face. She smiled, her teeth gleaming whitely in the candle light and for a moment I was tempted to believe that she chewed animal bones as some people claimed she did.

'Pay attention now, Catrin,' she said and there was a mischievous look in her eyes. 'You must be careful with mint because it stirs up bodily lust, do you understand?' She crushed a leaf suddenly and the fresh smell surrounded me. 'Mix the leaves with mead, water and a bit of honey and it will cure pains in the ears.' She stared at me shrewdly. 'You must know every plant, girl, otherwise you could make a mistake that could kill instead of cure a body.'

We worked steadily for an hour or two, the time passed so quickly that I had no time to feel tired. At last, Mrs Lloyd washed her hands and indicated that I should do the same.

'You've got everything that is needed to make a good nurse, Catrin,' she said in satisfaction, 'run along home now and come again tomorrow.' She came with me to the door. 'Don't worry, Catrin, I'll teach you all about the herbs and plenty that will be of use to you in curing Dylan Morgan.'

I smiled to myself in the darkness of the street, she was a wise old woman, all right. 'Good night Mrs Lloyd,' I said, 'thank you very much.'

It was cloudy and dark as I turned the corner into Tip Row and tired though I was, joy flared inside me when I walked straight into John's arms.

'Catrin!' he held me close, 'I was just coming round to fetch you home from Mrs Lloyd's.' He looked closely at me, 'You seem a little pale, are you driving yourself too hard?'

I shook my head, 'Oh, no, I'm fascinated by everything Mrs Lloyd tells me.'

His hand smoothed my hair from my face. 'But I scarcely see you these days, are you avoiding me deliberately?'

'Don't be so soft, boyo!' I said a shade too quickly and John sighed.

'Well you won't have to go out of your way not to see me, I'm going up to London tomorrow.'

Fear opened inside me like a flower. I stared up at him trying to read what was in his eyes, he couldn't go away from me, not now.

He sensed my panic, 'It's only for a while, Catrin, I promise I'll get my business over and done with as quickly as possible.' He drew me so near that I could feel his heart beating. 'You do need me just a little don't you?'

'I need you, John,' I said shakily and I did not turn away when his lips came down on mine. He released me with a sigh.

'Go on inside, now, your parents will be anxious about you. I'll see you as soon as I return.'

I watched him walk away from the row and part of me wanted to call him back. But Dylan was lying down at the infirmary and it was my responsibility to see he got well again. I turned my back on the row and went inside.

The sun was a pale disc in the evening sky as I made my way into the infirmary. Dylan was sitting up against the pillows, his face drawn but with something like the old gleam in his eyes.

'Here,' I held a small pot towards him, 'take this but don't show anyone or I'll be thrown out on my ear!'

'What is it, girl?' he said, attempting to smile, 'are you trying to poison me?'

'Never mind the questions, drink it before anyone comes in.'

He moved a little under the sheets wincing with pain. 'Well it can't do any harm, I suppose,' he said, 'and it may do a little bit of good.'

He drank the remedy in one gulp and with a grimace handed me the pot.

'Good boy.' I took his hand, 'Dylan, I can't tell you how sorry I am that you got hurt by the copper. Your mam blames me and she's right, it is my fault.'

'Hey cut it out!' Dylan said urgently, 'and I don't want you hanging around because you feel guilty and sorry mind.'

'Don't be soft,' I kissed his lips briefly but inside I was trembling.

'*Duw*, there's mam.' Dylan closed his eyes as Mrs Morgan her back ramrod stiff, marched up to us.

'I've had a talk with the doctor, Dylan,' she said with not so much as a look in my direction, 'he says you can come home next week. But,' and she emphasized the word, 'there must be no visitors for a while.'

Dylan winked at me, 'Catrin will have to come, mam,'

he said in all innocence, 'she is bringing me medicine and it is doing me good already.'

Mrs Morgan was sharp. 'What medicine, what rubbish have you been giving my boy, Catrin Owen?'

'It's all right,' I said, 'Mrs Lloyd has done the mixture for me.'

She set her lips in a thin line of anger, she would say nothing against Mrs Lloyd just in case she needed her some time.

I moved away from the bed, 'I'd better go now but I'll bring you more medicine tomorrow.'

Outside, I sank down on to the softness of the sand that was silver and jewelled in the moonlight, trickling the pale grains through my fingers. There was a feeling of despair inside me, I was as fickle as the wind, now that Dylan really needed me, I wanted John more than I'd ever done before.

I became adept at making up potions and Mrs Lloyd was pleased because my fingers were nimble and because now I could tell the name of every herb she possessed.

'*Darro*! You'll be better than me if I don't watch out.' She sounded angry but I was beginning to know her and there was pride in her because I was turning out to be a good pupil.

Mam grumbled to me because I was hardly ever home. 'If you are not down at the infirmary, you are with Mrs Lloyd in that stuffy kitchen of hers. You need air in your lungs after a day in the copper sheds, girl, see how pale you've grown?'

Mam sank down on a stool, her elbows on the table. 'Oh children do bring worry to a body, between worrying about you and missing our Huw I'm in a proper mess.'

'You worry too much, mam,' I said gently, 'we've got to

live our own lives, you can't carry us on your back for ever.'

'I know, girl,' mam said softly, 'but it's a hard thing for a mother to learn that the children she brought into the world are grown up.' She was suddenly impatient. 'Anyway, we were talking about you, when are you going to take a few days off from that place, that's what I want to know?'

'Now, now,' dad said, 'she can't go taking days off, she's needed in the sheds.'

Mam rounded on him, 'Don't talk, Will Owen, a woman has enough work to do all her life, cooking and cleaning up after men. You won't be satisfied till you see our Catrin brown as the copper like you.'

Dad got to his feet, 'Hush woman, and who was it asked me to get the girl a job in the first place?'

'It was me,' mam said, 'and wrong I was, there are you satisfied now?'

'A man can't win against a woman's tongue,' dad took his hat from the hook on the door. 'It's down to the beer shop with me and the devil take you and your tongue, woman.'

The door shut with a bang and mam looked at me a bit sheepish. Laughter bubbled inside me and I leaned against the wall too weak to say anything to mam and after a few minutes, she began to laugh with me.

Dylan came home from the infirmary in great style. Reece the death lent his funeral cart and a bed was made on it with clean sheets smelling of sunlight. One thing I'll say for Lizzie Morgan, she keeps a clean house.

The whole of Tip Row was out waiting to see him as he lay pale but smiling, waving his hand to everyone just like he was royalty.

I went in to help Mrs Morgan get him into bed and for the first time I saw where the copper had caught him. The flesh on his back and legs was angry and red and I could tell that every step he walked brought him pain.

'We'll soon have you better,' I whispered, 'Mrs Lloyd and me.'

He looked up at me from the bed, his eyes almost black and his hair like a sheaf of dark corn across his forehead.

'While mam's gone down to see the visitors out, you can make me feel better by giving me a kiss,' he said, 'only take it easy, mind, I'm in no condition to get excited.'

I pretended to hit him. 'There's a devil, you have only one thing on your mind and you supposed to be sick, too.' I leaned over and pressed my lips to his mouth gently, his hand touched my breast and I jumped back startled, I'd forgotten how much his nearness thrilled me.

'There's a pretty colour in your face,' he said teasingly, 'just wait until I can run about a bit, you won't get away from me, I promise you!'

Mrs Morgan bustled into the room, her eyes upon me were like chips of coal. 'I expect Dylan would feel better for a bit of a rest.' She said folding her hands across her thin waist and waiting by the door for me to move.

'I'll see you tomorrow after work,' I said touching his arm and ignoring his mother's loud sniff of disapproval. 'It's time I got along to Mrs Lloyd's anyway.'

She was seated in the doorway, her fading eyes watching for my approach.

'Here I am, Mrs Lloyd,' I said, 'I hope I'm not late.' I followed her inside and she waved her ebony stick that was clutched in her hand like an extension of herself.

'Been with the Morgan boy, have you?' she said staring at me like a vengeful cat, her eyes half closed. 'He's not the one for you, mind, but you are determined to make his accident your business so I suppose I'd better help you.'

She moved to the table and the faint pleasant scent of lavender drifted from her.

'I'll show you how you can heal burns with the herbs,' she said, 'and try to settle down, you're like a mettlesome pony there.'

I blushed and made a great business of rolling up my sleeves, Mrs Lloyd always seemed to know just what I was feeling.

'See this white beet?' she asked as I stood beside her, 'slice it up very thinly like this.' She worked neatly dropping the slices into a bowl, 'Soak it all in water with a little drop of vinegar.' She smiled at me, 'Now get the cups out, we'll have a drink of tea because the beet has to soak for at least an hour before it's ready.'

We sat near the fire, the tea was fragrant, made of herbs and very refreshing.

'I see good things in store for you, Catrin,' Mrs Lloyd said suddenly. 'You have a star of luck over your head and there is much love in your life.' She smiled gently, 'Well there's no need to look as miserable as a dead fire, go off home with you now and get a bit of rest, everything will turn out right, you'll see.'

I felt tears sting my eyes as I let myself out into the heaviness of the night air.

'Close your door, Mrs Lloyd,' I said gulping a little, 'the sparks are flying all over the Hafod tonight and the smoke is like a dirty blanket.'

'I never shut my door, girl,' she said, 'night and day it stands open so that folks will know I'm here to help. Anyway, I could not stand being shut inside a house, like a coffin it would be to me.'

I walked home slowly, coughing a little as some of the

96

dust went down. I was glad to reach the house and to let myself into the cheerful kitchen.

'Oh, there you are, Catrin,' mam said and she looked a bit strained. 'Here have a drink of cabbage water, I kept some for you.'

'What's wrong, mam?' I said quickly, 'something has happened hasn't it?'

She sank down into her chair and twisted her apron between her fingers.

'Our Huw's home,' she said at last and her eyes as they met mine were full of pain. 'And he's brought his wife with him.'

TWELVE

The kettle sang on the live coals as I entered the kitchen, rubbing the sleep from my eyes. Rhian, round as a dumpling, her breasts almost meeting her belly under her apron stood over the fire slices of bacon laid out on her hand ready for the pan.

'Oh, please let me do the breakfast,' she said to mam, 'being a farm girl I'm well used to cooking.'

With a shrug, mam reluctantly sat down at the table. 'Well please yourself, though your face is flushed now and too much overheating is bad for the baby, mind.'

Huw leaned over the table and whispered to me, 'It is great fun to see them fighting about who is going to cook my breakfast.'

I put my hand on his arm, 'Take my advice boyo and have a word with Rhian. Two women in a kitchen never works well and mam likes to have things her own way in her own house.'

Huw laughed, 'I'm not saying anything, let them sort it out between them, I'm likely to have my ears boxed if I interfere.'

I stifled a laugh behind my hand and dad looked up from his newspaper.

'Come on, Catrin or you'll be late for work, get some food into you and quick.'

I was silenced by dad's anger, he had been in a rage ever since Huw had turned up and if it had been his choice, neither Huw nor Rhian would have set foot inside the house.

I watched as Rhian expertly forked the rashers of bacon out of the pan. Mam was watching too but you'd have thought Rhian was doing it all wrong from the look on my mother's face.

'What's the matter, Mrs Owen?' Rhian said quickly, 'Isn't the bacon cooked to your liking?' She was not backward in coming forward but it was foolishness to put mam in her place in front of us all.

'I like my own ways best,' mam was huffy, 'no doubt when you have a place of your own you won't want strangers messing it up.'

Huw shook his head warningly at Rhian telling her with his eyes to keep her mouth shut. Things were difficult enough already, I had given up my bed in the slope and was sleeping in the kitchen and mam didn't approve of that arrangement at all.

I finished my food and moved away from the table and as Rhian went to take my place, Huw pinched her playfully. Mam tutted her eyes angry and Huw started to laugh.

'Go on mam, don't tell me that dad never pinched your ass.'

Mam rose from the table affronted but filled with dignity.

'We will have none of that talk at my table,' she said on her high horse, 'taking oaths is against the Lord's command I'll have you know.'

Dad pushed his plate away. '*Duw* this place is enough to give anyone the belly ache,' he complained. 'Are you coming to work, Catrin?'

I went to the door after dad and Huw came to stand beside me so that I was like a tiddler in a sandwich between the two of them.

'Any jobs going down the sheds for me, dad?' Huw said and there was tension in the room so thick it could have been cut with a blunt knife.

'You should have given a thought to your job before you ran off,' dad said, anger burning in his eyes. 'You can't come back here as if nothing has happened.'

Huw bunched his great fists and there was a fear inside me, if the men quarrelled now murder might be done.

'Oh come on, dad,' I said coaxingly, 'Huw hasn't been away long, he hasn't being doing any harm, just getting Rhian pregnant!'

In spite of himself, a smile crept into dad's face. He was proud to think of his son as a virile man following in his own footsteps.

'Aye, come on then,' he said, 'you're not such a bad copper man and I dare say Mr Vivian will never notice you've been away.'

As we set off for work, it was like it used to be, me, dad and Huw walking along in the gritty morning light and Huw whistling a merry tune. The sound of many boots echoed on the cobbles around us, all making for the copper works that sprawled like a voracious monster, waiting to swallow us up.

In the sheds there was the roaring heat to greet us and Huw loosened the button at the neck of his shirt.

'*Darro!* I'd almost forgotten what a hell hole this is.' He rolled up his sleeves past his elbows the light of the furnaces turning the hair on his arms to the colour of gold.

'You heard about the accident, did you?' dad asked and Huw shook his head.

'It wasn't too bad this time.' Dad held out his canvas sleeve for me to dampen the clay around it. 'Young Dylan Morgan was hurt, though we never did find out who was to blame.'

Huw's eyes glowed red, 'We know who's to blame,' he said fiercely, 'the blasted owners should be spending some time and money making the place safer. We slave our guts out for them isn't that enough?'

'Hush, boy,' dad said, 'there's time for the airing of opinions and this isn't the time or the place. Get on with your job and be lucky you've got one.'

Huw gave him a bitter look, 'Aye thank the bosses for giving me a job that fills up my lungs with dust and turns my face copper.'

Dad stared at him. 'Remember the wife you've got and the child she is expecting,' he said, 'shooting off your mouth is very good if you don't have responsibilities but you are tied now like any other married man.'

Huw's anger faded, 'Aye, you are right dad,' he said softly, 'people might change but the copper will go on for ever.'

The noises coming from the slope were enough to curl up the straightest hair and I shook with fright as I put the kettle on the fire. Rhian's time had come.

Mam came out of the slope, 'I think you'd better bring Mrs Lloyd, now girl, the child is almost ready to be birthed.' Mrs Lloyd was sitting in the doorway as usual, smoking her pipe.

'My brother's wife has come to her time,' I said breathlessly and she picked up her bag as if she had known I was coming and had made her preparations.

'Now, girl,' she said leaning heavily on her stick, 'see if you've learned anything from me. What do we give the mother to help the birth along?'

I took a minute to collect my thoughts. 'The seeds of columbine steeped in wine,' I said, 'and later, some cocks head to bring out the milk.'

'Good,' she said, 'come along then, don't linger here, let's be on our way.'

Rhian was lying on her back with her hair streaming like strands of silk down her face, clinging to the sweat that mingled with her tears. Her swollen belly was uncovered and she began to arch her back with the fresh onslaught of pain.

'Wash your hands, Catrin,' Mrs Lloyd said, 'and come and help me by here. You'll always be able to turn an honest penny if you can birth a child.'

Mam was a bit alarmed that I was allowed to assist in the birth but she would not gainsay Mrs Lloyd's authority.

'See, Catrin, how the child's head appears with every push the mother gives? When it comes far enough, grasp it and I will show you how to bring out the shoulders.'

She took up some dried herbs rubbing them on to my hands and her own. 'Keeps away evil vapours,' she said to mam.

The columbine seeds had eased Rhian's pains and she relaxed a little her heavy lashes resting against her smooth cheek.

'Lift up your leg, there's a good girl,' Mrs Lloyd said kindly, 'and when I say bear down, you do it good and hard and then it will soon be over.'

Rhian gasped her assent, her lips pursed as another pain gripped her. I watched Mrs Lloyd's old hands gently smooth Rhian's belly, it was as if she would squeeze the child into the world herself. 'Bear down!' she commanded and Rhian's face reddened with the effort she was making. Her moan became a strangled murmur and then the baby's head, wet and slippery was in my hands.

'Turn it gently, Catrin,' Mrs Lloyd said, 'that's the way, ease those shoulders out.'

It was over, the child crumpled and red lay on the sheet. I felt tears rise to my eyes at the miracle of it all.

'Rhian,' I said softly, 'you have a fine boy, he has dark hair just like our Huw.'

I stood back, washing my hands in the bowl trying to blink away my tears. Childbirth was a marvellous thing but let no-one tell me it was easy, it was the hardest thing on this God's earth.

The men were in from work and Huw paced across the room biting his lip ferociously as he waited for the news. It was mam who spoke.

'Go in and see your son,' she said and he waited no longer darting into the slope like a dog released from a chain. Mam started to cry and dad took her into his arms his cheek against the darkness of her hair.

Mrs Lloyd pulled her shawl around her shoulders and for the first time, I realized that she was quite old and bent.

'Are you going to see me to my door then, Mr Owen?' she asked, 'my sight isn't as good as it should be.'

Immediately, mam reached for the tin on the mantelpiece, her hand still shaking.

'How much do we owe you, Mrs Lloyd?' she said, 'not that money could ever repay you for what you've done.'

'I won't take money from this house,' Mrs Lloyd said full of dignity, 'teaching Catrin my secrets is enough payment for me.'

She moved forward as dad opened the door with an eagerness that had me smiling. I think he was just a little nervous of Mrs Lloyd and her powers.

'Shall I come with you?' I said and dad nodded his head smartly. 'Yes come you, girl, a little walk might settle you down after all the excitement.'

He began to cough as the smokey night air reached his lungs and Mrs Lloyd tutted.

'Remind me to give you something to ease that cough of your father's,' she said as if he wasn't there, 'good deeds are best done for those near and dear to you, Catrin, remember that now.'

She bid us a curt good night at her door and I could tell she was tired even though she tried not to lean too hard on her stick. As dad and I turned back up the row, a shower of sparks lit up the sky and dad coughed again.

'*Duw*, we eat, live and sleep the copper, I wish some times we could all move away from here and breathe in the good sweet air the Lord meant us to have.'

I slipped my arm through his. 'Hey dad, this is not a night for complaining, tonight you have become a grandfather for the first time.'

He sighed. 'That is what makes me think, do I really want my grandson to grow up where the dust kills the flowers before they can bloom?'

I looked up at the ever present mountain of slag that leaned over the houses and for the first time it struck me that it was like a wall imprisoning us in ourselves, we were stuck like flies in a web.

The thoughts were foolishness that disappeared when I was once more in the brightness and warmth of the house.

Mam's eyes were shining with pride. 'You'll never guess what Huw has decided,' she said glancing up at dad, 'he is going to call the baby William, after you.'

Dad sniffed a little, scratched his head and stared into the fire to hide his pleasure.

Mam poked at the coals, 'I've just had such a job getting Iorwerth to bed,' she said. 'He did nothing but stare in delight at the baby and him little more than a baby himself.'

104

When at last, I climbed into my makeshift bed, it was only to find that I was too tired to sleep. I thought of the baby and tried to imagine how it would feel to have a child of my own. I tried to see Dylan's face but there was the persistent picture of John's blue eyes staring into mine.

THIRTEEN

The sun was brilliant in the cloudless sky. I lay against the warm boards of the barge as it moved slowly forward bending the tall reeds, jolting to a stop when the horse bent his head lazily to crop the grass.

'*Duw*, it's good to be out in the fresh air, Catrin,' Dylan stretched out his arms skyward, 'the day must have been especially ordered for me.'

I turned over on my side so that I could look at him. 'It's a nice feeling, being lazy like this, it's a great pity that life isn't one long outing.'

'Well this is for me,' Dylan said, 'no more sodding copper sheds, not for all the money in the world.'

'Dylan! Don't swear like that.' Even as I reprimanded him, I knew with certainty that he was going to talk about marriage and the thought discomforted me.

He put his arm around me, drawing me close so that his cheek rested on my hair. I felt the old sweet thrill at his touch and it was not love.

'You did a good job of patching me up after the copper caught me.' His hand was touching my breast and excitement fluttered like a bird inside me.

'You were very amiable,' I said trying to laugh, 'you didn't complain not even when I covered your back in sliced beets.'

He tipped my face up and kissed me with practiced thoroughness and like the fool I was, desire stirred in me, taking away my breath. In a quick movement, I sprinkled cold water over him, sitting up quickly away from his searching hands.

'Remember, boyo, you are still an invalid.' I leaned forward and called to Dai who was at the other end of the barge nodding in the warm sunlight.

'Dai! How far have we come now?' He sat upright, shifting his hat to cover his eyes.

'Just a couple of miles, girl, are you enjoying yourself?' Before I could answer, Dylan pulled me back into his arms.

'I want you to marry me, Catrin,' he said seriously, tangling his fingers in my hair so that I could not turn away. 'What's your answer?'

I closed my eyes and rested my lips against his warm neck. 'It's too soon to think of that,' I said unsteadily, 'we must make you well and strong first.'

He released me and turned over on his stomach and I could see the whiteness of his back where the copper had marked him for ever.

'Of course I'll marry you,' I said quickly tears stinging my eyes, 'when could I ever resist you?'

He took me in his arms holding me fiercely against him. His body was hard against mine and I could feel his desire for me, start him trembling.

'Behave, boyo,' I said though my senses were swimming, 'would you do it here in the open with people staring at us from the bank?'

'Don't tempt me!' he said, the fun twinkling his dark eyes. I leaned against him determined not to worry about the future but to enjoy the sun and the heat and Dylan's masculine presence beside me.

The day was beginning to slide into evening by the time I got home to Tip Row. I walked into the kitchen with a song on my lips only to drift into silence as I saw that John was sitting there waiting for me. He stood up and I realized how tall he was, quite an inch taller than dad and that was tall indeed.

'Hello,' I said hearing the reserve in my own voice, 'you are quite a stranger aren't you?'

I felt suddenly shy of him and I avoided his eyes as he came forward to take my hand.

'Yes, my business trips have kept me busy of late,' he said gently, 'regrettable but quite unavoidable I'm afraid.'

He continued to hold my hand and I risked a quick glance. He was smiling down at me, his eyes so blue and steadfast that my heart turned over.

'I have asked your father's permission to take you in marriage.' John's voice was soft and smooth like chocolate spread rich upon a cake and I was hypnotized by the sound of it so that for a moment the sense of his words escaped me.

'Catrin,' he said, 'I'm asking you, will you marry me?'

I looked round, seeking a way of escape, I wished I could vanish into the smoke above the stacks but there was no way out, I had to face John some time and give him my answer.

'I can't marry you, John,' I said very low, 'this afternoon I promised to marry Dylan Morgan.'

My voice fell into the silence like pebbles into a deep pool and then dad scowled at me.

'You can't marry the boy just because you feel guilty about his accident. Think girl what you are giving up.' His voice rose and from behind him in the slope I heard Rhian's baby cry out.

'Shush, dad,' I said quietly, 'you know as well as I do that Dylan only went into the sheds because I said I'd marry him, I can't go back on my word now can I?'

I looked at John miserably. 'It's better this way. I can't make myself into a fine lady for you however much I might want to.'

'Don't be silly, Catrin,' John said impatiently. 'You are a real flesh and blood woman and that is what I want.'

I shrugged helplessly. 'But I'm a copper girl born and bred, I would be out of my depth if you took me away from it.'

Huw came out of the slope suddenly and I knew he had been listening.

'Tell him what he would be taking you away from, Catrin,' he said harshly, 'lung disease, the retching cough that wracks dad every morning. The smoke that smothers babies at their birth. Is that what you want for the rest of your life, Catrin, is that what you want for your children?'

'Stop!' I said putting my hands to my ears, 'do none of you care about love?'

There was nowhere to run to hide my tears so I went out into the night and crouched against the smoking tip. It was familiar if not loved, a part of me since the day I was old enough to toddle outside the door and look at it.

'Catrin,' John's voice came softly and for a moment I remained where I was trying to ignore him. 'Catrin, I must speak to you.'

Reluctantly I came out of the shadows and stood before him, afraid to look at him.

He took me in his arms holding me as if I was precious and fragile. 'We could have such beautiful children, Catrin,' he said, 'they would speak Welsh and English and they would have your black eyes and my fair skin.' He rubbed his cheek against my hair so tenderly that tears came to my eyes.

'I'm going now,' he said, 'walk along the row a little way with me.' He pulled my hand through his arm and I laughed at the staid picture we must have made. As my fingers curled round the fine cloth of his sleeve I could not help contrasting the feel of it with the rough flannel I was used to. It seemed to emphasize the difference between us and my spirits sank.

At the end of the row John stopped walking. 'I believe you love me,' he said seriously, 'and I can be a patient man, I won't stop asking you to be my wife, you'll say yes one day.'

'Oh, John,' I leaned against him for a moment, my head just reaching his shoulder and he smiled down at me.

'You are my woman, Catrin, nothing can alter that however much you may protest.'

'Goodbye, John my love,' I said in Welsh and he looked at me as if he understood my words.

'What demon is driving you, Catrin?' he asked, 'why do you feel you must tie yourself to Dylan? You may have loved him once in an immature way but that is over.'

He took me in his arms there in the middle of the street and kissed me so tenderly that I wound my arms around his neck without realizing I had moved.

He released me then. 'I'll be back tomorrow and the day after, every day, and soon you will find out who it is you love.'

I saw in the corner of my eye a movement in an upstairs window and I knew Mrs Morgan had seen what had happened.

'Stay away from here John,' I said, suddenly afraid for him, 'these are my people but they are not yours.'

He shook his head. 'Good night, Catrin.'

As he walked away from me I knew that mine wasn't the only pair of eyes watching him.

Mam was concerned when I returned to the house,

'Catrin you've been out there ages, I was just going to send dad out to find you.'

I sat on the stool by the fire and closed my eyes and mam came and sat next to me.

'Don't tear yourself to pieces, Catrin,' she said quietly, 'just do what your heart tells you.'

'And what about my conscience, mam, what do I do about that, just ignore it?

'It couldn't work between me and John even if there was no Dylan. John works for Mr Vivian, keeping us in the copper works to make money out of us, you can feel sure that Mr Vivian won't die of dirty lungs, or dirty hands either!'

'That's fine talk, Catrin!' mam said indignantly, 'have you tried pulling a tram through the stifling darkness of the pit, stripped to your waist and so dirty it does not matter? That's how I started off and many girls are still doing it so count your blessings that you are decently employed.'

I stood up shaking a little, 'Mam, mam,' I said shaking my head, 'you haven't seen how the copper bites into the flesh and hardens there, or felt the heat that's like hell itself. Oh maybe it's better than the pits but not much, mam.'

Mam turned away, tears in her eyes. '*Duw*, I don't know what the world is coming to, there's Rhian with child before Huw is decently married to her and now you arguing with me like a fish wife, there's no respect for your elders these days.' She sighed and there was nothing I could say to her. 'Well, Catrin, I'm going to bed out of it,' she said and without a backward look went up the stairs.

When I was alone, I lay down and covered myself with a blanket, I was too tired to even think any more and I

111

closed my eyes and fell into an immediate sleep with the ease of a baby.

I sat on the Town Hill, looking out over the river, it was the same spot where I'd first lain with Dylan and now it seemed like a hundred years ago. I wondered what it would have been like to wear fine clothes and go out to tea parties like Mrs Vivian but that was a fruitless track and only led to painful thoughts of John. I had to put him right out of my mind, I was decided on marrying Dylan and that was that.

I heard footsteps, quick and firm coming towards me and there was Dylan as if conjured up by my thoughts. As he drew nearer, I could see the fury on his face and I got to my feet frightened by the intensity of his anger.

'You've been carrying on with the Englishman behind my back, you whore!' He lashed out and caught me across the cheek so hard that I fell to the ground.

'All the time you were pretending to look after me and giving me lies about us marrying, you were fooling around with him.'

He knelt over me, his eyes glowing red in the light from the stacks.

'He asked me to marry him it's true,' I said almost spitting the words out, 'I refused, I told him I was marrying you.' I tried to sit up but he pushed me back straddling me so that I was pinned to the hard ground.

'Bitch!' he said, 'no doubt you've been giving him the same as you've been giving me and I was fool enough to want to make an honest woman of you!'

Anger scorched inside me, I pushed at him not knowing my own strength and my nails raked the side of his face. He swore ferociously and then his weight was upon me and his voice was so full of pain that it took away my will to fight him.

'I loved you so much, Catrin, I wanted you to be my wife and all the time you were laughing behind my back with the Englishman.'

He pushed up my petticoats and I screamed as he thrust against my unyielding body.

'You act like a whore so I'll treat you like you,' he said breathlessly.

At first I tried to scream as he lay over me threshing wildly like an animal, there were tears on my face but I didn't know if they were mine or Dylan's. I lay still then and waited until at last he rolled away from me releasing me from the pain and humiliation he had been inflicting on me.

I sat up trying to cover myself with my skirts and as we looked at each other in the dark like two strangers I was calm.

'I am free of you now, Dylan,' I said and there was a hardness to my voice I did not recognize. 'You were so wrong and you have hurt me more than the copper hurt you so now I'm free.'

He stared at me for a moment as if uncertain what to say or do and then he lunged to his feet and ran down the hill as if the devil was at his heels.

I washed myself in the coldness of the stream, it's very iciness seeming to cleanse me and at last I was able to walk quietly down the hill.

The moon came out from the clouds, silvering the road and the tip glittered like a pile of jet beads. I took a deep breath and brushed down my hair and went into the house. I talked and ate my supper as if there was not a cloud on my horizon to worry me but deep inside I was trembling and uncertain wondering if my life would ever be good again.

FOURTEEN

Rhian was up from her childbed and to me she looked like a beautiful goddess from some old legend. Her blonde hair hung like ripples of honey over her shoulder and her cheeks were warm with the bloom of health. In her arms she cradled her son and it was beautiful to see.

It irked me sometimes that I no longer had the privacy of my own bed in the slope but apart from that, the house seemed little different to what it had always been. And yet to mam it seemed that everything was changed, she moved around with the stealth of a cat watching Rhian with critical eyes waiting for her to make a mistake. Had Rhian been a bad tempered girl there would have been murder done long ago but somehow she managed to remain serene through it all.

The baby grew like a mushroom, sitting up and taking notice of us all but especially of dad who was making a fool of himself over little William.

Mam's resentment fanned into flame and I saw her looking at dad with a strange darkness about her eyes as he played with the baby. I tried to speak to my father about it.

'Do you think mam is still grieving for the little one she lost, dad?' I asked and he shook his head.

'Don't ask me, girl, I never did understand your mam's moods and these days she just shuts me out.'

'Do you think she is jealous of Rhian's baby, you do give him a lot of your time?'

Dad ruffled my hair, 'Stop worrying like an old woman, your mother will come out of it, it's just difficult us being so crowded as we are.'

Dad had a typical man's attitude, what he couldn't mend he tried not to see but I knew a storm was bound to come and come it did.

Rhian was washing the baby, the water dripping over his plump body, he was wriggling naked and gurgling with the fun of it. Mam got up suddenly and threw a blanket on to Rhian's knee.

'Cover the boy up decently,' she said her eyes snapping with anger, 'the door is open for all the world to look in and anyway, the child could catch the ague or the cholera, the good Lord only knows what blows into the house with the smoke on a day like this.'

Rhian wrapped the baby up without a word and moved into the slope. Mam was confounded for a moment and I held my breath praying she would let the matter rest but she could not. She went into the slope, her voice raised hysterically.

'Don't walk away from me, my girl!' she shouted, 'can't a woman offer a piece of advice in her own house without being insulted?'

Rhian got on with the job of dressing little William, her eyes regarding mam almost with pity.

'It's all right, Mrs Owen,' she said softly, 'I won't be a burden to you any longer, I'm going home to my father. I was a fool for thinking such an arrangement could work out.'

She lifted the baby in her arms and stood up, almost a head taller than mam.

'Oh, *Duw*, what will Huw say?' Mam was unsure of her

ground now regretting her outburst but unable to apologize to Rhian without losing face.

'Huw must decide for himself what he will do,' Rhian said calmly, 'but I can't stay here any longer, there's nothing more sure than that.'

'Well, perhaps you'd better wait at least until Huw gets home from work.' Mam was really worried now but Rhian was steadfast in her resolve.

'It will all come out right,' she said, not even angry, 'please don't worry about us, Mrs Owen.'

She wrapped the shawl wide around herself and William tucking the end of the shawl under her arm so that the baby was supported.

'I must thank you for all your kindnesses,' she said and her gaze included me. She set out down the row at a good pace proud and dignified and I think in that moment, mam felt more respect for her daughter-in-law than she had ever done.

She sat down on a chair, hands clasped in her lap and she jumped, startled when I touched her gently on her shoulder.

'I didn't mean to drive her out,' she said bewildered, 'I didn't want to lose little William like this. *Duw*, what will the men think of me when they come home?'

We soon found out. They came in together, dad and Huw and looked straight away for the baby.

'Where's William?' Huw said puzzled, 'and where is Rhian come to that?'

Mam looked silently down at her apron and it was left for me to answer Huw.

'She's gone,' I said breathlessly, 'she's taken the baby with her and gone home to her father.'

Huw was white. 'Gone, how could she have gone? She would never leave without me.'

I shrugged not knowing what to say and mam spoke at last. 'It was my fault,' she said flatly, 'I was picking on her again that's the truth of it. She had the patience of a saint, otherwise she would have gone long since.'

'I must go after her!' Huw stood up looking for his hat and then we all froze as there was a gentle tapping on the door.

Huw flung it open, the joy on his face a rare sight indeed as he saw Rhian standing out the front.

'We've come to take you home with us,' she said, 'my father is waiting outside with a cart to carry our bits and pieces.'

Huw looked over her shoulder, his face settling into lines of hardness.

'The last time your father and I met, I was not at all welcome,' he said with sarcastic understatement and Rhian nodded.

'I know, but a bit of time alone has changed his view, he wants us with him, I promise you.'

Dad took charge. 'Come inside, Rhian and your father, too, we can't conduct our private business with all the row looking on.'

Mam tried her best to act as though nothing was wrong. She put food on the table and boiled the kettle, calm enough but there was a high colour in her cheeks that told me she was disturbed.

The food was like sawdust in my mouth and the only one who ate with any real pleasure was Iorwerth, the rest of us were too busy falling over ourselves to be polite.

One thing I found to like in Rhian's father was his obvious delight in the baby, his eyes lit up with pride whenever they rested on little William and Huw was not slow to notice it either.

At last, Rhian rose to her feet, pulling her shawl round her full breasts.

'It's time we were starting back,' she said firmly though her eyes were on Huw, pleading.

Huw stood up, 'All right,' he said speaking directly to Rhian, 'I'll come up to the farm, aye and work my guts out on it but I won't stand any interference mind.'

Her father coughed a little into his yellow spotted kerchief, he blinked his eyes rapidly, his colour high.

'Forgive and forget, boyo, is it?' he said awkwardly, and Huw nodded.

We followed them outside and I noticed with a smile that Huw climbed into the driving seat, forcing his father-in-law to take a backseat. He went a bit red round the earlobes but he kept a silent tongue in his head and I could see that so long as Huw was strong there would be a good life ahead for him.

Later, as we sat around the table drinking a quiet cup of broth, mam looked up, her face smooth now and free of worry.

'Good luck to them, I say,' she smiled, 'I don't say I was in the right, mind, but everything seems to have turned out for the best, doesn't it?'

Dad grinned. 'Aye your precious boy will grow up to be a property owner and isn't that what you wanted all along?'

Mam looked at him teasingly. '*Duw*, you think you know my mind better than I do, there's arrogance for you.'

It was peaceful in the kitchen with the coals shifting in the grate and the light rain tapping on the windows outside. I sighed a little, mostly from contentment, now I would have the privacy of my bed in the slope again.

Dylan was waiting for me when I came out of work. I looked up at him pulling my shawl closer round my shoulders, shivering a little in the cool of the evening breeze.

'What do you want?' I asked, suddenly hostile and he stood hunched miserably in his coat, his hands thrust deep into his pockets.

'Catrin, please let me speak to you,' he said and the usual air of cocksureness was missing.

'I can't stop you talking,' I said tartly, 'but I'm going to walk towards home while you are doing it.'

He caught my arm in a way that irritated me and I was too tired to make a fight of it.

'Catrin,' he said his voice low and pleading, 'don't you feel anything for me any more?'

'You've got a damn cheek!' I said stung by the tone of reproach in his voice. 'After what you've done to me you can ask that.'

'Think, Catrin,' he said, 'think of the beautiful times we've had on the Town Hill. You loved me well enough when we lay together.'

'I was ripe for a man's love,' I said bleakly, 'and you are the one that happened to come along, that's all there is to it.'

'That's not true, Catrin,' he said. 'I know there was more to it than that.'

He twisted me suddenly into his arms and his lips came down on mine while his hand explored my breast. I felt a sudden answering response in myself, I made a half hearted attempt to pull away from him but he held me fast. His tongue probed my mouth and he skilfully caressed me so that my body ached to receive his love.

'You see, Catrin?' he said triumphantly against my lips. 'We are tied together by our needs, two of a kind we are, you and me.'

He drew me into the shadow of the bushes that grew

stunted but thick on the edge of the road and lowered me gently to the ground. My body betrayed me and welcomed him but when at last we lay silent side by side, there were tears on my face, salt and bitter.

That night as I lay in bed in the darkness of the slope, I tossed and turned condemning myself for my weakness and telling myself I had no right to think of John as a husband when my body still ached and cried for Dylan's love. I could not sleep and at last I went into the kitchen to make myself a potion of rest giving herbs, perhaps it would calm the turmoil in my mind.

From the bedroom upstairs, I could hear dad coughing. It was a sound I'd grown accustomed to but now I realized that the cough had grown worse.

I took him some gin in hot water and when he saw me, his eyes gleamed his appreciation. At his side, mam was sleeping deeply, her shoulders rising and falling under the bedclothes. I sat cross legged on the floor and dad stretched out his hand to smooth back my hair.

'What's troubling you, Catrin?' he said softly and I looked up at him his face angular and strong in the flickering candle light.

'I am so mixed up about Dylan and John, dad,' I said wearily, 'perhaps I should marry neither of them.'

'There is a great deal of difference between them,' dad said, 'John is more of a man than Dylan Morgan will ever be.'

'But dad,' I said in bewilderment, 'I am drawn to Dylan by some force, as if we were meant to be together.'

Dad smiled gently. 'That is just bodily attraction, you could feel that for half a dozen men, just like a bull will service many cows.' He laughed a little, his voice low. 'Good thing your mam can't hear me, she'd wash my tongue for me and tell me not to speak vulgarities.'

He handed me the empty cup. 'No, you must look beyond that, girl, find a real love that will last through all manner of trials and tribulations. Go back to your bed, now, before you catch cold.'

Obediently I got to my feet and tip-toed back down the stairs, I was no nearer to solving my problem but I felt better now that I'd spoken to dad.

Mam was up before the cockerels in the morning, frying great rashers of bacon. Suddenly the smell of it turned my stomach and I rushed out into the yard and splashed cold water into my eyes trying to clear the mists that rose before me. Mam came behind me and caught me round the waist.

'Are you all right, Catrin? You look so white and ill come and sit down before the fire a minute and have something hot to drink, perhaps you have a chill coming on you.'

Sitting by the fire, I sneezed a few times and mam looked at me with relief.

'There!' she said in triumph, 'I knew it was the cold that had got you.'

She brought out a flannel petticoat for me. 'You young girls these days don't wear enough clothes, no sense of modesty, well you'll do as I say in future.'

'But mam,' I said, 'I'll boil to death wearing that in the sheds, you've no idea how hot it is.'

'I don't care a jot about that.' Mam was determined. 'The weather has turned colder now and you need more clothes, you can always take it off while you are at work, can't you?' She pushed the petticoat into my hands and with a sigh of resignation, I went into the slope to put it on.

'A proper fool I'm going to look when I get into work and take the stupid thing off again,' I complained and I heard dad laugh as he came into the kitchen.

'Just watch you don't show an ankle and get all the men excited,' he said good naturedly and mam rebuked him.

'Will, don't talk like that, it isn't nice.' She turned to look at me, to assure herself that I was all right and I tried to smile.

It was a foggy morning with the smoke crouched low over the houses and before we had gone very far, dad was seized by a violent spasm of coughing. He looked up at me trying to regain his composure. 'I'm all right, girl,' he gasped and I clutched his arm as if trying to drag him back from the edge of an abyss.

FIFTEEN

The air was cold with a touch of winter about it and the trees were shedding the last of their leaves. They lay in mounds on the streets, colourless and tattered.

John had suddenly turned up on the doorstep, his skin fresh from the wind and his eyes shining as they looked down at me.

'You are growing into a fine looking woman, Catrin,' he said gently, 'I feel I have missed the transition, last time I saw you, there were still some of the soft contours of girlhood in your face.'

I avoided his direct gaze and stood aside for him to come inside. 'It's not my fault if you have to go away on business so much of the time,' I said lightly but we were both aware that my words carried a reproof. Only I knew that some of my anger was because of the way my conscience was bothering me.

I had been seeing Dylan regularly, we had fallen into a sort of pattern meeting several nights a week. Sometimes, if it was very cold, I would let him through the window of the slope when everyone else was in bed and we lay together until it was almost morning. It was impossible for me to go on this way, holding the two men and unable to let either of them go.

'You are very far away, Catrin.' John spoke so suddenly that I jumped. He tipped my face up and studied me gravely, 'I'd like to know what you were thinking about.

Won't I ever know your true feelings, Catrin?'

'It's not wise to show too much,' I said quickly, 'if you knew all about me you might not love me any more.'

'And would you care very much about that, Catrin? Be honest with me.'

I looked directly into his eyes. 'Yes, I would care if I lost your love, I would care very much.'

He drew me to him and kissed me tenderly. 'Do you know that your nose is cold?' he said, and there was a twinkle in his eyes.

'Oh, John,' I pushed him away, 'you can't be serious for two minutes together.'

'Oh, I can be serious,' he looked down at me, 'but I warn you I wouldn't be responsible for my actions. I think you'd prefer me to stay as I am.'

'I can't see you being carried away with passion.' I was a bit affronted because he found it so easy to resist me.

'There is a time and a place for everything,' he said lifting his eyebrows, 'and I don't think your father would altogether approve of me seducing his daughter under his own roof.'

'So clever always, aren't you?' I said, huffy like and he laughed outright.

'Wait until we are married, you'll learn a great deal about me, I only hope you have plenty of stamina.'

From the kitchen came the sound of dad coughing and John and I looked at each other, I was frightened and he was sympathetic.

'I am trying my best to see that conditions are improved at the works and in all fairness to Mr Vivian he wants the bad effects of the smoke eradicated.'

I leaned against him, 'I know that, John,' I said, 'but it will come too late for my father, his lungs are already weakened by the smoke.'

John smoothed back my hair. 'Try not to worry too much, Catrin, it may take some time but conditions will eventually be improved and that is the only comfort I can offer you.'

I reached up and kissed him. 'I know. You'd better be going now, I'll make dad some herb tea to ease the pain in his chest. Good night, John, God bless.'

He was tall in the moonlight and I watched until he disappeared out of sight. Suddenly I felt unbearably alone, I shut the door quickly and returned to the warmth of the house.

Dad insisted on going to work. We walked slowly along the row and I could see that he was short of breath and there was a fine coating of sweat on his face even though the air was chill. Another bout of coughing seized him and I caught his arm tightly.

'Please, dad go back home,' I said almost in tears, but he shook his head stubbornly.

'I'm just a bit tired, girl that's all,' he said, and there were lines of strain around his mouth. 'I've no doubt caught a bit of a chill, nothing to make a fuss about.'

As always, it was hot to the point of suffocation in the sheds. I rolled up my sleeves waving anxiously to dad as he went to join his tew gang. There was a chorus of greeting as I started my rounds with the water, Tom Williams jumped away from the furnace and was first at my side.

'It's the end of my shift, little missy,' he said rubbing his eyes, 'but I'll have a drink of water all the same, thank you.'

He gulped down the water with a gasp of pleasure. 'You serve the best water this side of heaven,' he said with a grin. 'I'm off home now, glad to shake the dust of this place off my boots.'

I watched as he walked from the sheds, crouched as if to evade the heat of the furnace, fashioned that way by years of copper working that sapped the strength from the strongest of men in the end.

I turned to where dad was working just in time to see him thrust another pole into the shimmering heart of the furnace. The clay had dried on his glove, showering to the floor like dust. His eyes met mine for a moment and I could see his pain clearly.

'Dad,' I moved towards him anxiously, shielding my eyes from the glare, 'are you all right, dad?'

He barely nodded seeming too exhausted to answer me. He just held out his arm and indicated that I cover the clay with water.

Reluctantly I left him, I needed to refill the casks with water. The air was crisp and there was a coating of frost on the ground and I was glad of my warm shawl and the extra petticoat mam insisted that I wear.

Dai the Quay was on the river bank and I could see Dylan lifting the copper ore in hands that were red with the cold. He waved when he saw me and jumped from the barge, whistling as he came towards me.

He slipped his arm possessively around my waist. 'You've got a long face this morning, what's wrong?'

'I'm worried sick about dad,' I remained in the warm circle of Dylan's arm, 'he's coughing so much and I'm sure he's got a fever.'

Dylan shrugged, 'The same thing could be said of all the men working in the sheds, girl, that heat is enough to destroy anyone, try not to worry.'

He used the exact words that John had used and somehow the thought annoyed me. When his hand fumbled at my bodice, I slapped it away.

'Do you have to treat me like a whore?' I asked. 'Oh get on with your job, man, and leave me to get on with mine.'

I hurried back to the sheds and the men were ready and waiting for another round of water. I was making my way towards dad's gang when I saw him stagger and pitch forward on to his face.

'Dad!' I cried, leaving the water and falling down on to my knees at his side. 'Dad, are you all right?'

He opened his eyes and they were dark with pain. 'It's my chest, Catrin,' he croaked, 'I can't breathe.' I looked round me frantically for help and it was Tom Williams who came forward.

'It's a good thing I came back here, little missy,' he said kindly, 'I can help you to get your father home and into bed.' He took dad's weight in his strong arms and somehow we staggered out of the works.

'*Duw!* There's daft I feel,' dad revived a little out in the crispness of the air, 'fainting like a sickly woman, what ever next?'

When dad was seated in a chair at his own hearth, he seemed a little better. I helped mam to pull off his sweat soaked clothes and wrap a blanket round him then I poured a drop of gin between his pale lips.

'I'll be all right,' dad's eyes were on mam's white frightened face and even in his pain, he wanted to comfort and reassure her. 'A little bit of a cold shouldn't bring me all this fussing, though I must say, I like it.' He tried to smile.

'Come on mam, let's get him into bed, he'll rest better there.' I knew that mam would be all the better for having something to do.

'I'll be off, little missy,' Tom Williams slid his hat on to his head, 'but if you need help you know where to find

127

me.' There was a lump in my throat as I closed the door behind him, he was a good man and a good friend to me and mine.

Dad's breathing was still difficult as we got him into bed so I helped mam sit him up against the pillows. I brought him a bowl of steaming water and held it near his face and after a while he seemed somewhat easier.

'Come on, mam,' I whispered, 'let him sleep, it will do him good.'

We returned to the kitchen and mam had a lost look on her face. I poured her a glass of gin and she took it with trembling hands.

'Your dad has always been such a strong man,' she said looking at me almost pleadingly, 'he's not going to die, is he?'

'Don't think of such a thing.' I pulled on my shawl. 'I'll run around to Mrs Lloyd, she can cure anything.' I wished I felt as sure as I'd sounded but as I ran down the street, fear was like a stone inside me. I panicked for a moment when I saw that Mrs Lloyd wasn't in her usual spot by the door but as I stepped into the dim little kitchen I saw she was asleep before the fire.

'Mrs Lloyd, I need your help.' I put my hand on her arm and she was instantly awake, her eyes like shiny black beads. 'Dad is ill,' I said, 'I'm afraid that it's the lung fever.' Her face was difficult to read as she studied me thoughtfully.

'I'm not going to promise a cure, girl,' she said slowly, 'but I will do all I can to help you.' She pointed to the table, 'see those herbs there, girl? Water agrimony they are, you know what to do with them don't you?'

I looked at her questioningly, 'aren't you coming with me then?'

She shook her head. 'No, you can do all I can and most

likely more. My legs are growing old, Catrin, the spirit is willing but the flesh is weak.' She puffed on her pipe for a moment. 'You remember all I've taught you, girl, and God go with you.'

Dad's fever was worse. I boiled the herbs and gave him the juice to drink, rubbing the leaves on his chest. His eyes flickered open and he smiled at me.

'You are a good girl, Catrin, but I think I've had it this time.'

I shook my head vigorously. 'No, dad, not if you fight, the fever can be beaten, you'll see.'

I sat beside him bathing his face in cold water, changing his clothes frequently, anything to keep him cool. His face remained flushed and his eyes seemed smaller because of the puffiness around them.

I gave him more herb juice and as a last resort, I opened the window so that the cold air encased him. I watched at his bedside well into the night, insisting that mam went to bed to at least try and rest. 'I'll call you the minute there's any change,' I promised and she nodded her head helplessly relying on me with touching faith.

The cockerels in the garden were just setting up their morning clamour when I could see that the flush had gone from dad's cheeks and he was breathing more naturally.

'Mam!' I called, and she came immediately, her feet swift on the boards. She looked down at my father and tears made rivulets along her tired cheeks.

'He's going to be all right, mam,' I said shakily, 'the fever is broken, he's out of danger.'

Mam fell down on her knees at the bedside. 'Thank God!' she said and layed her face on dad's hand so that he stirred and smiled weakly at my mother. I think in that moment I knew what love was all about.

The next day, I decided to return to work, mam would

need my money more than ever with dad off sick. As I pulled on my shawl I gave mam instructions about boiling the herbs.

'Keep them tender,' I said, 'and don't think dad will be well all at once, it's going to take time and good nursing.'

'I know, love,' she said, 'I wish you could stay at home you are so good and clever with everything.'

She followed me to the door and kissed my cheek. '*Duw* there was I calling the pits everything and now the copper's got dad's lungs, it's like a punishment because I made you all go to work there.'

'Nonsense, mam,' I said, 'it's no good thinking like that, none of us can see into the future.'

It was strange walking down the row on my own, first Huw had gone away and now dad was sick that made me the only worker left in the family. It was a frightening thought and I gulped back the tears.

'What's wrong, little missy?' Tom Williams fell into step beside me, 'your dad's not worse, is he?'

I shook my head. 'No he's over the worst now, thank God.' I brushed the tears away with the back of my hand. 'He'll never be a furnace man again, though.'

Tom patted my shoulder. 'Well, don't you worry about that, we'll see that your father gets fair treatment from Mr Vivian, there are light jobs your father will be able to do, we copper workers look after our own, remember.'

He caught my hand and pressed some money into it, 'here's a little something to help out until things are brighter and don't offend me by saying no!'

I walked along the road crying like a baby and Tom walked beside me, silent and strong but I think his eyes were a little moist too.

'You can't get out of it now, Catrin.' John sat at the table in our small kitchen, his hat in his hands and his face fresh from the cold wind. 'I've promised Mrs Vivian that she shall meet you today.'

'But what could I wear, John? My flannels would not look fine beside her silks and velvets.'

Mam came and stood by my side. 'I've an old velvet dress that your grandfather bought me, it's still as good as it ever was and I was smaller then, it should fit you.'

Against my wishes, mam dressed me up fit to kill, the velvet gown was too big but mam's needle made short work of that excuse. John smiled happily as I tied my hair up in a ribbon of green that matched the gown.

'There,' he said with pride, 'you look beautiful enough to eat.'

It seemed that the whole row turned out to watch me climb into John's carriage. Feeling like a queen, I waved as the horses moved forward, slipping a little on the icy road.

Soon we had left the streets of the Hafod behind us, John paid the money at the toll gate and then we were out on the open road. I pressed my hands together to stop them trembling. I was worried that I would make a fool of myself and shame John.

The house was beautiful, built of a stone that seemed to hold the sunshine in its walls. We drove beneath the trees and John looked down at me.

'You've been so silent and still,' he said with a twinkle in his eyes, 'I thought you had fallen asleep.'

'Oh, John, boyo, I'm frightened out of my wits, my place isn't here, I don't believe in anything Mr Vivian stands for, I was a hypocrite to come at all.'

He drew the horses to a stop, ignoring my outburst and a man came from the house to take the reins and he bowed to me as if I was a lady.

Laughing at my expression, John lifted me to the ground, leading me through the large doors into a cool, high ceilinged room that reminded me of a church.

An elegant lady smelling of some beautiful scent came towards us, her hands outstretched, smiling a greeting.

'How lovely to see you John and at last we are able to meet your young lady and very beautiful she is too.'

I could not take my eyes off Mrs Vivian as she led me into a smaller room. Her hair was dark glossy ringlets and there was a smoothness and innocence about her face that made her seem young even though I judged her to be about my mother's age.

'It was very kind of you to invite me.' I spoke slowly, glancing round at the pieces of marble and the innumerable vases of leaves that seemed to be everywhere. 'It's the most beautiful room I've ever seen,' I said spontaneously.

Mrs Vivian's face lit up. 'How kind of you to say so, my husband is very indulgent. Ah, here is John Henry.'

I saw a tall man in a black coat and my first impulse was to get to my feet.

'Tut, tut, sit down, my dear,' he said, 'how good of you to visit us.'

He turned to John and the two men were soon in a deep discussion of which I could understand only a very few words.

'Come, Catrin,' Mrs Vivian said in mock anger, 'let us leave the men to talk business, I will show you my beautiful plants.'

I began to tell her, a little shyly, about the herbs and their virtues and she was fascinated.

'Oh, my dear, I simply must write this all down,' she said eagerly, 'how wonderful to have such knowledge, let me share just a little of it.'

After tea, during which I was in an agony of embarrassment lest I tipped crumbs of cake on the white carpet, John rose and said it was time we took our leave.

'I must see Catrin safely home to her parents before it gets dark.'

I sighed with relief as the carriage rolled down the drive astonished to see that both Mr and Mrs Vivian waved until we were out of sight.

'There, it wasn't so bad was it?' John laughed down at me. 'Did you imagine they would eat you on toast for breakfast?'

'It was like a dream, John,' I said seriously, 'and dreams are not for the like of me. You must have a wife who is a true lady.'

'When will you get it into your pretty head that I want you, Catrin. Now we'll have no more of that foolish talk if you don't mind,' he said firmly.

It was good just to lean against the smooth cloth of his coat and to breathe in the sweet air that had no trace of copper dust to mar it. It would be a hard thing to go back to Tip Row after such a day.

SIXTEEN

'I think I'd like to sit in the old doorway for an hour, Catrin, will you give me a hand?'

It was with difficulty that dad pushed himself up from his chair and walked towards the open door, leaning on me heavily.

'It's a bit cold, dad.' I brought a shawl to cover his shoulders and he smiled at me wistfully.

'*Duw*, girl, would you make an old man of me already?' he said but the shawl remained around him.

'Have I salted the chicken, Catrin?' Mam dipped her finger quickly into the pot and sucked it. 'It needs more but just a pinch.'

She smiled at dad. 'There's goodness in that, Will, it will put new strength into you, if only you'll promise to eat a bit.'

Dad stared down the row allowing his womenfolk to fuss him but detaching himself from the proceedings, his eyes searching the distance.

'Well, I'll be blowed!' he said, 'Catrin, you've got better eyes than me, isn't that our Huw and his wife coming this way? See them, him driving a cart like a dandy?'

I leaned out of the door past him. 'Yes, it's them and just look how big the baby has grown.'

There was a lot of noise in the kitchen then what with dad slapping Huw on the back and Rhian telling us all how much the baby had eaten for his dinner.

Mam quickly put more vegetables into the broth to stretch it for another two mouths.

'There are things here for you, mam.' Huw put a huge basket on the table and mam leaned forward to look, her eyes wide.

'Just see the size of that chicken.' Mam's cheeks were red and her eyes shone but I knew it wasn't the basket of goodies that had excited her but the sight of our Huw looking so brown and healthy.

'Look at that, Will,' she said, 'there's enough food to keep us going all winter.'

Rhian smiled. 'And plenty more where that came from, don't you worry.'

I knew at once she'd said the wrong thing, a gift was one thing but mam would never have anyone believe we were in need, not even her own daughter-in-law.

'No, don't bring anything else,' she said firmly, 'not unless we can pay you.'

'But mam,' Huw put his arm around her, 'we just want to help you out.'

Mam frowned at him. 'We don't need helping out, Catrin is bringing home money enough to get us by and soon dad will be well enough to go to work.'

Dad spoke up. 'Don't be so proud, girl, it's a son's place to mind his parents and I'm happy to see the children thinking of us.'

Mam made a face and for a moment I held my breath thinking she was going to protest but she shrugged. 'Well, only stuff left over, that's all I'll take.'

She picked up baby William and he sat on her knee as good as gold, his chubby hands reaching up to pull the wisps of hair that hung down mam's cheeks.

'He's a lovely boy.' Mam looked at Rhian her eyes knowing. 'You are with child again,' she said, and I looked quickly at Rhian to see if she was offended by mam's outspokenness but she just nodded, smiling.

'I didn't think it showed yet, I'm hoping for a daughter this time.'

Mam tutted. 'You should go carefully, too many mouths to feed calls for trouble.'

William was curled up against my mother's breast his eyes drooping as mam, quite unconsciously rocked him to and fro.

Dad came to stand beside her. 'Going all broody are you girl?' he said softly, a smile on his face. 'Just say the word and I'll do my best.'

'That's enough of that talk, Will,' mam said but there was a small sad smile on her face as she spoke, 'I know well enough there will be no more children for me.' She turned to dad. 'Now for goodness sake sit down and stop cluttering up the place!'

Dad grinned. 'You can tell I'm getting better by the way your mam shouts at me.'

Huw looked at dad in concern. 'You had us worried there for a while but I might have known an old war horse like you couldn't be kept down for long.'

Mam reluctantly handed the baby back to Rhian. 'I'd best put out the broth before it thickens too much,' she said, 'and perhaps eating will stop dad from talking so much!'

It was quite like old times with all of us sitting round the table. I studied Huw covertly noticing that he had filled out to good advantage and his skin was brown not with copper dust but with the sun and the wind on it all day.

'Marriage and farming seems to suit you boyo,' I said quietly, pinching his arm in fun. He turned to look at me his eyes alight with amusement.

'Bedding a good woman puts life into a man,' he

whispered, 'when are you going to pick a husband and settle down?'

'Stop whispering together you two.' I think mam had caught the gist of what we were saying and her next words seemed to bear me out.

'Catrin, tell them about your visit to Mr Vivian's house.'

Huw raised his eyebrows, speaking through a mouthful of broth. 'Going up in the world, and what was it like there? A palace I shouldn't wonder.'

I laughed, a bit self conscious. 'It was beautiful, like a church, all coloured marble statues around the place and rooms so big you could put our house inside one of them.'

'Well, you could be living like that if you married John Richards.' Huw shook his head, 'I can't understand why you are hesitating.'

'I don't know why everybody wants to interfere in my life, I'll decide for myself and in my own good time.' I knew the hot colour was in my cheeks as I bent over my bowl.

Huw put his hand on my shoulder, 'If you want my advice, go for respectability rather than the sins of the flesh.'

'Huw!' Mam glowered at him not quite sure what he was getting at but feeling a reproof was due anyway. 'Watch your tongue boyo, little ears are listening.'

Mam nodded towards Iorwerth who wasn't paying us a bit of notice anyway, he was too busy floating pieces of bread on top of his broth.

Huw reverted to our previous conversation. 'What was it like in the lions den, then, was Mr Vivian very uppity?'

I shook my head. 'He was very kind to me, he bent over my hand as if I was a lady. It was a queer feeling I can tell you.'

Huw made a wry face. 'I've got to admit that he treats

137

his workers very fairly in every respect except that of cleaning up the copper works, that smoke and grit will be there till the day I die.'

A bout of coughing seized dad and I watched helplessly as his face turned red and his hands started to shake with the strain.

'Aye,' he said at last, 'the copper has made an old crock of me before my time, I'm good for nothing now but sitting in a corner with a shawl over me.'

'Now dad, don't be silly,' I said quickly, 'you're not an old crock, you'll be right as rain given time.'

'You can't fool me girl,' he shook his head. 'I'll never work the sheds again, my lungs are gone.' He lit up his pipe which made him cough even more but he kept it firmly in his mouth through the spasm, sinking back against his chair at last weary like an old man.

'Mind I'm not complaining,' he gasped, 'the copper has brought me a good living for many a year, I knew the hardships of the job and accepted them along with my pay, no-one gets anything he doesn't work for.'

A loud rapping on the door brought us all to silence and for a moment no-one moved. Then mam straightened her apron tucking a wisp of hair in place and opened the door.

John stood on the step, smiling, his eyes finding me immediately.

'Oh, come in,' mam said all of a fluster, 'you'll have to excuse us we've just been eating our dinner.'

John sniffed appreciatively. 'It certainly smells good, it's enough to make my mouth water.'

Mam glowed. 'Come and sit down and you shall have a bite, squeeze in there by Catrin.' She went to the hob and ladled the steaming broth into a bowl.

John removed his topcoat and sat next to me, his blue

eyes smiling at me in a way that warmed me. Huw grinned and shifted up and it was obvious the two men liked each other. John ate with relish and when we had all finished eating, mam quickly cleared the table, prodding Huw to build up the fire.

'I'm glad everyone is here,' John said rising to his feet. 'I'd like to formally ask permission to propose marriage to Catrin.'

Dad nodded. 'We are willing and more than willing, it's the girl herself you've got to convince.'

I sat in silence embarrassed and rather pleased at the way John had forced me into a position where I had to give him an answer. He might be a gentleman with impeccable manners but he wasn't soft by any means.

'Say you will have me, Catrin,' he said taking my hand. 'I've even chosen a house for us to live in. Perhaps you will come with me to see it,' he looked round. 'Would you all like to come?'

No one listened to my small protest, there was a lot of movement in the kitchen, the pulling on of shawls and coats amid a deal of excited laughter. I stood back watching as if none of it concerned me until mam threw me a shawl and told me to hurry myself up.

It was a strange procession that set off down the row. Huw driving the cart and Rhian in the back with Iorwerth and little William. In John's carriage was mam and dad and me like a lady beside John in the front seat.

We rode through the Hafod and down the strand, I had a fleeting glimpse of the sea and then John turned the horse in the direction of a small hill set on the west side of the town.

We came to a stop before a house with roofs that pointed to the sky and many windows reflecting the pale sunlight giving out a feeling of warmth. Excitement stirred within me as John lifted me down from the carriage and led the way through the curved polished doors.

There were high ceilings just like those at Mrs Vivian's though the rooms here were smaller, more cosy with large dark furniture that gleamed with abundant polishing.

Mam stood just inside the door, her eyes wide as though she could not believe what she was seeing.

'*Duw* Catrin, there's grand you'll be, he must love you very much indeed to buy you a fine house like this.'

I sighed, 'But mam, can you see me living here? I'd be lost in all this space.'

John put his arm around my waist. 'You would soon become accustomed to it, Catrin, come let me show you the room that will be ours.'

He took my hand leading me up the cool staircase and with a grand gesture, he flung open the double doors. The bedroom was magnificent, decorated in pale shades of blue and in the centre was the biggest bed I'd ever seen.

'Here our sons will be born,' John took me in his arms, 'all you have to do is say you'll marry me.' He kissed me full on the mouth and I clung to him, shyly at first, feeling as if a hundred stars were lighting up the heavens. When we drew apart, I was trembling and John took my hands in his.

'Can you tell me now that you don't love me?' he said, and I shook my head.

'I love you all right,' I said leaning against him with his cheek warm against my hair.

'I knew I would win you over in time,' he said softly. 'I have loved you from the first moment when I saw you dressed up as a dirty faced boy with your glorious hair streaming over your shoulders.' He caught my hand and drew me to the door.

'We are going to be married,' he announced from the

140

head of the stairs and he took me down to where my family waited in the airy hallway.

Dad coughed. 'You have my blessing, you know that. I pray that God will make you very happy together and look after her mind, she's very special.'

Mam came up to me hugging me and kissing my cheek in a rare to-do. 'Oh, our Catrin, I just can't believe it, you are going to be the mistress of this fine house! I'm so proud of you girl.' She nudged my arm. 'But take no nonsense from him, mind, he's still a man and they need keeping in their place now and again.'

I had tears in my eyes as I looked down at my hand as it lay in John's broad fingers, he made me feel cherished and cared for. I struggled to make him understand.

'I'd love you even if you didn't have this fine house for me, do you understand John?'

He pinched my cheek. 'I know you are not after my money, if that's what you mean. I've told you, Catrin, I know you better than you know yourself.'

Outside, there was frost on the grass, I looked anxiously at dad but he seemed to be standing up to the excitement very well, there was some colour in his cheeks and his eyes were shining. I went up to him and squeezed his arm.

'How will you manage, dad, with no money coming in?' I said quietly and he winked at me, saucy, like his old self again.

'Don't you worry about that. I'll work again. Oh not in the furnaces granted but I'll have a job and bring in regular money for mam to keep the three of us on. You just be happy, girl, that's all I ask.'

We were all a little subdued on the homeward journey as if the afternoon's excitement had drained the energy from us. Huw and Rhian turned off before we reached the Hafod and waved their farewells. 'See you soon!' Huw called. 'And all the best to you, John and Catrin.'

It was good to be back in the warmth of the small kitchen and I wondered if I would ever learn to live with the big rooms and tall windows of John's house. My feelings were in a turmoil, one minute I was on fire to leave Tip Row behind me and the next I wanted the safety of the sameness of mam's kitchen.

John picked up his hat, 'I'd better be going now,' he said, 'thank you for everything, Mr and Mrs Owen. Catrin will you see me to the door?'

We stood for a moment in the crisp evening air, the light was dying from the sky and I looked upwards to where the flare of the stacks illumined the hill above us.

John tipped my face up to his. 'Promise you will not change your mind,' he said softly, somehow vulnerable. I put my hands on his cheeks and drew his lips near mine.

'I promise *cariad*,' I said tenderly and we clung together for a brief moment.

'I will make all the arrangements,' he said, 'we will be married as quickly as possible, I'm not taking any chances.' He turned then and climbed into his carriage, lifting his hat to me before starting up the horse. The gesture seemed to put him miles away from me and as I watched him ride away, out of sight, there was a fear inside me that I would never match up to his expectations.

'You will be all right, Catrin,' dad said, sensing my feeling as soon as I returned to the fireside. 'John is a good man and a strong one. He knows what are the true values in life.'

I ruffled his hair. 'I'm going to bed now, I'm worn out with everything.'

I lay on my bed staring upwards not seeing the cracked ceiling or the small window but trying to imagine myself walking through the great rooms of the new house. At last

I pulled the bedclothes over my head shutting out the little bit of light that managed to seep into the slope, hoping to shut out the thoughts that plagued me. I fell asleep in the end only to dream about marble statues and long graceful stairs and me on my hands and knees scrubbing as though my life depended on it.

The next morning I woke to see that sprinkling of snow had fallen. Mam was already puffing on the embers of the fire trying to bring some warmth to the kitchen. Iorwerth was crouched beside her watching intently and I realized suddenly how big he was growing, his face was changing from its baby roundness and he was the image of Huw.

'Wrap up warmly, girl,' mam looked at me over her shoulder, 'make a good breakfast before you go out.'

Later as I walked along the streets towards the works, yesterday seemed little more than a dream. This was my real life, the cold of the streets and the heat of the sheds. Men in flannel shirts and women in spotless aprons struggling to keep their homes clean in the face of the copper cloud that hung forever over the houses. Within me was an emptiness and a feeling of sickness that I could not explain.

'Hello, little missy,' Tom Williams greeted me with a none too gentle pat on the back, 'what is this I hear about you riding round in a fine carriage as idle as a rich man?'

I laughed wryly, 'News travels fast as ever, doesn't it? I had a good time and I wish I was out riding today instead of sweating in the heat of the sheds.'

Tom tapped his finger along his nose. 'Ah, you won't be here much longer though, will you? A little bird tells me you'll soon be married and quite right too, a pretty girl like you.'

I took out a slice of cake from my pocket. 'Here, a little

something from mam,' I said, which wasn't strictly true, the cake had been meant for me but I couldn't face it.

'Lovely,' he said, his mouth full, 'give me some water to wash it down, I'm cruel thirsty.'

As I went round the tew gangs, the teasing continued, the men who had worked side by side with my father for years felt almost a vested interest in what happened to me. I was from Tip Row and I was going to get away from it which was a subject for rejoicing.

Although the banter was well intended, I grew tired of trying to smile and an awful listlessness seemed to hold my limbs as if I was trying to walk through honey. I hardly knew how I got through the day but at last it was time for me to finish work and never had I been so glad.

The ground was hard with frost that struck with a terrible bite after the heat in the sheds. I walked along carefully watching where I was putting my feet and I looked up startled by a whistle to see Dylan and Dai the Quay walking towards me.

'Hello there, Catrin girl.' Dai pulled off his hat and stroked back his streak of green hair and Dylan just stood, hands to his side, staring at me as if he would like to land me one.

'I thought all the nonsense with you and Mr Fancypants was over,' he said without preamble, 'galavanting you were yesterday, side by side with him for all the world to see.'

I wasn't in the mood to argue, I made to walk past him but he caught my arm tightly.

'I could tell your fine boy friend a thing or two. How to keep you happy by giving you your oats regularly, hey?'

'Now then, boyo, there's no need to go talking like that to the girl,' Dai the Quay was red to the ears with embarrassment, 'calling names never did anybody any good.'

'Shut your gob!' Dylan growled, 'before I shut it for you, this is my business so keep your beak out of it.'

'John knows all about us,' I said wearily, 'I haven't hidden anything from him.' I drew my arm away as he stepped back from me.

'Liar!' he said, 'you wouldn't tell him, he wouldn't take you after that.'

I shrugged. 'If you don't believe me tell him yourself. I don't love you Dylan, I love him.'

There was a desire in me to hurt him, to take the stupid, arrogant look from his face. Once lay with a man and he thinks he owns you body and soul.

He looked down at me with dark, burning eyes, they were red rimmed as if he wanted to cry and suddenly I felt sorry. I put out my hand.

'I didn't mean to hurt you, Dylan,' I said huskily but he thrust me away.

'You'll come back to me, Catrin,' he said with conviction, 'however far you try to run you'll come back because you belong with me, we're two of a kind.'

I was suddenly afraid. I turned from him hurrying over the slippery ground scarcely noticing the cold rain that was beginning to fall. Deep within me was a question that dug like a knife. What if Dylan was right, what if I married John and still longed for the touch of another man's hands? I wanted to cry but the tears were locked inside me like a cold hard pain.

SEVENTEEN

There was a sickness within me, a deep searing pain that gave me no rest, I had lain with Dylan once too often and now I was pregnant with his child. The irony of the situation did not escape me. I had made up my mind to be with John only to find I was tied to Dylan with unbreakable chains.

I could not tell mam, her hair was turning white at the temples through worrying about dad, I couldn't place yet another burden on her shoulders.

My father was a little stronger now, but his breathing was laboured and he walked slowly, bent like an old man. Nevertheless, he had made up his mind to accept a light job down at the works and I knew what it cost him in pride.

'Are you sure, Will, sure that you are fit to go back to work?' Mam fussed over him, spreading out his scarf to cover his chest, her hands saying what her tongue could not.

'Don't be soft girl,' he smiled but not with his eyes, 'it's a boy's job I'll be doing, of course, I'm fit, woman.'

Mam opened the door for us, 'Look after him, Catrin, see he doesn't take on anything too hard.'

I nodded fighting the nausea that had churned within me ever since I'd smelled bacon frying for breakfast.

We walked in silence, dad his hands thrust deep into his pockets, hunched his shoulders as if to protect himself from the cold wind. 'Here we are again, Catrin,' he said with a bleak smile, 'treading the old familiar path to the copper works.'

'Aye, dad,' I said rubbing my hands to keep some warmth in them, 'I feel I've been walking it all my life.'

He put his arm around my shoulders. 'But not for much longer, girl, soon you'll be a fine lady in a great house. John Richards is right for you, he'll be good to you.'

'I know that dad,' I said dispirited, 'but I feel I will always be tied to Tip Row.'

'Well,' dad said heavily, 'there's no need for you to forget your roots or be ashamed of them, you are as good as anyone and a damn sight better than most.' He laughed and ruffled my hair, 'You've always had a good head on you and you are a pretty girl even though I do say it.'

I smiled up at him warmed by his praise. 'I can see now where our Huw gets his charm from, you old flatterer!'

I said goodbye to dad and he stood for a moment watching me walk into the heat of the sheds. There was a strange lost look on his face and I realized with surprise that he was really going to miss working at the furnace with all his friends.

Tom Williams nodded to me, his face reddened from the heat, 'Fair freezing out, isn't it girl? You look as pinched as a penny chicken.'

'I'm all right,' I said quickly. 'I'll soon warm up in here.' I stood still for a moment. 'What job will dad be doing, Mr Williams, is it something easy?'

'*Duw*, of course it is, little missy, he'll be in the wash house rubbing sawdust over the copper to clean it, he can sit down in there all day if he wants to.'

My eyes were suddenly full of tears, my father was used to being strong, the leader of the tew gang and now he would be working among the boys, what shame he must be feeling.

'This old place has got a lot to answer for, Mr Williams,' I said sniffing a little and he nodded.

'Aye, the copper beats us all down in time, I shouldn't wonder if I was to end my days breaking up stones for a few pence a day.'

He took his water in one huge swallow and went back to work, dipping the ladle into the brilliant copper and deftly turned it into pots. It suddenly struck me that all the men were like ants crawling from furnace to pots and back again in never ending slavery to the molten copper.

I scolded myself for having such strange fancies and went on to the next tew gang. The heat was like a wall and I wiped away the sweat from my eyes with the corner of my apron. Suddenly, everything was spinning round me and the ground came up to meet me as I pitched forward into a silent darkness.

Someone was dabbing cold water in my face, I struggled to sit up gasping with shock and Tom Williams was bent over me, a crowd of the men standing behind him.

'*Darro*, little missy, that was a rare fright you gave me, are you feeling bad?'

I tried to stop the buzzing in my ears. 'I'm all right.' I said, 'I think it was the heat after the freezing cold outside, really, I'm better now.'

Tom Williams took the water casks from me. 'You go and sit down for a minute, I'll see to these.'

I watched him, tears threatening to overflow, he was a huge man, built like an ox but he had the simple goodness of a child.

I don't know how I managed to get through the rest of the day, Tom Williams kept an eye on me and it was an effort to hide from him the fact that I could barely stand for the faintness that attacked me every time I went near a furnace. It was a great relief to finish my shift and go outside into the greyness of the evening.

Dad was waiting for me, stamping his feet and rubbing his arms trying to keep some warmth in his limbs.

'Have you been waiting long?' I asked anxiously, 'you should have gone straight home not stand here asking to catch a chill.'

Mam had a piece of steaming ham ready for us but my stomach rebelled immediately at the greasiness of the meat. I turned away from the table, my hand over my eyes.

'What's wrong, love?' Mam asked anxiously putting her arm around my shoulder. I was tempted to turn to her and blurt out the truth, beg her for comfort and reassurance but Iorwerth was sitting at the table, eyes large in his pale face and I knew I couldn't do it.

'I'm just tired, that's all,' I said. 'I think I'll go and lie down for a while.'

Mam brought a dish of bread and warm milk in to me, her eyes anxious as they rested on me. 'Eat this love, it will put some warmth into you.'

I ate a little just to please her and then burrowed under the blankets like an animal making a nest and soon I drifted into a deep sleep.

It was dark when I woke, I felt rested and much better, there was no feeling of sickness, much to my relief. I washed my face in water from the bowl at the side of my bed and pulled a comb through my tangled hair. A ray of hope had sped into my mind, I would slip out and go to Mrs Lloyd and ask her what I should do.

She was sitting near the fire, her feet drawn up under

her flannel petticoats, her kitchen warm and sweet scented and very welcoming. She smiled when she saw me but her shrewd eyes missed nothing.

I sat down. 'You know why I've come, don't you?' I looked into the heart of the fire unable to face her.

'Yes, I know,' she said softly and picked up her pipe and I noticed with surprise that her hand was shaking. 'What are you going to do about it?'

I shrugged my shoulders, taken aback by her question, I had thought she would have told me what course to take.

'You know I have herbs that would make you slip the child,' she said calmly, 'if that is what you want.' There was an air of waiting about her. I shook my head vigorously.

'No, I don't want that, Mrs Lloyd, I couldn't ever do that.'

She nodded her head as if well pleased. 'Right, then you must tell him, not Dylan Morgan, the other one, he'll forgive you if he loves you as much as he says he does.'

I rested my head wearily on my knees. 'He's been prepared to give me so much, how can I ask any more of him?'

She pushed herself up from her chair with an effort and poured me a drink that shone amber in the fire light. 'Drink this, it will do no harm, I promise you but it will calm you so that you can think properly.'

I drank the liquid quickly, it was bitter and I shuddered as it clung to my lips.

'Tell him everything,' she urged, 'better that than he should find out from someone else.'

'Yes, you are right,' I said, 'I owe it to John to tell him to his face.'

Mrs Lloyd's eyes glowed in the firelight as she stirred up the coals. 'That's one secret you can't keep for long, girl you know that as well as I do. Go home now and rest.'

She saw me to the door and I walked along the empty streets in the darkness feeling as though I'd like to crawl to the top of the tip and throw myself down. The thought was an evil one and I banished it quickly but the haunted feeling lingered long after I had climbed into the safety of my bed.

John came for me on Sunday and we went together to see the new house again. I was on pins, searching my mind for a way of breaking the news to John that I was pregnant by another man. However I managed to say it, the news was bound to be unpalatable to him.

'This will be your own private room.' John flung open a door and there was a cheerful fire in the grate making the room homely and bright. Deep comfortable chairs stood like sentinels either side of the fireplace and the tall windows were dressed with velvet curtains that touched the floor.

'You will be able to entertain your family and friends in here whenever you like if you want anything altered please let me know.'

I sank down into one of the chairs, my heart heavy. 'Come and sit down, John,' I said in a small voice, 'there is something I must tell you.'

It was the hardest task I had ever been set and I looked down at my clasped hands struggling for the right words to begin.

'What is it, Catrin?' John said in concern, 'is something wrong at home?'

I shook my head, 'No, it's nothing like that, I don't know how to say this to you, John.' I looked up at him trying to read encouragement in his expression but his eyes were guarded.

'I'm going to have a child, John, there is no other way I can say it.'

The words sank into the cold silence of the room like pebbles in a pond and John rose to his feet and walked across to the window, his face averted from me.

'I can't begin to tell you how ashamed and sorry I am,' the words were dragged from my dry throat sounding hopelessly inadequate. 'I can only say that I love you with all my heart.' His back was stiff and there was something defeated about the set of his shoulders. I went to him on an impulse and put my arms around his waist, my head against his broad back.

'Oh, John how can I say words that will make you understand me when I don't even begin to understand myself?' I moved away from him then and went to the door. He followed silently holding the door politely for me to pass through.

'John,' I tried to keep from crying. 'I told you I could not make a fine lady, didn't I?'

He barely glanced at me, 'I did not expect you to behave like a wanton.'

'I do not deserve that!' I said hurt and angry. 'I did not want Dylan to make love to me, I just couldn't help it, somehow I can't resist him but that is not love.'

John held his hand up, 'Spare me the sordid details, Catrin, I'm not a solid block of wood, I'm a man and right now I'd like to beat the living daylights out of the both of you.'

'What good would that do?' I stood watching as he locked the door, the gesture was one of finality, he would never live in that house now, with or without me.

He took me to the end of Tip Row and without speaking another word to me spun on his heel and walked away. I went to Mrs Lloyd's cottage, I couldn't face the inevitable questions there would be at home.

'A drop of gin is what you need now,' Mrs Lloyd fussed over me as if I was a baby myself. 'There, not enough to harm the baby but just enough to warm you through, you look so peaked and white.'

She brought me a muslin bag with herbs in. 'Steep these in water tonight, the liquid will help you to sleep.'

'It was asking too much of any man.' I made no explanation none was needed. 'He was so hurt, I couldn't expect him to forgive me.'

'What will be, will be.' Mrs Lloyd sank down on to her stool by the fire and I saw suddenly how frail and ill she was looking.

'What's wrong?' I said, suddenly jerked from my own miseries. She smiled at me a little wistfully.

'Old age, mostly, girl and there's no cure for that except death.'

'Don't talk like that!' I said quickly, 'what would I do without you?'

She waved her hand around the kitchen. 'All this is for you, Catrin, there's no-one else would do any good with it.'

'Why talk like that?' I asked distressed, 'you have many fine years ahead of you yet.'

She looked at me, a hint of laughter in her eyes. 'I have had my fill of years, girl, and I am going to choose the time I will die.'

My throat was suddenly dry and my heart began to pound sending the blood rushing to my cheeks. 'You are not thinking of doing anything silly are you?' I said fearfully and she shook her head.

'You need not worry on that score, girl, to take a life,

even my own is a sin against God and man, I will do nothing of that sort so rest easy.'

'I do not understand you, then,' I said and she waved her hand to me.

'Go on home, now and do not worry about anything, it will all work out for the best, you'll see.'

Troubled I slipped out into the street and the coldness of the night settled around me. I shivered, the world was full of miseries and they all seemed to be resting on my shoulders.

Dad was in the rocking chair when I let myself into the kitchen, his eyes were closed and he was singing a soft, haunting tune. I went and sat on the floor beside him resting my head against his knee the way I'd done as a child. His hand smoothed my hair and I wanted to stay that way for ever, my worries being soothed away as I grew sleepy.

Mam came in from the back, putting the kettle on the fire. She smiled and I saw that she was pretty and colourful in a red dress.

'Hello, *cariad*,' she said to me and dad opened his eyes and smiled benevolently, happy and contented. I saw that it was impossible for me to tell them about the baby and to splinter their fragile moment of beauty.

I went into the slope and undressed in the dark, slipping into bed with a sigh of relief. My body ached and my head was thumping, I just could not sleep.

From upstairs, I heard mam's soft laugh and the creek of the old bedsprings and in the face of their happiness I was the more lonely and lost.

I rose and went into the kitchen remembering the herbs Mrs Lloyd had given me, it would take no more than a few minutes to steep them in water and find the benefit of the juice.

I went to the door and looked out on to the darkened world sleeping, insensible to my pain. I sank down on to my knees, my dry eyes aching and finding no relief of tears, there was the world and I was the bottom of it.

EIGHTEEN

My petticoats were becoming tight around me and I was bound to tie the strings of my apron loosely to conceal the thickening of my waist. It was a great wonder to me that mam noticed nothing wrong, she was usually so keen eyed and perceptive. I dreaded the mornings when my breakfast was left practically untouched and the sickness that drew me to the privy down the back.

But mam was living in a world of happiness because dad was coughing less and he was sticking his new job down at the works bringing home money, albeit less than before, like any other man in the row.

Her cheeks had taken on a new bloom and she bustled around the kitchen with new zest in her steps and every day I shrank from bursting her bubble of happiness.

In the copper sheds I was finding the work almost more than I could bear. The intense heat was sapping every ounce of strength from me and at last the men began to notice.

It was Tom Williams who was elected as their spokesman. He placed a brawny arm around me and he smelled of sweat and copper, his shirt, where my cheek rested was damp against the heat of him.

'Come on, little missy, something is wrong, you can surely tell old Tom about it.'

He spoke softly and there was such a wealth of kindness in his eyes that I burst into tears.

'There's a good girl,' he said, 'have a good cry and if I can do anything, anything at all to help you then you know I will.'

I shook my head, 'You can't help, Mr Williams, I'm in trouble and it's my own fault.' I looked up at him but I could see he had not grasped the situation at all.

'What sort of trouble, girl?' He was bewildered, his honest face wrinkled as he tried to imagine what could be wrong.

'I'm going to have a young 'un,' I said bluntly. 'I don't know how I can bring myself to tell mam and dad, it will kill them, they were so proud of me.'

His eyes were angry as he smoothed the hair back from my hot face. 'Tell me who has done this to you, little missy, I will strangle him with my own hands.'

'No!' I said quickly, 'please Mr Williams don't be angry I realize now that I don't love the father and I don't want to marry him, he doesn't even know about the baby yet.'

He tried to think, rubbing his sweat grimed hand over his face.

'Shall I talk to your dad, then, try to explain things to him?'

'I'll tell them but thank you for listening to me and for being so kind.'

'Well, after all it's not the end of the world, is it?' He smiled forcing himself to be cheerful, 'many's the girl have found herself in a spot like you are now but everything works out in the end, you'll see.' He looked round him at the tew gang working doubly hard to make up for his absence. 'I've got to get back to work but remember I'm here if you need me for anything. Go off home now and I'll make some excuse for you.'

I shook my head, 'I must get the men some water, first, then I'll go home.'

It was cold outside and as I made for the well, I could see that the clouds were heavy with the promise of snow. I shivered, pulling my shawl tightly around me and my hands were red as they clutched the casks.

I did not linger, it was cruel to stand in the bitter cold, even the heat of the sheds was preferable. In the distance I caught sight of three men in tall hats and well cut coats and with a dip of my heart I saw that one of them was John.

I leaned against the grimy wall of the shed trying to overcome the waves of faintness that advanced and receded like the tide, blotting everything out from my vision.

'Are you all right, Catrin?' John's voice was so impersonal that I flinched.

'Yes, I'm all right, thank you.' I pushed myself away from the wall, willing myself to be strong.

'You should be at home, not working in your condition.' He took my arm. 'Come along, I will bring the casks for you.'

I tried to pull away from him, 'A fine fool you'd look in the sheds, casks are women's work.'

'I want no argument,' he said, 'I will bring them.' He gave me a gentle push and with no more to say, I began to walk towards the sheds. Seeing John again had shaken me and such a feeling of love and respect rose within me that I could hardly breathe, I wanted to be close in his arms, to stroke his hair, hear him say he would make me his wife in spite of everything but that was just a hopeless dream.

Tom Williams came and took the casts from John, 'I'll see that the men get their water, little missy,' he said, 'don't you worry about anything.'

'Just a minute, Tom,' John said, 'perhaps you'd like to tell the men that Sir Humphrey Davy is here with the intention of studying the smoke. He hopes to find a way to diminish the ill effects of the copper dust, perhaps the people of Hafod will see better days in the not too distant future.'

Forgetting all that was between us, I put my hand on John's arm.

'Oh, John I expect you are very pleased, from the first time I met you down at Carmarthen you have wanted to help the people who lived under the smoke.'

His face wore a closed look. 'Yes, well those days are long gone, aren't they?'

I felt the colour wash into my cheeks. He thought I was trying to win him round with talk about the past, a fine fool I had made of myself.

I watched him stride away and the pain cut deep into me, if only I could turn back time and drive out the shameful weakness in me that had allowed me to lay with Dylan even when I knew I loved John.

Tom Williams put his hand on my arm. 'There, go on home with you, little missy, try to put everything out of your mind for now, have a good rest.'

I smiled at him, 'Thank you Mr Williams.' The words were hopelessly inadequate but I could think of nothing else to say. He seemed to understand, he squeezed my arm and winked cheerfully at me, waving as I left the sheds.

'You are not going out on a cold night like this, are you?' Mam looked up from her sewing as I pulled on my heavy flannel shawl.

'I'm just going to see Dylan, I won't be long.' I went to the door, hoping to escape without further explanations but mam came and stood by me.

'Something is very wrong, isn't it, Catrin?' her face was pale with concern. 'Have you quarrelled with John we haven't seen him for over a week?'

In that split second, I wanted to lay my head on mam's shoulder and unburden myself but the sight of dad, his feet stretched out to the blaze of the fire made me hold my tongue.

'Don't be such a worrier, mam,' I tried to smile, 'I won't be long, I promise you.'

The streets were empty and for once the cloud that usually hung over the houses seemed to have rolled away, revealing a stark moonlit night. The ground was crisp with frost and I shivered beneath my shawl.

Mrs Morgan opened the door to my knock and I think she would have closed it again in my face except that Dylan had already seen me. He led me through the kitchen and into the slope ignoring his mother's murmured complaints about people pushing their way where they weren't wanted.

I suddenly became aware of how much Dylan had changed, it was as if I was seeing him with new eyes. He was taller, heavier with great breadth to his shoulders. His face was strong and angular, from a boy he had changed almost overnight into a man and I felt the old treacherous stirrings of desire. It seemed my emotions would always betray me when I was with Dylan.

I took a deep breath. 'I'm going to have a child,' I said simply, looking up at him after a moment or two trying to anticipate his reaction.

'Is it mine?' he asked, and there were no anger or bitterness in him, just the polite enquiry.

Hot colour flooded into my face. 'Of course it's yours Dylan otherwise I would be a million miles away from you by now.'

He considered my words for a moment and then nodded, 'All right, I accept the responsibility.' Suddenly an imp of mischief seemed to dance in his eyes, 'It's a wonder to me you didn't fall pregnant long ago.'

He took my hands in his, 'We'll be married as soon as possible,' he said and even through my rush of gratitude, I felt as though a trap had been sprung and I was inside it. I could see the years rolling away before me with the copper dominating my life and the lives of my children.

Dylan took my face in his hands. 'You have always been my woman, Catrin,' he said gently, 'perhaps now you will see it too.'

I clung to him but deep inside me was a pain, I felt foolishly, that I was betraying John. Dylan kissed my throat and my lips and I responded instinctively, perhaps we would have a good marriage, I knew I would always find joy in his embraces and as for love perhaps I didn't even know the meaning of the word.

He pulled on his coat. 'Come on, *cariad*, I'll take you home, I don't want you to fall on the icy streets.' He laid his hand over my stomach, 'you have my son there and you must be careful of him.'

We walked along the street in silence and I could hear men's voices, raised in song coming from the doorway of the beer house on the corner. It was a sad song telling how the copper ate into everything including the souls of the men who worked it. Suddenly I was crying, deep gulping sobs that shook my whole body. Dylan held me, unable to understand my tears but doing his best to comfort me.

'Go on into the warm now,' he said at last, 'and don't worry about anything we will be married in good time so that the baby will have my name.'

I mopped my face with the corner of my apron, I did not want mam asking questions now, it would be almost impossible for me to keep my tongue still. Far better for me to break the news of the baby when Dylan and I were safely wed.

161

I curled my fingers into his big hand. 'It will work out for us, won't it, Dylan?' I asked and he nodded, his voice gruff with emotion.

'I have loved you for as long as I can remember, Catrin Owen. You are a great prize to me and I will work with all the strength within me to make you happy.'

I put my hand over his cheeks and kissed him gently and he took my fingers kissing the tips so gently that I almost started to cry again.

He turned away then and for a moment I stood listening to the ring of his footsteps against the slippery hardness of the street.

NINETEEN

I stayed in bed all the next day, convincing mam that all I had was a chill.

'There you are, see,' she waved her finger at me, 'you would go visiting Dylan Morgan in the freezing cold, I told you it would only do you harm. I suppose I'm lucky you didn't slip and break your neck!'

It was good to stay in my bed and listen to the everyday homely sounds of the household. Iorwerth popped his head in and when he saw that I was awake he sat on the bed beside me.

'Are you feeling bad, Catrin?' he asked his eyes wide with interest and I caught his warm hand in mine, laughing a little but with tears not far behind as I realized that soon I would be leaving everything familiar behind me.

'I'm not so bad that I can't tell you a story if that's what you want.'

He nodded eagerly and I held back the blankets, 'Come on then, in here with you or you'll freeze.'

His feet were cold on my bare legs and I shivered but didn't move away.

Iorwerth was bright and responsive and as I looked down on the black silkiness of his hair I prayed that he would never have to work in the hell hole of the copper sheds. It occurred to me that had I married John, he would have no doubt been pleased to help my family in any way he could. Such thoughts were painful and fruitless and so I applied myself to the task of keeping my small brother happy until mam had a chance to get the fire glowing in the grate.

During the afternoon, I must have slept a little, I was brought back to consciousness with the sound of mam calling me.

'Catrin, get up and dress, girl,' mam was greatly agitated and my hands shook as I threw on my clothes.

'What is it mam?' I asked fearfully, 'is dad taken ill again?'

'No, love,' she said, 'it's old Mrs Lloyd, she's sinking fast and she's asking for you.'

'Mrs Lloyd?' I could hardly clear my mind, 'what's happened to her?'

Mam gave me my shawl. 'Mrs Price the *pisio* called there and found that the poor old thing had taken a funny turn.'

I hurried out into the street with mam coming behind me, my heart was in my mouth and I didn't dare face the possibility of losing Mrs Lloyd.

She was lying in her bed, frail as a child beneath the covers. Her face was so peaceful that for a moment I thought I was too late. Then she opened her eyes and smiled faintly at me.

'Come here, girl,' she beckoned with a shaking hand and her voice was thin and threadlike. My mouth was dry as I knelt beside her. She was wrinkled, like a dry leaf in Autumn and I knew she had decided this was her time.

'Not till midnight,' she said, reading my thoughts. 'I am going at midnight, I wanted to see you first.' She waved her hand towards an old tin box in the corner. 'There's money for you,' she said softly. 'It's a lot of money and a

164

will written out all proper, like. I want you to get away from this place, set yourself up in a smart house, you won't be beholden to anyone.'

She lifted herself up a bit, her eyes shining like beads. 'They didn't know I had come from a rich family, the folks round here thought of me as poor Mrs Lloyd and that suited me. I was from a family who farmed this land before the copper came and spoilt it. Oh you should have seen it then, girl.' She fell back against her pillows.

'Mrs Lloyd, is there anything I can get you?' My voice was unsteady but I managed to check the tears. She smiled up at me like a wicked child.

'A last puff of my pipe, Catrin, and stay with me until midnight, I don't want to be alone when I go.'

There was a movement behind me and I realized that mam and Mrs Price were standing in the bedroom doorway. Mrs Lloyd saw them too and waved her hand.

'Wait in the other room,' she said faintly, 'I'll be needing you later, Mrs Price, to lay me out and do it proper, the way I would do it myself, no skimping mind. There's a piece of money under the clock for your services.'

Mrs Price looked ready to throw a fit but she managed to nod obediently.

Mam stared at me uncertainly but Mrs Lloyd smiled, her eyes as bright as a bird's. 'Go on, she'll be all right with me, Mrs Owen. I wouldn't harm her while I was alive and I surely won't harm her when I'm dead.'

Mam went out, then closing the door quietly. I glanced at the clock as Mrs Lloyd closed her eyes wearily and saw that it was five minutes to twelve.

'It won't be long now, girl,' she said, 'humour an old woman and hold my hand.'

I took her dry, feeble hand between my own as if I could transfer some of my vitality into her veins. She smiled and shook her head.

'Don't be sorry, Catrin, I'm old, I want to die, I've had my life and I'm lucky to have some one who cares, to see me off.'

I smoothed back the wisps of hair from her forehead and held out her pipe but she waved it away.

'Listen to me carefully, Catrin,' her voice was almost gone, 'don't worry about your future, it is already decided in the stars. You weren't meant to live in Tip Row for ever, believe me, every word I'm saying to you is the truth.'

'Save your strength,' I said in a whisper, 'please don't try to talk any more.'

She gave a wry smile. 'What have I got to save my strength for, Catrin? I won't need it in the next world.'

I opened my mouth to speak to her and I saw that the light had gone from her eyes and her hand was suddenly heavy in mine. It was twelve o'clock. I rocked to and fro trying to contain the grief that was inside me. I told myself that she wanted to die now, she had chosen her time and accomplished her desire.

I felt hands on my shoulders then, and mam was helping me to my feet.

'Come on home now, Catrin,' mam said quietly, 'Mrs Lloyd has gone to her eternal rest.'

At the door, I paused for a moment to look back. She was just an old lady who had passed away in her sleep but I knew that part of my life had gone with her.

TWENTY

'What a day we chose to come and see you, mam.' Huw brushed the light dusting of snow from his coat and took off his scarf.

'*Duw* it's enough to freeze off my manhood.' He leaned over and kissed mam on the cheek and she pushed him away unable to control the laughter that made her eyes sparkle.

'Hush, boyo!' she said, 'you are not in the house two minutes and you're coming out with vulgarities.'

She drew him towards the fire and Rhian sat down on the stool with baby William on her lap. He was blue with the cold and I took his little hands in mine, rubbing them gently. Rhian's eyes flickered over me and I noticed the way that one of her hands rested almost protectively over the roundness under her apron, it was all right for her, I thought sourly she didn't have to worry about concealing her condition.

'Give me my grandson.' Mam took William up in her arm and he chuckled as she pinched his cheek. 'You are getting to be a great big boy,' she said proudly. 'I remember your daddy was a bonny child too, such beautiful, black curls.'

'Aye,' Huw grinned, 'and I haven't changed a bit, have I mam? I'm still the handsomest man for miles around.'

He settled himself beside me, his arm casually round my

shoulders. 'And how about your love life, little sister?' His eyes sparkled wickedly.

'Mind your own business,' I tried to laugh, 'you only think of one thing.'

'Still got two men on the go have you?' he said, 'and it's beginning to tell on you, I'd give one of them up if I was you.'

'Oh, hush!' I wrapped my skirt around my legs to keep out the cold. 'I'm fed up of men if you want to know the truth, none of them are worth a light.'

'Stop teasing your sister, Huw,' Rhian broke in and I glanced up at her. She met my eyes and I saw at once she'd guessed about my condition. There was compassion in her look mingled with speculation. Unable to sit still under her scrutiny I got up and put the kettle on the coals. 'I'll make us all a cup of tea,' I said, and as mam was still talking to the baby, Rhian came to my side to help me.

'Want to talk about it?' she whispered and I shook my head.

'There's nothing to be said, except be careful, I haven't told mam about it yet. I dread to think what she will say.'

Rhian, to her credit did not question me further. 'You know where we live if ever you need help,' she said and I smiled warmed by her kindness.

'I was sorry to hear that old Mrs Lloyd passed away,' she said. 'I know you were very fond of her. You'll miss her.'

'Yes, I'll miss her.' I blinked a little, 'I still can't believe that she won't be there sitting in her doorway, smoking her pipe.'

Rhian put her hand on my arm for a moment. 'Poor Catrin, you are going through a bad time but when you are down, the only way to go is up, remember. Everything will turn out for the best you'll see.'

I know she meant well but I could see no solution to my problem except to marry a man I didn't love for the sake of the child I was carrying.

'What are you two whispering about over there?' Huw said and Rhian turned to him, tapping her finger to her nose.

'That's your trouble, boyo,' she said, 'too much beak you should learn to keep your nose out of other people's business.'

'So that's the way of it!' Huw looked at dad. 'See what married life has made of that woman of mine? She's a real little shrew.'

Dad shrugged, a twinkle in his eye. 'The sooner you learn to keep your place, son, the better off you'll be.'

Huw did not know when to let things alone, 'Are you going to end up a fine lady, Catrin, that's what I want to know.'

My mouth was dry but I forced myself to make a face at him, ignoring his words and holding up my cup so that he couldn't study my face too closely but there was no putting him off.

'You don't exactly look blooming with health, girl, is there anything ailing you?'

Mam gave me a sharp look, her attention distracted from the baby.

'No, Catrin, you don't look very well, I'd been thinking the same thing myself. Are you still grieving over Mrs Lloyd?' She did not wait for an answer, she turned to Huw.

'The old lady left Catrin a lot of money, who'd have thought she had that much stowed away? A good woman she was, mind for all that some people thought her a witch.'

'Aye,' dad said, 'a fine woman when people got sick, I

only hope Catrin won't be expected to take her place.'

I took a deep breath and all at once I was clear about what I should do. I would move right away from the Hafod, it would not be a good marriage with Dylan not with me longing to have John for a husband. I opened my mouth to break the news before I lost my courage but as the words trembled on my lips there was a knock on the door.

Dad went to open it and I felt the blood drain from my face as John stepped into the kitchen, his head and shoulders covered with snow. His eyes met mine and hope blossomed in me like a flower in the sun. I wanted to cry and run into his arms, beg him to forgive me and love me.

Everyone seemed to be talking at once. Mam handed the baby to Rhian and hurriedly took John's coat and hat, hanging them almost reverently behind the door. She poured him tea and brought him flat cakes still hot from the gridle.

'*Duw*, it's good to see you, boyo,' dad said rising from his chair, 'but will you excuse me if I rush out down to the works?'

He wound his scarf around his neck ignoring mam's protests that he should not go out in such weather.

'A couple of the men are talking about this Sir Humphrey Davy and his ideas for improving the works. They've asked me to be at the meeting but I won't be long, keep something hot for me, mam.'

He went out leaving a blast of cold air behind him and I ventured a look at John. His eyes met mine and I held my breath as he smiled.

'Is this on the level?' Huw said and for a moment his meaning escaped me. 'Is Mr Vivian really trying to improve conditions, John, or is he on to a good thing for making more money?'

John's hand reached out for mine under the shelter of the table and I was shaking so much it was a wonder I didn't give myself away.

'It is not merely a scheme to make money,' John said quietly, 'Mr Vivian is offering a thousand pounds to anyone who can diminish the ill effects of the smoke. Of course, if the smoke can be used so much the better for everyone.'

'What do you mean "used"?' Huw asked in surprise. 'How can anyone use smoke?'

John was on a subject he knew well and his authority thrilled me.

'There are elements in the copper dust that may well be harnessed and turned to good account.' He spoke reasonably but Huw was in the mood for argument. 'And make a packet for the owners too, I dare say.'

John shrugged, 'Does that matter? The main thing is to be rid of the nuisance of the smoke, why complain if good money is made at the same time? We could all benefit from that in that more money could be put into the works.'

'Enlarge the sheds,' Huw said shortly, 'so that more poor sods can have lung disease.' He moved abruptly from the table knocking over his chair and starting little William off crying.

'Hush your noise, Huw,' Rhian said quickly, 'you are talking as if it was John who owned the works, not Mr Vivian.' John smiled good naturedly.

'I'm pleased to see Huw with so much fire in him but we are on the same side really so it's a waste of energy us arguing with each other.'

'Aye,' Huw said quietly, 'you are right boyo, how do we set about helping people who don't even know they need help?'

John picked up his hat, 'Well, I'd better get back to the

works myself, will you see me to the door, Catrin?'

I pulled on my shawl and went into the coldness of the night, closing my eyes with joyous wonder because John was near me again. He took me gently in his arms and we clung together wordlessly.

Suddenly the moment was shattered. 'Down with all bloody bosses!' A voice rang out in the darkness and I spun round to see Dylan walking menacingly towards us and behind him a small crowd of men who from the smell of them had come straight from the beer shop. As they drew nearer, John stepped in front of me.

'Get back into the house, Catrin,' he said urgently and I stood there in the flurry of snow wondering what I could do to protect him.

There was the sound of tearing cloth as several hands made a grab for John and I kicked the door screaming for Huw to come and help.

Light spilled into the row as the door was flung open and Huw sizing up the situation at once dived through the darkness, hitting out mercilessly, felling a few of the unwary men.

Mam was close behind him wielding a piece of log and I stood unnerved as she ploughed into the crowd. It was only when I saw the gleam of a knife that I came to life. I knocked the arm of the assailant and his blow was deflected, missing John's heart but etching a red line across his cheek.

'Let them fight it out!' Huw yelled, 'stand back everyone this is a private quarrel between two men.'

His words took effect. The men slowly moved back until there were just two figures battling in the snow that was tinged here and there with jewels of red blood. Dylan's fist crashed into John's face and I covered the scream that rose to my lips knowing that nothing on earth was going to stop them from beating the living daylights out of each other.

John brought his head down as Dylan made another rush and they locked together as if in an embrace and when they parted, Dylan was bleeding from a wound above his eye.

'Merciful God, can't someone stop this fight?' I said in anguish and Huw shook his head.

'They are men and they have a score to settle, let them fight it out, it's the only way.'

There was a crash as the two men fell against Mrs Price's door and immediately her upstairs window was thrown wide.

'Get away from here, you villains,' the old woman screamed, 'before you get bucket of *pisio* over you.'

No one took any notice of her and she hung over the sill, her narrow eyes watching the fight with avid interest.

John's eyes were both black and his cheek was still bleeding from the cut of the knife but slowly he was pinning Dylan to the ground.

Dylan spat some blood, 'She's mine!' he said and John caught him by the throat.

'Give up any idea you may have about marrying her,' he said, 'Catrin is going to marry me.'

With a superhuman effort, Dylan pushed himself upright. 'There is one thing you don't know, Mr High and Mighty!' He paused his eyes bright with triumph, 'Catrin is going to have my child.'

I heard mam give a small cry and I stood dry eyed unable to move or speak, caught up in a nightmare that seemed to have no end.

'I know all about that,' John said, 'so I'll tell you once more, leave her alone or I'll kill you.'

A deafening roar filled the night sky and sparks shot

high into the air raining pieces of burning metal and cinders upon us as we stood rooted to the spot.

There was an unearthly silence and then mam spoke, 'My God!' She moved forward, stumbling a little in her haste, 'One of the furnaces must have gone up and dad is down the works.'

The men were running then, the fight forgotten, boots slipping on snowy streets. The women came behind ghostly in shawls draped around their heads, silent in their fear.

Somehow my feet took me towards the works and I could see that one of the sheds had a gaping hole in the roof. Dust was beginning to settle and part of the shed was on fire, flames licking upwards into the night. As I stumbled over the rubble I could hear the moans of the men and boys who were injured.

John and Dylan were working side by side, along with the other men, lifting rubble to free those who were trapped.

Snow began to fall more heavily, covering the devastation so that the scene had an eerie, beautiful quality that only emphasized the horror of it.

Mam was in the midst of it pulling away at the stones with her bare hands trying to find dad. I went to her side and with her began to move the timbers and there was a sudden shout from Dylan.

'Catrin, your father is here.' Slipping, I found my way to dad's side, the men had moved all the big pieces of rubble and to my relief I saw dad sit up.

'Oh, thank God!' Mam rushed forward and fell in a heap on the snow, clinging to dad as if she would never let him go. 'Will, Will I never thought I would see you alive again.'

'Mind now *cariad*,' dad said, 'where's Tom Williams? He saved my life, held up a beam that was pinning me down.'

'Here he is!' One of the men moved a piece of wood and Tom's face, blackened by dirt looked up at us. They were busy then pulling at stones and spas until at last Tom's great body was freed. He did not move, his strong arms were broken and lifeless by his side and his smile was twisted.

'I'm finished,' he said and I bent down to wipe his face with my apron.

'Don't say that, Tom,' I said gently, 'what would we all do without you?'

'The explosion,' he gasped, 'it wasn't my fault this time little missy.'

I choked back the tears, trying to think of something to say, but it was too late, his head slipped sideways and the snow drifted down covering him with a soft blanket.

Some one caught my arm and I looked up to see John urging me to my feet.

'It's no use, Catrin,' he said softly, 'he's dead, come away.'

I nodded trying to understand what was happening, it all seemed unreal, a bad dream from which I was bound to awake.

People were moving away, some following the injured to the infirmary, the lucky ones returning to their homes. It had been just another explosion, something to be forgotten the next day or the day after when the furnacemen would return to their work as if nothing had happened.

'Well, Catrin girl,' Dylan was standing beside me, 'you've made up your mind for him haven't you?' He nodded to where John stood, unfamiliar in his dirty ragged coat, his face covered in sweat and dust.

'I love him,' I said simply and Dylan nodded his head sighing deeply.

'All right, girl, he's a good man, almost good enough for you.' He grinned fleetingly, 'but not as good as I would have been.'

He walked away stumbling a little over the snow and rubble.

John came to me and took me in his arms holding me tightly to him so that I could feel the beating of his heart.

'Will you take me as I am?' I asked unable to believe it. And he smiled.

'Just as you are, Catrin.'

His arm was around my waist then and he was leading me away from the blackened sheds, out on to the road. I turned to have a last look at my home, the moon was high, shining down on the fresh snow and suddenly Tip Row was very beautiful to me.

THE END

Part Two

RETURN TO TIP ROW

ONE

The graveyard was cold and bleak in the raw December wind.

'We must go home to Swansea, Davy,' Mam said to me in Welsh. 'There's no money left, *bach*; spent it all, I did, trying for a cure for your dad.'

She spoke to me as though I was still a child, not realizing I was tall now, past seventeen, with the urges of a man.

The trees bent and moaned over my head as I stared at the headstone in the freshly turned earth. It was a modest stone, all we could afford, but the inscription stood out fine and bold, black on white.

JOHN RICHARDS
GONE TO HIS ETERNAL REST
IN THE YEAR OF OUR LORD 1848.

'Come along.' I took Mam's arm. 'I don't want you catching a chill.'

'*Duw*,' she touched my cheek briefly, 'you sound so like John with your fine English voice.'

I saw the glint of tears in her eyes then, and she had not cried in all the weary months of my father's illness. I drew her gently to me.

'Don't worry, I'll look after you. I'll take you back to

Wales. There you'll have your family round you and perhaps find peace.'

'A poet's soul, my son has.' She took my arm as we walked through the arch of the church, leaving my father at rest in his native soil.

Two days later, we sat side by side in the mail coach that bumped its way towards Swansea. It was the last part of the journey and I glanced at my mother anxiously, knowing she must be tired. But she looked beautiful, small and dark, with fine eyes that saw right through you. She caught my gaze and rested her hand on mine.

'What's the matter?' she said softly in Welsh. 'Not regretting leaving England so soon, are you?'

I shook my head. 'I'm just admiring the most beautiful woman in the world, that's all.'

'You have a silver tongue,' she said, 'and a beautiful English voice.'

'That's natural enough,' I said with a smile. 'My father was an Englishman.' I spoke without thinking, and a shadow fell across my mother's face. I could have kicked myself for a tactless fool, reminding her so crudely that she was a widow.

'We are nearly home,' she said. 'Look, Davy, you can see the stacks of the copper works. *Duw*, I'd forgotten how bad it smelled when the wind was down.'

The acrid smell of sulphur offended my nostrils. I stared out in sheer wonder at the forest of stacks shooting sparks up into the clouds of smoke that rolled over the area.

'You'll get used to it, Davy,' Mam said. 'It gets so that you hardly notice it.'

'Surely the whole of Swansea isn't like this?' I asked in horror, and she raised her eyebrows, on the defensive, pride in her home town evident in every line of her body.

180

'Certainly not!' She sounded angry. 'The sea licks the shore like a giant tongue and soft mountains rise above the smoke. But I am not ashamed of the copper, mind. Me and mine have lived by it, eating and breathing it for good money.' She paused a moment for breath. 'Do you know, Davy, I once carried water to the men in the sheds? My father and my brother Huw were among the best of the copper men. Proud I was of them. God grant that I'll be as proud of you some day.'

Her words were a reproof. My hands were soft and white, my head stuffed with knowledge gained at the expensive college where my father had sent me. I had yet to prove my manhood.

'We will leave our bags at the Mackworths Arms,' Mam said, 'and we'll walk to Tip Row. It isn't far.'

'Are you sure you feel like walking?' I asked. 'Could you not stay at the hotel and let me bring a coach for you?'

'There is no coach to Tip Row,' my mother smiled, 'though my brother Huw would lend you a farm cart, I suppose. I'll walk, and don't you worry about me – a strong Welsh woman, I am, mind.'

The town had pleasant enough roads with gracious buildings and patches of grass that in summer would be green and restful. But as we came to the outskirts, the houses huddled together, grimy and insanitary, along narrow, unpaved roads. My mother sensed my dismay.

'Don't judge too harshly, there's a good boy,' she said. 'The copper houses are neat and clean, with decent privies, one to each house.' She slipped her hand through my arm. 'You just wait, you will come to love it here as I do.'

'You love the memories,' I said, 'but see, you are coughing at the smoke just as I am.'

'I am determined not to be put in a bad mood,' she said.

'Just think how lucky we are that my mother is going to take us in and give us shelter. It's better than the streets, isn't it?'

Tip Row was small and grimed with smoke like the rest of the houses. An enormous hill of black waste dominated the area, a monument to the copper works.

The doors stood open in spite of the smoke, and as we walked past curious eyes stared at us. We must have looked incongruous in our good town clothes.

At last, we turned into one of the doors, and the kitchen was surprisingly neat and clean, with a good fire burning in the hearth. A woman with leathered skin stared at me, and there was no mistaking those fine eyes; she was my grandmother.

'Come inside, Catrin,' she said in Welsh, 'and your boy with you. Don't give the neighbours a peep show, is it?'

'Oh, Mam, it's so good to see you.' I watched the women embrace each other, and then my mother drew me forward to be inspected.

'He's a quiet one,' my grandmother said, 'but with the very devil in him, I'd say.' She touched my cheek briefly. 'Yes, you'll do, boyo. You can call me *mamgu*, that's Welsh for grandmother.'

'He speaks the Welsh,' my mother said. 'I've brought him up right, you see.'

'Good, good,' my grandmother said. 'I'll just put the kettle on to boil. Sit down, the two of you, though you look so grand as to be out of place in my kitchen.'

'No, Mam, not out of place at all, there's silly you are.'

I stared at my mother as she reverted to the Welsh. She looked just the same, well groomed, elegant even, and yet there was an intangible difference, a vigour that replaced her usual quiet calm. She went to the back of the kitchen and lifted a curtain.

'This is the slope, Davy,' she said softly. 'It used to be my bedroom.'

It was difficult to believe. I was used to my mother sharing the large high-ceilinged room with my father in our town house. Could she be actually happy to come back to this?

'You seem a bit put out,' she said, 'but I've told you about my home many times; it shouldn't come as a surprise.'

But it had seemed magic in the relating, a dream, a story my mother told me to while away a dull hour.

'Huw will be coming over with Rhian and their boy,' Mamgu said. 'You know they only have the one, lost two fine babies, they did, to the scarlatina.' She went to the door, peering out short-sightedly, coughing a little as the smoke assaulted her lungs.

'They are coming,' she said triumphantly. 'They are just around the corner at the end of the row.' She looked at me and smiled dryly, reading my thoughts. 'No, I haven't got the gift of second sight,' she said. 'I can hear the wheels of the cart rumbling on the cobbles.'

We smiled at each other, and it was the beginnings of a sound friendship between us.

My Uncle Huw had massive shoulders and a leonine head; he was handsome, with the same dark cast of features that distinguished my mother.

'*Darro!*' he gripped my hand. 'He's the spit image of his father.' He spoke in Welsh, and to my surprise I saw the colour rise in my mother's cheeks.

'Davy speaks the Welsh, mind.' She put her arms around him. 'There's good it is to see you again.'

There was a momentary embarrassment on Huw's face, and then he grinned.

'I was paying you a compliment, wasn't I, boyo? You're

a credit to the Owen family with those looks.'

'Thank you.' I smiled. 'It's kind of you, but I know I'm not in the least like my father; I am coarser of feature and dark.'

Huw stared at me in silence for a moment and I wondered if he'd understood me because I'd spoken in English.

'What beauty in a voice,' he said at last. 'You're a real gent, Davy. You sound just like John Richards.'

He went to the door. 'Rhian!' he called. 'Stop fussing over that damned horse. It gets more attention than I do. Come in here, and bring our William with you.'

He grinned at my mother. '*Duw*, Catrin, you don't look a day older than when you left here. Just look at those fine clothes.'

A boy of about my own age, perhaps a little older, stepped in through the door and dropped a basket of farm produce on the table. Behind him was a statuesque woman with golden hair.

'Rhian, will you look at Catrin's boy?' he said. 'He's almost as tall as William.'

She smiled at me; her skin was fresh and pink and there was a sweet smell about her like that of new-mown hay. I took her hand and bowed, and she inclined her head graciously.

'And this is my son William.' Huw spoke proudly, and then I was face to face with my cousin. He stared at me, unsmiling, and I'd be willing to wager anything that he had my measure, the height and weight of me down to the last pound.

'Sit down, the lot of you!' Mamgu said sharply. 'It's like a cattle fair here with you men standing around.'

We all sat, even Huw was obedient to her voice. I expect she kept my grandfather on his toes when he was alive.

'Catrin,' Mamgu said, 'you know where the parsnip wine is, in the same place as it always was. Get us all a little drop, there's a good girl.'

My mother rose and did as she was bid, and the wine was sharp on my tongue, but with a cleansing quality about it that was refreshing.

Will drank his, staring at me all the while. I felt a little discomforted. He was almost hostile to me, though for what reason I could not tell.

'Let's hear all about your goings on in the big town, Catrin.' Huw put his arm around my mother's shoulder, and she smiled at him warmly.

'This is where it all gets a bit of a pain in the neck,' my cousin said quietly in my ear. 'Would you like me to show you round the place a bit?'

'All right.' I felt a bit annoyed at his disrespect for my mother, but I doubt if he intended his words to be construed as such. At any rate, I would give him the benefit of the doubt.

I rose. 'Will you excuse me?' I said, and behind me my cousin sniggered.

'Go on, you boys.' It was Huw who answered. 'No doubt you would rather be outside than listening to us, anyway. A bit of fresh air will do you good, Davy, after your long journey.'

My mother smiled and nodded, and together with William, I left the little house and strode out down the row. The air reeked and my eyes smarted at the onslaught of dust. William didn't seem to notice it at all; he was probably well used to it. I started to cough, and he laughed at me.

'I am forgetting that you are a gentleman!' he said scathingly, and anger began to grow in me.

'I am used to fresh air, is that a crime?' I said quickly.

'And does it make me less of a man?'

William shrugged, amusement plain in his eyes, but he said nothing. I followed him over a bridge into the heart of the copper works and stopped when he did at the entrance to one of the sheds where the copper was being smelted. The heat brought beads of sweat to my face immediately and I felt as though I couldn't breathe.

'Is this where you work?' I said, gasping a little, and he gave me a quick incredulous look.

'No fear! I work the farm with my father. There's nothing would bring me to the copper. It's a place for fools, man.'

We walked through the sheds and I was glad to come out once more into the coolness of the air. It was almost impossible to believe my mother had worked in such conditions.

'See the skin of the men?' I said, forgetting my hostility. 'Copper coloured, as though they had become impregnated with the very metal they are working. They stand before the full glare of the furnaces with no protection for their hands and feet other than the rough coverings of sailcloth. I can't get over it.'

My cousin seemed pleased with my reactions. 'Look.' He pointed to the river and to the canal that ran parallel with it. 'I bet you haven't seen the like of this, either. You seem to have spent most of your time round your mam's pinny.'

Before I could think of a suitable reply, he was at the edge of the canal.

'Dai!' he called. 'Dai the quay, come here, there's a good man. There's someone you ought to meet.'

The man reined in his plodding horse and as he stepped out of the barge on to the bank I saw that he had a broad streak of green copper dust in his hair. He stared at me in amazement and a grin spread over his face.

'*Darro!*' He spat on to the bank. 'It is Dylan Morgan's spittin' image or am I going senile at last?'

'What do you mean?' I said in Welsh. 'Who is Dylan Morgan?'

He stepped back a pace, his eyes wary. 'Oh, you speak the Welsh, then. That's very good, boy.' He rubbed at his hair with a dirty hand. 'You're Catrin's son. There's proud she must be of you, you've grown up a right fine boyo.'

He turned his back on me then and shakily climbed back into the barge, clucking a message to the horse that made it move slowly away down the muddy pathway.

'Well?' I faced William. 'What was all that about? You planned the meeting. Why?'

'There's strange that you don't know the name of Dylan Morgan when he's your natural father.'

Rage rose inside me as I stared at his mocking face. I felt as though my head was going to burst. I wanted to run away, not to listen to his poisonous words, but I had to know the truth.

'All right,' I said through tight lips, 'go on. You are obviously longing to tell me.'

'It's well known around these parts,' he said, 'common knowledge.' He grinned, and I could have killed him. 'Your mam couldn't make up her mind between two men. She was full up with Dylan Morgan's child when John Richards took her away from Tip Row. It's become a sort of legend.'

Cold rage caught me. I would bury his head in the mud, suffocate the life out of him for what he had just said. He must have seen my intention written plain in my eyes, because suddenly his great fist exploded in my face.

I staggered back, dazed, and for a moment could see nothing. The fighting techniques that I'd learnt at college came back to me then, and I successfully sidestepped the next rush he made at me. My fist clipped the point of his jaw and he went down like a felled oak tree. I could have laughed at the surprise on his face. I was upon him before he could get up. I felt no pain, even though blood flew from my clenched fists as they struck home. But he was strong, and a blow behind my ear had my senses reeling. I felt my lip split and my nose begin to bleed before I managed to catch him off balance. I was caught from behind then by strong arms and pinioned against the rise of the bank. Two men stared at me closely.

'*Iesu Crist*!' one of them said. 'Surely this is Dylan Morgan's whelp. Must be. I've never seen such a likeness, not in the years of my life.' He took the sweat cloth from his neck and handed it to me. 'Here, boy, wipe the blood from your face and tell me your name.'

'I'm David Richards,' I said, and the two men exchanged knowing looks. Heartsick, I knelt and dipped my head into the yellow water of the canal before straightening up and facing my cousin.

'We are enemies,' I said to him, 'now and forever, and one day I will teach you a lesson you won't forget.'

'Easy to speak, isn't it?' he said, but I'd turned away and headed up the bank in the direction of Tip Row.

My mother screamed when she saw me and would have put her arms around me, but I held her off.

'I know about my father,' I said abruptly. 'It would have been easier if I'd learned the truth from you.'

She put her hand over her mouth and there was a darkness in her eyes.

'Did William tell you this?' Huw was angry, the red colour running up his cheeks.

'Yes,' I said curtly. 'He went to great pains to convince me I was a bastard.'

Huw put a restraining hand on my arm. 'I know it has been a great shock to you,' he said, 'but there is no need to be ashamed of your natural father. Dylan Morgan is a prosperous man now, well liked and respected in the town.' His look included my mother. 'His wife died some years ago and he has brought up his four daughters with commendable courage.'

My mother stared at me, silently begging my understanding. I turned my back on her.

'It seems,' she said, 'as though I have lost a son as well as a husband.' And she burst into tears.

TWO

The morning was raw with a tang of frost in the air as I made my way down the row towards the Hafod copper works. I must have looked a wonderful sight in my grandfather's old trousers, several sizes too big for me and gathered in folds around my waist.

'If you want a job in the copper, it's no good you going down there looking like a gent,' Mamgu had said, 'and proud you should be to wear his clothes. A real man, he was, as any one will tell you. Just tell the manager you are one of the Tip Row Owens and he'll set you on, mark my words.'

It was a great deal to live up to, being the grandson of Will Owen, but I'd sure to God try.

The sheds were even worse than I remembered them from my brief visit with my cousin William; a haze of heat and choking dust took my breath away, and my eyes stung so that I could hardly see.

'Give the blasted furnace another pole!' a man shouted, and the copper hissed and sucked like a live thing. No-one took the slightest notice of me as I stood staring round. Sweat broke out on my face, beading the fine hair that covered my upper lip, as I forced myself to walk deeper into the shed.

I stopped, watching in fascination as a man with bulging muscles turned a ladle full of molten copper into a pot. There was strain on his dripping face and his singed eyebrows met across his forehead as he ducked the spitting skets of copper.

'Can you tell me where I'll find the manager?' I shouted as he rested his empty ladle. He was breathing heavily, unable to answer, and he jerked his arm in a gesture I failed to understand.

'Water, is it, Luther?' A young girl grinned and handed him a jar, and he swallowed it gratefully. I could almost feel the soothing action with him as it flowed into his throat.

'By God, Annie,' he gasped, 'I needed that. Listen you to the way this young buck speaks. What did you want, boyo?'

I felt rather foolish. 'I wanted the manager. Can you tell me where to find him?'

'*Duw*, there's musical,' he said. 'A foreigner, are you, come down here to find a job?'

'I'm from England,' I said, 'but my grandfather was Will Owen, and yes, I am looking for a job.'

He regarded me steadily for a moment and then nodded to the girl.

'I think he'll do, Annie, don't you? A fine set-up buck from good stock.'

The girl giggled. 'My name is Owen too, Annie Owen. I 'spects we're related somewhere.'

The big man held out his hand. 'I'm Luther Lloyd. Manager's office is over there, out of the heat, but he's fair and that's all can be asked. Tell him Luther Lloyd is a man short on the tew gang and will take you. You'll be all right.'

The manager was a red-faced man, sitting behind a high desk like a pouter pigeon nesting.

'I saw you in the shed, boyo,' he said, looking at me at a sideways slant as though his fat neck wouldn't turn. 'I suppose you want a job, but you're a bit thin, aren't you? Perhaps you should be in the wash-house with the boys.'

'No.' I shook my head. 'I want a real job. I need the money to keep my mother and myself.'

'*Darro!*' he said. 'With that voice you must be the son of Catrin Owen brought from England.' He studied me for a moment, and I could almost see his mind raking over the fact that I was illegitimate.

'None of my business where you come from,' he said. 'If you do the work, that's all I ask.'

'Luther Lloyd said he'd take me on his tew gang,' I said eagerly. 'I'll work, I promise you.'

'Come on, then.' He slid from behind the desk and I saw that he was surprisingly short in the legs so that he barely came up to my shoulder.

I followed him to where Luther was working.

'You'll take this young 'un on your gang?' the manager said, and as Luther nodded he moved away. 'Right, he's your concern now, boyo, and see that he does his share.'

We watched his portly, retreating figure, and Luther laughed.

'He's all right, is that one. No nonsense about him, mind, but I like a man that's fair. Come on, then, roll up your sleeves. You can take it slow at first, feed the poles into the copper, see? It's damn hot work, but it won't break your back.'

He thrust a slender tree trunk into the molten copper and it was devoured almost instantly. 'That's all there is to it, but come by here for me to bind up your arm first.'

He tied a piece of sailcloth over my hand and forearm and then moulded damp clay over it, and I picked up a pole to show that I was ready and willing. The heat scorched my face, the mouth of the furnace was like the

192

entrance to hell, I felt the sweat run between my shoulder blades, and my skin stung as though a thousand wasps were at me. I ignored the discomfort as far as I could and tried to listen for Luther's commands.

'Step down, boyo,' he called after about ten minutes. 'Look, there's Annie with the water. Drink your fill, you'll need it, and put more clay over your arm.'

Annie's eyes were on me, filled with mischief and curiosity. I tipped up the jar and drained it.

'*Duw*, there's a thirst for you. Even a gent with a proper English voice needs water then, is it?'

She brushed the sweat from her forehead, it glistened on her arms, running down the bodice of her dress where the buttons were undone. Her skirts were hitched up and tucked in at the waist, and I wondered if my mother had looked like this in her days as a water girl.

'How old are you, Annie?' I was surprised at myself for asking an outright question. I was afraid she might be offended, but she just laughed.

'As old as my teeth and a little bit older than my tongue, right, boyo?'

'Come on,' Luther roared. 'There's no time for talking to girls. There's enough work to take up all your strength so that there won't be any left over for sins of the flesh!' He laughed uproariously, and I was glad of the heat of the furnace so that the colour in my face would not be noticed.

By the end of the shift, there was no moisture left in my body; I had sweated it all away. My muscles screamed out in agony whichever way I moved, but inside me was a satisfaction that made up for it all.

Mamgu was ready waiting for me, and as I stepped over the threshold she helped me off with my coat and shirt. Before the fire was a flat-bottomed bath, and the steaming water looked inviting. I waited for Mamgu to leave me, but she stood, arms folded.

'Come on, Davy,' she said. 'I carried that water all the way up from the canal and boiled it nice for you. Don't let it get cold.'

'But aren't you going out?' I asked foolishly, and she laughed.

'Oh, shy is it? Well don't be so soft, boy. My father was a collier and I bathed him after my mam died, and I did the same for your grandad, bless his soul. You're the working man now. Will you deny me the right to see to you?'

I stripped off my trousers and stepped into the water, and it was surprisingly soothing to have the copper dust washed from my skin.

'There's not many round here that bothers to clean themselves of the copper,' Mamgu said, rubbing vigorously at my back, 'but pitmen bath every day, and it's a good habit, I say.' She tipped water over my hair, and I gasped. 'There,' she sounded satisfied, 'dry yourself and there's a good hot meal waiting for you.'

The smell of the food was enough to make my mouth water. Quickly, I dressed in the clean clothes laid out for me and went to the table.

The fish Mamgu had cooked for me was like I've never tasted before. It was wrapped in strange leaves with a taste of herbs, spicy and sharp to my mouth, and I ate with relish.

'Where's my mother?' I asked when at last I'd finished. The words were difficult to say, though they had been on the tip of my tongue since I'd come in.

'Oh, she's gone to see some people.' I could tell by the tone of Mamgu's voice that she disapproved. 'There's an

194

address that she left here somewhere.' She fumbled behind the clock on the mantelpiece. 'Here we are.'

I looked at the piece of paper. The address was that of a villa on the west side of the town.

'They're moneyed people, obviously,' I said scathingly, and then I was amazed at myself for the antipathy I felt to these unknown friends of my mother's. Until recently I had taken money and position for granted, and yet here I was acting as though I'd been a working man all of my life.

'Your mam wants you to go over there and bring her home,' Mamgu said. 'She wants you to look nice, that's why I put out your town clothes, make a good impression on her friends.'

'To hell with them!' I exclaimed, and though Mamgu clucked her tongue in disapproval I could see she felt the same as I did. She put her hand on my arm.

'I know it's difficult, Davy,' she said. 'You don't know if you're cow or pig, gentleman or worker, but try to have a bit of patience with your mother. She only wants what's best for you.'

'All right,' I said. 'I'll go and meet her fine friends and act like a gentleman, but just this once, mind. I'll not make a habit of it.'

The brisk walk refreshed me, I felt clean, and it was undoubtedly good to have the soft material of my good clothes against my skin instead of the rough flannel. Nonetheless, I was a copper man now, however little my mother thought of it.

The villa was set in a wooded hill just above the town. It looked remote and gracious – a stark contrast to the huddled houses of Tip Row. In the softness of the evening light, I saw the curve of the bay spread out below and the shimmer of the gas lights enhanced the town so that it was

195

like a vision of an unknown but beautiful land.

The door was opened to me by a pert young maid-servant. She looked into my eyes boldly.

'Shall I take your coat, sir?' She had her hands on my shoulders before I could reply.

'Thank you,' I said, disconcerted. Servants were another item I'd taken for granted in my old life, but now it seemed almost immoral to have such command over another human being.

'I'm Joanie,' she said, 'and you are Mr Richards. You are expected, so go right in.'

She opened a door for me and at first I thought the elegant room was empty. Then I saw a woman sitting near the fire, a high-backed chair almost hiding her from my view.

'Hello.' Her voice was low and musical, and as I moved closer to her I could see she was beautiful, older than I was by at least ten years. She held her hand out to me.

'I expect you are David Richards. Your mother is talking earnestly to my brother-in-law in the study, so I am to entertain you until their business is concluded.' She patted a stool beside her chair. 'Please sit here and tell me about yourself. I'm Susannah, by the way.'

She had a brilliant smile, and she gave out an aura of colour and warmth, her rose-coloured gown contrasting with her glossy dark hair. She leaned towards me, her scent was heady.

'I am a widow, David,' she said softly. 'My poor dear husband died some years ago now, I was little more than a child at the time. Life can become very lonely in such circumstances.'

Was there an invitation in her words or was I being presumptuous? I looked directly into her eyes and saw there a message clear and plain. I touched her thigh briefly

196

as if by accident and she smiled brilliantly, the colour delicate in her cheeks.

Suddenly I was coldly angry. She was no doubt intrigued by the irregularity of my background and thought she would amuse herself with me, while away the boredom of a life spent with not enough to do. I got to my feet and glanced at the clock and, strangely enough, the off-handedness of my manner seemed to impress her.

'I hope I may have the pleasure of meeting you at the assembly rooms some time,' she said, and I shook my head.

'I doubt it,' I said bluntly. 'I shall no doubt be working.'

She came and stood beside me, her hand on my arm, her face tilted up to mine. Before I could think of what I was doing, my lips were on hers and she was holding me close.

She moved away from me then, and I stood there foolishly, not knowing what to say or do, but she was not a bit discomfited.

'I shall be out walking Sunday morning after worship,' she said gently. 'I hope I may have the pleasure of seeing you at the green then.'

The kiss had stirred me more than I'd thought possible. I had never known an experienced woman, though I could look back with pleasure to the nights I'd shared with a young maidservant at the college. Dolly was a big, sturdy girl with healthy appetites and the liaison had been mutually satisfying until she had suddenly got married to the baker boy.

'Why so silent, David?' Susannah said, looking at me curiously, and I smiled.

'I was just thinking how beautiful you are,' I said, and bowed over her hand.

The door opened suddenly and my mother stood there, relief in her eyes at seeing me.

'Oh, Davy, you managed to come for me. I'm so grateful. I thought you might have been too tired.'

'It's quite all right, Mother,' I said formally, and she sighed.

'This is Mr Hatfield,' she said. 'He was a friend of your father. He has been kind enough to offer you a place in his shipping office.'

He came forward, smiling in a friendly way, holding out a broad hand.

'Yes, I knew John Richards very well, thought highly of him too, a man of rare integrity.'

I wondered if he knew that my real father was not John Richards at all. It seemed likely enough. All the occupants of Tip Row knew; it seemed common gossip.

'Thank you sincerely for your offer,' I said. 'It's most generous of you, but today I found myself a job, so I'm afraid I must decline.'

'Well, good for you, boy.' Mr Hatfield spoke jovially. 'To tell the truth, you've taken a weight off my mind. I have more clerks than I know what to do with as it is, but, of course, I couldn't let your dear mother down, now could I?'

'We must be going.' My mother's voice was small and I felt sorrow for her, mingled with anger. She had to let me make my own way. I didn't want help from people like the Hatfields, however kindly meant.

'Please, Mrs Richards, let me lend you my carriage for the journey home; it's too far to walk.' Mr Hatfield would brook no refusal, and so I helped my mother up the steps and into the comfort of the carriage. The muffled sound of the hoofbeats and the drum of the wheels on the road were enough to make me feel sleepy, but my mother had other ideas.

'How could you refuse such an opportunity?' she said angrily. 'There's no merit in being obstinate and pig-headed. How far will you get in the copper works?'

'Oh, leave me alone!' I said, and swung open the door of the carriage. 'I'll walk the rest of the way.'

The night air was cold on my cheeks, and when I saw the carriage disappearing into the night I cursed myself for being an impulsive fool.

The roads were crowded with people and along the Strand there were women in doorways waiting for a man to favour them. I almost bumped into an old woman; she was hobbling along, skirts held up, looking fearfully behind her. A young policeman caught her easily, talking to her gently.

'Come along now, old mother. A night spent out in this cold could kill you.'

'But I've only just come out of the house of correction,' she whined. 'I don't want to be taken back there so quick.'

He led her away still grumbling and whining, and I felt an impotent anger inside me, wishing that people like the Hatfields could be forced to witness what went on in their own town.

As I drew near to Tip Row, a burst of sparks shot up from one of the Hafod stacks, illuminating the houses huddled together. I felt a burning need to do something concrete for the working people, to put a stop to the system that forced women like my grandmother to walk for ten minutes to get a supply of water for their daily needs, carrying every drop over the rough ground back to the house.

My mother was waiting up for me. She seemed resigned rather than angry.

'I don't want you to work the copper, Davy,' she said.

199

'You don't know it like I do, how treacherous it can be, how it can mark and scar. I didn't give birth to you for the copper to eat you up.'

'But then, it was careless of you to give birth to me at all, wasn't it, Mother?' I said bitterly.

She was still for a moment, as though I'd slapped her, and I would have given anything if I could have taken the words back.

'All right,' she said, 'do what you will. I see I have no influence over you any more.'

I turned away from her white face and went into the slope, struggling to hold back the hot, bitter tears.

THREE

The New Year came in bleak and hard, and from Manchester came the news that a woman had died from Asiatic cholera.

'I will go into town,' Mamgu said anxiously, 'and lay in some tamarind wafers. I can well afford it now, Davy, with your money coming in.'

'The wafers do no good,' my mother said. 'I will make up an elixir of balsam herb. It is excellent for the chest and the stomach and is wonderful for anyone taken with dry agues.'

I stared at her in amazement; this was a side of my mother I had never seen. As usual, she read my mind; it was a trick she'd always had.

'You don't know very much about me at all, do you, Davy?' she said softly. 'And yet you presume to judge me.'

'A fact is a fact,' I said. 'And I am not who I thought I was; in short, I am a bastard. Nothing can alter that.'

'Isn't it odd?' My mother stared across the room at me as though I wasn't really there. 'You think the past is over and done with, but it catches up with you, never forgiving or forgetting.'

I pulled on my coat and Mamgu came to me, doing up the buttons as though I was a child.

'You're not right in the head, boy, going out in this icy wind. Freeze the marrow in your bones, it will.'

'I won't be long,' I said. 'You know I like to walk on Sundays.'

'So I've noticed.' She smiled. 'I'll wager you've found yourself a woman, though it's no-one local or I'd have heard. It's not one of those Irish girls from Greenhill, is it? Pretty enough, I know, but they do have a funny way of talking.'

I laughed. 'You've got a long nose, Mamgu, and mind I don't bring home a whole flock of Irish girls to share our Sunday tea.'

'Go on with you.' She aimed a slap at me. 'There's cheek I take from my grandson that I never took from my own boys!' Her face brightened and she turned to my mother.

'I forgot to tell you, Huw had a message from our Iorwerth. He's coming home from Neath and he's bringing a wife with him!'

'About time my little brother was married,' my mother said in delight. 'How old is he now?'

'Oh, let's see now.' Mamgu frowned in concentration. 'Seven-and-twenty years, sure to be. I'd given him up as an old bachelor.'

'I'm going,' I said, 'while the talk is about someone else!'

It was sharp and cold as I strode down the row, but anticipation quickened my steps. I had been meeting Susannah for several weeks now, both of us playing a game of cat and mouse, but now I was eager for some advancement in the affair.

There was no sign of her on the green, and my disappointment was intense. I was just about to walk away when I felt a hand on my arm.

'Good day to you, sir,' she said. 'It's me, Joanie. Miss

Susannah sent me to take you back to the villa. She's in bed, a slight chill, nothing to worry about.'

'Oh, I see.' I hesitated a moment. What if Mr Hatfield objected to me seeing his brother's widow?

'It's all right, sir,' Joanie said, smiling, 'there's no-one at home but us.'

When I entered the villa, it seemed spacious and elegant, much more so than I'd remembered it from my first visit. No doubt, by now I'd grown accustomed to the cramped conditions in Tip Row.

Susannah looked delightful sitting back against the pillows, her dark glossy hair spread round her shoulders. She looked no more ill than I was, but I deduced that this was the next step of the game.

'Are you all right?' I took her hand and kissed her fingertips. 'I hear you have a chill.'

'It's nothing,' she said, and gave me the benefit of her brilliant smile. 'In any case, I'm much better now you are here.'

She leaned towards me, pressing her lips against mine, and the softness of her breast touched by arm. Desire flamed within me, but I forced myself to take my time, and at last it was she who took my hand and guided it to the warmth of her skin beneath the bodice of her gown. This was no timid girl to be coaxed and cajoled; she wanted me as much as I wanted her, and I would not disappoint her.

Later, when at last we were quiet, she traced the outline of my jaw with her hand.

'You grow more handsome each time I see you,' she said in a soft, languid voice. 'Your shoulders have filled out, you seem more mature than when we first met.'

I moved away from her and sat up. 'Work does that, you

know. I receive a man's pay so I have to do a man's job.'

'Don't sound so sorry for yourself,' she said. 'You don't have to work in the copper. It's just a foolish sort of pride with you, isn't it?'

She smoothed my back. 'The copper will spoil your skin, my love. Why not take up my brother-in-law's offer and do a respectable job?'

'In a position conjured up for me out of pity, no thank you. I suppose as a copper man I'm not a suitable lover for you at all. You can't tout me round in public, can you?'

'Oh, David!' There was laughter as well as reproach in her voice. 'Do you think I lack escorts? I'm a wealthy widow and not unattractive. No, it was not company I lacked before I met you.'

She ran her fingertips over my spine and I knew she wanted me again as I wanted her.

'Are you not afraid of getting with child?' I asked, and she looked away from me.

'There was no child in nine years of marriage; there won't be one now.'

Her lips quivered and I kissed them gently, warming them to a response.

'Oh, David, David,' she moaned, and received me with delight.

My mother was waiting up for me, sitting before the fire, braiding her long hair. She looked so virginal, I could not imagine her making love to two men, having them both on a string.

'There's many a time I waited like this for my brother Huw to come home,' she said softly. 'You have the same blood in your veins.'

And so did she, I thought wryly, but did not speak my

thoughts out loud. However, she knew them anyway. I sometimes think she is a witch.

'I am only human, Davy,' she said. 'I have desires, just like you, but when I was married to John Richards I gave him all of myself, I was true to him.'

'Let us not talk now, Mother.' I took off my coat and hung it behind the door. 'I'm really very tired.'

She gave a wan smile. 'I expect I know what's taken your strength, too.' She came to me and placed her hand on my cheek. 'You are my son, Davy, and I love you dearly, but why do you impose on me such high standards that you yourself fail to live by?'

'Mother, please,' I said impatiently. 'I don't want to talk about it.'

'Oh, the devil take you then!' she said. 'You will work in the copper till it ruins you, and all for pride. You are as soft as a sheep's belly!'

She swept up the stairs, her head high, and I was sorry for my impatience. Tomorrow I would beg her pardon and put things right between us.

But in the morning I was late from my bed and had to run down the slippery streets to the works. The furnace seemed as hot as Hades and my mouth was dry from the heat and the excesses of the previous night. I was glad to see Annie come round with the water.

'*Duw*, there's a thirst you've got, gent,' she said, crooking her arm around my shoulder. 'You know what causes that, don't you? Too much rolling in the meadow.'

'I see you know all about it,' I said sourly. 'Now shut up and give me more water.'

'Go on, boyo,' she said, 'you don't frighten me with your words. Look, you still have bum fluff where your moustache should be.'

205

'Look out, there,' Luther said quietly. 'The manager is on the war path.'

'*Duw*!' Annie was flustered. 'I'd better be on my way. He's threatened to give me the boot once today already for talking too long with the men.'

I watched her hurry away, her small hips swaying, and then I felt a sharp dig in the ribs.

'Give it another pole,' Luther said, grinning. 'And I'm talking about the copper, mind.' He wiped the sweat from his face. 'Come on now, let's work, shall we?'

Work we did. I was as worn as a sweat rag when we left the sheds and made our way up the road.

'Davy!' A light voice shouted behind me, and I turned to see Annie hurrying to catch me up. 'The manager's done it,' she gasped. 'The bugger's laid me off, the old dry bread what he is!'

'*Darro*, Annie.' Luther looked concerned. 'What will you do now, girl?'

'There's no need to worry about Annie Owens,' she said. 'I've been caring for myself since I was a tot. I'll be all right.' She ran off up the road, her coarse flannel skirts flapping round her thin ankles.

'*Duw*, it's a bad job,' Luther said, 'carrying water round in that stink and heat, but at least it gave the girl food to put in her belly.'

'Come on, Luther, Annie will be all right,' I said. 'Swansea isn't such a bad place to live. There'll be other jobs she can do.'

'Maybe so, boyo, but if you can spare a little time, there's a few things I'd like to show you.'

'What now?' I asked incredulously. 'All I want to see now is a bath and a meal.'

'*Darro*,' Luther said. 'It won't take very long, and to me it is important. Are you coming or not?'

'I'm coming,' I said ruefully, rubbing at my face where the copper dust mingled with my drying sweat. 'But it had better be good.'

He led me away from the works down the hill, and for a large-built man he moved swiftly.

'Viviantown may be filled with copper dust,' Luther said, 'but it's not such a bad place.'

'Viviantown?' I asked in surprise. 'Where on earth does that name come from?'

'There's ignorance for you,' he laughed good-humouredly. 'Mr Vivian owns the Hafod works and the streets surrounding it are called after him. That's not so difficult to understand, is it?' He tutted. 'As I said before, it's not such a bad place except that the women have to walk down to the canal for every drop of water. Back breaking, that is, man.'

I thought guiltily of Mamgu, how she prepared a bath for me every day with never a moan from her.

'You'll have to hold your nose down by here for the stink.' Luther glanced at me. 'This place is called Little Ireland because of all the poor Irish living here. Green Row this tiny street is called, and nothing green in sight.'

'It certainly doesn't look or smell very pleasant,' I said.

'And no wonder!' Luther was angry. 'There are no privies and no sewers. Pigs shouldn't live like this. It's a sin and a crime, and does the damned Paving Commission do anything about it? No, by damn, they don't.'

'Well,' I said slowly, 'I don't know anything about the politics of the town, but I agree with you that something should be done for this place.'

'Oh, boyo,' he pulled at my arm, 'you haven't seen anything yet. This sort of condition spreads all the way down the High Street and the Strand, there are open cess-pools in some places, and Bethesda Court has an open ditch that every man, woman and child has to use for a privy. Sometimes the mud in the road is knee deep on a rainy day.'

'Well, Luther,' I said, 'I know you are not showing me all this just for the hell of it, so what do you want me to do?'

'Ah,' Luther said with a sigh of satisfaction, 'I knew I could count on you the moment I saw you. You write fine English, I'll wager, and we want letters written to prominent people in the town, as well as leaflets to push into doorways. You'll help, won't you, Davy, boy?'

I rested my hand on his shoulder. His earnestness had impressed me.

'Yes, Luther,' I said in resignation. 'I'll help you. I don't see how I can refuse.'

'Good.' He rubbed his hands together. 'The first thing we'll do is make out a petition to send to London for an inspector to come and see all this, and then perhaps Swansea will be put under the Public Health Act which will stop all the little councillors and commissioners mismanaging everything.'

I looked at him with growing respect. 'You're quite a man, Luther,' I said.

When I got home, Mamgu was anxiously peering down the row.

'Good God, boy, where have you been?' she said. 'I've been keeping the water hot for your bath this past hour. Quite worried, I was.'

I looked round the kitchen. 'Where's my mother?' I asked, but Mamgu didn't answer. 'Is she gone out?' I persisted.

'Yes. Now let's get on with the washing, is it?' Mamgu avoided my eyes. 'Save your jaws for eating.'

She obviously wasn't going to tell me anything, and I

spent what remained of the evening sitting next to the fire in silence.

'Going to sulk like a little boy, are you?' Mamgu had a twinkle of laughter in her eyes. 'Come on, Davy, I haven't had a chirp out of you all night.'

'Just tired,' I said. 'I think I'll go to bed. An early night will do me good.'

I lay on my bed in the slope, wide eyed in spite of my fatigue, wondering where my mother was. I didn't like the thought of her being out late. I lifted my head to listen. I heard the rumble of wheels and a cart stopping along the end of the row, then the sound of voices directly outside.

'Catrin, this evening has been such a wonderful one for me. I've never stopped loving you, not for a minute.'

'Hush, Dylan,' came my mother's voice. 'Someone might hear you.'

He gave a short laugh. 'Anyone would think we were young 'uns just walking out for the first time.'

I pulled on my clothes and went out through the kitchen, silently letting myself out of the house. They were in each other's arms, she thigh to thigh with him. My first impulse was to slam my fist against his jaw, and then I saw her face softened by love and I shrank into the shadows.

'Oh, Dylan,' she said, 'I have the same sweet longing for you that I had as a girl. If only Davy wasn't so set against you. He loved John dearly as a father. It's only natural for him to be hurt and angry now he's found out the truth.'

'You are forgetting one thing, Catrin.' His voice was low, but I heard every word. 'He is a man now, he must make his own decisions and stick by them. Already he is doing a man's work. I am so proud.'

Suddenly there was a lump in my throat. I shouldn't be standing here spying on them. It was despicable of me.

'Dylan,' my mother said softly, 'once he knows you he will feel differently about everything, you'll see.'

'I hope so.' He smoothed back her hair. 'I love my four girls, but a man needs to have a son.'

I turned away and went back into the kitchen. Mamgu was standing silently waiting for me, the glow from the fire giving her hair a reddish cast.

'Well, Davy,' she said. 'And what are you going to do now?' She shook her head. 'There's such beauty in their love for each other, don't spoil it.'

I was silent. I just could not speak. He was a big, handsome man, my father, and he wanted me. That knowledge would take a bit of getting used to.

FOUR

It was raining; hard, spiteful drops stung my face as I left the house in Tip Row. I turned up my collar, thrusting my hands deep into my pockets, shrinking into my coat for warmth.

'Davy!' Mamgu's voice stopped me. 'Take this old scarf of your grandad's; it will stop your ears freezing off.'

She laughed as she wound it round my neck. '*Duw*, it's good to have a man to take care of again. There's glad I am you came to me. Have I ever told you that?'

I kissed her cheek. 'Go inside out of the cold, Mamgu, the rain is soaking your shawl.'

'Oh, what's an old drop of rain, then?' she laughed, bright-eyed as a girl. 'It will take more than that to do away with me, never fear.'

I sighed. 'Will women never listen to sense? Go indoors, I say!'

Her laugh was merry. 'All right, then. I suppose it is a bit cold and wet for my old bones, but watch how you go now, Davy.'

I could not help laughing as I turned the corner of the row. She was a fine old woman, my grandmother.

The rain stopped quite suddenly and a weak sun came out from the clouds. The cobbles had a grey sheen that glistened, dazzling my eyes; perhaps that was the reason the place seemed more attractive to me than when I'd first seen it. Somehow even the copper smoke brought down by the heavy clouds wasn't as troublesome as usual. At the roadside, I saw the small white head of a flower, struggling through the soil. Spring would not be long.

'*Duw*,' I said ironically. 'I'll be liking the place if I don't watch out.'

It was good to be alone. The little house seemed to be always crowded, especially now that my mother had begun to bring Dylan Morgan there. He never came when I was at home, and that piqued me. I knew it wasn't because he was afraid to meet me – he wasn't that sort of man. It was probably my mother's idea to keep us apart until she knew what my reaction would be. I wanted to speak to her about it, but somehow the right opportunity never presented itself.

As I came into the town, I saw there was a huge crowd gathered. Several wagons stood in a row, packed to overflowing with bags and tea-kettles and various pieces of ironmongery. I wondered what on earth was going on.

'Hello, there. What's a gent like you doing here, then? Can it be you're as nosy as us common folk?'

'Annie!' I said in delight. 'It's good to see you again. You're looking fine,' I lied. Her face was pale beneath her heavy hair, and she seemed thinner than ever. 'Have you got a job? Are you working now?'

'Oh, yes, I'm working all right,' she said. 'I told you never to worry about little Annie, didn't I?' She drew out a pocketful of money. 'See?' she said. 'Not doing bad, am I?'

'Fine.' I gestured towards the crowd. 'What's going on here, then?'

'Latter Day Saints.' She grinned. 'That's the name they call themselves. They've come from Carmarthen and Merthyr. They're going to get a ship to California, lucky devils. I wish I was going with them.'

'The open seas are treacherous, Annie,' I said. 'They'll face a lot of danger before they reach their destination, if they ever do.'

'Well,' she shrugged, 'they've got their faith, haven't they? See that man over there, the one with white hair? That's Captain Dan Jones, their leader. He looks like a saint.'

'You're incurably romantic,' I laughed. 'He's just a man like any other.'

'There's gratitude for you,' she said. 'I tell you all the news and you just laugh at me. Come on, I'm going to the pier to see them off.'

I hurried after her. Her good spirits were infectious and, anyway, I had nothing else to do with my time. We weaved our way through the crowds of people who seemed to all have the same idea, and we arrived at the pier in time to get a good spot from which to watch the ship sailing.

The wind was bleak and the waves splashed cold spray over us.

'Look at you,' I said to Annie. 'No coat or shawl. You'll catch your death of cold. Come here.'

I pulled her under my own coat. She felt thin and frail as she leaned against me for warmth.

'They're going to Liverpool,' she said, 'and from there a ship will take them out across the sea to all that golden sunshine.'

'But first,' I said mischievously, 'think of all the high seas and icy winds they'll have to face. Sea-sickness is a very unpleasant thing to experience, so I've heard.'

'Oh, you!' Lost for words, she dug her small elbow into my ribs.

'Anyway,' I said, more seriously, 'if you really wanted to go, why don't you join the Latter Day Saints? I'm sure they are looking for new converts.'

'Huh!' she said. 'And do you think I'd be good enough for them?'

I was disturbed to catch a glimpse of tears in her eyes, but then she pushed at me eagerly.

'Look, they're coming. Oh, and, Davy, listen to that singing. Have you ever heard anything so lovely in all your life?'

The steamer *Troubador* sailed gracefully between the piers, crowded with people all singing their last farewell to their own country. It was a haunting, disturbing sound, and as the ship passed out into the open sea I found myself cheering with the rest of the crowd, waving my arms as frantically as though I had a loved one on board.

I looked down at Annie and her face was drenched with tears. I held her gently in my arms, a lump in my own throat.

'There's lovely, it was,' she said. 'I'll never forget it, and I'm glad you were here with me, Davy.'

I gave her my handkerchief and she mopped her eyes, smiling a little sheepishly. I put my arm around her and led her away from the pier, back on to the road, where the wind was not quite so keen.

'Come on,' I said. 'I'll buy you a hot toddy, how's that?'

To my surprise she shook her head. 'No, I've wasted enough time. I've got to do some work, mind.'

'What work, Annie?' I asked in curiosity, and she turned her head away from me.

'Oh, you, you're always so damn nosy, aren't you? What I do is my own business. You're not my keeper, though you act like one.'

'I'm your friend, Annie,' I said. 'Surely there's no job so bad that you can't tell me about it? Are you scrubbing in some fine house, perhaps?'

'Yes, that's it.' She spoke so glibly that I knew it was a lie.

'All right,' I said in resignation. 'You win. I won't ask you any more questions.'

She put her hand on my arm. 'Come on, you're not mad at me, are you?' She pulled at my moustache. '*Duw*, your bum fluff is growing!'

I laughed. There was nothing else I could do; she was entitled to her privacy.

'So long, then, Davy,' she said. 'I'll see you sometime, I suppose.' She looked as though she would say something else, but then suddenly she turned and darted away between the crowds.

I felt strangely restless. I didn't want to go home yet. I kicked at a stone and looked about me. Perhaps a brisk walk would rid me of my excess energy. I would like to have visited Susannah, but I had to stick rigidly to the plans she made, otherwise there was the danger we would be caught out, and that would never do, for either of us. I had no wish to be confronted by her brother-in-law, perhaps even forced into marriage, and to be fair to Susannah I don't think she would want that, either.

I made my way out of the town and began to climb the steepness of Kilvey hill. Stunted gorse bushes clung to my clothes, and I saw that the grass was brown and shrivelled as though it had been burned; the copper dust had spread its destructive fingers wide.

I stumbled upwards, stopping a moment for breath, and looking down I saw the harbour spread out below me. On the horizon I caught a glimpse of a ship, and I wondered if it could be the *Troubador* carrying the Latter Day Saints to their new life.

I sat down to rest on a flat stone and wondered about my

own life. It seemed I was no longer necessary to my mother. She had Dylan. And though Mamgu loved me, she would soon have her youngest son home again. I was of no use to anyone. Perhaps I should get out of it all and make a new life for myself, perhaps even go back to England. The thought left me empty. Swansea had become my home now; I did not want to leave it.

'Well, stay then!' I said out loud. 'Stay and make some sense of your life.'

Luther had shown me the way in which I could do something for the town; my education might as well be put to good use.

I rose and made my way back down the hill. It seemed I had sorted my chaotic thoughts into some sort of order. When I'd first agreed to help Luther, it had been a half-hearted gesture, but now I was eager to be active. I ran the rest of the way down the hill, arriving breathless at the bottom. I was surprised to see that it had grown almost dark and that the gas lamps of the town were lit, hissing gently above my head, a circle of mist around them because it had started to rain again, fine and soft.

The noise of singing and laughter came to me from the open door of a little inn. I hesitated for a moment, wondering whether a glass of ale might be a good idea. My coat was wet now and my hair hung lankly on my forehead.

I heard a cry then from a small alleyway, and as I hesitated it came again. I went forward into the gloom, my eyes trying to focus. I heard a muffled curse and I saw a girl pushed up against a doorway, her skirts above her waist.

'Pay me first,' she said, small fists beating against the back of the man who held her. Then I saw to my horror that the girl was Annie.

I caught hold of the man's collar and dragged him away from her. He came upright, his fist lashing out, his knee catching me where it hurt. I fell to the ground and saw his boot swing viciously towards my head. I rolled away and I felt the wind of it whistle past my ear. I staggered to my feet and pushed myself away from the wall against the shoulder of the man. We were face to face, and I felt sick as I saw it was my cousin William.

'I thought you were low,' I snarled at him, hating him with my guts, 'but I didn't think even you could sink as low as this.'

'Mind your own business, you bastard,' he said, and he laughed coldly. 'Bastard, the word suits you down to the ground.'

I jerked my head forward, catching him above the eyes. I'd grown taller and we were on a level now. Taking advantage of his bewilderment, I slammed him up against the wall, thudding my fist into his belly. He went down, and Annie began to cry.

'Why couldn't you keep out of it. I told you to mind your own business, didn't I? This was the reason why. This is my job now.'

'Come on.' I led her away from the alley and helped her to tidy her shawl before leading her into the inn. 'Sit down. I'll get you a drop of brandy. You'll soon feel better.'

She shook her head, her face stained with tears. 'You are such a child sometimes, Davy,' she said. 'So innocent there's no believing it.'

I brought her a drink and sat beside her. 'All right, Annie.' I smiled. 'I know I'm dumb, but I don't see why you have to do this. You say I'm a child, but you don't face up to the truth, do you? I could get you a job as a maid with a good family. Would that suit you?'

'I do face the truth, Davy,' she said soberly, 'and the truth is I don't want to be a maid. I'd only steal things again. Why do you think I went to the copper in the first place?' She smiled. 'I've got itchy fingers!'

I sighed. 'But, Annie, you're so young. You can't be above fourteen years of age. This is no life for you.'

'Wrong,' she said. 'I'm twelve years old exactly, and don't bother to preach at me. I know what I'm doing. I've made some good friends while I've been on the streets; they're not all like him back there in the alley. I knew he was going to be trouble when I set eyes on him. I know his sort off by heart.' She brushed back her hair. 'They think it's a laugh to take what they want without paying for it. They don't realize they're doing me out of a piece of fish or bread. Even whores have to eat.'

'Don't talk like that, Annie.' I took a deep drink of my ale. 'Come on, have another drink. It will bring some colour to your cheeks.'

She put her hand on my arm. 'I'd rather have the money instead, if it's all the same to you, then I won't have to work any more tonight.'

I felt sick as I handed her the money, more than I could really afford. She looked at me gratefully and I sighed in anger and despair.

'Have you no family?' I asked, and she shook her head. 'Not even an aunt or a cousin you could go to?'

'They all died of the cholera,' she said. 'It's a long time ago now. My grandad brought me up, but he got old and died, too.'

I stared at her in concern. 'Well, have you got anywhere to sleep tonight?'

'Oh, yes.' She smiled. 'I've a friend, Rosie. She's got a room for her customers; she's very respectable, not on the streets like me. She lets me sleep there when she's finished working.'

I saw her face change, her eyes widen and her mouth become a circle of horror. I turned round quickly, sensing danger. Then the earth split open inside my head. The last thing I saw before I lost consciousness was the face of my cousin William looking down at me, his eyes blazing with triumph.

FIVE

I tried to open my eyes, but the pain of it caused me to wince. 'Oh, my God!' I mumbled, and my lips stuck to my teeth.

'Easy does it, *cariad*.' The voice was soft, the hands that touched me were even softer. 'You look a pretty sight, I must say, but a strapping man like you shouldn't take long to get over a little beating.'

By squinting carefully through my swollen lids, I saw that I was in bed, in a small neat room, and sitting beside me was a woman with golden hair hanging loose to her waist. A big woman with a calm face and a feline grace that set her apart from other women.

'How did I get here?' I struggled to sit up, but she put her hand against my shoulder and forced me back against the pillows.

'Take it easy, good boy. There's no need for you to rush away anywhere, and, in any case, I don't think you could stand up just yet.'

It was good just to obey her and relax. I seemed to ache everywhere and my head was buzzing. Suddenly Annie appeared in the doorway, a grin on her face as she saw that I was awake.

'*Duw*, there's a beating you took,' she said, her eyes shining with anger. 'He would never have stopped kicking you if I hadn't hit him over the head with a jug.'

'William!' I said, remembering. 'Trust him to play the

coward and attack from behind. How on earth did you manage to get me here?'

Annie nodded towards the golden-haired woman. 'Rosie. She got a couple of her friends to come and fetch you. She's the friend I was telling you about, you remember? She lets me stay here at night.'

With a shock of understanding, I looked at Rosie. She looked too fine and proud to be selling herself to men. Like most women, she could read my thoughts.

'Why do I do it?' she said. 'It's because I need money to live, and what's more I like my trade.'

'Oh.' There seemed nothing more I could say to that. I moved my legs, and a pain travelled through my loins.

'Good God!' I said. 'He certainly kicked me very thoroughly before you hit him, Annie.'

'Sorry about that,' she said. 'I was trying to get behind him, see. I didn't want my teeth knocked out of my head. I'm not ready for sucking my food yet.'

'He could have ruined me for life.' I stretched my legs carefully, trying to assess the damage.

'No,' Rosie smiled, 'it's not too bad at all. I've had a good look and there's nothing a rest won't cure.'

I felt my colour rise, even though she spoke in a matter-of-fact way with no trace of embarrassment herself.

'Well,' I said awkwardly, 'thanks for everything. I hope that at least you'll let me pay you for the time I've taken up.'

She shook her head. 'Only customers pay, so pipe down and I'll bring you something to eat.'

She went into the back room and Annie sat down beside me, careful not to disturb me. She stared in frank curiosity at my face, so that at last I was forced to smile even though it hurt.

'*Duw*, you've got the best blacker I've ever seen.' She

sounded delighted. 'Your eye is like an egg, only bigger.'

Rosie returned, and the tempting smell of the broth she carried made me realize how hungry I was.

'There,' she said with satisfaction as somehow I managed to open my mouth enough to let the spoon inside. 'I knew your appetites would soon return, and I'll be happy to cater to them all.' She laughed and winked at me. 'There's a lot I could teach you, Davy.'

'Please,' I said, 'I'm not in a fit state to receive improper suggestions. Wait until a little while later.'

'All right,' Rosie's eyes were bright with mischief, 'but don't think you're getting out of anything, mind.'

I eased myself up until I was propped against the bed rails. Beneath the sheet I was naked, and I saw that my ribs were covered in bruises. Fortunately, nothing seemed to be broken.

'Stop admiring yourself, there's a good boy,' Annie said. 'I've got to go out now. Someone's got to work.' She pulled on her shawl, but Rosie caught her arm.

'Better stay with your friend here,' she said. 'I'll go out and find some work. The change will do me good. I've sat in this room far too long; about time I saw what the streets were like.'

'Oh, Rosie,' Annie's eyes were huge in her pale face, 'you will meet them rough out there, I can tell you.'

'Don't you worry,' Rosie said. 'I can handle any man, rough or not.'

I believed her. As she stood up I saw how statuesque she was, tall, and splendid of breast and hip. I did not want her to go out in the streets. The thought of a man using such beauty sickened me.

'Look,' I said awkwardly, 'I still have some money. No one need go out.'

Rosie shook her head. 'There's no money on you now, Davy,' she said, 'and you've only got half a coat left – torn to shreds, it was.'

Anger burned within me. William hadn't been content to beat me savagely, he'd taken my hard-earned money as well.

'Lay down and rest, boyo.' Rosie put her hand on my shoulder. 'I won't have to stay out very long.' The door closed quietly behind her, and there was nothing I could do.

I stared at Annie. She was pale and there were dark shadows beneath her eyes. She was just a child and should have been in bed long ago.

'Come on,' I said. 'You look cold. Come in here under the covers. You'll be all right, don't worry.'

Her eyes were soft.

'I know that, you don't have to tell me. There's daft, you are.'

She climbed on to the end of the bed and thrust her cold bare feet against my legs, and I winced as she touched a bruise.

'Sorry, boyo,' she said. 'Your cousin must really hate you bad to do this to you.' She leaned her chin on her hands. 'Do you know that William and I have the same family name? He's Owens and so am I, but no relation to each other, thank God!'

I was beginning to feel drowsy. I lay back and closed my eyes.

'Go on talking, Annie,' I said. 'Your voice is soothing, but forgive me if I drift off to sleep.'

She laughed. 'Sleep, you, boyo, while you can. There won't be much of that once Rosie gets home.'

It must have been morning when I opened my eyes

again because a grey light was creeping across the room. I moved a little and felt a soft warmth beside me. From the fresh smell of her I knew it was Rosie. I put my arm around her and she whimpered a little, moving closer to me in her sleep. I kissed the warmth of her neck, and her eyes came open.

'There, David,' she said softly, her hands busy. 'I told you it wouldn't be long, didn't I?' Her lips were warm against mine and I held her splendid breasts, ignoring the pain of my bruises in the sheer ecstasy of being with her.

At last, I stood up shakily and pulled on my trousers. There was still my job to think of and it was Monday morning.

'Not tired of me already, are you, Davy?' she said softly, the very tone of her voice an invitation. I groaned.

'Don't tempt me, Rosie. I don't want to lose my job.' I looked round helplessly, wondering what to put on. My shirt was nowhere to be seen.

'I threw the old thing out,' she said, sitting up, with no attempt to cover herself. 'If it's your shirt you're looking for, you're out of luck.'

She slid easily from the bed, her limbs long and pale with a sheen like marble.

'I think there's something here will fit you, Davy, boy.'

She brought a flannel shirt from the cupboard and helped me to put it on, and her nakedness was a torment to me.

'Get back into bed, for God's sake!' I said, half angry, half laughing. 'I'll see you tonight.'

I went then without looking at her, for fear of forgetting common sense and staying with her all day. I ran back up the hill towards the Hafod, trying to feel my face and judge what state it was in. Luther soon informed me.

'*Darro*! Have you been run over by six horses, boyo? There's a beautiful blacker you've got.'

I touched my eye gingerly. It didn't feel too bad and at least I could open it enough to see.

'Been fighting and sowing your wild oats in the same night,' Luther said. '*Duw*! There's strength for you.'

'How is it you always poke your nose into my business, Luther Lloyd?' I pretended to be angry, and he aimed a harmless punch at me.

'I couldn't care a toeless sock, boyo, but your mam's been looking for you. Worried, she is, that you've been out all night. Go on, slip up home; it won't take above five minutes. Put her mind at rest. I'll cover for you by here.'

I sighed. 'Thanks, Luther. Perhaps I can do the same for you someday.'

He grinned. 'Oh, I'll make sure you pay me back, boyo, don't you worry about that. I've already got plans for you to go to a meeting, but I'll tell you about that another time. Go on now.'

Up at the house, Mamgu was bent over a pot on the fire. She turned and gave a little scream when she saw my face.

'*Iesu Crist*!' She put her arm around me and led me to a chair. 'What have they done to you, and where were you all the night?'

Before I could answer, my mother stepped in through the door, her skirts held up in her hand, her hair coming loose, falling over the whiteness of her forehead.

'I can answer that,' she said angrily. 'He was fighting like a common bruiser and, what's more, he was fighting our Huw's boy, William. I can't even trust him not to cause trouble in the family.'

I was furious at the injustice of her words. She knew nothing of the true facts.

'*Darro!*' Mamgu took my arm. 'I'd say that what William got he rightly deserved. Look at your own son, will you, woman?'

'That's not all.' My mother spun round. 'He went off in the company of a street woman, a whore!'

I was coldly angry then. 'You are wrong, Mother.' I heard the hostility in my own voice, but could do nothing about it. 'I was with two whores, and both of them better women than many so-called respectable women.'

I left the house and ran along the row towards the works, not knowing if it was anger or hurt that twisted my stomach into knots.

I worked hard at the mouth of the furnace, the sweat running from my body, filling up my boots. The ache in my ribs gave me no peace, but I was determined to ignore it.

'*Duw!*' Luther said at last. 'You've got the devil in you, boyo. Don't work so hard. You'll have nothing left to spare for your lady friend.'

I realized then that I'd promised Susannah I'd stay over with her for the night. She offered me silken sheets, a delicate, sensitive and yet eager response, but there was Rosie now. Rosie had vigour, expert knowledge and a splendid body.

'Hey, Davy, boy!' Luther called. 'Keep your mind on your work, not on tom-catting. I can see how excited you are from here. Bigger trews you need, boyo.'

I laughed with him, but the hurt inside me was eased a little because of a woman my mother called a whore.

I ached all over when I walked from the works and up to Tip Row. I looked forward to Mamgu's hot bath. She winced as I stripped off my clothes.

'*Duw, duw*, there's a state on you, Davy. Your mother ought to see this! William may be my grandson, but he's a sour apple and that's the truth.'

226

She gently rinsed my back. 'Don't know where he sprung from. He's not like his father. Huw was never vicious.'

'Don't worry about it, Mamgu,' I said with a smile. 'It didn't stop me enjoying myself.'

'Oh, go on with you.' She gave me a gentle slap, but her eyes were twinkling. 'And I suppose you'll be out again tonight too. There's no keeping you young 'uns bridled.'

I dressed carefully. I knew I should keep my word to Susannah, but I also knew it would be to Rosie I would go.

It was early to be in town, but the streets were busy and I could hear singing from one of the ale houses. I stepped round an elderly woman who was lifting her skirts to let out a stream of water along the gutter, and wished I could take Rosie away from this to a beautiful house somewhere. My footsteps were eager as I went up the stairs to her room. I knocked on the door, waiting in a sweat of impatience for her to open it and come into my arms. The minutes seemed to drag by as I waited, then I knocked again, louder.

'Go away, there's a good man, and come back in about twenty minutes, is it?' It was a heavy masculine voice and I froze for a moment, not believing the evidence of my own ears. The bed began to creak, and I hammered on the door with my fist.

'You prostitute!' I shouted, which was absurd. Almost in tears, I ran back to the street and entered the nearest ale house. I took two jugs of the bitter liquid and felt better. Slowly, I left the noise of the streets behind me then and made my way towards the elegance of Susannah's villa.

Susannah was warm and full of concern when she saw my bruised face.

'Davy, you shouldn't get involved in street fights.' She reproached me as if I was a child. I grinned ruefully.

227

'I didn't intend to get involved, I assure you. It was very much of a surprise, but I won't be caught like that again. I'll keep my back to the wall.'

'Come to bed,' she said softly. 'I'll help you to forget all your hurts.'

She was soft and yielding, and she wanted me so much that it was a balm. Gratefully, I held her close.

'Sweet Susannah,' I said softly. 'I'm so happy to be with you.' And, surprisingly, I was.

In the morning, I was out of bed early, standing before the mirror, surprised at the way my body had filled out. My shoulders were broad and my neck thick, though my hips were as slender as ever they were.

'Vanity is a terrible thing.' Susannah turned over on her stomach, watching me with narrowed eyes, her hair spread over the whiteness of her skin like a silk cape. 'Come back to bed,' she said. I turned my back on her and began to dress.

'No,' I said. 'I have to work.' There was something about her that brought on a streak of cruelty I hadn't known I possessed.

'Oh, go on downstairs, then,' she said. 'Joanie will see that you have a good breakfast, but say goodbye to me before you go.'

Joanie looked at my battered face with undisguised curiosity.

'Where on earth did you get such a blacker?' she said, her finger pointing to my eye.

'I got it from sticking my nose into other people's business,' I said, and she shrugged and placed a plate of bacon before me.

Susannah was still in bed when I was ready to go. I hurried upstairs and kissed her lightly on the mouth.

'Oh, Davy,' she said, her eyes wide, 'I've just read in

the paper that the cholera is rife in Glasgow. It won't come here, will it?'

My stomach contracted at the very sound of the word, but I tried to look reassuring.

'Glasgow is a very long way from here.' I looked over her shoulder and the word sprang out at me, making my mouth dry. Cholera!

'I lost two sisters to the cholera when we were all very young.' She looked up at me. 'It is a terrible thing, a fearful sickness that just burns you up.' She shuddered.

'Try not to think about it.' I put my hand on her shoulder. 'It's no use worrying.' I smiled. 'The copper dust keeps the cholera away – at least, that's what the owners tell us.' She seemed to take some comfort from my light words. 'I shall have to go now, but shall I see you Sunday?'

'Yes, of course, and thank you, Davy, for being so kind to me. I know I'm very foolish sometimes.'

'Not foolish,' I said, 'just human.' And the word rang like a chant in my ears as I left the house and made my way down the street, echoing in time to my footsteps. Cholera, cholera, cholera.

SIX

I had told myself I would never visit Rosie again, but I just could not keep away. I stood outside the house where she lived, looking up at her window like a lovesick boy, wondering if she was alone. At last, I forced myself to go inside, and after a few minutes I timidly knocked on her door.

'Oh, Davy!' She moved aside to let me into her little room, and I could see she had been crying. 'I'm so glad you came. I need a friend, and so does Annie.'

'Why, what's wrong?' I held her shoulders, and she buried her face in my neck.

'Annie's been taken by the police, and there's awful I feel not able to do anything to help.' She led me to a chair and poured a glass of gin, her hands shaking.

'Sit down, Rosie,' I said gently, 'and tell me all about it.'

'Oh, God!' She rubbed her eyes with the back of her hand just like a tired child. 'She stole a tea-kettle of all things from the Ivy Bush Hotel. I went to see the landlord straight away, a Mr Dean. He was very kind, but it was too late. It was in the hands of the police, you see.'

'What do you think will happen to her?' I felt foolish of my ignorance of such things, but Rosie did not think my question silly.

'If it comes to the worst, she will be transported on a prison ship. Oh, poor Annie, what possessed her to do such a thing?' She stared at me, beseeching me silently to help.

'I'll do what I can,' I said, without the faintest idea of how I could put my words into action.

'If you could see someone in authority,' she suggested, 'a councillor or somebody like that, I know you could make an impression, Davy. You have such a fine voice.'

I sighed. People seemed to set such store by my way of speaking, as if it could get me anywhere.

'You know I'll do all I can, Rosie.' I took her hands in mine. 'Now try not to worry. Promise?'

She began to smile. 'I feel better already. Come, hold me close. There's one good way I know of to drive out unpleasant thoughts.'

She kissed me, pressing herself against me, moving sensuously. 'Oh, Davy, you are something special. Out of all the men I've known in my lifetime, not one of them has given me the magic joy I have with you.'

Her words thrilled me. I twisted my fingers in her gold hair and tipped her face up to mine.

'Why don't we live together, you and I?' The thought, once spoken, appealed to me enormously. 'I could find us a small house, perhaps, somewhere better than this area. How can you stand the sound of hammering that goes on night and day? It would drive me mad.'

She wriggled against me. 'It's just the building of the new railway, Davy. I don't mind the noise. It means there are men out there, men who need me.'

It was like a slap. 'Need you?' I said angrily. 'All they need is the use of your body for a few minutes!'

She moved away from me. Her eyes seemed as though a shutter had come down over them.

'I know that as well as you do,' she said quietly. 'Perhaps I know more than you could ever dream about menfolk. It is my job, and I'm not ashamed of it. Don't try to change me, Davy, because I won't let you.'

'One day you'll be old.' I knew I was being cruel. 'Who will want you then?'

'We all get old,' she spoke softly, explaining as though I was a child, 'and there will be many men who will be grateful to me for what I've given them. Aye, and their wives, too; they are thankful enough there are women like me to lighten the load.'

She came to me and held my face in her hands. 'Davy, come on and love me. Today is yours. There will be no-one else, I promise.'

She drew me down on the bed, beguiling me with her gentle caresses until there was but one thought and desire engulfing me, driving out conscious thought so that there were just feelings lifting me to heights I'd never dreamed of before. I think I screamed out her name as my back arched above her, thrusting my life into hers, and then I sank to rest, sleeping immediately, my head on her breast.

It was dark when I left the little room, promising Rosie once more that I would do whatever was possible to help Annie. I had arranged to meet Luther in the Gloucester Arms and he was waiting for me, leaning against the bar, his huge fist closed around a jug of ale.

'Hello, boyo,' he greeted me, with a grin. 'I've got some happy news. I've found a friend who will let us use his chandlers store to work on our petition, and the sheets carrying the latest information can be stamped out on some machine he's got. At last the workers will know what's really going on in the town of Swansea.'

'Good,' I said. 'When are we going to start collecting names for the petition?'

'Start? Start, boy? Why, look at this.' He carefully drew out of his pocket a sheet of paper with rows of names running down it. He chuckled. 'The paving commissioners are getting windy already, boyo, creating hell they are, in case their powers be taken away from them. They want to run Swansea in the chaos it is now; afraid, they are, of what an inspector from London would say if we got one here.'

'Have we much chance of getting an inspector? It might not be so easy, you know.'

'Nobody said it was easy,' Luther growled. 'Working the copper isn't easy, is it, man, and yet don't we do it every day?'

'Right,' I said, 'what do you want me to do now?' I took the jug of ale he handed me.

'Drink that first, boyo, then come with me to the chandlers and we will write a lovely letter to go with the names on the petition. We will see what action there will be when they get this in London.'

I followed him down through the town streets that as usual were thronging with people. They seemed so mindless, so bent on pleasure, with no thought for improving their lot. Luther caught my eye.

'I know what you're thinking, boyo,' he said, 'but remember that a little ale and a little pleasure makes the thought of working for a living bearable.'

'I suppose you're right.' I grinned at him. 'But for all that, you are trying to do something about conditions here, aren't you?'

He shrugged. 'I have no family, there's only myself to think about. I hurt no-one by my actions.' He saw my quick look and nodded to me. 'Oh, yes, there can be reprisals. Watch out for that, boyo.'

'You mean because we are fighting for some betterment of the town water supply and the sewage problem, harm could come to us?'

'Well, it stands to reason, doesn't it, boyo? Stir up water and muck rises.'

The chandler was a small man with sparse hair and a long miserable-looking moustache. He let us in one at a time, as though half-afraid of opening the door.

'This is Edgar Jones,' Luther said. 'He may not look much, but he's got a good head on his shoulders.'

The little man grinned and shook my hand. 'And you are David Richards,' he said. 'There's no mistaking you. Luther described you well.'

He led the way down a long passage to the back of the building. A lamp burned on the table next to a pile of papers.

'The Public Health Act came out last year,' Edgar said, 'but no town is beholden to have a local board unless the death rate is very high.' He gestured to a chair. 'Sit down, boys. I've got some ale that's gone a bit warm, but you're welcome to a drop.'

I looked at the slight man with growing respect. I had lived in London, but knew nothing about the Act, even though I was receiving a very expensive education.

'I don't really see why you need me.' I shrugged. 'You are doing very well on your own.'

'Ah.' Edgar brushed up the drooping ends of his moustache. 'You will be able to attend any meeting that might come from our petition. You can dress the part of a gentleman and speak it. You will be taken for granted, one of them, see?'

I nodded. 'Are you so sure there will be something done about your petition?' I looked from one to the other. 'It could very well be ignored.'

Edgar waved a paper towards me. 'We have signatures of some prominent businessmen here,' he said. 'It's not only the workers want improvements made. Oh, I think notice will have to be taken of us.' He winked. 'Especially when you write a proper English letter for us.'

I laughed. 'What a weight of responsibility you are putting on my shoulders,' I said, half-seriously, 'but I will do my best.'

Luther clapped my back. 'That's all any man can do, boyo,' he said. 'Now let's get down to the work and then we can go out and have a proper cold drink of ale.'

It did not take me long to compose and write an elegant letter – at least the college had taught me that much. I held it out and Edgar took it from me eagerly.

'*Duw*, see that beautiful hand,' he said admiringly, 'and such flowing sentences. You should be a poet, Davy. You have the gift of words.'

I felt strangely pleased by his praise and waited breathlessly while he finished reading the letter through.

'Well,' he said at last, 'if that doesn't bring an inspector down here, nothing will.' He stretched his thin arms. 'Come on, then, work's over for tonight. Let's get out of here and have some ale.'

It was late when I walked along the row towards home. I stood for a moment, slightly dizzy with drink, trying to see the stars between the rolling clouds of copper smoke. I thought of the past hours and a little of my elation faded. I had done something in general for the town of Swansea, written a letter that might or might not get to Mr Chadwick in London and bring his attention and that of the Board of Health to the problems of Swansea, but I had done nothing to help my little friend Annie.

My mother sat beside the fire, her skirt over her knees so that her legs were bathed in a rosy glow from the fire. She looked up at me, her eyes heavy with sleep.

'Oh, there you are, Davy. I was getting a bit worried about you. It's so late.'

'There was no need for you to wait up,' I said, shrugging off my coat. 'I'm quite old enough to take care of myself now, you should realize that.'

'That's good,' she said a little sharply. 'In that case you won't mind if I get married again then, will you?'

Her words fell into my mind like pebbles in a pool, and I shivered suddenly. I thought of John Richards, the man who had been my father all these years, and a bitter taste rose in my mouth.

'At last,' I said cuttingly, 'he intends to make an honest woman of you. Dylan Morgan is going to make amends for the harm he did all those years ago. Well, be his wife, but one thing is sure, I'll never be his son.'

SEVEN

Mamgu was up to her elbows in flour, there were stripes of it across her nose and forehead, and she was flushed with the heat of the oven.

'And where are you going, Davy, dressed up like a pig's head on a plate?' she challenged as I made my way through the kitchen. 'Out, out, out, that's all young people think about these days. Why, your grandfather would spend his time chopping wood for the fire.' Her eyes became dreamy as her fingers continued to knead the dough. 'Lovely apple-smelling logs, sparks shooting all over the place, mind. Beautiful it was.'

I kissed her cheek and tasted the coarseness of the flour.

'I won't be long, Mamgu. Keep some fresh bread for me. I love it soaked in your tasty cawl; fit for a king, it is.'

'Go on with you, and stop speaking Welsh. It sounds so strange with your English voice. They lie together like sunshine and snow, lovely but not right somehow.'

I went outside and a pale, smoke-filled day greeted me. It was spring, and wild chamomile flourished on a dung heap at the side of the road. It was symbolic somehow of the town itself, beauty and poverty hand in hand.

I knew my thoughts were scattered, jumping from one subject to another without cohesion, and I knew full well what the reason was. I had to see Dylan Morgan.

I had tossed and turned during the night, wondering how best I could help Annie. I thought of approaching

Susannah's brother-in-law, but decided he was too ineffectual to be of any good. I had known the answer all along, but I had been reluctant to face it, until now. Dylan Morgan was well liked and respected in the town. If he could be persuaded to speak up for Annie, someone might listen.

I stood at last outside his shop. It was larger than I'd imagined, with double windows and a large black-painted door that stood open. Outside were baskets of dishes, warm brown, glistening in the sunshine that had warmed me once Tip Row and the copper smoke was left behind.

My heart beat rapidly and I hesitated, wondering if I could bring myself to speak to the man who had betrayed my mother all those years ago. Even the thought of it brought a bitter taste to my mouth. I almost turned away, but the thought of Annie's poor, thin frame being dragged on to a prison ship brought back my resolution.

It was dim inside the shop after the brightness of the sunshine, and a pleasant mixture of smells hung in the air. I couldn't have put a name to any of them, but it was fruit and spice and beeswax mingled with bacon and tea and soap.

A tall girl, slim and dark, came out of the shadows and stared at me in a friendly way. A strange feeling, almost like a pain, made me tremble. She was probably my sister, blood of the same blood, come from the same father as me.

'I'm David Richards,' I said softly, and her eyes widened. 'Could I see Mr Morgan, please?'

She stared at me in silence for a long moment, a mixture of expressions crossing her face. She was incapable of guile, and at last she burst out:

'I know who you are. You haven't come to cause trouble, have you?'

'No, of course not,' I said quickly. 'As a matter of fact, I have a favour to ask of him.'

She smiled and held out her hand. It lay cool and firm in mine, and I liked her immediately.

'I'm Kate,' she said, 'and I think I'm going to like having a brother.'

'Half-brother, really,' I corrected, 'but thank you for being so kind.'

'Come on.' She pulled my arm. 'I'd better take you to the parlour while I look for Dad. Goodness knows where he's got to.'

She left me alone, and I looked around me. The parlour was heavy with furniture, thick curtains covered the window, and from the musty smell of the room I guessed it was rarely used.

Kate came back into the room. 'Dad's in the stables,' she said breathlessly. 'He's seeing to a sick horse, and he says will you come out there to him?'

I got to my feet and followed her, my heart beating rapidly. What would he be like face to face, this man who was my father?

He was crouched down beside a beautiful bay horse, his sleeves rolled up exposing huge arms. He looked up at me, one man sizing up another.

'The beast has got the copper disease,' he said conversationally. 'I tried bleeding through the feet and that did no good, so now I'm putting on a mixture of tar and feathers.'

'How can you tell the animal's got the disease?' It seemed easier to talk about the sick animal than to say what I came for.

He lifted the animal's mouth. 'See how the gums bleed? And the poor thing's joints are swollen. Well,' he got to his feet and plunged his arms into a barrel of rainwater, 'that's all I can do for now.'

We stood in the sunshine and I could see how closely we resembled each other. It was uncanny, a sort of looking into a mirror that reflected myself twenty years ahead. He grinned.

'*Duw*! There's a likeness for you. Two peas in a pod, boy. What is it you want of me?'

I swallowed hard. 'It's a favour, for a friend of mine. Her name is Annie Owens.' It was getting easier to talk. 'She was caught stealing, just a silly tea-kettle, but she may be transported.'

He looked at me for a long moment. 'You say she is guilty of stealing this kettle. There's no doubt about it?'

I shook my head. 'No doubt at all, she did steal it, but she's just a child, twelve years of age.'

'Ah.' He nodded his head. 'I think I can help you there. The girl is too young to be transported.' He smiled. 'A friend of yours can't be all bad. I'll see what I can do. How about some tea now? It will give us a chance to talk.'

In the parlour, Kate had set out a white cloth and on it some fresh-baked cake; the smell of it made my mouth water.

'Have a cup of tea, David.' Kate smiled at me and I felt a little easier. 'Lotty, the youngest of us all, made the cake and she especially wanted you to taste it.' I was warmed by the welcome I received at my father's house and it was hard to reconcile the calm, considerate man he was with the picture I'd had in my mind of a rogue who played on a young girl's feelings.

He met my eyes, and it was as if he read my thoughts there.

'You know how hard your mother is to resist,' he said gently. 'I could refuse her nothing all those years ago, and even now, at my age, I am like a foolish boy in love for the first time.'

I looked away from him, liking him, even at such a short acquaintance, but unable to quite forgive him for the past. I got to my feet.

'Thank you for everything. I am indebted to you for your promise of help.'

'*Duw*,' he said softly. 'John Richards gave you everything I could not, a fine education and the bearing of a gentleman. He has done you proud.'

I left him then and, turning, saw the four girls, my half-sisters, framed in the shop window. The youngest one raised her hand to wave, and I waved back. My mind was a jumble of bewildered thoughts and impressions. Meeting my father had been so different to what I'd expected.

It became a day for meeting people, because when I returned home to the row, my uncle Iorwerth had arrived from Neath.

'Look at Catrin's boy, then!' Mamgu excitedly drew me into the room. 'Isn't he a man, then?'

'*Duw*, let the boy breathe,' my uncle said with a laugh. 'And I'm telling you now, Davy, please do not call me uncle and you towering two heads above me!'

'Indeed,' I said and meant it, 'you look far too young to be an uncle.'

'*Duw*, he speaks so beautifully, Catrin, you must be proud of him. What are you working at Davy, school-teacher is it?'

'He's in the copper,' my mother said, 'though I think he's a fool when he's been offered better.'

'Hush now, Catrin.' Iorwerth smiled at her. 'I'm going into the copper. At least it pays good money, doesn't it?' He turned to me. 'You'll put in a word for me, won't you, Davy?'

241

'Certainly I will,' I couldn't help laughing, 'but I don't think the manager sets a lot of store by what I say.'

'Well,' Iorwerth looked me over, 'with those shoulders I think anyone would be a fool not to listen to what you say.'

At the table, I found myself sitting next to my uncle's wife. She smiled up at me trustingly somehow, almost like a child.

'I couldn't help hearing you speak. You are English, I believe? Well, so am I.'

'That's a difficult question to answer,' I said. 'I was born and brought up in England, certainly.'

'Oh,' she clasped her hands together. 'It's so good to listen to you, though it makes me quite homesick, I must confess.' She glanced across at Iorwerth. 'Of course, I wouldn't want to return to England, not now.'

He met her gaze. 'If that nephew of mine is whispering sweet words in your ear, ignore him. They don't mean a thing. It's just that no Welshman could resist a beautiful woman.'

'She is beautiful, too,' I said with a smile. 'I envy you, Iorwerth.'

'Tut!' Mamgu snorted. 'There's enough women sick for you as it is, Davy, without you envying your uncle. There's a tom cat for you, Iorwerth; reminds me of Huw when he was a boy.'

'And that's good enough for me,' Iorwerth laughed. 'You just keep away from my woman, Davy boyo, or I'll have your liver for breakfast!'

Later, when tea was over, I excused myself and went into the slope. There was no real privacy, I could still hear the family laughing and chattering, but at least I could be alone and close my eyes and think my own thoughts.

'Sorry, am I disturbing you?' I looked up to see my mother standing above me. Her face was flushed with the heat of the kitchen and the excitement of having her brother home again, and she looked beautiful. How could Dylan Morgan resist her? I could not blame him, after all, for what had happened.

I sat up and moved aside so that she could sit next to me. She remained standing, her hands clasped in front of her, a look of disapproval on her face.

'I went to Siop Fawr just after you left,' she said, 'and Dylan told me about this girl you want to help. Have you no shame? The girl is a thief and probably worse.'

My mother had the knack of touching me on the raw and, as always, I responded by being cruel.

'Yes, she is worse; she's a prostitute as well. Now are you satisfied?'

'Davy, you're not – not sleeping with this girl, are you? Surely even you couldn't sink that low.'

'You always get the wrong end of the dog's bone where I am concerned, don't you, Mother?' I spoke sharply. 'The girl is just twelve years old.'

She looked at her hands. 'I'm sorry, Davy. Dylan told me you were helping a friend. I should have taken his word for it.'

'Oh, Mam,' I said softly in Welsh, 'can't you have a little faith and confidence in me?'

'I do try, Davy,' she brushed back a wisp of hair, 'but I can't seem to reach you at all, these days. It's as if we are strangers.'

I reached out to take her hand, but just then Mamgu called from the kitchen.

'Catrin, come and help me make up a bed for Iorwerth and Elizabeth, there's a good girl.'

She went out then, not looking at me again, and with a sigh I leaned back on the bed. I wondered what her life had been like when she was a child. The house would have been full as it was now, a close, warm family, loving hard and living hard. She loved my father, of that there was no doubt, and they could be happy together now if I didn't put obstacles in their way. I closed my eyes and, in spite of the chatter from the kitchen, I drifted off to sleep.

Sunday was a glittering day; for once the smoke seemed to have rolled away, and the air felt almost fresh. I ate some bread and cheese and was just about to start out for a walk before meeting Susannah when Mamgu came downstairs.

'Going out, Davy?' she asked, and I nodded, my hand on the door, waiting for her to continue.

'Do a favour for your grandmother, then, is it?' She raked up the fire and set the kettle on to boil. 'Go to Huw's farm and tell him that his brother is home.' She stared at me. 'But keep away from that evil cousin of yours. I don't want you coming home with a pair of blackers.'

'All right,' I said. 'I promise I won't lay a hand on him, not unless he hits me first.'

She laughed. 'Oh, get away with you, there's a good boy. It's too early in the morning to put up with your good humour.'

It was good to be outdoors beneath a sky that was bright once I was away from the Hafod. I tramped across the soft grass, anticipating my meeting with Susannah. She would be doubly welcoming because we hadn't been able to meet the Sunday before.

The sun was warm on my back, and once I was away from the streets and courts of the town there was the sweet smell of grass. Swansea could be a wonderful place, resting as it was on the edge of the sea with two fine hills protective each side of it. But I had seen its other face.

Huw's farm was quite large and it took me half an hour to walk from the gate to the warm stone house. The door stood open and Huw, looking up from the table, saw me and his face split at once into a grin.

'Davy, boyo, there's good it is to see you. Come and sit here with me and have some fresh cooked eggs and my own bacon. Put your mouth in shape for a feast.'

I sat with him at the table, and it was obvious that he knew nothing of my last fight with William. Rhian, however, stared at me with guarded eyes as she put a plate of food before me. She took her son's part against me, as was natural. I could only wish that my own mother was of like mind.

'I have a message for you,' I said between mouthfuls of tasty egg and bacon. 'Your brother Iorwerth is home.'

'Well, damn me!' Huw thumped the table in his delight. 'I'll ride over there later and see the old devil! What's this wife of his like?'

'Very beautiful,' I said. 'He has good taste, I'll give him that.'

'Ha!' Huw was amused. 'A good judge of womenfolk, are you? Quite right too. Glad to see there's red blood in your veins, boyo.'

He leaned his elbow on the table. 'Your mam was lovely as a girl, mind. Take some beating for looks, she would. Had her pick of the men around here.'

'How did she meet John Richards?' I asked, trying to sound casual, and he grinned.

'*Duw*, that was a day. A crowd of us walked to Carmarthen, Catrin dressed as a boy, to hear the copper trial. Some poor man said the smoke had affected his wife's lungs, as it probably had, but the Vivians won the case, of course.'

'I can't imagine my mother dressed as a boy!' I was incredulous. 'How on earth did she get away with it?'

'Oh, she was all right after I'd rubbed some dirt into her

245

face.' Huw laughed at the memory. 'How John fell in love with her that day I'll never know.'

I got to my feet suddenly, grieving that the man I'd called my father all these years had died without ever becoming really close to me, never confiding the truth about our relationship.

'Where are you rushing off to then, boyo?' Huw said quickly. 'You've only just come, man.'

'I would stay,' I grinned, 'but I don't like to keep a lady waiting.'

Huw gave a bellow of a laugh. 'Oh, it's like that, is it? Away you go, then.'

The air was fresh and clear as I stepped out sharply down the path towards the gate. I lifted my face and felt the warmth of the sun like benediction. It was a lovely day.

Suddenly, behind me, I heard a cry and the drumming of horse's hooves on the dry ground. I spun round in time to see a large black stallion bearing down upon me. I flung myself to one side and the breath was knocked out of me as I hit the ground hard. Then Huw was helping me to my feet.

'That young fool William could have killed you!' he said in fury. 'I've told him that animal is too spirited to be ridden yet. I'll flay the boy alive when I get my hands on him.'

'No harm done,' I said, brushing the dust away, and behind my uncle I saw Rhian. Her face was white and in her eyes was the terrible knowledge that what had just happened was no accident.

EIGHT

Susannah sat up in bed and stretched her slender arms luxuriously above her head. Her fine, pointed breasts lifted high and free above the sheets were marble white in the chill of the morning air. She looked virginal, untouched, and for a moment guilt pressed upon me as I wondered at the harm I might be doing.

'I'm delighted that my brother-in-law is away so often. He could not plan his trips better if he tried.' She flung herself back against the pillows and laughed, her narrowed eyes offering a challenge, and the illusion of childish innocence vanished.

I reached for her, but she held me away. 'Davy,' she whispered, 'why be stubborn? Why not work for my brother-in-law? The Hafod copper works is no place for you. You should take your rightful place in society.'

'As your lover?' I said dryly, and before she could speak again I took possession of her. The act was swift, almost impersonal; it was as if I wanted to punish her, though what she had done wrong wasn't clear, even to me.

She clung to me, her arms warm and smooth against my neck.

'Davy.' She spoke my name softly, with a wealth of feeling, and I kissed her with tenderness, an act of contrition. 'Will you do something for me, Davy?' With a woman's intuition, she had sensed my momentary weakness.

I rolled on to my back and put my hands beneath my head. With my eyes closed it almost seemed as though I was floating far above the earth.

'Come on, Davy,' she tickled my chest, 'there's no use in pretending to sleep. I mean to have a promise from you.'

'A promise of what?' I said warily, and she laughed outright.

'Not of marriage, I assure you! No, I am quite happy to be as I am, independent and wealthy. My first husband took good care to leave me well provided for. I wouldn't hand all that over to a husband, so be easy. You are safe with me.'

I sighed in resignation and sat up. 'All right, what do you want?'

She hugged her knees. 'There's a grand soirée at the Royal Institute. Say you'll come with me. It would make me so happy.'

'I thought you never lacked for male companions.' I couldn't resist the gibe, but she just laughed.

'True, but they begin to bore me. I'd like you to take me. Come on, Davy, just this once. You never know, you might find it all quite interesting yourself.'

'But how will you explain me away?' I was curious. 'You can hardly introduce me as your friend the copper man.'

'You will be an out-of-town cousin,' she said, her eyes full of amusement. 'You speak so beautifully I'm sure no one will question you.'

'But your brother-in-law knows quite well who I am. I'm sure he wouldn't be at all pleased.'

'In all probability he won't come to the soirée,' she had an answer for everything, 'but if he does, I'm sure he'll think it all a fine joke.'

'Oh, I see,' I said with mock severity. 'I am to be a joke.'

She fell over me, her hair brushing my face, her lips sweet and demanding on mine.

'All right,' I said, my arms tight around her, 'I'll come to your damn soirée.'

Returning to work the next day was like going into hell. The smoke was down, blowing into the sheds in choking gusts. I stood before the mouth of the furnace and cursed myself for being all sorts of a fool. I should have ignored the voice of pride and take a job somewhere right away from the smell and heat of the copper.

'*Iesu Crist!*' Luther coughed as though he'd never stop, his face was red with strain and heat, the sweat dripping from his arms like tears.

'I'm not long for this world,' he joked, thumping his chest with a huge fist. '*Duw*, you young bucks don't know you're born, working all week and then still having the strength to cross a woman on your day off!'

I laughed. 'You being nosy again, Luther, or just remembering old times?'

His bout of coughing subsided and he crouched down on his heels for a moment, struggling to draw breath.

'Don't take any notice of me, boyo,' he said at last. 'Envy is a terrible thing, but I must confess it burns in me on times.' He nodded towards the furnace. 'Best give it another pole.'

I fed a slender tree trunk into the voracious mouth of the furnace and leaned back as far away from the heat as possible, sweat soaking my face and chest, running down my legs.

'Right, boyo,' Luther called, 'step down to have some water. As for me, I could drink the canal dry!'

I wiped my face with my sweat rag and felt the bite of the copper dust in my skin. Soon, I would have a shell of copper particles, like the other men in the sheds. I'd be branded for anyone to see what my trade was.

The manager came across the floor and nodded to me, drawing Luther to one side. He spoke softly in Welsh and I could only catch a word or two, not enough to be able to make sense out of it. Luther nodded vigorously, and when the manager went trundling away on his short legs, back to the coolness of his office, Luther caught my arm in great excitement.

'There's good news, Davy.' He could hardly tell me, so great was his excitement. 'An inspector is coming down from London next month, and it's all because of our petition.'

'We've won, then?' I said eagerly. 'I can't believe it is that easy.'

'Hold your horses, boyo,' Luther said. 'It isn't that easy, not at all. The inspector will have to give his judgement, then we will see if Swansea will be placed under The Health of Towns Act.'

'Surely the inspector will be convinced once he's seen some of the streets and courts in the town,' I said quickly, and Luther shook his head.

'If he sees them, boyo. It will all depend on who shows him around.'

'Then we will have to make certain his attention is drawn to the right areas,' I said, smiling. 'I still have my good town suit at home.'

Luther slapped his thigh. '*Darro!*' He grinned at me. 'It will be a good sight to see, a copper man mixing with the nobs. Do you think they'll sniff you out?'

'I shouldn't worry about that,' I said. 'Just trust me.' I smiled to myself. Susannah had done me a favour by offering to take me to the soirée and introducing me as her cousin. My face would be known in the right quarters, but not too well known.

'You're up to something, Davy, boyo,' Luther said, 'but I don't give a damn what your plan is, so long as it works. Come on, now, let's get on with the copper smelting, is it, before we're thrown out by our necks.'

I watched him take the molten copper in his ladle – the sight of his bulging muscles fascinated me – and tip the glowing stream into the pot to cool. It hissed as some of it sket on to the floor, and then I felt a bite like that of a horse sear on my leg.

I fell back and Luther bent over me, quickly loosening the sailcloth that was tied around my trousers. The copper had gone deep into my skin and set hard there, a bright jagged ornament in my singed flesh.

'Get off home with you, Davy,' Luther said. 'Your mam is the best one I know for curing burns.' He held me back for a moment as I made to rise. 'No, first I must get the metal out.'

He took his knife from his belt and a flask of whisky from his back pocket. I watched fascinated as he poured the amber liquid over the blade. A few of the men had gathered round, and I felt beads of moisture run down my face that had nothing to do with the heat of the shed.

'Take a good swig of this.' Luther handed me the flask, and I obeyed him, feeling the hard liquor bite the back of my throat.

The knife dug deep and I felt the pain of it right up into my belly. I grasped the flask, my hands sweating so much that it nearly fell from my fingers. I took another drink, a longer one, as Luther's knife probed round the copper that by now had become part of me. I wanted to scream out with the agony, but after a few minutes the pain seemed to vanish and I was aware of nothing except the will to remain conscious, not to lose my dignity before my fellow workers.

'There, boyo,' Luther said at last. 'Do you think you can manage to get home alone?'

'Yes.' I nodded and handed him the flask, but he gestured for me to keep it.

'Go on, take it with you. Your need is greater than mine.'

The manager was waiting for me as I left the shed. He nodded. 'Lift up your trouser leg, man,' he said. 'Let me see what has happened.'

I showed him, but did not look down myself. He did not seem surprised or even concerned.

'All right,' he said, 'an hour off from work is all that I can allow. It's only a very small sket, isn't it?'

I managed to walk past him without reaching out and hammering my fist in his face. What did he know about skets, sitting in the comfort of his office all day?

My mother was sitting before the fire, a piece of sewing in her hands.

'Davy, what are you doing home at this time of day? You're not hurt, are you?'

'Don't worry,' I said as she got to her feet. 'It's just a small sket. The manager has given me an hour off to have it seen to.'

'Let me look, then.' She examined the wound carefully and nodded. 'That won't take very long to heal.'

I was piqued by her attitude. 'It stings enough anyway, and Luther's probing to get the metal out wasn't much fun.'

'Before you feel too sorry for yourself,' my mother said, placing some beets on the table, 'let me tell you about Dylan.' She glanced at me guardedly. 'I sent him to work

252

in the copper when he was a boy, not much more than your age, maybe even less. Well, there was a big explosion and he caught the copper all down his back. He has the scars to this day.' She chopped up the beets and put them in a bowl with some vinegar. 'I tended him when he came out of the infirmary, and I wouldn't let him go back to the works. Now perhaps you'll see why I've been so against you working in the sheds.'

The mixture of beet and vinegar stung the wound for a moment and I gritted my teeth. She wound some clean strips of linen over the reddened surface of my leg, and almost at once it brought me ease.

'Mam,' I said softly, taking her hand, 'I know I've been difficult just lately; I've acted like a child, but perhaps if you give me time I might manage to grow up a little.'

She took my face in her hands and kissed me. 'There's soft you are sometimes, Davy,' she said. 'I don't know when it is I love you the most, when you are gentle like this, or hard like a headstrong man. You are very much like Dylan, you know.'

There was a mixture of feelings inside me at her words. Would I ever get over the guilt I felt now because I was suddenly proud that Dylan Morgan was my natural father? What of John Richards who had brought me up and cared for me all these years?

'Oh, leave me,' I said irritably. 'I'm going back to work.'

I walked as quickly as I could along the row. The pain in my leg had settled to a dull ache, but there was a hurt inside me that was far worse than that; it was something I couldn't control, couldn't even understand properly.

The manager was standing at the gate, his hands behind his back, his stubby legs astride.

'You've come back, then?' His tone was dry, as if I'd

253

been a silly child to even bother going home for such a small matter.

'Yes, I'm back.' My voice was hostile, and his eyebrows rose. 'Are you going to give me the boot, just like you did with Annie Owens?' I heard the challenge in my voice, and so did he.

'What's the reason for bringing Annie Owens into this discussion?' He thrust his hands into his pockets. He wasn't in the least angry, just curious.

'Do you know what happened to her after she left here?' I said. 'She became a street girl, at twelve years of age. Do you feel no guilt when you think of that?'

He rocked to and fro on his heels. 'I knew nothing of that,' he said, 'but I did what was right in sending her off. I'm sorry that she turned bad, though.'

'There's worse,' I said tersely. 'She's in trouble now for stealing. She might even be transported.'

'Oh?' he said. 'Is that so?' He rubbed his chin thoughtfully. 'I'm glad you told me, but back to work now or the shift will be over.'

He walked away on stocky legs, his head sunk into his chest, not looking back at all, sure that I would obey him. For one moment I felt like running after him and telling him to stuff his job where he liked, but then common sense prevailed and with a sigh I made my way back to the sheds. Copper working might not be much of a job in some people's eyes, but for the moment it was all I had.

NINE

The sound of hooves and the rumbling of wheels as a stream of coaches drew up outside the Royal Institute gave me a feeling of excitement and anticipation. I stood in the brilliantly lit entrance, waiting for Susannah to arrive, aware of curious looks that came my way, feeling like a small child at a party.

At last I saw Susannah step from a coach, and my heart sank as I saw that her brother-in-law was with her.

'Davy,' she stood on tiptoe and kissed me lightly on the cheek, 'you look so handsome,' she whispered in my ear. She looked wonderful herself; her hair shimmered in the light and there was a sparkle in her eyes that made me want to take her in my arms and hold her close.

'Good evening.' Her brother-in-law bowed to me rather stiffly. 'I trust your dear mother is keeping well.' He didn't wait for an answer, but turned to where a crowd of richly dressed ladies stood waiting for their menfolk.

'Old crows!' Susannah said, following my gaze. 'With their stuffy old husbands, they'll be so envious of me.' She laughed lightly and took my arm. 'Oh, isn't the vestibule decorated beautifully? Look, there's so much greenery about the place it's almost like being in the woods.'

'I don't know why you are so excited,' I said dryly. 'You attend so many functions I'd have thought you'd be bored with it all by now.'

'I don't ever allow myself to become bored,' Susannah

looked at me reprovingly, 'and I do hope you are not going to be in one of your strange moods tonight; you'll spoil everything for me and I shan't love you any more.'

I laughed at her puckered face. 'All right, I'll give in and admit I'm as excited as you are.'

'Good.' She drew me closer to her side. 'No flirting with any of the other ladies. Tonight you are all mine, remember.'

'A very willing captive.' I smiled. 'I don't think you have anything to fear.' I looked round at the women in their bright dresses and elaborate hair styles and thought of Rosie, her golden hair loose to her waist, her magnificent body dressed simply. If Susannah had anyone to fear, it was a girl who spent her life whoring. It was so ironical I almost laughed out loud.

'You are miles away.' Susannah tapped my cheek. 'Were you thinking of another woman?'

'Certainly not,' I lied. 'I was just listening to the music. Can't you hear it?'

'I'll believe you.' Susannah pulled at my arm. 'Come along now, it's almost eight-thirty; we don't want to be late for the address.'

I had to admit that after a few minutes of listening to a pompous speech about literature I grew bored. At one time I would have listened as readily as the next man, keen to voice my own opinions, but in the light of my new experiences as a working man, it all seemed irrelevant to the real issues of the town.

Later, in the library, several of Susannah's friends came to pay her their respects and to give me a good looking over in the bargain.

'I'm Mary,' one of them said softly, her beringed hand resting on my arm. 'Where has Susannah been keeping you, the selfish girl?'

'I've been out of town,' I said quickly, 'though I must say I'm charmed to meet you all now I'm here.'

Susannah drew me away in a proprietary manner, her eyes promising me the earth.

'They are all amazed at my audacity in bringing you here,' she said. 'They guess of course that you are more to me than a cousin.'

'But they do not guess I am an impostor here and in the daytime I am a copper man,' I said, rather piqued at being treated like a prize stallion.

At ten o'clock it was decided that the company would retire to the theatre, where tea and coffee would be served. I took Susannah's arm and drew her outside into the garden.

'Come on,' I said, drawing her into my arms. 'Kiss me. That's what you want, isn't it?'

'Oh, David!' She spoke angrily. 'Let's go back inside. I don't want to lose my reputation altogether. We must be discreet.'

I was chilled by her attitude. 'You may be able to switch your feelings on and off,' I said, 'but I'm made of different stuff.' I pulled her roughly, but she shook my arm away.

'I am not prepared to make love in a field like an animal,' she said haughtily. 'Keep that sort of activity for the women in the copper district.'

She walked away, her head high, her shoulders stiff. I didn't know whether to laugh or be angry with her. I caught her up easily and drew her gently into my arms, kissing her mouth, my hands exploring inside her bodice.

'No, David, please.' Her breath was ragged, and she was still protesting as I drew her down on to the sweet-smelling grass.

'What could be a better bed?' I asked softly. 'It's so

257

romantic with the stars looking down on to us, don't you feel that, Susannah?'

'Oh, David,' she moaned my name as I slipped the soft material of her dress from her shoulders, 'what spell is it that makes me unable to resist you?' She reached up, pressing her mouth against mine and we were moulded close, like part of the earth itself.

She was beautiful when we returned to the theatre, glowing with happiness, and it must have been apparent to anyone who cared to notice that she was a woman who had been made love to. I drank bitter coffee out of delicate porcelain just to please her and gave her all my attention, and in return she favoured me with her brilliant smile until with a shock I realized that she was falling in love with me. Maybe she didn't even begin to realize it herself. It was an impossible situation, and long after she had climbed into her carriage and driven home, I brooded on the best way to end the affair.

Working the copper, the next day, seemed harder and dustier than ever, and I was glad to get home to Tip Row and have Mamgu pour the warm bath water over my aching shoulders.

'Well?' she said after a few moments' silence. 'Are you going to tell me where you went last night in all your finery?'

I sighed. 'There's nothing can be kept from a nosy woman, is there?'

She slapped my chest with a wet cloth. 'There's no need of cheek now, is there? Asked a civil question, that's all I did.'

I bent my head as she poured water over my hair, rubbing the copper dust out of it.

'The Royal Institute,' I said, and her hand paused in mid-air.

'What?' She almost shouted the word. 'And what business do you have there, indeed?'

'I was with a lady,' I said slowly. 'We've been sort of fond to each other, if you know what I mean.'

'Oh, yes,' Mamgu said sharply. 'I know what you mean, all right, and I'm shocked. I thought ladies allowed no-one but their husbands in their skirts.'

I tried not to laugh. 'The trouble now is she's falling in love with me,' I said slowly.

'And now you've had your fun and want to go on to pastures new, I suppose.' Mamgu folded her arms across her chest. She sounded angry, but her eyes were sparkling. 'Well, serve you right, that's what I say.'

I stood up, and the water ran in streams down my body. I brushed back my hair and grinned at Mamgu.

'But you wouldn't want me to marry someone who I didn't love?'

'Love? You don't know the meaning of the word yet. You're only a cub. It takes a man to be in love.' Mamgu frowned. 'Get dried before you catch a cold.'

The door opened suddenly and Elizabeth stood there, her face growing crimson.

'I'm so sorry,' she mumbled and banged the door shut again. I burst out laughing, but Mamgu frowned at me.

'I don't want no trouble in that quarter, mind,' she said quietly. 'All other women are fair game, but not Iorwerth's wife.'

'But I wouldn't dream of doing anything like that. What an opinion you have of me, Mamgu.'

'It's the opinion I have of all men, Davy. Tempt them enough and they can't say no. I'm not blaming you for anything, but I saw the look in Elizabeth's eyes when she saw you. You're a fine figure of a man, Davy, but you've a great deal of growing up to do yet, mind.' She waved at me

259

impatiently. 'Oh, come out of there before you catch your death of cold.'

I shook the water from my feet before stepping out on to the old flannel shirt Mamgu had put ready for me. I still found it hard to accept the way my grandmother waited on me; she was so stern and strong and yet she bathed me as though I was a baby.

'*Duw*, that burn is sore.' She wiped at it gently. 'Catrin will have to see to it again. We don't want it going bad on you.'

I lay on my bed in the slope for a while, staring up at the cracked roof. Somehow the picture of Elizabeth intruded into my mind and I was impatient with Mamgu for putting foolish thoughts into words. Restlessly I dressed and let myself out of the house. It was a cool evening and the smoke didn't hang so suffocatingly near to the houses. Even through the rolling green clouds I caught a glimpse of the stars, and they seemed close to me, just above my head, so that if I reached up I could touch them.

As I turned the corner of the row, I almost bumped into Kate. She was hurrying along, head bent, trying to ignore the shouts and whistles of some copper boys.

'Oh, Davy,' she said breathlessly, 'Dad sent me to see you. There's some news of your friend.'

I took her arm and led her away from the narrow streets out into the bank that led up to the Town Hill.

'What news?' I asked eagerly as we sat side by side on the grass.

'Well,' Kate twisted her slim fingers together, 'it isn't as bad as you feared. She will not be transported, but she has to go to gaol for a month. Dad said the manager from the copper works spoke on her behalf; said he'd take her into his house in service when her sentence was finished.'

I sighed. 'Well, I suppose the old devil has some good in

him after all. He must have a conscience like any other man.' I turned to her, and she smiled warmly.

'Dad said to tell you he did his best for the girl, but it was for your sake mostly, though of course he felt sorry for her, she being so young.'

'Tell him how grateful I am for his help,' I said. 'If he hadn't put a word in the right quarter I'm sure she wouldn't have been let off so lightly.'

'No,' Kate said gently, 'I won't tell him. Tell him yourself. He wants to see you again, I know he does. He needs a son, Davy.'

I got to my feet abruptly, the old war fighting inside me again. Where did my loyalty to John Richards end and my wish to recognize my natural father begin.

'Oh, Kate!' I said. 'If only it was so simple, but it isn't. Am I to forget my upbringing? Forget that my mother was having Dylan Morgan's child and he allowed her to marry another man?'

'Hush, Davy, there's a good boy.' Kate spoke sharply. 'You don't know anything about it, do you? Your mother chose to leave Tip Row. My father would have married her in a minute if she would have taken him.'

I sighed and shook my head. 'I'm so mixed up, Kate. I can't understand it myself, so how can I make you see how I feel?'

'Well,' she rose, 'I must be getting home. Dad is not well. I think he's got a bit of a fever, but he will keep on working in that shop as though the place will fall apart without him.'

I watched her go, and within me there was a wild impulse to run after her, to tell her I would come to the shop and see my father, but she turned the corner out of sight and I sighed heavily. The moment was past.

Slowly I made my way down High Street. I would see

Rosie. I would tell her about Annie, that she would not be transported after all, and together, Rosie and I would be happy in a world of our own making.

She was sitting at the window, magnificent in a gown of pale blue muslin. Her hair was gold in the sunlight, and she could not have looked more gracious if she was decked in diamonds and silk.

'Davy.' She kissed me, the warm scent of her heady in my nostrils. 'Oh, Davy, I felt inside me that you would come today.'

She drew me down beside her and I kissed the pink tips of her fingers, brushing the soft hair away from her neck so that my lips could dwell on the sweetness of her skin.

'Have you any news of Annie?' She took my face in her hands and forced me to look at her.

'Yes,' I said softly. 'She will not be transported and she has only to serve a month in gaol. When she is released there is a place waiting for her in service with the copper manager, so don't worry your pretty little head any more. Annie will be all right.'

'A month can be a very long time,' Rosie said, frowning. 'I only hope the poor girl can stand up to it.'

'It's better than the streets.' The words were out of my mouth before I could stop them, and Rosie pushed me away.

'You are not going to start on about that again, are you?' she said, her voice rising. 'Why can't you accept me as I am and not try to change me?'

I drew her to me. 'I'm sorry, Rosie. I didn't mean to say that, but now the words are spoken won't you think again about living with me? I'd be good to you.'

'There's stubborn you are.' She brushed the hair away from my face and kissed me so that the breath left my body. I held her tightly in my arms and, laughing a little, she led me towards the bed.

'Come on, Davy, boyo,' she whispered. 'I'll give you something to remember me by.'

'Remember you by?' I said. 'You surely don't intend to go away from Swansea, do you?'

'No, no. There's a one for the questions, aren't you? Come on, stop thinking so much, just enjoy yourself. Too serious for your own good, you are.'

I closed my eyes, breathed in the scent of her and held her close.

'Don't worry, Rosie,' I said fiercely. 'I'll give you something to remember *me* by!'

TEN

'There's grand you look, Davy, man.' Luther straightened my collar, fussing over me as though I was a prize hog. '*Duw*, I've never spent a Monday morning like this one.'

'Nor have I!' I moved away from him impatiently. 'My head aches as though a hundred men with hammers were inside it. I should never have agreed to stay with you last night. I might have known we'd spend the time drinking instead of sleeping.'

'This way is better,' Luther said. 'Now I can be sure you've gone to the meeting.'

I sighed. 'You are like a proud mama sending off her first daughter to the ball. Stop worrying, will you?'

'I can't help being excited,' Luther grinned. '*Duw*, at that last public meeting I thought we'd had it; everyone was against us. It's a miracle the inspector is coming here at all, so allow me some excitement, will you?'

I nodded. 'Yes, there was nearly a riot. You'd think Swansea was about to be burned to the ground, not put under the Health of Town Act.' I sighed with satisfaction. 'Well, we won this inquiry at least, so stop fussing and let me go to the Assembly Rooms before I miss it all.'

It was a fine day, a good day for leaving behind the choking sweep of the copper smoke brushing through the valley. I lifted my face to the morning sky, and the spring sunshine bathed me in its glow which was so much kinder than the glare of the copper furnace.

Luther had surprised me by gaining support from the works manager of all people. He had stood on his short legs, looking me up and down, his face red with the effort of gathering his thoughts, but at last he'd agreed to allow me time off.

'But no taking advantage, mind!' he'd warned, and I had nodded, trying my best to keep a straight face. And now here I was acting the gentleman in my good clothes, striding down the Strand in the direction of the Assembly Rooms.

To my surprise, the meeting was a small one. With all the opposition to the inquiry, I'd expected the room to be crowded to the door. I sat down near the back and stared at Mr Clark who had been sent here from London to determine whether Swansea should come under the operation of the Act or not. Beside him sat Mr Michael, resplendent in his mayoral robes. But if I'd expected excitement, I was doomed to disappointment. A few questions were asked and were answered with courtesy. The inspector had a quiet manner, but I could see that he meant to be thorough. After a short time, he left the Assembly Rooms with about twenty of the town's most prominent businessmen to start his examination of the sanitary conditions of the town.

Luther was silent when I told him how little had happened.

'Don't look so down in the mouth,' I said. 'It's early days yet and, anyway, I have the feeling that Mr Clark is a man we can depend on.'

'I only hope you are right, boyo,' Luther said. 'The question is will he be allowed to see the worst areas of the town?'

'I can set your mind at rest on that score,' I said quickly. 'Mr Clark has asked for maps of the town boundaries; he

265

won't miss anything out, I'd put my last shilling on that.'

'Well, go on home now,' Luther patted my shoulder, 'but don't forget to attend the meeting again tomorrow.'

I laughed. 'I'm not likely to forget with you nagging me like a fishwife!' I strode up the road then, and though the door of the little house in Tip Row stood open as usual, there was no sign of Mamgu, no sign of anyone.

Carefully, I built up the fire that had sunk low in the hearth and boiled the kettle ready for when Mamgu returned. I felt drowsy after the excesses of the previous night and went into the slope, stretching out on my bed with a sigh of contentment. I must have dozed then, because the next thing I was conscious of was my mother shaking my arm.

'What's wrong?' I said at once, seeing how white her face was. 'Is Mamgu ill?'

My mother shook her head. 'No, it's not your grandmother, it's Dylan. He's taken a fever, probably caught from that damn horse he's been nursing.' She twisted her slim hands together, avoiding my eyes. I sat up and brushed the hair from my eyes.

'What can I do to help?' Even as I spoke, there were mixed feelings inside me. I would help, of course I would, but a little knot of jealousy seemed to tie my tongue.

'If you could come up to the shop, Davy, there's no telling how grateful I'd be. Kate works hard, and so do the other girls, but the place needs a man.'

I searched my mind for something to say, some reassurance, but there was nothing inside me except a blank. At last I managed to nod my head and she, understanding how I felt, touched my cheek softly.

'Thank you, Davy.' She went to the window and stared out, though there was nothing to see; the copper smoke was down over the houses, obscuring everything else. 'I'll pack some of your clothes. You'll need to look tidy if you're to serve customers in the shop.'

I touched her shoulder lightly. 'How bad is he? Is it serious?'

'Not serious,' her tone was full of mixed emotions, 'but if he doesn't get the rest he needs there's no telling what will happen.'

'All right.' I smiled at her. 'You go on ahead. 'I've some apologies I have to make to a friend.'

She shook her head, a wry smile on her face, as though she understood me too well for my own comfort.

'Don't break too many hearts, Davy.' There was the glint of tears in her eyes. 'Fate has a strange way of catching up and expecting payment.'

'Don't worry about me, Mam.' I smiled, though I felt like crying, knowing there was a gentle reproof in her words.

There was a sudden bustle of movement in the kitchen. I heard Mamgu's voice and the softer tones of Elizabeth. I took my mother's arm and together we left the slope.

'Hello, there's a fright!' Mamgu clutched the starched white bodice of her apron. 'I didn't know anyone was in.'

There was a small silence. Elizabeth's eyes met mine for a second, and then she looked away. I moved forward and took the heavy basket from her arm.

'We've been to the market.' Mamgu began to unpack the vegetables, her movements quick and deft. 'Put the kettle on the fire, Davy, there's a good boy. I'm parched.'

'It was boiling it's head off when I came in,' my mother said. 'I wondered where everyone could be.'

'That was my fault.' I put the kettle once more on to the flames. 'I didn't think I'd sleep this long. Sorry, Mamgu.'

'*Duw*,' my grandmother stopped her work to look at me, 'I can't get used to you talking posh, even after all this time. Tickled to death, I am, to have such a grandson, and proud too, though it wouldn't do to tell you that very often.'

'I've asked Davy to come and help us at *Siop Fawr*,' my mother said suddenly, and I realized that she was nervous. 'I'm sorry to take him away from you, Mam, but Dylan is ill and we need a man about the place.'

Mamgu was silent for a long moment, her hands still over the basket.

'Well,' she said at last, 'he knows that my door is always open to him. This is his home for as long as he likes to call it that.'

I wished I could find the words to tell Mamgu how fine a woman she was. Instead I put my hand lightly on her shoulder for a moment, and I think she understood.

'I've got to go,' I said, moving towards the door, 'or I'm going to be late for my appointment.'

Mamgu snorted. 'Late for your tom catting, you mean. Go on with you, boy, though I don't think it's wise of you to sow wild oats in the light of day!'

My grandmother was wrong about one thing: it was not still daylight, but a blue-grey twilight that softened the stacks of the works so that they were slim and tall, fingers pointing at the stars. Strangely, the place had become my home and now I was reluctant to leave it.

Susannah was waiting for me on the green. She came towards me, hands outstretched, skirts billowing, and I took her hands in mine, feeling a rush of emotion I couldn't have begun to explain. How could I ever have wanted to end the affair?

'I want to kiss you,' I said softly, and the delicate colour came into her cheeks.

'Behave yourself,' she whispered. 'You are supposed to be my cousin, remember.'

'I think I'm going to have difficulty with my memory,' I laughed. 'Perhaps it's a good thing I'm not able to stay with you long.'

She turned quickly, her eyes large as they rested on my face.

'Why, what's wrong?' She sounded anxious, and I cursed myself for being a clumsy fool.

'Nothing too bad, I assure you.' My hand curled round hers. 'It's just that there's a sort of family crisis and I've been asked to help out.'

'Oh.' She looked down at the ground. 'Are you sure you are not bored with my company?'

'Of course not!' I kissed her mouth quickly. 'We will meet next week as usual, won't we?'

'I'm not sure.' She held her head high in childlike defiance, and it was difficult to believe she was so much older than I.

'All right.' I tried not to laugh. 'I'd better leave it to you to arrange our next meeting.'

'Oh!' She almost stamped her foot. 'You can be so infuriating at times. I must be mad to bother with you.'

'But you can't do without me.' I spoke jokingly, but she stared up at me, her face serious.

'I think I'm falling in love with you, David.' She spoke the words simply, and I took her into my arms.

'Oh, Susannah, what can I say?' I brushed a strand of glossy hair that had escaped from under her bonnet and she caught my fingers, holding them to her cheek.

'Don't say anything.' She smiled at me. 'I'm not so foolish as to think you would want to marry a woman my age, but I'm willing to take what you can give me.'

In that second, I think I did love her in my own way. I held her close.

'You are very special to me,' I said gently. 'I don't think

there will ever be anyone quite like you in my life again.'

She pushed me away, suddenly her usual smiling self. She tied her bonnet more securely and brushed the folds from her skirts.

'Come to the villa on Thursday night,' she said brightly. 'I'll be alone then.' She walked away briskly, her shoulders straight, and I smiled to myself. There was no understanding the moods of women. I turned then and made my way up the hill.

The meetings at the Assembly Rooms dragged on for three more days, and I was torn between attending them and helping out at Dylan's shop. I had been given a small bedroom of my own over the stables, but I scarcely laid my head down before the early hours of the morning. Of Dylan, I had seen nothing.

At last, Mr Clark announced that he had completed his enquiries and all that remained was for him to draw up his report. Luther was almost jumping with impatience when I told him about it.

'Calm down,' I said. 'The report will be sent up to London and then copies of it will be circulated in Swansea.'

'Aye,' Luther said sourly, 'if all goes well, that is, but I'm not a believer in counting chickens before they're hatched.'

'Well, Mr Clark spoke strongly against the lack of privies,' I said. 'He found it objectionable that men and women should use the street as a convenience.'

'So do the men and women,' Luther said loudly, 'especially in the rain when the road is covered with enough mud to bury them.' He coughed into his sleeve. 'Fine words all right, but do they mean anything?'

'I think Mr Clark is a man of integrity,' I said patiently, 'and he said that the expense would amount to about a penny a week for each house, and this the owners would have to pay.'

He stared at me, unmoving. He was not a man to be swayed by words or promises; he wanted action, and the sooner the better.

'The summer is coming,' he said suddenly, and I stared at him in surprise. 'The hot weather always brings some sort of pestilence with it. Haven't you noticed that, boyo?'

'Come to think of it,' I said, 'you're quite right, but what of it?'

'If the town was properly cleaned up, perhaps there would be less sickness.' He shook his head. 'The doctors always say to keep away filth, don't they? Well, there's plenty of filth around here.'

'It will come,' I said. 'Just bide your time, Luther. We'll win, you'll see.'

'Yes, and while I'm biding my time, the scarlatina and perhaps even the cholera may come like it did in the thirties. How can I be patient?'

I yawned. 'I'm sorry, Luther.' I put my hand on his shoulder. 'It isn't that I lack sympathy, but I think you are looking on the gloomy side, and apart from that I'm so damn tired!'

'Go home and rest, then, boyo.' Luther managed a smile. 'See you in the sheds tomorrow, is it?'

I nodded. 'Aye, but before that I've got to move some sacks of grain from the store room into the shop. It'll be midnight before I go to bed.'

Luther gave a bellow of a laugh. 'What are you talking about, man? It's just past six of clock, not yet dark.'

'Ah,' I smiled at him, 'but I have other business to occupy me before I go home, a promise I have to keep to a certain lady.'

I thought of Susannah, soft and warm, with scented skin and glossy hair, waiting in her comfortable bed for me, and guessed I would be very late stacking grain that night.

ELEVEN

'Oh, Davy, thank God you've come.' My mother grasped my hands as I entered the large kitchen at *Siop Fawr*. I had let myself in as quietly as possible because of the lateness of the hour, and I was startled to see my mother standing before me in her nightwear, her hair hanging down her back.

'What's wrong?' I made an effort to tidy myself, brushing back my hair and straightening my collar. I need not have bothered; my mother did not notice.

'Dylan is worse,' she said. 'His fever is high. I'm making him a cordial of borage roots to expel the poison from him.' She poured a strange-smelling liquid into a cup and I wrinkled up my nose.

'He's not going to drink that, surely?' I followed her from the kitchen and down the long corridor to the stairs. She gave me a stern look.

'Take the candle – I can't carry everything – and don't despise what you don't understand.'

Dylan was shivering in his bed, even though the fire was built high, roaring up the chimney like a monster.

'Catrin,' he mumbled, but his eyes were glazed and it was obvious he saw no-one. 'The copper burns my back, Catrin, girl. Take away the pain for me.'

She put her arm around his shoulders, lifting him up from the pillows.

'Drink some of this, *cariad*. It will soon make you feel better, I promise.'

Obediently, he took it and my mother put the empty cup down.

'Help me to change his shirt,' she said briskly. 'This one is soaked with sweat.'

As I held my father and stripped off his shirt, I saw a huge livid scar across his back. My mother saw my look.

'Copper burns,' she said. 'My fault for sending him to work in the sheds. Perhaps you can see now why I didn't want you working the copper.'

'Why did you send him to work in the sheds?' I asked, and her eyes were misty.

'Money.' She dabbed at her cheeks with the corner of her gown. 'I thought he was not earning enough as a bargee. Well, he had not been there long when there was a blow up; took the roof off the sheds and killed and maimed some of the men. It was a bad day.'

Dylan moaned and his head fell against my shoulder. He opened his eyes and for a moment there was recognition and something else, a sort of tenderness that reached inside me, twisting me in knots. I think it was then I began to realize I could love him as much, if not more than I had loved John Richards.

'There.' My mother settled him back against the pillows and covered him over. 'He should sleep for a while. Go on to bed, you look tired.'

'I'm all right.' I spoke as if I was in a daze, and indeed I was because of the feelings churning inside me. 'I think I'll do some work on the books. I had some difficulty getting the figures to balance.' I touched her arm. 'You go to lie down for a while. I'll call you if there's any change.'

It was a long night. The work on the books had taken me only a few minutes, then I had gone to sit beside the bed, watching my father struggle for every breath. But at last morning came, stretching pale fingers through the window, and Dylan seemed past the crisis.

Kate crept into the room with some tea for me, her eyes wide.

'How is he?' She looked down at him and he opened his eyes, smiling when he saw her face.

'I'm going to be all right, Kate.' He tried to sit up, and I slipped my arm round his shoulders to help him. 'There's good to be cared for so well. I'm a lucky man.'

The room was suddenly crowded. I stood back as my four half-sisters sat on the bed, staring in undisguised joy at their father. My mother put her hand on my arm and we smiled at each other. It was a moment to remember.

'I'm still not sure of their names,' I confessed in a whisper. 'They seem to be absent whenever I'm at the shop.'

'The youngest one is Lotty. She's always too pale for my liking, but I'm giving her plenty of liver to build her up. She's almost twelve.' My mother pointed. 'The red-haired one is Vickie and well named too – she acts like a queen on times! You can't mistake Caroline, she's the image of Dylan, and of course Kate is the oldest. You know her well enough.'

She moved towards them. 'Come along now, girls,' she said with a laugh in her voice. 'Let your father have some peace. He's still quite weak, you know.'

Lotty came and stood beside me. 'Shall I cook some breakfast for you, Davy?' she said shyly, and I smiled down at her.

'I would be honoured.' I bowed, and she burst out laughing, covering her mouth with her hands.

'There's manners for you!' Vickie slapped her sister's arm lightly. 'Anyway, I'm going to cook the breakfast today.'

Kate led the way downstairs. 'You can all help,' she said firmly, and I could see she was used to taking command. I noticed that Caroline had hung back. Her eyes as they rested on me were hostile. She sat close to her father on the bed, as though to protect him from me.

'I'm glad to see you so much better,' I said, stopping for a moment in the doorway. I would have liked to call him father, but the word stuck in my throat.

He raised his hand for a moment before closing his eyes. My mother was right, he was still very weak.

'Can I go and tidy your bedroom, Davy?' Lotty sat on the very edge of her chair, staring at me anxiously. I nodded.

'That would be very kind of you, but I don't think it's very untidy. I didn't sleep in there last night.'

Vickie brushed back her red hair. 'Oh, you, Lotty!' she said in exasperation. 'You know I wanted to do Davy's room.'

'Come on, then,' Lotty said, generous in her triumph. 'You can help me.'

Caroline came into the kitchen slowly, almost reluctantly, and sat as far away from me as possible. Kate handed her a plate of bacon and then served me with an extra portion.

'Huh!' My mother glanced at me. 'I see you are going to be spoiled while you're here.'

Caroline pushed away her breakfast and stared at the table. I could almost feel her unhappiness, even though I couldn't understand it.

'Caroline is the moody one,' Kate said, unperturbed. 'I think it's because she's so clever and writes poetry all the time. Makes her look inward too much.'

'Oh, shut up!' Caroline left the table abruptly and ran out of the room.

'Do you think I've offended her in some way?' I asked anxiously, but my mother shook her head.

'She's always been very close to her father,' she said softly. 'She knows he's always wanted a son, and now you are here she has the very natural fear that you will take his affections away from her.'

'You are clever,' Kate said, her eyes wide. 'I would never have realized all that.'

'Well,' my mother smiled, 'I am a little older than you, don't forget, but you have the makings of a very wise woman, Kate. Perhaps you would like me to teach you some herbal lore.'

'Oh, I would!' Kate smiled at my mother and I got up from the table briskly in case I gave away my feelings.

'I'd better get off to the works, then. And no lifting anything heavy until I get back, right?'

'Just a minute, Davy.' My mother stared at me as though she had difficulty in gathering her thoughts. 'I won't keep you a minute, but I'd like to have a few words with you.'

She came with me to the door and she seemed ill at ease.

'How would you feel about coming here to stay?' She forced the words out in a rush. 'Dylan could do with your help; he'll be weak for some time yet, and in any case the business is doing so well there's room for a partner.'

I stood in silence for a moment, trying to imagine myself running the shop alongside my father. Would it be so bad?

'I can't think straight.' I looked at my mother. Her eyes were large with pleading. 'Can I let you know tonight?' I said quickly, and she nodded in resignation.

'There's no need for you to rush into anything,' she said, 'and I'm grateful for the help you've given us up to now.'

I strode away down the hill. The thought of leaving the

copper sheds should have filled me with delight, but strangely I knew I would miss the companionship of the men I'd grown to like and admire.

It was a crisp morning with a touch of frost in the air, and the roads were slippery underfoot. I could see my own breath in the coldness, and I huddled inside my coat. I must be all kinds of a fool to even hesitate about giving up this sort of life.

I was surprised to see Iorwerth waiting at the gate of the works, stamping his feet and flinging his arms around his body in an effort to keep warm.

'Hello,' I said, 'what's my uncle doing out in the cold morning air?'

'Looking for a job, boyo.' He blew on his hands. 'Seems I was a bit eager, like. I must be the first one here.' He fell into step beside me. 'Anyway, I thought if I came in with you, a word could be dropped in the right ear, perhaps?'

'I'll be glad to put in a word for you, not that the manager will take a lot of notice of me. He just tolerates me, thinks I'm still a boy.'

The manager shook his head when I took Iorwerth to him.

'No room for another man, see.' He rubbed his chin and coughed. 'No offence, mind, and I'll let you know when anyone leaves, all right?'

Iorwerth looked at me, shrugging his shoulders hopelessly, and I knew what I had to do.'

'I'll be leaving at the end of the week,' I said quickly. 'I've been offered another job, so how about Iorwerth taking over from me?'

'All right.' The manager stared at me and I could almost believe he was sorry to lose me. 'Let him come on the tew gang with you and Luther, then, so that by the end of the week he'll be pulling his weight.'

'Thank you, Davy!' Iorwerth gripped my hand so hard it hurt. 'Are you sure you've got another job to go to?'

I nodded. 'Yes. Dylan Morgan needs a man in the shop now, and my mother asked me to work there.' I smiled wryly. 'And don't thank me. The furnaces can be hell on earth when the smoke is down; there's not a clean bit of air anywhere to breathe into your lungs.'

Luther clapped me on the back when I told him that I'd be leaving.

'There's sorry I'll be to see you go, boyo.' He wiped the sweat from his eyes. 'But you'll still come down to the chandler's shop and help us with our papers, won't you?'

'Try to stop me!' I said fiercely. 'I've gone along with you this far, I won't back out now.'

'That's all I wanted to know.' He turned to Iorwerth and shook his hand. 'Welcome. Any kin of Davy's is bound to be all right.'

The news spread fast that I was leaving the sheds, and many of the men came over to the furnace to wish me well. I hadn't realized how completely I'd become accepted as a copperman.

I felt a shove against my shoulder blades as I was about to dip the ladle into the shimmering heat of the copper, and I turned quickly. A man who was a stranger to me stood there.

'Careful, you damn fool!' I said. 'You could have caused an accident then.'

Luther stepped forward. 'What do you want here anyway, Edward Phillips?' he said. 'You have never been any friend of mine or my gang's, so what do you want now?'

'I want to tell this young buck a few things before he goes.' Phillips stood before me. 'You've been treated special, like, ever since you came here and we all know it's because of your fancy way of talking. Well, yesterday, I asked for a job for my son, and the manager said there was no room, yet you come along today and get your uncle in just like that. How do you explain it?'

'It's simple,' I said. 'I'm leaving and he's taking my place, all right?'

'*Duw*,' he leaned closer to me, 'do you think I'm a child to believe in such fairy tales? You won't leave here to go to work at *Siop Fawr* for the simple reason that Dylan Morgan wouldn't take a bastard to work with him.'

Iorwerth sprang forward, his fists upraised. 'Pick on me if you want a fight, is it?' he said angrily. 'Not on a youngster like him.'

'Let us get on with our work,' I said quickly, 'before the manager comes to see what's going on.'

I leaned forward and scooped up some of the molten copper on to my ladle, straining every muscle to tip it into the pot. Just as I was about to turn my wrist, Phillips stuck his foot in front of me and for a terrible moment I thought I was going to drop the copper and fall into it. Miraculously I regained my balance and tipped the ladleful straight into the pot.

Sweat ran down my face, clouding my vision, but I heard Luther's voice low with menace.

'Clear off from by here, Edward Phillips, before I land one on you, and no more trouble or, by God, I'll fix you good.'

I wiped my face in my sleeve and the copper dust stung my cheeks.

'Look out,' I said, 'the manager is coming. Get back to work, Iorwerth, or you'll be out of a job before you're in one.'

'Any bother, then?' The manager was watching Phillips

return to his gang. 'There's some around here I wouldn't trust further than I could throw them.'

Luther grinned. 'Nothing that I can't handle, like. Just a bit of an argument, that's all.'

I was just about to speak when Luther caught my eye, shaking his head warningly, and I got his message clear and plain: the men could fight amongst each other but no squealing to the manager.

'All right, then.' The manager turned away with a shrug. 'But let's do our work instead of standing around, is it?'

I watched him walk away on his short legs, his belly thrust out before him. He didn't miss a thing, that man.

'We'd better do as he says,' Luther clapped me on the shoulder, 'but I'm warning you to watch out for Edward Phillips; he's a bad one.'

'I'll watch out for him too,' Iorwerth said quickly. 'If there's trouble brewing, I want to be in on it.'

I grinned and went back to work. It was good to be accepted, to be one of the men. It was a feeling I would never have experienced if I'd remained in my college in England. Looking back on those days, I couldn't believe how ignorant I'd been; I'd learned a lot of academic subjects, but nothing about life itself.

We walked home together, Iorwerth and I, and it amused me that I had to shorten my strides to match his. The smoke was low over the houses as we neared Tip Row and Iorwerth began to cough.

'*Duw*,' he said, 'I'd forgotten how the copper dust catches in the chest, man. It will be a good thing for you when you're up at *Siop Fawr* and away from it all.'

'I suppose you're right,' I said doubtfully, 'but I'll miss the old place for all that.'

'Oh, you don't belong in the copper, Davy.' Iorwerth looked up at me. 'You can do better for yourself than slave your time away getting your lungs hardened like an old tin pot.'

'Yes, but can't you see that at least now I'm independent, I'm earning my own money and asking charity from no-one?'

'You're too damn touchy!' Iorwerth's voice was sharp. 'Dylan Morgan will pay you an honest wage for a job that you'll do well, can't you see that?'

'I suppose you're right,' I said slowly. 'I'd never looked at it quite like that.'

'Look here.' Iorwerth stopped walking and stared at me. 'If he was any other man, would you hesitate a minute before taking him up on his offer?'

'No,' I said, 'I have to admit that the knowledge he's my father does have a bearing on how I feel.'

Suddenly Iorwerth laughed. '*Duw*, you talk like a damn lawyer on times, man. Let's get on home and have our food, is it? I'm famished.'

The kitchen was full of the rich smell of rabbit, spiced and boiled in a pot hanging over the fire.

'*Darro!*' Iorwerth flung off his coat and his sweat cloth and caught Mamgu in his arms. 'That smells good enough for Queen Victoria herself to eat!' He swung her round before setting her on her feet again, and she slapped at his arm.

'Wash first in this house,' she said severely, 'and don't talk about the good Queen like that. Get on with you, who's going to be first in the bath?'

'Davy can have that honour.' Iorwerth chuckled and looked at me. 'I suppose you're out tom catting again tonight. I enjoy my pleasures at home, being an old married man.'

Elizabeth came in from the yard, her sleeves rolled above her dimpled elbows.

'Come on,' she said, 'I've got a tin bucket filled with water outside in the yard; a drop of cold won't hurt you for once.'

Mamgu looked at her in approval. '*Duw*,' she said, 'you may be English, but there's some common sense inside that head of yours.'

Iorwerth winked at Elizabeth. 'That's some compliment, my girl,' he said with a smile.

I washed quickly, not as meticulous as Mamgu would have been had she not been busy seeing to the stew. When I was dressed, I went into the yard to tip the water from the bath, and saw Elizabeth's hand, small and white, rub at the broad expanse of Iorwerth's back.

'*Duw*,' I said in Welsh, 'you're a pretty pair of lovebirds. The sight of you is almost enough to make me want to give up my freedom and become a married man.'

Elizabeth blushed and stepped away from her husband, her arms dripping water.

'Don't let me disturb you,' I said quickly. 'I'm just going back inside.' As I returned to the kitchen, I suddenly felt very much alone, which was absurd. I had two fine women to love and I'd now become part of a large family. I did not recollect ever feeling alone like this before.

'Some goose stepped on your grave?' Mamgu said, pushing me towards the table. 'Sit down and get some good food into your belly and you'll soon feel better.'

The door swung open and my mother stepped into the kitchen. She was smiling, and the lines of strain that had been on her face recently seemed to have vanished.

'He's much better,' she said happily, not even mentioning his name, so certain was she that we all knew who her thoughts were centred on. 'That's a lovely smell. Give me a huge dishful, Mamgu. I'm starving.'

She sat next to me at the table, her eyes sparkling, her voice light and quick, and I felt a stab of jealousy that Dylan could evoke such a response in her.

'I'll be glad when you come and settle up at the shop,' she said. 'Even though he's much better now, Dylan's still weak enough to appreciate a strong help around the place.'

I looked at my grandmother; she stared at me as though she'd swallowed a sour plum.

'Will you be staying up there for good, then, Davy?' She spoke casually, but I could see she was anxious to hear my reply.

'You won't see the back of me as easily as that,' I said quickly. 'I'll be round here pestering you for a long time yet.'

She brightened up, but I could see that my mother bent her head over her dish so that I couldn't read her expression. I knew she was displeased, but I didn't want decisions made for me. Perhaps I would stay up at *Siop Fawr*, but if and when I decided, I would be the one to tell Mamgu.

I lay awake in the slope that night, staring out of the square window, trying to see the stars. I would try to make a go of working for my father. I might even invest the little money I had saved in the shop; that way I would feel less dependent. From my study of the books I could see there was room for expansion in the business; I would have to give it some thought. I turned over restlessly, not wanting to admit even to myself that what I really wanted to do was impress my father.

It was a sad moment when I left the heat of the furnace for the last time. Luther wrung my hand warmly, the sweat still dripping down his huge forearms.

'I'll expect to see you soon,' he said meaningfully. 'We still have a great deal to do, mind.'

'I know,' I said, 'and don't worry, I won't let you down. You can trust me.'

'Aye,' Luther said, 'I know that.' He mopped his face with his sweat rag and followed me out towards the doors.

'Going into trade, then?' The manager stood staring at me over his tight stiff collar. 'A step up for you, my boy. You never know where it will lead.'

To my surprise he held his hand out to me and I shook it so vigorously that he winced.

'Damn,' he said, 'at least we've made a man of you since you've been here, and if ever you want your old job back, just ask.'

I went through the gates for the last time and stood for a moment staring round me, and it was good to know that if things didn't work out at *Siop Fawr* I always had the copper to come back to.

TWELVE

'Come on, Davy, this sack of potatoes is just about breaking my back. I asked you five minutes ago to give me a hand moving it.' Kate stood, hands on hips, hair swinging over her face. She was red from the exertion of trying to lift the sack alone.

'Good God!' I tried not to laugh. 'I didn't know that having sisters would be such hard work. I might as well go back to working the copper. Just look how thin and drawn I've become in the last week.'

'Huh!' Kate raised her eyebrows at me. 'You're getting like a bull, and anyway, whose idea was it in the first place to change the shop around?'

I took the sack and lifted it easily, stacking it back against the furthest wall.

'We need more storage room,' I said thoughtfully. 'Perhaps I could get some timber and set up a slope behind the shop.'

'That's a good idea,' Kate said. 'You could get Caroline to help you. She's got good hands for wood.'

I looked at her in surprise. 'But building is a man's job. I couldn't expect your sister to do anything like that.'

'Who do you think helped Dad before you came along?' Kate said shortly. 'And besides, you don't want Caroline to feel left out, do you?'

'No,' I said thoughtfully, 'I suppose not.' I touched Kate's shoulder briefly. 'Thanks for putting me wise. I'm not very popular with her as it is. I wouldn't like to antagonize Caroline even more.'

The bell on the shop door clanged and a woman came into the dimness, almost falling over a bale of cloth.

'*Darro!*' She steadied herself. 'Here I am falling about the place and not touched a drop of gin yet! Why don't you light a lamp in here? Saving oil, are you?'

'Oh, Mrs Rees.' Kate pulled the bale up on to the counter. 'Sorry, we're changing things around a bit and we hadn't noticed how dark it was.'

She lit several lamps and went to the back door. 'Lotty!' she yelled. 'Come and serve Mrs Rees. My hands are dirty, so I can't do it.'

'Don't worry, girl.' Mrs Rees pulled her shawl around her shoulders and leaned over the counter. 'I'm not in any hurry, and it's just a bit of flour I want.'

Lotty came in from the kitchen tutting in exasperation. She was small for her age and was forced to stand up on a box in order to see the customers.

'Why couldn't you have called Vickie or Caroline?' she said to Kate in a fierce whisper. 'It's always me, isn't it? You put on me because I'm the youngest.'

'Less of your lip,' Kate said good-humouredly. 'You know the girls are busy enough cooking our supper, and anyway after Mrs Rees is served I'm locking the door. We've done enough for one day.'

Mrs Rees settled her arms under her copious breasts that strained against the bodice of her gown, seemingly in danger of bursting through at any moment.

'Have you heard about Edward Phillips?' she said, her eyes bright with the anticipation of telling us all her news. Kate shook her head.

'No, Mrs Rees, what about him? Has he been caught pinching again?'

The woman's face fell. 'Oh, *Duw*,' she said, 'you've guessed it.'

'Well, not all of it.' There was a glimmer of a smile on Kate's face. 'What was he robbing this time?'

'Coal, of course!' Mrs Rees said, consoled by our interest. 'Pinching Mr Vivian's coal, and him employed as a copper man, too. They say he'll get solitary this time, and serves him right too, I say.'

She folded her shawl more firmly around her. 'If you're going to steal, do it right, don't get caught.' She took her bag of flour, willing to go now that she'd told us her news, and Kate went behind her, slipping the bolt across the door.

'Why are you grinning like that?' she said suspiciously, and I sat on a sack and burst out laughing.

'Edward Phillips got what he deserved, and I think I can guess who put the police on to him.'

'What do you mean?' Kate sat beside me, staring up into my face, avid with interest, and Lotty leaned over my shoulder, her hair brushing my face.

'He tried to cause trouble down at the copper works,' I explained. 'Just before I left, it was, when Iorwerth had been given my job. Nearly had me face down in the copper pot, he did, and Luther said he'd fix him good.'

'Well,' Kate frowned, 'Luther had better be careful when Edward Phillips gets out of prison. He's a nasty, vicious man, and I've always been afraid of him.'

She moved to the door and gave Lotty a gentle push. 'Come on, wash yourself ready for supper, and you can sweep up the mess you've made with those sacks before you get anything to eat,' she said to me.

'Right, boss,' I said, and when she turned her back on me I whacked her with the brush.

She spun round and slapped my arm. 'Good thing

you're only my brother,' she said with a laugh. 'Any other boyo would have had the back of my hand across his face.'

It was strange to walk down the long passage into the kitchen. I still hadn't grown used to the largeness of the house after the cramped conditions of the little cottage in Tip Row.

'Hello there, Davy.' Vickie brushed back a strand of red hair and grinned at me. 'Supper's nearly ready.' She had accepted me with warm friendliness, as had the two other girls, but Caroline alone still treated me with suspicion and what almost amounted to hostility. She stared at me now with her dark eyes that were so much like my own, and did not even acknowledge my presence.

I rolled back the sleeves of my good white shirt. 'Can I help?' I asked. 'Perhaps I could carry a tray up to your father?'

It was Vickie who answered. 'Yes, just put a jug of ale on the side and it's ready.' She grinned at me, her lovely eyes changing from amber to green in the flickering light.

The stairs were steep and wound upwards at a sharp angle and I had to balance a candle in one hand and the tray in the other.

'Oh, Davy, there's a good boy.' My mother held the door to the bedroom open for me. 'The smell is just about driving Dylan mad with hunger. Anyone can see he's better.'

He was looking well, his fever had gone and there was a healthy tinge to his skin, though he seemed thinner, with a gauntness of face that only made him more handsome.

'How's the shop doing?' he said, taking the tray from me. 'I heard the bell clanging a few minutes ago. You'll be spoiling my customers, keeping open so late.'

'We're moving everything around,' I said. 'I hope you don't mind, and I was thinking of building a slope outside if you're agreeable. We need more room for stores.'

He nodded and took a deep draught of ale before answering; his moustache was coated in white foam, and my mother laughed, wiping it away from him as if he was a child.

'Carry on,' he said approvingly, and for an instant he met my eye. 'My children make me proud.' He cut into his pie, and I turned to the door.

'Will you come up and speak to us after you've had your supper, Davy?' My mother put a restraining hand on my arm. 'There's something we want to talk over with you.'

I covered her fingers with my own. 'All right.' I smiled. 'I'll fit you in between doing the books and starting on my new slope.' I laughed at the startled expression on her face. 'Yes, Mother,' I said, 'I'll admit there's a great deal more to running a shop than I ever believed possible, but don't worry, I'll be up to see you later.'

After supper, I went into the parlour and spread the books out on the table. Dylan had a simple method of accounting and it was easy to see at a glance that the profits were good. The shop was well situated, being on the border of the copper town where the works had money to spend and were not bound to any company shops. In that respect, Mr Vivian was a fair and just owner.

An idea was growing in my head as to what form the new trade in the shop would take. I would have to discuss it with Dylan and with my mother, but I had every confidence that my views would be well received.

When I'd finished the books, I went out into the backyard and searched among the bits of timber that were propped up against the wall.

'Caroline,' I called, and she came to the door, her face registering her surprise.

'Yes?' she said coolly. 'What do you want? I'm busy with the washing-up.'

'I won't keep you a minute,' I said, 'but I'd like to ask your advice about where to build a slope. The store room isn't big enough now; something has to be done.'

'Then why not wait until my father is ready to see to it himself?' She was not going to thaw that easily.

'I thought I would save him the exertion,' I said, 'especially when he's been so weak with the fever.'

She nodded, seeing sense in my words, and in spite of herself she was drawn to the timber, picking pieces out with an excellent eye for quality.

'I think these will do,' she said at last, 'and the slope would be best put against the west wall – it's cooler there for the perishables – but perhaps it would be better if we looked again when it's properly light.'

She went indoors then, her back straight, and she had not smiled once, but I thought I sensed a chink in her armour. I closed the back door and bolted it, and then took the stairs two at a time; my mother would think I'd forgotten my promise.

At the open bedroom door, I paused. They were sitting close together, holding hands, and my mother had the look of a young girl about her.

'Sit down, Davy.' Dylan indicated that I take a place on the bedside. He seemed nervous, his eyes searching my face anxiously, and I knew I had to make things easier for them both.

'You are going to get married,' I said gently, and even as I spoke the words it was like a knife turning within me, but I tried to smile.

'Oh, Davy,' my mother took my hand, 'say you don't mind about it, please.' She laughed nervously. 'Some people would say it's high time I became respectable.'

'When's it to be?' I asked quietly, and I saw Dylan giving me a worried look.

'We thought as soon as possible,' he said decisively. 'We intend to marry whether or not you approve, but we would rather it be with your blessing.'

'Then I give it,' I said, trying to keep my voice light. 'I know you'll both be happy.'

Back in my room, I sat down on my bed that was softer by far than the one at Tip Row and looked out at the night sky. Could I bear it, to have her sleep in the same bed as him, I who had seen her so happy with John Richards? Suddenly, in spite of my manliness, I found I was crying, hot bitter tears that rolled unasked down my cheeks.

The wedding which started out as a quiet affair became like a circus, with all the Hafod, it seemed, joining in. After my mother and Dylan had left the chapel, Dai the Quay started playing his fiddle as if the devil himself sat on his shoulder egging him on.

My four half-sisters had prepared a feast that would have done justice to Queen Victoria herself and had decorated the yard and the outside of the shop with bright squares of cloth that fluttered in the warmth of the breeze, and my mother looked more beautiful than I'd ever seen her.

Someone touched my arm lightly and I looked down in surprise to see Susannah smiling up at me.

'Don't look as though you'd seen a ghost,' she chided. 'It's only right and proper that I be invited to the wedding feast; I am a friend of your mother – well, at least, my brother-in-law is a friend,' she corrected herself, 'though I must admit I was happy to come if only for the chance of seeing you again.'

In the soft night air, her scent was intoxicating and I

wondered at myself for keeping away from her for so long. But then, I had been busy at the shop.

'I don't know how I could have been so ill mannered,' I said lightly. 'Perhaps you will allow me to make up for it sometime?'

'I insist you make up for it.' She smiled at me through half-closed lids. 'I'll see you on Monday evening, all right?' Without waiting for a reply, she left me and went to speak to my mother, kissing her lightly on the cheek. I could see her brother-in-law, a head shorter than Dylan, talking to him earnestly, and suddenly a great sense of belonging swept over me; somehow, it seemed right that I should be in this place on such a festive day. I sat down, a little way from the rest of the party, and watched contentedly. The lights that Dylan had strung up gleamed softly in the blue of the night air, and there was a spicy smell drifting from the open shop door.

I saw my mother smile and come towards me, and I got to my feet, offering her my chair. Instead, she put her arm around my waist and smiled up at me.

'I'm so happy, Davy,' she said, 'almost too happy. Why should life have given me such fine men to look after me?' She shivered a little, and when I glanced anxiously down at her I saw that her face had grown pale.

'What is it, Mam?' I said softly in Welsh. 'You look almost frightened. Is anything wrong?'

'I don't know, Davy. I had a strange feeling, almost a premonition.' She gestured around her. 'Something tells me to make the most of all this, I won't have it for long.'

'That's silly, Mother!' I touched her cheek lightly. 'You are just tired, that's all. You've spent most nights sitting up nursing Dylan, remember.'

'I expect you're right.' She gave me a small hug, but her eyes still held a trace of fear.

'Hey, step aside and let a man dance with his sister!' Iorwerth stepped in between us, a huge smile on his face, and it was obvious the ale had made him merry. He gave me a playful push. 'Go and dance with my Elizabeth, and that's an order.'

'My pleasure,' I said, taking a blushing Elizabeth into my arms. She was light as a feather, and as the fiddle played faster I twirled her round so that her skirts flared out round her trim ankles.

'Slow down!' she begged, her hair tumbling from its ribbons and falling over her shoulders. 'Remember that I am older than you.'

'Ha!' I stared down at her. 'By three years only. That's nothing at all.'

The fiddle stopped, and then Dai was playing a soft, haunting tune, his voice rising true and strong on the evening air. I looked down at Elizabeth, about to say something inconsequential, but our eyes met and the words died on my lips. In that instant, I knew I was in love with my uncle's wife, and though not a word passed between us, I think she knew it too.

'Davy, you haven't danced with me all night. If you're not careful I won't love you any more.' Susannah stood beside me, her eyes on Elizabeth as she put her hand in a proprietary manner on my shoulder.

As I danced her away, she looked up at me, her eyes serious.

'There's nothing but trouble if you go in that direction, my dear,' she said softly, and I knew there was genuine concern in her voice.

'I know,' I said, 'and there's no need to worry yourself. I'm far too wise to do anything so rash.'

'And far too honourable, only you won't admit it. Davy, I know you better than you know yourself.'

There was a sudden noise at the back of the house, and then the sound of a woman's scream. I left Susannah and ran through the shop into the back yard. Dylan stood there in the light from the hanging lamps, his face white with anger, and his fists bunched as though he was about to strike someone.

'Keep your foul-mouthed whelp away from me or, by God, I'll kill him.' He spoke in a low voice that was cold with anger, and I saw my uncle Huw hold out a placating hand.

'I apologize for my son,' he said. 'He had no right to speak as he did.'

'What's wrong?' I moved forward and caught my mother's arm as she stood shrunken against the wall, her face pale. 'What is it, Mother?'

'It's nothing for you to bother about,' she said quickly. 'Young William is a bit drunk, that's all. He'll be sorry in the morning when his head has cleared.'

'Sorry for what?' I asked impatiently, and then William moved directly towards me.

'I called you a bastard,' he said with a sneer. 'Can you deny that you've been one ever since you were born? No marriage is going to change that.'

Fury rose up in me like a sickness, catching my guts and twisting them so it was like fire in my belly. I lunged forward, but before my fist could connect with William's jaw Huw had grasped my arm.

'No, boyo,' he said, 'not now, even though I do not blame you for wanting to leather the fool.'

My mother clung to me. 'No fighting,' she begged, her eyes wide. 'Not tonight, please God, not tonight.'

'Don't worry, Catrin,' Huw said. 'I'll take William home. There will be no more trouble.'

They took their leave quietly, but even though Dai the

Quay started up with the fiddle again, the joy had gone from the gathering and people began to drift away homewards.

Anger was still deep within me as I took down the lanterns and put out the flames. My mother sat in the kitchen when I put away the lanterns, looking down at her feet beneath the cream skirt of her gown.

'I was wrong about you picking on William,' she said quietly. 'I can see it clearly enough now, but I should have trusted you before. I'm sorry, Davy.'

I knelt down before her. 'Don't worry about it, Mam.' I kissed her fingers. 'I don't care what William says about me, it just does not matter.'

She leaned towards me. 'But it matters to me. I thought once Dylan and I were married, people would forget about the past, but how can they when your own kin goes about talking in that evil way?'

'Go on up to bed,' I said. 'Remember, tonight you're a bride and don't give a jot for what anyone says. You be happy, that's all I ask.'

She stood up, her eyes alight with tears. 'Good night, son. I'll see you in the morning,' she said, and as I watched her leave the room, for the first time in my life I saw that her proud shoulders were bowed. Inside me, a determination flared, and I knew that one day William would pay for his cruelty.

The next day, I sprung my surprise. I led my mother to a corner of the shop where I had built some shelves and a small counter and filled the place with earthenware pots and jugs.

'What's it for?' she said in astonishment. 'It looks very fine indeed, but what are we going to do with it?'

'This,' I said importantly, 'is where you, my dear mother, are going to sell your herbal remedies. Why waste such a talent as yours when you could be helping people cure their ills?'

Dylan leaned over and picked up one of the jars. 'You know,' he said thoughtfully, 'that's a wonderful idea. I'm surprised I didn't think of it first!'

The four girls had crowded round to see my mother's reaction, and they burst out laughing at their father's words.

'I know why,' Kate said, putting her arm through his. 'It's because Davy's a born businessman. He'll make this shop into a goldmine if you'll listen to him.'

I was warmed by her praise. I hadn't known she thought so highly of me. Dylan nodded his head.

'I do believe you're right, Kate. I've always trusted your judgement and I'd be a fool not to believe in you now. All right, Davy, you'll have a free hand in making decisions for the improvement or expansion of the shop, and I've been looking at your figure work, too – you are so much better at it than I am. Can I depend on you to continue to do it?'

My mother began to laugh, but it sounded pretty near to tears, too. 'I'll work so hard!' she said, clasping her hands together. 'I may be a bit rusty on herb growing, but I'll soon get back to it.' She gave me a hug. 'Oh, Davy, this is the best wedding present you could have given me.'

Over her shoulder, I saw the set face of Caroline. Her dark eyes were staring into mine almost with hatred, and suddenly there was a cloud over everything.

'I'm glad you're happy,' I said quickly. 'Please excuse me.' As I hurried through the door and down the hill towards the town I knew I'd been foolish to let a young girl spoil my happiness, but somehow, deep inside me, there was an answering antagonism towards Caroline, and I wondered if we could ever live together in the same house.

THIRTEEN

'*Duw*, the beer's good tonight.' Luther bent his great arm and took another swallow from the jug, drinking it down as if it was water. 'It's so hot in here, it's almost as bad as the furnaces.'

'Nothing could be that bad,' I said, laughing, 'and we all know you're using the heat as an excuse to drink your fill.'

'Well, boyo,' Luther peered over the jug at me, his eyes alight, 'I've got something to celebrate. I heard today that the Board of Health are moving and that Mr Clark's report should be out sometime in July. What do you think of that?'

Iorwerth looked up in interest. 'What's all this about, then?' he said. 'You been dabbling in politics, Davy?'

Before I could answer, the chandler leaned forward, shaking his head warningly.

'You're loose mouthed, man,' he said to Luther. 'If I were you I'd lay off the drink.'

'Good God, Edgar Jones!' Luther stared at him in amazement, 'I can speak freely in front of Iorwerth Owen. I've known the family for years. I'd bet my last Swansea Penny on their loyalty.'

'Well, don't forget,' Edgar said slowly, 'it's my shop we're using to write the leaflets and do all the business from, and it will be me to suffer if we're found out.'

'Steady, boys,' Iorwerth said good naturedly. 'I'm with

you all the way if you're trying to improve things for the poor of the town.'

'Well,' Edgar looked round doubtfully at the crowded room, 'men who look as if they're the worse for beer sometimes have ears like a donkey, so be careful.'

'*Darro!*' Luther stared at him in disgust. 'You're as weak as a woman's petticoats, man. If we don't talk, how are we going to get people on our side?'

Edgar lapsed into silence and swiftly Luther explained how we had sent a petition to Mr Chadwick and how, as a result, an inspector had come to Swansea to examine the sanitary conditions.

'Of course,' Luther said, 'if he's an honest man, he'll tell them what conditions are really like here, and then we should have some action.'

'If the paving committee don't put the top hat on the idea,' I said quickly. 'They're dead against us because they don't want to lose their power.'

'This is all very interesting.' Iorwerth's eyes were bright. 'I'm all for a good fight, so count me in with you, right?'

'Another couple of beers, here!' Luther banged on the bar. 'Good God, there's a thirst I've got tonight. I could drink the sea dry.'

'Don't get a beer for me,' I said quickly. 'I'm just going. There's a friend I've kept waiting far too long as it is.'

'*Duw*, do your thoughts never raise above the level of your trews, boy?' Luther slapped me on the back so hard I almost fell. 'If I was twenty years – no, ten years – younger, I'd come with you.'

I could hear his laughter as I pushed my way to the door, but once outside, in the warmth of the night air, my thoughts were all on Rosie. She would think I wasn't coming, perhaps even go out and find a customer, and that would never do, not the way I was feeling tonight.

She was cool towards me when I took her in my arms. I felt her splendid breasts move against me as she struggled to loosen my hold.

'I know I'm late,' I said between kisses. 'I really am sorry. It just couldn't be helped.'

'No, Davy,' she pushed harder, 'please listen to me, just for a moment.'

But I couldn't wait. Her protests went ignored as I undid her bodice and rested my lips on the swell of her skin, breathing in the intoxicating scent of her. It was quick, too quick, but I brushed the hair from her face and when I saw tears glinting on her gold lashes I reassured her.

'Don't worry, I shall stay with you all night. You will be happy too before I leave you.'

'Oh, Davy.' She moved away from the bed and sat on a chair near the window, and I couldn't help the fleeting thought that it was there she touted for customers.

'What's wrong?' I leaned up on my elbow and stared at her, realizing for the first time that she was pale and that there were dark shadows beneath her eyes.

'You are not ill, are you?' I said anxiously, wondering how I could have been so insensitive.

'No, I'm not ill.' She paused for a moment, twisting her fingers together. 'But I have to tell you something, and I know you will be angry.'

I began to feel exasperated. 'Well, for God's sake put me out of my misery and tell me!'

'I'm going to be married!' The words burst from her, and then she sat silently, waiting for my reaction. I wasn't sure, for my part, how I felt. I enjoyed Rosie, in a way I loved her, but it was not the all-consuming feeling I had for Elizabeth.

'Well,' I said uncertainly, 'I've no rights over you,

Rosie, and though I can't say I'm happy to see you tied to some man, I suppose it's the best thing for you.'

She began to cry then, soft, noiseless tears that rolled down her high cheekbones and into her mouth. I went to her, taking her in my arms, thinking that I would never understand women if I lived to be a hundred.

'I don't love him, Davy.' She took my face in her hands, and in her eyes I read her true feelings for me. I drew a sharp breath and moved away from her, taking a cup of gin from the bottle on the shelf.

'Drink this,' I put it before her, 'and tell me why you are getting married if you don't really want to.'

'I do want to be respectably married,' she said. 'I know I'm lucky to be asked at all, but at least I can ease my feelings of guilt by giving him all the money I've saved up.' She drank some of the gin. 'Some people might say it's dirty money, but it will be enough to set us up somewhere away from Swansea where no-one knows me.'

'Don't sell yourself short, Rosie,' I said gently. 'You are a fine woman and any man would be proud to make you his wife.'

She looked at me for a long moment, and the silence seemed to stretch between us almost like a barrier. There were so many things left unsaid in that short time, and later I was to regret it.

'Now,' she said briskly, drying her eyes on the corner of her robe, 'what about you. How are you making out up at *Siop Fawr*?'

'It's all right,' I said, with less show of enthusiasm than I really felt; somehow I didn't want to talk about the growing affection between me and my natural father, not even to Rosie. 'Caroline continues to resent me, I'm afraid, but then, how can I blame her?'

I sat up and pulled on my trousers. It seemed wrong to

301

be here like this now that I knew Rosie was going to be married.

'When are you going to name the great day?' I said lightly. 'Be sure to let me know, because I'd like to buy you a special gift before then.'

Her eyes shone like a child's. 'Oh, Davy, what will you give me?'

I laughed. 'A bale of muslin, a sackful of ribbons; you name it and I'll get it for you.'

'I'd like a silver locket,' she said slowly. 'I could wear it around my neck always; it would remind me of you.' She came and stood before me, loosening my trousers with practised hands. 'Don't go yet,' she said softly, pleadingly. 'This may be the last time we'll ever have together, and remember, you told me that you would make me happy before you left.'

I could not resist her and it was a better union this time, fulfilling and gentle, and we moved together sweetly like a song that's well learned.

At last I knew I had to leave, and she came with me, silent and glowing, to the street door.

'Well, Rosie,' I said gently, 'I suppose this is goodbye, but you know I wish you every happiness, and if ever you are unhappy, or you need anything, please promise you'll send for me.'

She stood on tiptoe and kissed my mouth before stepping back into the dark passageway and half-closing the door.

'I have to tell you this, Davy,' she said, in a tight voice, 'and I know you are not going to like it, but there's nothing you can say to change my mind. I'm going to marry your cousin William.'

Before her words had properly sunk into my consciousness, she had slammed the door shut and I heard the sound of a bolt being drawn across. I hammered at the solid wood uselessly.

'Rosie, don't be a fool! You know what he's like. You can't trust a man who's lower than a rattlesnake!'

There was silence from behind the closed door and at last I gave up and walked away along the street. By the time I reached *Siop Fawr* I was calmer, and I knew I had to go back and see Rosie again, convince her that she would never find happiness or even security with William.

The family were gathered around the table, an aura of gloom hanging over them that distracted my thoughts from Rosie.

'What's wrong?' I said quickly, and Dylan looked at me over the paper he was reading.

'Cholera.' The single word struck fear into me, but I tried to hide it as I took my place at the table.

'Is there anything in the *Cambrian* about it?' I said, trying to control my voice. Dylan shook his head.

'No, I was just looking and there's nothing. They don't want to alarm the people so soon, I suppose, and anyway it might be an isolated case. Let's pray to God it is.'

My mother coughed. 'It's down the Greenhill,' she said, 'and that's where all the sicknesses seem to start. Poor Irish people, their houses are so crowded. Do you know there are thirty people living in one small cottage that I know of?'

She looked around at us anxiously. 'I don't want any of you going down there, mind.'

Among the chorus of agreement I noticed that Vickie bowed her red head and avoided Mam's eyes. I could hazard a guess that she had met someone from the Irish quarter who had become important to her.

My mother got to her feet. 'I'll bring in the supper now that you're home, Davy. We've been waiting for you ages.

303

If I'd known you were going to be this late we'd have started without you.'

'I'm sorry,' I said. 'I didn't think to tell you I'd be late. I'm so used to Mamgu's easy ways, I suppose it just didn't cross my mind you would all wait for me.'

'Well, never mind now.' She busied herself with the food, her brow crinkled. 'You know that we mustn't sell anything in the shop that's the least bit stale,' she said. 'It's often bad food that carries the cholera disease, and we must clean out the house and keep the windows open wide.'

Dylan looked up at her. 'But surely we'll be letting in bad air as well as good?'

'Leave it all to me now, Dylan, there's a good boy,' she said. 'I shall make up plenty of cordials for the shop as well as our own use. Dried periwinkle is a soothing remedy for the bowel disorders and helps healing too, and we mustn't have any strawberries; they cause fits if eaten when you have a fever.'

'For God's sake, girl!' Dylan sounded exasperated. 'There's only one case in the whole of Swansea. Don't worry so much. It won't spread as far as here.'

Caroline leaned towards my mother. 'Don't worry,' she said gently, 'you know that the copper dust keeps away the cholera; everyone knows that's true.'

'I don't know,' my mother said doubtfully. 'When I was young, two boys died of cholera even though they lived in the very heart of the copper. It doesn't pay to believe all that the owners tell us.'

'Well, that's enough gloom for one day,' I said quickly. 'There's a fair in town tomorrow. Who's going to come with me?'

'I'll come, Davy.' Lotty jumped to her feet excitedly. 'Will there be piglets? I love piglets.'

'I daresay there will be,' I said, 'and if there's not I shall make such a fuss about it that they will always have piglets in any future fairs just to please Lotty Morgan!'

'I'd like to come too, if you're willing,' Vickie said shyly. 'I want to buy some new green ribbons.'

'Willing? Of course I'm willing,' I said. 'What about Kate and Caroline, are you coming too?'

Kate shook her head. 'No, I'm not much for all that pushing and shoving, and crowds just frighten me. I'd rather stay at home, and in any case I'll be needed here at the shop.'

I looked at Dylan. 'I'm sorry,' I said. 'I suppose really I should have asked your permission to take a day off. I just didn't think.'

'No, indeed, boyo,' Dylan said. 'You are more like a partner to me. You take the day off and enjoy yourself.'

Kate came to me and wound her arms around my neck. 'Silly Davy,' she said. 'I wasn't saying that to make you feel guilty, really I wasn't.'

'I know,' I said, grinning at her, and in the confusion none of us noticed that Caroline said nothing at all.

'Well, I'm going to bed now,' Lotty said, getting to her feet, 'and I'm going to make a very special prayer to God so that the sun will shine tomorrow.'

I pinched her cheek. 'I'm sure the Lord won't refuse you,' I said. 'I couldn't.'

It seemed that Lotty's prayers were answered with interest; there wasn't a cloud in the sky when we set off from *Siop Fawr* the next morning. It was a breathless day, with the drone of bees loud on the stillness of the air, and we walked slowly, taking our time, so that it was a good hour before we reached the field where the fair was being held. I found us a place under a shady tree and Lotty immediately began to attack the basket of food.

'I'm going to look round the stalls before I eat,' Vickie said, and the colour was high in her cheeks.

'Ah!' I smiled at her as she brushed the strands of red-gold hair away from her forehead and put my arm around her waist. 'I think there's a young man waiting round here somewhere.'

She couldn't help smiling in spite of her shyness. 'Well, he said he'd be here, but he may not show up.'

'He'll turn up, you daft thing!' Lotty said scornfully. 'Why, Davy, the boy's cracked on her. He has the same colour hair as Vickie and he's Irish. Do you want to know his name?'

'Little cat!' Vickie said. 'It's a good thing I don't mind Davy knowing. His name's Patrick O'Brian. I've seen him round for ages, but he's only just noticed me.'

'That's because your lillies are growing big,' Lotty said wisely. 'You'll have to have bigger bodices soon.'

'Oh, you!' Vickie turned and ran away across the fields, her petticoats flying, her hair shining like copper under the sun.

'I don't know why she's so touchy about it,' Lotty shook her head in bewilderment. 'I only wish my lillies were growing. I hope I won't always stay like this.' She looked down at her own flat bodice in disgust. 'If I do, there's no boy going to come to fairs chasing after me.'

'You'll be all right,' I said in amusement. 'It's my experience that girls begin to grow up quite suddenly when they're least expecting it.'

'Do you know a lot about girls, then?' Lotty looked up into my face, avid for a bit of gossip. I playfully pushed her away.

'Go and look at some silks or buy yourself a cordial, anything, only leave me alone. I don't feel like answering questions; it's too hot.'

Lotty delved into the basket of food and brought out a pie still hot from the oven. She bit into it with obvious enjoyment, and I began to feel hungry myself.

'Here.' She saw my look and handed me a pie wrapped in a cloth. The crust was delicious, it melted under my teeth. I ate it quickly and took another one.

'Huh!' Lotty grinned at me. 'You look so funny with flour all over your moustache. Oh, look!' She pointed to something behind my back and I turned to see Elizabeth, beautiful in a blue gown.

I got to my feet quickly, brushing the flour from my face, holding out my hands to her. She took them, smiling in delight.

'Oh, I'm so glad to see you. I went up to *Siop Fawr* to see if anyone could come with me to the fair because Iorwerth has to work, and Catrin told me you'd gone just a few minutes before.'

'Sit down,' I said, feeling awkward and ungainly against her delicate stature. 'Have something to eat. I can recommend the pies.'

Elizabeth leaned across me to take the pie Lotty was offering and her perfume tantalized my senses. I longed with an overwhelming desire to take her in my arms and lay her in the sweet grass.

'I'm going to find the piglets.' Lotty got to her feet, brushing crumbs from her skirts. 'You look after the food now, and don't eat it all.' Her finger was pointing at me, and I nodded to her seriously.

'I give you my word of honour I won't touch another morsel unless handed to me by your own fair hands.'

'Go away!' she said. 'You talk so funny at times it's hard to understand you.'

I watched her run pell-mell over the grass, her skirts beating a tattoo against her small ankles. I don't know where she summoned such strength from on a day so hot and airless. I lay back, my head on my hands, and closed my eyes. I could feel the soft material of Elizabeth's dress against my fingers, and even such a small contact made me feel absurdly happy. She sighed softly.

'Your grandmother misses you very much, Davy. I wish you would come down to Tip Row and see her. It would make her so happy.'

'I will come tomorrow,' I said promptly, 'after my work in the shop is finished.' I opened my eyes. 'I miss her, too. She's a fine woman. There are so many fine women in Swansea.' I tried to laugh, but it stuck in my throat. I couldn't look away from Elizabeth's eyes, and she too seemed to sit frozen, as if incapable of movement.

After a silence that seemed to last for an eternity, she turned her face away from me.

'I wish Iorwerth would try to find a job away from the copper works. It wears him out. I know it, even though he doesn't say anything.'

I knew what she was doing by mentioning my uncle's name; she was reminding me there was an insurmountable barrier between us.

'Come and look at the cattle,' I said, getting to my feet and brushing the dried grass from my clothes. 'It's better than sitting here doing nothing.'

Nothing but long for you, I thought almost desperately. I had never felt like this for any woman before. It was not simply desire, or even tenderness; it was a feeling so inexplicable that I didn't quite know what it meant myself.

'I'd better bring the basket of food.' She bent down in a graceful movement and put it on her arm. 'Lotty would never forgive us if it was stolen.'

People of every description thronged round the cattle pens, farmers and coppermen rubbed shoulders, and colliers with their blue scars identifying them poked at calves with knowledgeable fingers.

'Oh!' Elizabeth wrinkled up her nose. 'What an awful smell, I don't think I can stand it.' She laughed helplessly as she was pushed forward by the surge of people behind her. 'If I don't watch out I'll be in the pens along with the animals!'

I caught her arm firmly and pulled her free of the crowd; her fingers had twined in mine, and we stood with the hot sun beating down on our heads, close and tinglingly aware of each other.

'Davy!' Lotty ran up to me. 'I've been looking for you. I've found the piglets. Come and see them with me. I want you to lift me up on your shoulders so's I can have a better look.'

'All right,' I said in resignation, 'I'll play the pack horse if it will keep you quiet.'

She sat on my shoulders squealing like a piglet herself, wriggling in her excitement until my neck began to ache.

'You must be thirsty,' I said loudly, 'and if you're not, I am, so come on down from there.'

She came down quietly enough and I could see she was tired. The field was clearing now and some of the cattle were already being driven homewards.

'Where's Vickie?' I said in sudden concern. 'We haven't seen her since we arrived.'

'Oh, don't worry,' Lotty said. 'I expect, if Patrick didn't turn up, she went to see him.'

I was suddenly cold, in spite of the sun that was still warm, although lower in the sky.

'Where does he live?' I tried to keep my voice light, not to startle anyone, but Lotty's eyes met mine and I knew our thoughts were the same.

'He lives in Greenhill,' she said in awe, 'and that's

where the cholera has struck. We were told not to go down there, weren't we?'

I looked at Elizabeth. 'Will you take Lotty home? I'll go and look for Vickie; we may be getting worried about nothing. Go on, I'll be all right.'

I watched them walk away from me and I tried to push back the dread that twisted my inside into knots. One case of cholera didn't make an epidemic, I reminded myself, and yet hadn't Luther complained that the summer heat always brought out the pestilence?

I quickly climbed the grassy hill towards the place the locals called 'Little Ireland', and stopped to get my bearings.

The courts and streets were narrow, dry and dusty in the heat of summer. I don't know what instinct led me, though when I stopped outside a tiny cottage and saw a priest inside the door I knew I had found Patrick.

A woman turned when I entered. 'Oh, Mother of God protect you, sir,' she said in a soft voice. 'There's bad sickness in this house, but come in if you must.'

'I'm sorry to intrude,' I said, 'but I'm looking for my sister Vickie. Is she here?'

She pointed to the stairs. 'She's up there with my son. The father has just gone to give Patrick what comfort he can. Go you and get your sister; take her away from here. It's the kindest thing you can do.'

The bedroom was dark and airless and it took a few minutes for my eyes to become accustomed to the gloom. A priest was bending over the boy on the bed and Vickie sat beside him, a haunted look in her eyes.

The priest looked up and nodded to me. 'He's bad,' he said gently. 'I've given him a little laudanum, but I fear the worst.'

I took Vickie in my arms and held her close. I think I

310

knew already what was wrong with Patrick, but it still sent a chill through me when he actually looked up at me and spoke the word we all feared to hear.

'It's the cholera,' he gasped. 'For pity's sake get Vickie out of here. I don't want her to see me like this.'

I looked questioningly at the priest and he nodded again, a world of weariness in his stooped shoulders.

'Go from here, my son,' he said. 'There is nothing you can do and you only put yourself in danger.'

Vickie pulled herself free and went to Patrick's side. There were no tears in her eyes.

'I will stay here,' she said, and there was a determined set to her chin. 'I won't leave until I know Patrick is over the crisis.'

He died at two o'clock in the morning.

FOURTEEN

Cholera spread insidiously through the villages, and fear blazed up like a forest fire. People closed their windows and doors which, according to my mother, was the worst thing they could do.

Vickie did not parade her grief, though she became silent and withdrawn. Her small face took on a set expression that lay oddly on one so young.

When we had returned from the house in Greenhill, my mother had taken our clothes and burnt them, insisting that we wash ourselves all over to rid our bodies of any contamination. Whether her methods had any sound basis I did not know, but at least cleanliness would do us no harm.

It was a soft summer evening and I had arranged to go to meet Susannah. I set off from *Siop Fawr* with little enthusiasm. I was too much in love with Elizabeth now for any other woman to interest me very much. Still, I could not be unkind to Susannah; I would have to break off the relationship as gently as possible, allowing her to keep her pride.

I was unprepared for her outburst of hysterical fear as she drew me quickly inside the door of the villa, closing it with a resounding bang.

'Oh, Davy.' She clung to my arm, her face upturned to me was pale and her eyes dark ringed. 'I'm going away. I just can't bear to stay in Swansea any longer. Did you know that a merchant living not half a mile away from here has gone down with the cholera?'

I smoothed her hair back from her face. 'Where will you go?' I was trying hard to be kind and understanding, but the thought was inside me like a knife that people like my grandmother were not so fortunate as to have somewhere to run.

'My brother-in-law has a cottage down the Gower coast; it's isolated there and the air is fresh and pure. Davy, why don't you come with me?'

'It's impossible,' I said slowly. 'I'm needed at the shop, and in any case what would people say? You would lose your reputation.'

She twisted her hands together. 'Oh, that. I'm going to lose that anyway.' She glanced quickly away from me, and I frowned.

'What do you mean? Has someone found out about us?' I led her to a chair. She seemed on the point of fainting, and there was a fine beading of sweat on her cheeks.

'No,' she shook her head, 'but, Davy, I'm going to have your child.'

'Oh, my God!' I stared at her in amazement. I'd thought her barren after what she said about her marriage not producing any children.

'Oh, don't fresh yourself!' She spoke sharply. 'I shan't ask anything of you; no-one shall even know who the father is.'

'That's nonsense!' I said angrily. 'I shall marry you, of course, and give the child my name.'

'No!' She sounded resolute. 'I don't want that, Davy, much as I think of you. It just would not do at all.'

'But why?' I said in surprise. 'I can look after you both, give you some security.'

She turned her face away from me. 'My first husband's

money is all the security I need, and if I married you I would lose it all; he put a clause in his will to the effect that if I married again, his money would go to another branch of the family.'

'I see.' I spoke rather coldly, and she shrugged her shoulders in exasperation.

'Just think, Davy,' she said reasonably. 'How would we manage on the pittance you earn? I am used to expensive clothes and an easy life. I don't want love in a cottage. In any case, I could give the baby a better life on my own.'

'Aren't you afraid of what people will say about you, a widow with a child?'

'I'll go somewhere I'm not known, and then the child will be accepted because no-one will find out how long I've been a widow,' she said quickly.

She wound her arms around my neck and her face was suddenly radiant. 'Davy, you don't know how happy you've made me. I feel fulfilled as a woman now that I'm going to have a child.'

I wondered bitterly if it could have been anyone's child; did the father really matter to her at all? She must have sensed something of my feelings.

'Look, Davy,' she said softly. 'You really don't want to be married to someone like me, do you?' She kissed me lightly as if she was already beyond my reach, made unapproachable and chaste by her impending mother-hood. 'I'm so much older than you, for a start, and I'm utterly selfish. You need a robust woman, one who would follow you to the ends of the earth if need be. You don't need me.'

She drew me towards the door. 'Go home now, Davy, and look after yourself. I will try to let you know when the child is born.'

'Thank you,' I said sourly. 'You'd take me along if I'd

just be content to live in sin with you, but you will not marry me and give the child a name.'

'I will give the child everything it needs, never fear. Now go quickly, Davy. I'm afraid to hold the door open long in case some evil humours find their way into the house.'

I found myself standing outside the villa with the door closed firmly against me. It seemed that my life held nothing but partings these last few days. Everything was suddenly changing, and it seemed that no effort on my part could make any difference at all.

As I walked over the grass back into the town, I thought seriously about the fact I was going to be a father. It gave me a strange feeling to know my child would be born illegitimate; it was a case of history repeating itself. I could see now that Dylan would have had very little say in what became of me; it seemed to be the mother's privilege to decide the child's fate.

The streets of the town were crowded with people, as usual, and inexplicably I began to feel uneasy. I couldn't fathom it out at all. Was I getting fanciful, like a woman huddled in a shawl on a stormy night?

I strode briskly past the Assembly Rooms and down on to the harbour. The breeze blew, fresh and salt, from the sea, and as I stood there I wondered what it was I really wanted from life. One thing I knew, it was time I grew up and acted with responsibility instead of going my own sweet way, disregarding the feelings of others.

At last the peaceful action of the sea calmed me and I felt able to return to *Siop Fawr*. I had the books to do, and there were sacks of meal to be carried from the store room into the shop. I would be dog-tired by the time I got to bed and so at least I should be able to fall asleep with little trouble. But I couldn't fall asleep. I lay awake in the heat of the darkness thinking of Susannah carrying my child, driven away from her home by the fear of the cholera. Perhaps I should have gone with her, looked after her, but now she was better off without me; there would be less talk. I thumped my pillow and closed my eyes tightly, but I felt as sleepless as if it was the morning.

The herb counter at the shop was kept busy all day with people seeking remedies for the cholera. My mother worked hard, brewing up herbs so that strange smells penetrated into all the rooms of the house.

'Will any of it really help?' I asked as my mother strained some juice through a piece of muslin into a jug.

'The remedies I make will check fever and soothe a sickly stomach, but once the cholera gets a hold, there is not much anyone can do.'

My mother gave me a little push. 'Get some brandy into the shop and tell anyone that needs it they can pay when men are recovered and back at work again.'

I stared at her soberly. 'Mam, you know as well as I do that some of them will never see work again.'

'Well, all right!' she said sharply. 'Are we going to deny them the right to a little help with their dying? After all, some folk can't even afford to send for a doctor. We're the only help they've got.'

'Yes,' I nodded, 'you are right, of course. I'll put the brandy up on the shelf straight away.'

'If only we could get some laudanum,' she worried. 'It greatly eases pain. Perhaps you could ride over to the doctor's villa and buy some, Davy.'

I smiled down at her. 'And then, I suppose, we will give it out free with the brandy?' I didn't wait for her to think of an answer. I hugged her tightly and she pushed at my arms, a reluctant smile on her face.

'All right, I'm an old fool,' she said, 'but, Davy, I've

had so much goodness in my life, I feel I owe it to other people less fortunate to give them all the help I can.'

The shop bell clanged and a woman carrying a baby in a shawl came up to the counter. The baby was crying fitfully, and my mother drew back the shawl to look.

'Don't worry, Mrs Phillips.' My mother smiled reassuringly. 'It's just a touch of colic in the stomach, nothing more serious than that. I'll give you some medicine that will soon put him right.'

'Oh, thank God for that.' Mrs Phillips sighed heavily. 'I thought it could be the start of something bad, and with my Eddie in prison I haven't much money to buy cures.'

I realized that this must be the wife of the man who had tripped me when Iorwerth started in the copper works. He'd resented the manager giving my uncle a job, and yet shortly afterwards he'd been caught stealing from Mr Vivian. If I remembered rightly he'd stolen some coal, not very much, but he'd had a previous conviction which was bound to tell against him.

'How long did he get?' I asked, and then, seeing her surprised look, I thought I'd better explain a little. 'I'm only asking because we used to work in the copper works together,' I said quickly.

'Oh, God!' she said, raising her eyes heavenward. 'My Eddie was a fool and no mistake. A good job he had down the works, furnace man, and a good one too, but he couldn't keep his itchy fingers to himself and, of course, he was caught in the act.'

'Here you are, Mrs Phillips.' My mother handed her a packet. 'Give the baby some of the powder three times a day; he'll soon be over his little bit of stomach trouble, don't you worry.'

The woman delved into her pocket for some money, but my mother waved her hand away.

317

'Give it to me some time when your husband's out of prison. There's no hurry.'

'Thank you, good girl.' Mrs Phillips quickly put the money away. 'My Eddie got six weeks in solitary, and that's cruel, that is. I went down to see him, but they sent me away again; they were just getting a crowd of men in from Cardiff gaol, and a scruffy, seedy lot they looked, too. There wasn't a pound of meat between the lot of them.' She went to the door. 'Well, thank you again, Catrin Owen. Oh!' She put her hand to her mouth. 'Excuse me, it's Catrin Morgan now, isn't it? It takes a bit of getting used to.'

My mother's face was pink and her lips were pursed as she closed the shop door and bolted it. I could see she was annoyed, and somehow I couldn't help seeing the funny side of it.

'Why are you grinnin' then, boyo?' she said sharply. 'Don't just stand there. Come and do up the top bolt for me, will you?'

I put my hand on her shoulder and grinned down at her. 'That will teach you not to show too much charity to the likes of Mrs Phillips!'

She searched about for something to say, but then she caught my eye and started to laugh. She leaned against me, tears running down her cheeks, and she wiped them away with the corner of her white apron.

'Oh, Davy,' she said at last, 'I suppose I did deserve that. I was being a bit pompous, I dare say. But then, she was quick enough to keep her money in her pocket, wasn't she?'

'Come on,' I said, 'let's go in and get some supper. I'm starving, and the smell coming from the kitchen is enough to drive a hungry man mad!'

The girls were just putting out the food. Vickie, her red

hair tied back, her face pale and strained, was cutting huge chunks of bread, and Caroline served out meat and vegetables.

Dylan put down his pen and smiled up at me, and I realized what a handsome man he still was in spite of the grey at his temples. It gave me a feeling of pride that I could not deny.

'You've been keeping the books well, Davy,' he said, 'and I hope you don't think I was interfering by doing them for you tonight. I just thought you were looking a bit tired, that's all.'

I was aware of Caroline sitting facing me, her eyes betraying nothing, but I sensed she was daring me to give her father a sharp answer.

'I am tired,' I said truthfully. 'It was so hot last night I couldn't sleep, and I'm glad you did the books because Mam wants me to ride over to the doctor's and buy a little laudanum.'

I ate my meal with relish, and Lotty sitting beside me pushed her plate towards me.

'You can have mine as well, if you like, Davy,' she said, leaning against me. 'I don't feel much like eating.'

'You haven't any pains in your stomach, have you, child?' My mother left her seat and put a hand on Lotty's forehead. 'You seem a little hot, but nothing unusual for this time of the year.'

'I feel all right, thank you,' Lotty said, but her voice was slow and she seemed about to drop off to sleep any minute.

'She's just tired, I expect,' I said. 'Don't worry, I'll take her up to bed. The rest of you get on with your supper.'

I swung Lotty easily into my arms and carried her upstairs. Her eyes were almost closed, but I shook her shoulders gently.

319

'Now, Lotty, tell me if you have any pains at all. Is your stomach hurting? Do you feel sick?'

I was worried because I'd been in Patrick's house the night he died. What if either Vickie or I had carried some ill humour back with us?

'I don't feel bad.' She tried to smile at me. 'I'm just very, very tired.' Her small fingers curled around mine and I sat by her side seething with impotent rage. Why didn't Swansea have proper sewerage and clean running water as other towns had? Luther was right when he said that the paving committee, by their ignorance and greed, were keeping the poorer parts of Swansea in constant risk of illness.

The door opened and Vickie looked in. 'She's all right, isn't she, Davy? I'm so afraid that she may have what Patrick died of.'

I shook my head. 'No, I don't think so. Look at her. She looks too well for that. No, I think she's just tired out with the heat; she's not very strong, and she should rest more.'

Vickie sat beside me and stared down at her sister, her eyes moist.

'If Lotty died, I'd want to die too, because I'd know it was my fault.'

'No!' I said sharply. 'Don't ever think that. The fault lies with people who run the town and with men sitting up in London hesitating over a decision that could bring great improvements to Swansea.'

'What do you mean, Davy?' she said. 'I don't understand what you are saying.'

'We need a privy to every house, for a start,' I said. 'It's wrong that people have to squat down in the mud of the streets like animals. And we need good sweet water, not the dirty, foul water from the canal.'

'But people have always put up with things like that,' she said in surprise. 'We are lucky we have the canal. Some folks have to stand and wait at a pump for an hour sometimes just to get some water to drink.'

'That's just what I'm against,' I said. 'It's those sort of conditions that bring illnesses and help them to spread. The epidemics are always worse in the most crowded areas.' She looked towards Lotty, who by now was fast asleep.

'Patrick lived in a crowded house,' she said. 'I knew that, and yet I still went there, but I didn't think I'd be risking anyone's health except my own.'

I got to my feet. 'Anyway, cheer up, Vickie. There's nothing wrong with Lotty that a good night's sleep won't cure.' I moved to the door and stood for a moment looking at the two girls; they were blood of my blood, my half-sisters, and I loved them with a fierceness that surprised me.

Vickie met my eyes and she smiled, a gentle, wistful smile that made me feel I'd fight the whole world to protect her.

'You're very young yet,' I said gently. 'You'll meet someone else you can love. Look at my mother; she loved two men, didn't she?'

Vickie smiled. 'Yes, I suppose you're right, David. I'll get over Patrick in time.'

But in spite of her forced cheerfulness, I had the strangest feeling that she never would love anyone else as she had loved her Patrick.

'Davy!' Kate stood at the bottom of the stairs, holding a candle above her head. 'Your mam says to go to the doctor's before it's too late and he'll be gone to bed.'

I ran down the stairs two at a time. 'Go to Vickie, Kate,' I said quickly. 'I think she's in need of some company.'

Kate was the sort of girl who didn't need explanations. She moved away immediately up the stairs, her shadow wavering on the wall made grotesque by the candlelight.

'Come on, Davy!' My mother held some money out to me. 'Dylan has saddled one of the horses for you, and no calling at the beer shop, mind.'

'All right, I promise,' I said, 'though a mug of ale would go down very well on such a hot night.'

Dylan gave me a hand up on to the huge chestnut horse and patted the animal's rump.

'He's a big chap, but gentle as a lamb,' he said. 'He'll give you no trouble.' He looked up at me as if trying to see me clearly in the darkness. 'You know the real reason your mother doesn't want you to go into town, don't you, son?'

'I can guess,' I said, pleased at his unselfconscious use of the word 'son'. 'She's afraid I'll get mixed up with my cousin William again.'

'Yes, there's that, but she's afraid of the cholera too, and that's an enemy it's almost impossible to fight.'

'But, Dylan,' I said, 'I am going to have to visit town on some occasions; it's unavoidable.'

'I know that,' he said, 'but humour her for tonight. Let her get over her worry about you and Vickie being in contact with the poor boy who died.'

'All right,' I said. 'I'll ride straight to the doctor's and back, I promise.'

As I rode away into the calm warmth of the night I didn't think I would be breaking my promise. I arrived at the doctor's house to find he had just arrived home. He greeted me cordially enough when I told him what I wanted.

'We are going to need people like your mother,' he said wearily, 'if the disease gets a hold on the town. I've just witnessed the death of a young serving girl. Worked for

322

the manager of the copper works up at the Hafod, she did. Poor child, she didn't have much of a life, by all accounts; been a prostitute and even served time in prison for her crimes, and now to die so young.' He shook his head sadly. 'I sometimes wonder if the good Lord is asleep when such things happen.'

'The girl,' I said in a harsh whisper. 'What was her name? It was Annie, was it?'

'Why, yes.' He seemed surprised. 'Annie Owens, a thin, dark little thing, quite pretty at one time, I suppose.'

I took the laudanum and put it carefully in my pocket and handed the doctor the money.

'Thank you,' I said, and hurried out of the villa, climbing on to the chestnut's back so suddenly that the animal almost took fright. I knew that I had to go to see Rosie, tell her what had happened.

FIFTEEN

The streets of the town were, for once, deserted. I rode the chestnut horse so hard that steam rose from the animal's flanks and the shoes sent sparks shooting against the stones in the road. My mind was still unable to completely grasp the fact that poor Annie was dead. It would be hard breaking the news to Rosie, but it was better it came from me than that she should perhaps hear it from a stranger as I had.

The downstairs door of the house where Rosie lived swung open, which surprised me; it was normally shut tight, sometimes even locked. Many times I'd had to knock on the door for several minutes before anyone heard me.

'Rosie!' I shouted loudly up the stairs, but there was no answering call and, spurred on by a feeling of apprehension, I took the stairs two at a time. Her door opened at a touch, and when I saw the chaos in the room I knew something terrible had happened.

She was lying huddled beneath the table, her arms outstretched, and when I managed to light one of the candles I saw that she had been badly beaten. Her face was so swollen and discoloured that it was difficult to recognize her. Her leg was folded under her at such an angle that it was sure to be broken.

But there was something more. The way she was breathing was fearful; it had a rasping sound as if her throat was constricted. I brought some water and held it to her lips, and when I helped her up to drink, she was burning up.

Her eyes flickered open and a gleam of recognition came into them.

'Davy,' she mumbled, 'you must get away from here.' I could hardly make out what she was saying, her lips were so cut and swollen. 'I've got the cholera, Davy.' She paused for a moment, trying to control the ragged breathing. 'I told William to fetch help for me, but he was drunk – he beat me, I couldn't stop him – took my money.'

Outrage was rising like a sickness inside me as the full import of her words became clear to me. I would make him suffer the tortures of the damned for this; killing would be too good for him.

'I'll bring a doctor,' I said softly, 'but first let me make you more comfortable.'

I put a pillow under her head, and her eyes looked up at me like those of an animal in pain.

'Don't go, Davy,' she said. 'It's no use, too late. Just stay with me, hold my hand. I don't want to die alone.'

I crouched on my knees beside her and held her for more than an hour. Even when I knew she'd breathed her last, I could not bring myself to leave her. I stood for a moment in her doorway, looking back at her crumpled form. She had been so splendid, such a woman as I'd never met before or could ever hope to meet again. And there were tears in my eyes as I went down into the street. Besides me, who would care about Rosie? She would be just another prostitute who had got what she deserved.

As I mounted the horse and made my way through the town, a coldness came over me and an iron determination to find William and punish him tonight. In my mind I went over ways of crippling him, ways that would give him most pain so that he would never be allowed to forget what he'd done to Rosie.

The lights from Uncle Huw's farm-house spilled out on to the scented night air; it all looked so peaceful, and yet here was I forced to bring violence into innocent people's lives. But then, William should have thought about his family before he beat up a sick girl and robbed her of her savings.

I knocked on the door, restraining myself from the urge to kick it in, and it was opened almost immediately by my uncle.

'Where's William?' I could not keep my voice low. The words came out clipped and hard, and Huw looked at me in amazement.

'*Darro!* What's happened, boyo? You look like the devil himself.'

'I want William,' I said again, 'and this time please do not try to stop me from doing what I have to do.'

Rhian came and stood behind Huw. Her face was pale as she looked at me.

'Go from here,' she said sharply. 'We don't want you causing trouble. Leave William alone, will you?'

'It's he who's caused trouble,' I said, 'and more trouble than he can cope with, because after I've finished with him I'm going to the police station.'

William came out then. He swaggered to the door and I saw deep scratches on his face. He stared sullenly at me, and when I moved towards him he raised his fists.

'Wait now.' There was such command in Huw's voice that instinctively both William and I obeyed. 'What's all this about? I know you two boys don't like each other, but surely there's no need for fighting.' He turned to me.

326

'Now, tell me, Davy, what has William done to make you look like this?'

'Tell your father what you've done, William,' I challenged, 'or are you afraid he'll give you a beating too?'

William sneered. 'And what have I done? Slapped a whore about a bit after she tried to steal my money. Is that so unusual? Men are doing it all the time.'

I couldn't believe my own ears. How could he stand there and lie so blatantly. I felt anger rise up and almost choke me.

'You bastard!' I ground the word out. 'You fooled Rosie into thinking you'd marry her, so that she'd tell you where her savings were hidden, then you beat her up like the animal you are. When I found her, her leg was broken and her face was so bad I hardly knew her.'

'It's all lies,' he said. 'You go and ask her to tell you the truth, Dad. It wasn't like that at all.'

'No one can ask her anything,' I said bitterly. 'While you were so drunk that you didn't know what you were doing you overlooked the fact that she was sick. She died of the cholera in my arms not an hour ago.'

William's jaw sagged and I saw Rhian cover her face with her hands. There was silence for what seemed a long time, then suddenly William pushed past me, running as though his life depended on it, towards the stables.

I caught the chestnut's reins, but just as I was about to mount, Uncle Huw caught my arm.

'You can help me catch him,' he said quickly, 'but please leave him to me then. I'll see he is punished.'

I shook his hand off. 'You didn't see the way Rosie died,' I said. 'I'm sorry, I can't do as you ask.'

I galloped in the direction of the road just in time to see the dust from William's mount as he turned a bend in the road. Huw came quickly after me, passing me easily on a well-bred stallion that seemed to have wings for feet. Apart from that, Huw was more used to the roads than I was, and he knew every twist and turn, and soon he was well ahead of me.

The moon had slid behind the clouds, so that now the darkness was thick and intense. I slowed the horse, trying to listen for hoofbeats or the snatch of a voice on the still air, but there was nothing.

I rode on desperately and tasted the salt of my tears as they ran into my mouth.

'I will avenge you, Rosie,' I vowed, 'even if it takes me the rest of my life. William Owen will not get away with what he's done tonight.'

I came out on to a broad road and saw a shape in the dimness. I strained my eyes to see who it was, and a voice called out to me.

'Davy! Is that you?' I knew it was Huw and I rode towards him.

'Where is he?' I asked, but I knew what Huw was going to say even before he opened his mouth.

'We've lost him. He must have cut across the fields. He knows every inch of this farmland; he grew up on it, remember.'

I sighed heavily and Huw put his hand on my arm, and through the darkness I could just make out that there were tears on his cheeks.

'A man will make many excuses for a son,' he said slowly, 'but I can think of no more. From now on my door is barred to him.'

'I'm sorry,' I said, and I was, sorry for him to have such as William born into his family. 'What shall I do about Rosie? I can't just leave her lying there.'

'You must make up your own mind on that,' he said. 'I

can't go to the police about my own flesh and blood, whatever he's done. But I will pay for the girl's burying, that's the least I can do.'

He swung his horse around and rode away slowly, his shoulders bent, and he looked like a very old man.

I rode back into town and along the street where Rosie lived, wondering what I should do, but it was all decided for me because the house was thronging with people and I caught a glimpse through the doorway of an officer in uniform. I swung the horse away; there was nothing more I could do for her now. Rosie was lost to me for ever.

At the nearest beer shop, I stopped the horse and tied him up at the doorpost. Rage still boiled within me, grief too, and there seemed nothing I could do about either of them at the moment.

The ale was good and cold against my throat and I drank mug after mug as though it was water. I heard the voices of the people around me, but it was as if I was in a world far removed from them.

At last, I had drunk my fill, my head was spinning and I felt sick to my stomach. I stumbled out into the soft night air and untied the patiently waiting horse. But when I made to climb up into the saddle, he moved away from me nervously and I fell into the dust of the road. For a moment I was winded, but when I looked up it was just in time to see the flying hooves of the chestnut horse disappearing into the distance.

'Blast the animal!' I said, and pushed myself up, leaning dizzily against the beer shop doorway.

'Come on, lovie,' a voice said near my ear, and I tried to focus my eyes on the woman who stood face to face with me. She was as tall as I was and her skin was chocolate brown, shining like silk in the light from the lantern hung over the door.

'What did you say?' My words sounded thick and hazy, and I wondered if she had understood me, but she took my arm and hung it around her neck, her shoulder under mine.

'I said come on, lovie.' Her soft voice reassured me. 'I'll take you back to my place.'

'The horse,' I said foolishly. 'I've lost him, he's run away, and there'll be hell to pay when I get home.'

'Ah.' She smiled, and her teeth were the whitest I'd ever seen. 'It's my experience that a horse, like a drunken man, usually finds someone to take care of him.'

She almost carried me down a small lane; her strength was unbelievable. I shook my head, trying to clear the mistiness that clouded my eyes.

'Don't worry, lovie,' she said. 'I'll give you some nice coffee, black like me. It will soon make you feel better.'

I went with her unquestioningly, putting myself completely in her hands. She led me through the quiet narrow streets and down into the Strand which broadened out, hissing gas lights bathing us in brilliance.

'In here, lovie.' She pulled me down some basement steps, steadying me when I would have fallen, and took me into a tiny room. It was clean and sweet smelling, but looked strange to my befuddled eyes. Instead of carpet on the floor, she had long-stalked grass so dry that it crackled as we moved over it. There was no bed, just a brightly coloured quilt spread out for sleeping purposes. I suddenly wanted to laugh, thinking how far I'd come from the graceful town house where I'd lived with John Richards as my father for all the years of my childhood.

'Lay,' she commanded, and she crouched down in the corner and picked up a pot. 'I'll bring coffee in a minute.' I almost fell on to the quilt and found it was filled with something like straw. It was very comfortable, and I think I dozed off for a few minutes.

'Drink this, please.' I opened my eyes and saw the dark handsome face above me, the eyes so brown they were almost black.

'You're beautiful,' I said, and took the scalding coffee, almost burning my mouth as I drank it.

'You are beautiful, also,' she said. 'Skin so brown for an Englishman.'

'I'm not an Englishman,' I said, returning the mug to her. 'I am Welsh.' I watched as her graceful body bent over the small fire. She was slender in the waist, but wide of hip and breast. She filled the mug once more and brought it to me.

'It's very bitter,' I said, 'but I am beginning to come to my senses again.'

'You are not used to coffee,' she said, smiling, 'but I brought it with me when I came from my country on a ship to England.' She smiled. 'I brought a baby in my belly too, a white sailor's baby. I thought I would find him, but, of course, I never did.'

'And the baby?' I said, not really curious, but because somehow it seemed expected of me.

'He died,' she said without any trace of expression. 'He was born sickly. I knew all along I would not keep him. It was only to be expected; the crossing over the sea was a nightmare.'

She crouched down beside me and her eyes were bright with knowledge. I felt she knew my innermost thoughts, and I sat up, my head against the wall, trying to pull myself together.

'Why did you bring me here?' I asked. 'Are you offering to sell yourself?'

331

She shook her head. 'No, I do not sell myself,' she said casually, with no sign that she was offended by my question. She touched my hand. 'I will give myself to you if that's what you need, but I don't think it is.'

I was surprised to realize she was right; in spite of her beauty and the exotic quality of her physique, I had never felt less like making love in my life. Too much had happened to me. Rosie's death and the way William had escaped had made me heartsick.

'Tell me your troubles,' she said. 'I perhaps may be able to help you.' Her voice was throaty with just a trace of a strange accent.

'No one can help,' I said, and suddenly there were tears in my eyes, running over my cheeks and into my mouth. I had no power to stop them, so I just sat unashamedly crying.

She took me in her arms as gently as if I was a baby. She crooned in a strange language and kissed my temples, almost as if she was bestowing a blessing on me.

After a while she cupped my face in her hands and made me look at her.

'Black Pearl will help you,' she said. 'I ask nothing in return because I can see you are a good man. Tell me what is grieving you.'

I found that I was pouring out all my grief and bitterness about Rosie's death. I kept nothing back, not even the way I wanted to cripple William so that he would always remember what he'd done. When at last I stopped talking, she nodded her head.

'I am satisfied that you are telling the truth now. I am a friend of your Rosie and I saw you leave her place. I wanted to find out if it was you who beat her.'

I stared at her in amazement; I would never have believed anyone could be so cunning.

'I was going to kill you,' she said without emotion, 'but I had to find out the truth first. You didn't look like a bad one, so I bided my time.'

'I'm glad you did!' I said feelingly. 'How William would have laughed if I'd been blamed for what he'd done.' I looked at her closely. 'But I rode away, up to the farm to find William. How could you know I'd come back.'

'I knew,' she said. 'Now I will do what has to be done.' She moved away from me and took some candlegrease out of a bag, making a roughly shaped figure of a man. I saw her wind a strand of hair around the head.

'What are you doing?' I asked in surprise. 'It looks like what people call the black art.'

She gave me a quick look. 'I found this hair in Rosie's hand,' she explained. 'It isn't one of yours, the colour is wrong; that is how I knew you were telling me the truth.'

She had finished with the figure and she laid it on the ground, murmuring something I couldn't understand. Suddenly there was silence, and then she lifted a stone and smashed the figure with it. She remained with head bowed for a moment or two and somehow I found myself shivering; it was as if the small room had become permeated with all the vile smells imaginable.

'Black Pearl,' I said, 'what have you done?' I sat transfixed as she came over and squatted beside me.

'William has been dealt with,' she said. 'His fate will catch up with him in a very short time, never fear. And now for you.'

She placed her hand on my head, forcing me gently back so that I was lying down. She sort of pinched her fingers together at my temples and I felt the world fall away from me into deep darkness.

In the morning when I woke quite suddenly to find the sun streaming in through the window, picking out all the bright colours of the quilt on which I lay, I was alone; there was no sign of Black Pearl.

I got to my feet wondering if I'd dreamed her. Had I somehow stumbled into the house of a kind-hearted whore and in my drunken state let my imagination run riot? I felt no ill effects, indeed I felt full of life and vigour. I went to the door and found it open, and I was just about to let myself out when something on the floor among the rushes caught my eye. It was a piece of candlegrease, and around it was tied a hair.

SIXTEEN

My mother had met me at the door of *Siop Fawr* in the fresh air of the early morning.

'Davy,' she said, 'I've been so worried about you.' She put her arms around me and leaned against my shoulder, and I felt warm and comforted by her nearness.

'I'm sorry, Mam,' I said gently, 'something happened to make me break my promise. I'll tell you about it some time, only not now.'

We stood in silence for a moment, and I could hear the sounds of breakfast being prepared in the kitchen. My mother moved away from me.

'Dylan wants you to go down to the docks later on, if you don't mind, to check on the arrival of some spices he ordered.'

'Of course I don't mind,' I said quickly. 'Indeed, it will be a pleasure to have a breath of sea air on a day like this.'

'Well,' my mother looked at me doubtfully, 'don't go too near the sailors – a lot of them carry the Yellow Jack fever, and that's almost as bad as the cholera.'

'All right,' I smiled, 'but come on, let's get something to eat. That bacon smells delicious!'

Now, as I strode out down the hill, the sun was pleasantly warm on my bare head. So far, I had managed to keep at bay the thoughts of Rosie and her tragic death. I knew that if I let myself dwell on it, I would be full of impotent rage.

Suddenly, as I passed through Greenhill, I heard the plaintive sound of somebody wailing. I stopped in my tracks, and it was as if my blood had suddenly turned cold. Coming towards me were four women; their heads were covered with shawls and between them they bore a roughly made litter and on it was the body of a man.

As the women walked past me, I could see the dust kicked up by their bare feet. They chanted something, and I could tell by their speech that they were Irish women.

The man was young and there was a fresh tinge to his skin that told me he had not been dead for long. I wondered if I should approach the women, offer my help, but they didn't even see me as they walked on down the hill, heads bowed.

'*Darro!* Did you see that, boyo? It's not right for women to see to their dead.'

I spun round to see Iorwerth standing behind me, copper dust clinging to his hair and skin, glinting like gold in the sunlight.

'What are you doing here?' I asked in surprise, wrinkling my nose at the smell of sulphur that was about him.

'The manager sent me to collect some special cargo from one of the ships.' Iorwerth grinned. 'I think I'm about the only one he can trust not to rob him!'

'I'm going down to the docks,' I said. 'We can walk together.'

We fell into step and Iorwerth slapped his fist into the palm of his hand.

'God, the sickness seems to be spreading and there's not a damn thing being done about it. It's the poor Irish I feel most sorry for. If it wasn't for the priest working himself to death, they would have no help at all.'

We came out into the pleasant space where the Guildhall

stood, graceful and pleasing to the eye, and suddenly my senses seemed to leave me. I ran up to the big doors and pounded on them with my fists.

'Come out, come out into the streets and see what you are doing to the people!'

A startled face appeared in one of the windows for a moment and then disappeared.

'Yes, I mean you, you fat, idle, rich men, sitting in your ivory towers, not seeing what's going on around you.'

Iorwerth pulled at my arm. I brushed him aside, past caring what anyone thought of me. I stepped backwards and, picking up a large stone, threw it with all my might at one of the windows. There was a crash, and pieces of glass scattered over the ground.

There was a crowd around me suddenly and I heard someone call to me to run. Iorwerth gave me a push. 'The peelers!' he said. 'Get out of here, you.'

I pushed my way through the crowd, and then heard a commotion behind me. I turned to see Iorwerth being held, his arms pinioned to his sides. I moved to go to him, but I felt someone pull at my sleeve.

'Come by here, boyo!' I recognized the voice as Luther's even before I saw his face. He drew me away from the press of people and I found myself in the dimness of the chandler's shop.

'You're wasting your energy doing that, boyo.' Luther grinned. 'Get him some ale, Edgar. He looks as if he needs one.'

'What about Iorwerth?' I said. 'I think he's been taken. What will he think of me just deserting him like that?'

'He'll think it was damned sensible of you to get away. What's the point of you both going to prison?'

'My God!' I sat down suddenly. 'Do you think it will come to that? I've been a fool, haven't I?'

Luther nodded. 'Yes, but I don't think any harm's been done. If you'd been taken before a magistrate our chances of getting you into any other meetings would have gone down the privy.'

I drank the ale gratefully and thought about Elizabeth. How would she feel if she found out that I was responsible for her husband going to prison?

'What are you doing down here anyway, man?' Luther took the mug of ale from me and refilled it from the barrel that stood on the floor. 'I thought you were working up at the shop.'

'Yes,' I said, suddenly remembering that Dylan would be waiting for me. 'I'm supposed to be picking up some cargo he's been waiting for. I seem to do nothing but fail in my duty these days.'

'Oh, come off it, man.' Luther punched at my arm. 'You haven't let us down, have you?'

'I haven't done you much good either,' I answered quickly. 'We are no further on than we were before the petition was sent.'

'Well, you could be wrong there.' Luther sat down on the edge of the table, his big arms folded across his chest. 'Mr Michael has passed on a piece of news that has come back to me, and very encouraging it is, too.'

'Who is Mr Michael?' I asked, completely at a loss to understand what Luther was getting at.

'Well, he's only the Mayor of Swansea. What's the matter with you, boyo? Did you go to the meetings with your ears and eyes closed?' Luther shook his head in exasperation.

'Oh, yes, I remember,' I said quickly and not quite truthfully. 'What about him?'

'He's let it be known that his nephew, Dr William

Henry Michael, has been called upon to prepare a report on the cholera.' Luther smiled at me in triumph. 'The College of Physicians have asked him specially, so Swansea must be of interest to them.'

'Yes,' I said slowly, 'you must be right. At least someone is sitting up and taking notice.'

'There you are, see, boyo. Nothing's as bad as it seems. Perhaps after this a new and bigger waterworks company will come to Swansea, giving everyone clean drinking water instead of just the few.'

When I left the chandler's shop, I made my way up the hill and past the copper works towards Tip Row. The dust was thick in the air and I began to cough; my lungs had grown unaccustomed to the copper smoke already.

It gave me a strange feeling of nostalgia to step in through the door of the little house and to see Mamgu standing over a pot on the fire, her cheeks rosy and lined like an over-ripe apple.

'Davy, boy!' She came towards me, her eyes showing her delight. 'About time you came back to see me, you dandelion, you!'

I bent to kiss her cheek and she held my shoulder for a brief moment. She was not a woman for emotional demonstrations.

'Come and sit and have a glass of my parsnip wine.' She drew me to a chair and pushed me into it, then stood back, hands on hips, studying me.

'Big, you've grown. You are going to be even taller than your grandad was. But there is a look of trouble about you. Come on, Davy, tell me what's wrong.'

I sighed. 'There's no keeping anything from you women, is there?' I took some wine, trying to find a palatable way of explaining what had happened.

'It's Iorwerth,' I said slowly, and I saw alarm leap into her eyes. 'He's all right,' I said quickly. 'He's not hurt or anything, but he's been taken into custody.'

Mamgu sank down into a chair, rubbing the perspiration from her face with her apron.

'*Duw*, what's the boy done, then? Taken into custody, I can't believe it. My Iorwerth was always the quiet one of the boys.'

'It's partly my fault,' I admitted. 'I threw a stone at the Guildhall windows and, in the mix up that followed, he was arrested instead of me.'

She shook her head. 'What's going to happen to him? He won't be sent to the gaol, will he?'

'I don't know, Mamgu,' I said, 'but I'll speak to Dylan when I go back to *Siop Fawr*. He'll know what to do.'

'They sometimes keep men inside that gaol for weeks without bringing any charges. What if that happens to Iorwerth? Losing his freedom would drive him mad.'

'Try not to worry,' I said quickly. 'Something will be done to get him out of there as quickly as possible. If it comes to the worse, I can always own up and tell them it was I threw the stone.'

'Don't do that, Davy, boy,' she said quickly. 'They will only take you in too, it won't make them let Iorwerth go, not once they know you're from the same family.'

I knew she was talking sense – that was one thing I could rely on my grandmother for.

'Well, I'll think of something,' I said decisively, 'so don't fret about it.'

I had just finished speaking when Elizabeth stepped in through the doorway, a basket on her arm. She smiled when she saw me, and I got to my feet quickly, taking the basket from her just for an excuse to be near her for a moment.

'It's nice to see you.' She removed her bonnet and a piece of shining hair fell down to her shoulder so that she looked little more than a child. With impatient fingers she tucked it back into the ribbons. 'What brings you here?'

'Well—' I paused, uncertain how to tell her. 'It's Iorwerth. He's been arrested, but don't worry, we'll soon have him free again.'

'Oh, my God!' She sank down into a chair and looked up at me with large eyes. 'What did he do?'

'It was nothing,' I said. 'A bit of a disturbance, that's all. It wasn't even his fault really, it was mine.'

She looked at Mamgu. 'What's to be done?' She bit her lip, and I could see she was struggling hard not to break down and cry. Weakness of that sort was something my grandmother would not approve of.

'We will go up to *Siop Fawr* with our Davy, see what Dylan thinks about it. He knows all kinds of people, and if anyone can get Iorwerth out of that filthy gaol it'll be Dylan Morgan.'

She pulled on her shawl and tied a bonnet round her hair, and Elizabeth got to her feet, offering her arm.

'No, thank you.' Mamgu was determined to be independent. 'I'm quite able to manage a little walk without help.'

We went down the Row and Mamgu nodded to everyone we passed, calling out greetings in Welsh, knowing everyone by name. The thickness of the dusty air did not seem to bother her, though both Elizabeth and I began to cough as soon as we left the house.

'You youngsters are such weaklings!' she said in amusement. 'We old ones were bred with tough roots that cling on to life, come what may.'

She was a wonder. I watched her bravely climb the hill to the shop, gasping for breath, but too proud to admit to any weakness. She might be an old woman, but her courage and spirit were that of a young girl.

My mother gave a cry of astonishment when she saw us all arriving. She hurried out of the kitchen and led Mamgu inside, making small anxious clucking noises as my grandmother struggled to get her breath.

'*Duw*, why didn't you let Davy come up and fetch the horse and carriage?' she said. 'Mam, you'll kill yourself with your obstinate wish to be independent.'

'Hush, Catrin,' Mamgu waved her hand at me. 'Davy, tell you mother what's happened.'

'It's about Iorwerth,' I said, growing weary of the repetition. 'He's been taken by the police constables. We got in a bit of a disturbance down at the Guildhall. Nothing very much happened, but they've taken him to the station house, and we thought perhaps Dylan might know someone who could put in a word for him.'

'Dylan isn't here, Davy.' My mother looked at me reproachfully. 'You were gone so long he was worried about you, and with good cause it seems. You are not a child now, but still you can't be trusted to do a small errand.'

'Catrin, that's enough of that!' Mamgu was getting her breath back. 'You've heard the boy tell you there was some disturbance. Aren't you glad he's not in the hands of the constables too?'

'Oh, I suppose so, Mam, but why you always have to take Davy's part I don't know.'

'Sometimes you are unjust,' Mamgu said reasonably, 'and I do hate to see anyone being made the underdog for no good reason. What time do you expect Dylan back?'

'Any time.' My mother went to the window as if by sheer strength of will she could bring him home. 'He's taken Lotty with him, though she was complaining of a tummy-ache earlier and I'm a bit worried about her.'

'You worry too much.' Mamgu folded her hands across her lap. 'Where are the other girls? The house is very quiet.'

'Caroline is in her room doing some mending, and Vickie is helping Kate in the shop.' My mother stopped talking and stared at Mamgu. 'Are you all right?'

I noticed then that my grandmother was very white and her forehead was beaded with perspiration. She was holding herself stiffly erect, her mouth pursed as if in pain.

'Don't fuss,' she said, but her lips were turning blue, and even as she spoke she pitched forward, her hands pressed to her chest.

'Bring me some crushed foxgloves from the herb counter, Davy,' my mother said sharply. 'Mamgu is suffering from a fainting of the heart.'

SEVENTEEN

'If I'm going to die,' Mamgu said, 'I'm going to die in Tip Row, the same as your dad, so please help me get ready to go home, Catrin, there's a good girl.'

My mother sighed. 'There's a stubborn old woman you can be on times. You know it will be easier for me to look after you if you'll only stay up here at the shop for a while.'

Mamgu pushed back the bedclothes and swung her legs to the floor, and no-one would think to look at her that she had lain at death's door for almost a week.

'I'm grateful to you, girl.' Mamgu's tone was gentler. 'I know if it wasn't for your nursing I wouldn't be here now, but try to understand; there's nowhere like Tip Row for me. I've lived a lifetime there, after all; your dad took me there when we were married.' Her voice shook a little and I saw my mother give in.

'All right,' she said in resignation. 'I'll ask Dylan to hitch up the horses.'

'Good girl!' Mamgu said in satisfaction. 'Now you're talking sense. Come here, Davy. Get your shoulder under my arm and steady me a bit, there's a good boy.'

I moved forward and swung her into my arms; she was small and light, an easy burden.

'*Duw*,' she winked at me, 'forgetting you're a man grown to maturity, I am. I still think of you as the thin little lad who came down from England last year.'

Just as I reached the bottom of the stairs, Caroline came

344

in from the shop and her eyes widened as she saw me carrying Mamgu.

'You're not going home yet, are you?' she said, and her disappointment was obvious. Mamgu with her outspoken, no-nonsense ways had drawn an answering response from the moody young girl who, though only my half-sister, was the mirror image of me.

'I know,' Mamgu said with enthusiasm. 'Why don't you come home with me to Tip Row for a while? We'd be good company for each other. My poor Elizabeth tries her best, but she doesn't speak the Welsh and sometimes it's very hard to understand her, and now that Iorwerth is in gaol I expect she'll be grieving her heart out.'

Her words were doubly painful to me because, though I hated to think of Elizabeth being distressed, there was also a stab of bitter jealousy in me that was unworthy and despicable. I pushed the thoughts away and tried to appear cheerful.

'I think it would be an excellent idea. My mother would feel better for knowing that Caroline was with you.'

I placed Mamgu in a chair in the kitchen, and my mother came back into the room carrying a small bag.

'Dylan is very reluctant to see you go home, Mam,' she said, 'but we both know you'll have your own way sooner or later. Here, take these crushed herbs and steep them in water and take a cupful each night.'

'Right, girl,' Mamgu took the bag, 'but I may not have to do it for myself. I may have a little helper. I've asked Caroline if she will come and stay with me at Tip Row for a little while, that is if you and her father are willing, of course.'

Dylan came through the door just in time to hear what she said.

345

'Willing about what?' He bent over Mamgu's chair. 'What are you up to now?'

'Mamgu wants me to go and stay with her,' Caroline said soberly. 'I'd like to go, if you can spare me from the shop, Dad.'

'Yes, of course I can, though I'll miss you, mind. You've never been away from home before.'

'*Duw!*' Mamgu grinned. 'It's only down the road, Dylan. I'm not taking the girl to the ends of the earth.'

'I know.' He smiled at Caroline and ruffled her hair, and as she smiled back at him I had a glimpse of the real Caroline as she must have been before I came along, a fun-loving girl and the apple of her father's eye. It was no wonder she resented me.

'Well, come along, ladies,' Dylan said. 'I've got the carriage waiting outside.' He took Mamgu's arm and I hurriedly went to the other side of her, helping her from her chair and out into the bright sunshine.

She sank down into the coach and I could see that she wasn't as strong as she pretended to be. I pressed her hand gently.

'I'll be down to see you before very long. Now you be sure to rest and look after yourself. No standing for hours over the heat of the fire, cooking.'

She slapped at me playfully. 'There's a nerve of the boy to go telling me my business. I'll do what I like in my own home, and you can like it or lump it!'

Caroline and my mother settled themselves beside Mamgu, and Dylan clucked to the horses.

'Come on, you lazy animals!' He flicked the reins and the horses were spurred suddenly into movement. 'Don't forget to fetch the supplies from the docks, Davy,' he said, 'and don't worry if you've got to wait for the unloading. I'll be back to look after the shop in less than an hour.'

346

It was strangely quiet in the house when I went back inside. I peeped into the shop and saw Lotty standing on a box serving a customer with a packet of herbs.

'Where are the other two?' I asked quietly, and she jerked her head towards the store room.

'In there. I think Vickie is crying over Patrick again. There's nothing anyone can say to stop her crying, is there?'

She looked at me hopefully, her large eyes full of childish trust. I took a deep breath.

'I'll see what I can do, Lotty, but don't pin too much hope on me, will you?'

Vickie was sitting on a sack of meal, twisting a handkerchief between her white fingers. Her face was swollen and red from weeping, and at her side Kate was talking quietly.

'There is a time for everything,' she said gently. 'It says so in the Bible. A time for living and a time for dying, and we can't change it however much we might want to.'

'But Patrick was so young,' Vickie said brokenly. 'He hardly had any life at all.' She began weeping again, and Kate took her sister in her arms.

'There, there, cry it all out. You will feel better then, I promise you.'

There seemed nothing I could do, so I went quietly out into the shop again.

'She'll be all right,' I said softly to Lotty, who had finished serving and was sitting on the box, her skirts wound around her thin knees. She looked pale and upset, and I patted her shoulder awkwardly. 'Don't worry about Vickie,' I said. 'People do get over things in time.' I pinched her cheek. 'Go on, I'll watch the shop for a while; you go and get a cordial for you and your sisters, all right?'

The sun shimmered in through the doorway. I went and

stood for a while looking out into the streets. I wondered if I could manage to go and see Black Pearl again when I picked up the goods from the docks. She fascinated me; she was a strange exotic creature, and my body was feeling the need of relief that had been denied to me now that Susannah had left town and Rosie had been so tragically taken away from me.

Suddenly I was eager to be gone. I strode back into the shop and called through into the kitchen.

'Kate! I shall have to go down to the docks in a minute. Could you and the girls hitch up the horse and cart for me?'

She came down the passage holding out a cup. She smiled when she saw the heat in my face and gave me a dig in the ribs.

'What ails you then, why so impatient suddenly? Is the sun driving you mad with lust?'

'God!' I said in amazement. 'You are just as bad as my mother and Mamgu, reading my thoughts before I'm aware that I have them.'

'Drink this cordial,' she said. 'We'll see to the horse while you cool down a bit.' At the door she turned. 'There's only slow old Charlie left, mind, but if you take it easy he'll pull the cart nice and steady for you, but don't expect a great speed out of him and don't load the cart up too much or you'll kill him, right?'

'Right!' I said. 'I shall obey you to the letter, you bossy old woman, you.'

She laughed. 'Watch your tongue, Davy, or you'll come off the worse, I'm warning you.' She poked her tongue out at me. 'And please don't call me old; I'm the same age as you are.'

I served a customer or two before Lotty came to tell me the horse and cart were ready for me. She giggled behind her hand as I climbed up on the cart, and I wondered if my shirt tail was hanging out. Vickie and Kate stood in the doorway watching as I clucked my tongue at old Charlie. He obligingly moved forward a pace and then came to an abrupt stop. I frowned in bewilderment and clucked at him again, but he stood perfectly still, leaning forward slightly, as though a great weight was holding him fast. I jumped down and looked at the wheels to see if any of them could be caught against a stone. And when I looked up, the three girls, even Vickie who had forgotten her tears for a moment, were leaning against the shop wall convulsed with laughter.

'All right,' I said, 'I give in. What have you done to poor old Charlie?'

Lotty pointed to the railings, unable to speak, and when I looked I saw that the cart was on the other side with only the arms coming through to be hitched up to the horse.

'Very funny!' I said grumpily, knowing I'd been made a fool of, but then my sense of humour came back and I started to laugh too. Old Charlie seemed so bewildered with his ears pointing forward as he waited patiently to see what I would do to release him.

At last I was on my way to the docks. It was good to be up on the cart, feeling the sun and the cooling breeze against my face. I passed some of the courts in Greenhill and saw the scavengers picking up the refuse from the streets with their hands and carrying it down the narrow lane to where their carts stood. One of the men had dropped some damp ash and rubbish over his trousers and he stank to high heaven. He laughed jovially as he saw me wrinkle up my nose.

'Aye, it's not pleasant, is it, especially in this heat, but there's no other way of cleaning the courts, you see, man. They're too narrow to run the carts down, so we have to carry the stuff by hand.'

'I don't envy you,' I called as I spurred Charlie forward. God, I hadn't thought anything could be worse than working the copper, but I wouldn't be a scavenger for a year's wages paid each week.

I found Black Pearl sitting on her doorstep, her skirts up over her knees revealing her dark shimmering skin, and I felt desire so fierce it was all I could do not to leap down from the cart and possess her there and then.

'Come inside,' she said, and once in the cool dimness of her room she calmly drew off her clothes and stook naked before me. She was beautiful, her limbs long and clean with a shine like black marble. I put my hands out to her, almost afraid to touch, but she had no such inhibitions and she drew me down quickly on to the brilliant patchwork quilt.

'You have never tasted black fruit before?' she said, smiling. 'And I believe you never will again, Davy, so savour it well.'

I gave myself up then to the sweet longing that drove all sense of time and obligations from my head. She was so different from all I had experienced before, a vigorous and active partner, almost masculine in the fierceness of her desire, and when finally it was over, I don't know which of us was the more exhausted.

I touched her black breast with my fingertips and she smiled lazily, reaching out and brushing back my hair with a maternal gentleness that surprised me. 'Will you see me again?'

'Will I see you again?' she said, and shook her head. 'No, it is not meant for us to meet after today.'

'Why not?' I asked, disappointed. 'We were so good together, didn't you think so?'

She looked at me, her dark eyes inscrutable. 'After what

350

will happen tonight, I will go away, far from here, perhaps back to my own land.'

'What do you mean?' I asked, bewildered, but she shook her head and would say no more. I began to dress, and when I was ready to go I took her hand and kissed it. 'I'll never forget you.'

She smiled and nodded, and then closed her eyes and leaned back against the coloured quilt. Her breathing was deep and regular, almost as though she'd gone to sleep.

Outside, poor Charlie was standing, head bowed, trying to find a bit of shade. I led him out of the streets and down towards the docks where a cooling breeze came in from the sea. I breathed deeply of the tangy air and watched the bustling activity of the sailors unloading the ships. But as for my own cargo, I was to be unlucky; part of it had been mislaid and it seemed I would have to come back later when everything was sorted out.

The few sacks of goods I did have I loaded on to the cart, and gently led the horse out of the harbour and back up the hill. The carriage was outside *Siop Fawr* and it was clear that Dylan and my mother had only just returned from Tip Row.

'Oh, God!' My mother took off her bonnet and stared at me, her face white. 'Iorwerth has been sent home from the gaol, but he's not half well. You should see the colour of him.'

'What's wrong?' I asked. 'Haven't they been feeding him properly?'

'Well,' my mother considered my question. 'I suppose that's half of it, but I'd say he's going down with a fever. I'm very worried about him indeed.'

Dylan came into the kitchen just then and he sighed in exasperation.

351

'Don't be so daft, girl. You can't expect a man to spend a week in gaol and come out the same as he went in, can you?'

'I know,' my mother said, 'but you didn't hear what he told me about the prisoners who'd been sent down from Cardiff gaol.'

'What was that?' Dylan sat beside my mother and covered her hands with his own, and I saw her fingers curl around his.

'They were pushed straight into a part of the prison far removed from the rest of the inmates. The rumour went around that these men had the cholera.'

'Nonsense!' Dylan said, though there was a frown between his eyes. 'At times like this there are always rumours.'

My mother seemed reassured by his words. 'Yes, I suppose you're right. Anyway, I can't sit around the kitchen all day like this; I've got work to do.'

When she had gone into the shop to talk to the girls, Dylan looked across at me.

'I did hear about the rumours,' he said slowly, 'but it wasn't from Iorwerth's lips. One of the gaolers himself told me, but don't let on to your mother.'

I sat in silence for a moment, feeling a weight of guilt press down on me because it was my fault that Iorwerth had been sent to the damn place.

'Don't look so worried,' Dylan said quietly. 'It is just a rumour at the moment. Only time will tell if there is any truth to it.' He got to his feet. 'Now come and show me what stock you managed to get for the shop.'

Later that evening, I took the cart down to the docks again, but this time I had a younger, stronger horse who pulled on the rein, wanting to trot all the way. The cargo had been sorted now and it took me about an hour to load he cart. There was enough stuff there to last for several months.

Coming back through the town, the docks just a few yards behind me, I suddenly saw a door to the right of me pushed open and to my amazement William stood there, dressed for a journey. He saw me in the same instant, but he might have seen the devil himself, so white did he turn. He backed away and ran full tilt towards the road. I heard a scream and the frightened sound of horses, and I jumped down from the cart. But I was too late. William was lying dead, crushed beneath the wheels of an enormous carriage. Black Pearl had done her worst.

EIGHTEEN

It was a deep summer night in June and the scent of the flowers in the small garden outside drifted in through my open window. In spite of the comfortable bed in my father's house, I lay wide awake, the sheets pushed back from my limbs for coolness.

Over the last few weeks, the cholera had spread out thin fingers of fear and death encompassing not only Swansea but the surrounding areas of Merthyr and Neath. Nowhere was free of it, and there were whispers of hasty, indecent burials and even mass graves. There was no remedy that would work against the disease except, in some cases, the victim's own strength and over-riding will to live.

I sat up and pulled on my trousers. I might as well admit that sleep would not come and go downstairs. Perhaps a drink of brandy would set my nerves at rest.

I wandered through the darkened rooms that were familiar to me now, as familiar as the cramped rooms at Tip Row had been just a short time ago. I sat down in a chair and leaned back, closing my eyes, and I might have drifted off to sleep right there if I had not been startled by a sudden banging on the door.

When I opened it, Elizabeth stood on the step, her hair flowing free down her back, a shawl pulled on hastily to cover her shoulders. Her eyes were wild with fear.

'Oh, God help us!' She stumbled into my arms and I drew her inside, kicking the door closed with my foot.

'What's happened, Elizabeth?' I shook her gently. 'Try to calm down and tell me.'

She began to cry. 'Oh, Davy, help us. I think Iorwerth's caught the cholera!'

'I'll call Mother,' I said quickly. 'Sit down here and drink this brandy, and don't let yourself get upset. It may be a false alarm.'

I ran up the stairs two at a time and knocked on the door of my parents' bedroom. My mother had heard the noise and knew in her intuitive way that something was wrong.

'Iorwerth's ill.' I couldn't bring myself to speak the dreaded word, but my mother's eyes told me of her fear.

'Dylan,' she said gently to my father, 'would you hitch up the horse and cart? I shall have to go down to Tip Row and see what can be done.'

'I shall come with you,' he said at once, and I saw the naked fear in his eyes that he might lose her, and it was only then I realized the depth of his love.

She shook her head. 'No, the girls will need you here with them.' She hugged him briefly and he buried his face in the whiteness of her neck.

When they released each other, I spoke up. 'I will come with you, Mam. You might need a strong arm to help lift Iorwerth when you see to him.'

She looked at me steadily. 'You know the dangers, my son, but you're a man and must make your own decision.'

'Come on,' I said, 'let's get the things you will need. There's no time to lose.'

I helped Elizabeth up on to the cart. She had calmed herself a little, but when she saw my mother she clasped her arm tightly.

'Catrin, thank God you are willing to come. I don't know what I'd have done if you'd refused.'

'Iorwerth is my brother,' Mam said simply, and I felt a

lump come to my throat. Dylan looked up at me as I took the reins.

'God go with you both,' he said. 'Come back safely to us all. We'll be waiting.' He leaned across me and took Elizabeth's hand. 'If anyone can work the miracle, Catrin can. So keep your spirits up.'

I clucked my tongue and the horse moved away, and I noticed my mother craning her neck to look back at Dylan until we turned the corner and he was out of sight.

It took little more than a quarter of an hour to reach Tip Row, but it seemed an endless journey, with all three of us silent and restrained. I jumped down from the cart, and Mamgu was at the door waiting to take my mother straight to Iorwerth's room.

'He's bad, Catrin,' she said in a low voice, but even her warning did not prepare me for the shock of seeing Iorwerth's condition.

His cheekbones stood out gaunt with deep hollows beneath them, as if the flesh had already melted from his bones. His colour was bad and his breath came in harsh bursts. Mamgu moved forward and wiped the sweat from his forehead.

My mother wasted no time in rolling back her sleeves and setting to work. She took some flannel pieces and a jar of vinegar from her bag.

'Poke up the fire, Davy.' She handed me the vinegar. 'And heat this up for me.'

She mixed some mustard with the hot vinegar and made a poultice of it, spreading it thickly on one of the pieces of flannel.

'Pull back the bedclothes, Elizabeth,' she instructed, 'and you, Davy, pour some of the hot vinegar into a bowl.'

She placed the poultice on Iorwerth's stomach, and as he moaned she forced some laudanum between his lips.

'Come on, Iorwerth,' she said loudly, 'fight the damn cholera, there's a good boy. Don't let it beat you!'

She began rubbing his legs and feet with the hot vinegar.

'You work on his arms, Elizabeth,' she said. 'We must keep the warmth in him.'

They worked all through the night, and Mamgu, weariness overcoming her, dozed in a chair. The scene took on an air of unreality for me. I don't know how the women continued in their tireless efforts, but work they did, renewing the poultice and heating up more vinegar. I think I must have fallen into a light sleep, when suddenly I heard fear, hard and cold, in Elizabeth's voice.

'My God, Catrin, is he dead?' She leaned over the bed, staring into her husband's face, and when I moved nearer I too thought we had lost him.

'No!' My mother spoke crisply. 'This is all part of the sickness. It's bad, I won't pretend otherwise, but people have been known to overcome even this stage of the cholera.'

'It's daylight.' She looked towards the window. 'Go you, Elizabeth, down to Thomas the medicine shop and get some pills made up.'

Elizabeth looked startled. 'But, Catrin, shouldn't I stay here to help you?'

My mother shook her head. 'Davy can help me. Now go on with you, the walk in the fresh air will do you good. Tell Thomas I want twelve grains of cayenne pepper, six grains of opium, six drops of oil of cloves, and enough aromatic confection to make twelve pills.'

She looked up at me. 'Give Elizabeth sixpence, Davy; it shouldn't cost above that.' She was still working swiftly, rubbing Iorwerth's limbs, and I couldn't tell what she was thinking. I saw Elizabeth to the door and watched her mingle with the copper men as they made their way down the Row, silent in the early morning warmth.

'It's better for her to have a break,' my mother said when Elizabeth was gone. 'There's really nothing we can do now but wait.'

'The pills,' I said, 'won't they help? You made them seem so important.'

'They can help a bit at the outset of the sickness, but I'm afraid Iorwerth is too far gone.'

'Will he pull through?' I asked in a whisper, and my mother's fine eyes looked straight at me.

'I can't answer that, Davy. Only God knows.' She sank down into a chair and Mamgu sat up, at once wide awake, and in a movement poked up the fire and settled the kettle on the coals.

'A nice cup of tea,' she said, 'will do us all good. Catrin, wash the smell of vinegar from your hands before you drink, otherwise it will turn your stomach.'

My mother obediently washed her hands in the bowl placed on the table. Her hair was falling forward and Mamgu gently drew it back, tucking it into place.

'It reminds me of when you were a girl, Catrin,' she said softly, 'and all the men from miles around were busy trying to court you.'

'That was a long time ago,' my mother said sadly. 'I'm feeling as old as the hills today, Mam.' They stood close together, each trying to infuse strength into the other, and even though flowery words were never spoken in this house, love was like a strong gold thread woven into the lives of the people in it.

The door opened quietly and Elizabeth stood there. She paused for a moment as if afraid to enter, and my mother smiled reassuringly at her.

'There's no change. Come on in and give me the pills.

358

I'll try to get him to take two straight away, and you can rub his legs and feet again.'

Elizabeth went to the foot of the bed and stood staring down at her husband.

'I tried to get the doctor to come,' she said. 'I've enough money put by to pay him.' She looked quickly at my mother. 'Not that I doubt your ability, Catrin, don't think that for a minute, but I wanted to give Iorwerth every chance.' She brushed her hair back from her forehead wearily. 'The doctor was too busy, out on his calls to his regular patients, and all of them rich, I dare say.'

'Don't fret yourself,' my mother said, taking Elizabeth's arm. 'A doctor couldn't do any more than we ourselves have done. There's not enough known about the sickness, you see, girl. We're fighting in the dark, so to speak, and that applies to rich as well as poor. In this we are all equal.'

'Come and drink your tea before you start working again.' Mamgu placed the cups on the table. 'You too, Elizabeth, you'll be no good to anybody if you faint away, will you?'

We sat at the table, avoiding each other's eyes, and I felt sick and helpless as I saw the way Elizabeth's small hand trembled.

Iorwerth moved slightly in the bed, and immediately Elizabeth was kneeling down at his side. He looked at her, his eyes alight, and then he smiled weakly at the rest of us.

'Don't cry after me,' he whispered. 'There's no pain now, only peace, and I'm grateful for it.'

'You are going to be all right, my love.' Elizabeth took his hand in hers. 'See how the fever has left you?' She made an effort to smile. 'Catrin has worked so hard over you, you're not going to let her down?'

'She has brought comfort to me.' His voice seemed

359

fainter. 'She knows my feelings better than I do.' He looked at me. 'Comfort Elizabeth.'

He stopped speaking, too weary to go on, and Elizabeth touched his face.

'Do you want me to rub your feet again, my love? You feel so cold.'

He touched her hair for a brief moment and then his hand fell back on to the cover and his eyes were without light.

Elizabeth leaned across his body, gathering him close to her, as if she could hold back death itself. My mother spoke to her softly.

'Come away, girl. There is nothing more we can do for him now.'

I expected Elizabeth to become hysterical, at least to break down and cry, but she simply drew the blanket up over Iorwerth, tucking it round him as if he was a child asleep.

'God rest his soul.' Mamgu touched his forehead gently with her fingertips, her eyes closed as if she was in physical pain.

I took Elizabeth's arm and led her to a chair. She was passive, obeying me as if she had no will of her own. She sat staring down at the ground, her head and shoulders bowed, her hands still, almost lifeless as they rested in her lap. I longed to hold her to me, to comfort her as Iorwerth had instructed me to, but I knew there would be no answering response in her. Her shock had been too great.

Wearily, my mother packed her bag and tidied up the room, burning the pieces of flannel on the fire. When she had finished, she looked at me. 'Take Mamgu and Elizabeth up to *Siop Fawr*,' she said. 'I'll do what is necessary here. And tell your father I won't be long.'

'I'm staying here, too,' Mamgu said flatly. 'I saw my son

360

come into the world and I will see him into the next with proper ceremony.'

'Please, Mam.' My mother frowned. 'You know your heart isn't as strong as it once was. Why not go with Davy on the cart?'

'The only way I'll leave Tip Row is feet first to the cemetery. I'm a stringy, tough old bird, make no mistake about it. I'm staying, Davy, so you may as well go now.'

'What about the funeral arrangements?' I asked in a low voice, trying to spare Elizabeth's feelings. I need not have worried; she didn't seem to hear a word I said.

'Dylan will know what to do,' my mother said calmly, though I could see she was almost overcome with grief and tiredness.

Her hands were shaking and I put my arms around her, so proud of her unfailing courage and yet unable to speak to her of it.

For a moment she leaned against me, sighing softly, her head dropping against my shoulder. Then she was practical once more.

'Do you think you could bring the cart back here for me later?' She glanced at my grandmother, and I knew she was hoping to persuade her to change her mind about coming up to the shop.

'Of course,' I said quickly. 'Give me about an hour to get Elizabeth up there and settled, and I'll come straight back.'

I opened the door and, taking Elizabeth's arm, led her outside. The sun was warming the cobbles in spite of the early hour, and the smoke hung like a pall over the houses, low and menacing, the particles of copper dust glinting like gems.

'So much for the owners' argument that copper keeps away sickness,' I said ironically, but my mother couldn't answer; she just shook her head, and I could see she was very close to tears.

Just as I was helping Elizabeth up into the cart, I felt a tap on my shoulder and turned to see Luther. He took off his cap and scratched his head.

'There's sorry I am to hear there's the cholera come to your family,' he said. 'It's a bad sickness, man. Saw it before, in the '30s, I did. There's not much to be done against it.'

'It's bad all right,' I said. 'I'm just taking my sister-in-law back to the shop; she's suffering from shock.' I was about to turn away when Luther stopped me.

'I know this is a bad time, but it may hearten you to hear that Mr Clark's report is out. *Duw!* He says it all, man, the filth of some of the courts he describes in detail, and his recommendation is that Swansea be put under the Health Act.'

I tried to feel pleased for Luther's sake, though it seemed to have come a little bit late for my family.

'Very good indeed, Luther!' I shook his hand warmly. 'Now please excuse me.'

I climbed up on to the cart, and Elizabeth was sitting motionless beside me. She did not even move when I flicked the reins and set the horse moving.

'Elizabeth!' I spoke her name sharply, the events of the long night catching up with me, making me impatient. 'For God's sake speak to me. Say something!'

She did not turn her head, but I saw her lips tremble and I leaned closer to hear what she was saying.

'Oh, God.' Her voice was almost unrecognizable. 'It's a sad thing to die in summer.'

NINETEEN

The grip of the cholera had tightened its hold and no-one was spared. It came to young and old alike, and only occasionally left a live victim in its wake.

Elizabeth, mourning grievously for her dead Iorwerth, saw none of it because every morning, after being forced to rise from bed, she would sit in the window staring sightlessly out and growing more gaunt as the days progressed.

The *Cambrian* published an article on the methods of avoiding cholera, but these were the selfsame means adopted by my mother weeks ago. The people were told to keep their homes clean and to open windows wide, to eat only fresh food, and throw away stale bread or fish. Avoid drunkenness. The instructions went on and on, and at last I threw down the paper in exasperation.

'Hell and damnation!' I said bitterly. 'Can't the authorities see that we need fresh clean water supplies and proper drainage in the town?'

'Get down off your soap-box, Davy.' Kate gave me a small push. 'There's enough work to be done by here without you wasting your time reading and cursing. Give me a hand with this sack of meal, will you?'

'God!' I said. 'You are learning fast how to nag a man. Getting ready for marriage, are you? Getting that sharp tongue of yours in shape.'

'Ha!' She put both hands on her hips and stared at me.

363

'And who would have me? I'm not exactly the beauty of the family, am I?'

I looked at her properly then, and was startled to see how pale she was. There were dark shadows under her eyes, and lines of pain etched themselves from nose to mouth.

'What's wrong, Kate?' I could not quite hide the alarm I felt, and Kate made an effort to smile.

'Nothing's wrong,' she said, 'except that I'm working too hard, and that's more than can be said for you!'

In spite of her words I could see she was far from well. She bent over the sack of meal as if to lift it, but she staggered and if I hadn't been there to catch her she would have fallen.

'Silly damn legs of mine,' she said, leaning against me gratefully. 'I don't understand why they're so weak.'

'And who's swearing now?' I sat her gently on a chair. 'Some lady, this sister of mine. How long have you felt like this?'

'A day, maybe two, it's hard to say. I thought I could work it off.'

She seemed to sway away from me and her eyes closed suddenly as I tried to steady her with my arm.

'Mam,' I called through to the shop, keeping my voice steady; there was no point in frightening everyone to death. 'Could you come here at once?'

My mother stood in the doorway, her eyes wide as they rested on Kate.

'Oh, my God, no!' she said in a low voice, and for a brief instant she just stood there, eyes closed, as if she was summoning up all her strength. 'Bring her upstairs, Davy,' she said at last. 'I'll give her two of the cholera pills straight away, just in case.'

Kate began to shiver in my arms. 'I'm sorry,' she said,

and her eyes were over-bright as they looked into mine. 'I don't want to be any trouble. I'm sure it's just a chill and it will go away in a day or two.'

My mother undressed her and tucked her into bed, talking soothingly all the while.

'We'll build the fire up in here,' she said softly, 'and you just take these pills for me and we'll soon see an improvement.'

She nodded to me. 'Bring more fuel for the fire, there's a good boy.' She followed me to the door. 'Ask Dylan to come up, but try not to alarm him. We have to decide whether it would be better to close the shop or not.'

'I'm going to be all right, aren't I?' Kate said, lifting herself up in the bed. 'It's not going to be anything serious, is it?'

'Of course you're going to be all right.' My mother went to her side quickly. 'You are a young healthy girl. You have plenty of spirit, too. You'll be fine.'

Dylan was just unloading some goods from the cart, stacking them into the store room. He handled the sacks easily, and even in the stress of the moment I couldn't help feeling a dart of pride in his youthfulness.

'It's Kate,' I said, 'she's not very well. Mam has put her into bed. She would like you to go upstairs.'

He stared at me for a moment and I think he read my fear in my eyes. He dropped the sack he was wielding and ran, and I heard him taking the stairs two at a time.

I finished the unloading and unhitched the horse, rubbing him down before leading him into the stables. Shortly after, Dylan returned, and he looked grey and harassed.

'It might not be what we fear,' he said. 'There are other fevers that start off with the same symptoms but are not so virulent. Let's pray that Kate be spared.'

I wanted to take his mind off it. 'Shall we keep the shop open?' I said. 'After all, we do sell only good food, and the remedies seem to be much in demand; perhaps we owe it to the people to keep going as long as we can.'

Dylan shook his head as if to clear it. 'Yes,' he said, 'I think you're right there, son. Oh, Christ!' He put his hand over his eyes. 'It can't be the cholera, not in this house.'

By evening it had become clear that Kate did have the cholera. Her shivering had become a thing of dreadful violence; she jerked and shuddered beneath the sheets and sometimes her eyes would open and she would stare ahead, but see nothing. My mother worked hard over her, rubbing her limbs with hot vinegar as she'd done with Iorwerth.

'I think I'd better give her some laudanum,' she said at last. 'She'll use up what little strength she's got if she keeps shivering like this.'

Gradually Kate seemed to become calm. She lay pale and fragile against the pillows, her face small and pinched under the cloud of her hair.

Vickie came upstairs with a bowl of thin broth for Kate; she sat at the bedside and looked questioningly at my mother.

'No, don't try to give it to her now.' My mother rested her hand on Vickie's red hair. 'Keep it warm for later. I think she needs to rest for a while.'

'Well, come and have supper, then,' Vickie said softly. 'You have to keep up your strength too, Mam. We would all be lost without you.'

'You go, Davy,' Mam said. 'You need to eat. You've been working in the shop all day. I'll come down in a little while when I'm sure Kate is well and truly asleep.'

At the bottom of the stairs I came face to face with

Caroline. Her usual hostility was gone and there was a look almost of pleading on her face.

'Will she be all right, Davy? Please tell me the truth. I'd rather know what I have to face.'

'I won't lie to you, Caroline,' I said gently. 'She's young and strong, and my mother is giving her the best attention it's possible to get. It all depends on her own strength.'

She closed her eyes and leaned against me, her head on my shoulder, and we stood there for a few minutes, more close than I ever thought we'd be.

We sat round the table in silence, each of us making a pretence of eating, and at last it was Lotty who pushed her plate away.

'I'm sorry, Vickie,' she said, 'I know you cooked mutton pies specially, but I just feel full up.' She got down from her chair. 'May I be excused, Dad?' she said sombrely, and Dylan nodded.

'Yes, of course, girl, no-one is going to force you to eat. To tell the truth, I don't feel much like eating, myself.'

We all watched in silence as Lotty left the room and went slowly up the stairs, and we all knew that she was leaving so that she wouldn't show her tears in front of us.

Dylan got to his feet. 'I'm going for the doctor,' he said resolutely. 'He's got to come to see to my Kate, whatever objections he may put up.'

Vickie left the table, too, and stood beside him, her arm encircling his waist.

'Let me come with you, Dad,' she said. 'I will be company for you.'

He ruffled her hair. 'No, Chicken, stay here. I will ride faster alone.'

Vickie's eyes filled with tears, but I could see she was struggling to hold them back.

'I feel it's my fault,' she said in a small voice. 'If I hadn't visited Patrick when he was ill, this might not have happened.'

'No, Vickie,' Dylan tipped her face up, 'that is foolish talk. I might have stood next to someone on the docks who was sickening with the cholera, and Davy here might have touched hands with a customer in the shop who was infected. And wasn't Catrin down at Tip Row nursing her own brother?' He smiled at her reassuringly. 'You can't blame yourself any more than the rest of us. I'm going now, but I won't be long.'

We all listened in silence to the sound of horse's hooves against the cobbles as Dylan rode away, but I don't think any one of us believed he would return with the doctor. When he did, Vickie led the way jubilantly up the stairs, and Caroline put her hand shyly on my arm.

'Trust our father to get his own way,' she said. 'He could charm the chickens from their eggs, he could.'

The doctor's visit did not last long. He did not come into the kitchen, but I could hear him outside in the passage talking to Dylan.

'The girl is getting the best nursing I've ever seen in Swansea,' he said in a dry voice. 'If anyone will pull through this dreadful scourge, she will.'

Dylan came into the kitchen. 'Well,' he seemed bemused, 'I paid the man just for the privilege of hearing him tell Catrin she was doing all the correct things!'

We all laughed. I think it was relief in knowing that everything possible had been done. Vickie made a pot of tea, and it was almost like a celebration, especially when my mother joined us, saying that she could leave Kate now that she was sleeping naturally.

In the morning, Kate was able to sit up and drink a little cordial; she was still pale and very weak.

'Please God the cholera has finished with *Siop Fawr*,' my mother said, tucking back a strand of hair. 'I think I can go to bed tonight and really sleep for once.'

The next day I found Lotty in the stables, lying on the ground, her knees drawn up to her stomach, a grimace of pain distorting her small face.

'How long have you been like this?' I said quickly, alarmed by the heat that came from her body.

'Only a day or two, Davy,' she said in a thin voice. 'It's only my old stomach, a bit of gripe, I expect. I couldn't say anything, not with Kate so bad.'

I picked her up in my arms and carried her into the house, and my mother, taking one look, undressed Lotty and put her straight into bed. Lotty lay there, looking over the sheet with the eyes of a frightened animal.

'It's the cholera, isn't it?' she said with such a sense of resignation that I wanted to hit out at someone, those faceless councillors who opposed any new ideas of improving the town.

'Come on, Davy,' my mother said, knowing as always what I was feeling. 'Don't waste valuable energy on hating, just help me with Lotty.'

Even as I helped my mother to rub hot vinegar into the pitifully small limbs, I had a feeling it was all useless, but for my mother's sake I kept on trying. One by one, the girls crept into the room, and then Dylan, who had been closing up the shop, came and stood by the bedside.

'Oh, God, Catrin,' he said in a whisper, 'we're going to lose her.'

I couldn't bear it. I handed the vinegar and a cloth to Caroline and left the room, going as silently as I could down the stairs.

No one was in the kitchen except for Elizabeth, who as usual was sitting in the widnow, staring at nothing. In sudden anger I took her hands in mine, drawing her to her feet, forcing her to look up at me.

'How can you be so selfish?' I said, and shook her hard so that her tangled hair flew across her face. 'You just retreat into a world of your own grief, when that little girl upstairs is dying with dignity and courage! The rest of us who so far have escaped the cholera may go down with it at any time. You could be of help, don't you realize that?'

Tears ran down my cheeks, and though it may not be manly, at that moment I did not care. Suddenly I felt Elizabeth's hands touch my face.

'Do not cry, Davy, love,' she said, but there were tears in her own eyes and we clung together in mutual need and grief. I don't know how long we stood like that, but when we drew apart the clouds that had been in Elizabeth's eyes had vanished and she was her old self.

'I will wash and clean myself up,' she said, 'and then I will see what help I can give Catrin.'

We went upstairs together, and even from the doorway I could hear that Lotty's breath had grown harsher. Her skin was cold to the touch, as though she was already dead.

'I'd better give her a little more laudanum.' My mother went to the bedside, but Lotty's eyes flickered open and she shook her head almost imperceptibly.

'No,' she gasped, 'I want to be with you all for as long as possible. I will go to sleep soon enough.'

Vickie turned away from the bed with a muffled cry, and Caroline put a protective arm around her.

'Please,' Lotty could barely whisper, 'I want to see Kate just this once.'

Dylan nodded. 'I'll wrap her up in a blanket and bring her in to you, Lotty, *cariad*. You shall see Kate, don't fret.'

He returned quickly and I could see by the high lift of Kate's head and the firm way her mouth was set that she had been warned what to expect. She sat on the edge of the bed, still so weak she could hardly hold herself upright and had to be supported by Dylan's arm.

'Well, Lotty,' she said gently, 'the cholera thinks it can play merry old hell with us, but we'll prove it can't.'

I couldn't take any more. I left the room and went silently down the stairs. At the door I stopped, and Elizabeth had come behind me.

'Davy,' she said in anguish, 'it was cruel of you to wake me out of my stupor so that I had to see this.'

'It is life,' I said, past all dissembling. 'It just has to be lived, but now and again we all need a reprieve from its harshness.'

'Where are you going?' There was fear in her voice, and I touched her hand gently.

'Just out walking for a while. No harm shall come to me, I promise, and when I return perhaps I will be better able to cope with everything.'

I walked out in the cool of the evening air, surprised to find it had almost grown dark. I walked through the streets that were emptier now that the cholera had visited the town with such a voracious appetite, and soon I came out on the green where I used to meet Susannah. That seemed to be a hundred years ago, not merely a matter of months.

'Excuse me, sir.' A woman was tapping my arm, and at first I thought she was looking for customers. Then I saw it was Joanie.

'What are you doing here?' I said in surprise. 'I thought you would have left town with Susannah.'

'I did, sir.' She began to cry softly. 'Oh, sir, I've come here looking for you night after night. She begged me to tell you what had happened.'

'Tell me, then,' I said gently, 'whatever it is. I'm not going to bite your head off.'

'She died, sir. The cholera got her after all, and she said to tell you that in the end she wasn't frightened at all, just sad that she didn't bear the child after all.'

'Oh, God!' I said, and for a moment I was silent, not believing the appalling toll the cholera was taking. 'You did right to tell me, Joanie,' I said.

Dispirited and bone weary, I returned to *Siop Fawr*. The lights were all on and for a moment I hoped that against all odds Lotty had recovered. One look at my mother's face told me I was wrong. She took my arm, resting her head against my shoulder.

'It's all over,' she said. 'Lotty is dead.'

TWENTY

Lotty's death left a gap in all our lives. The house seemed empty without her sharp, bright chatter, and yet each of us tried to hide our grief so as to spare the rest of the household.

I saw my father cry just once when we were washing ourselves down after working in the shop all day. He had walked into the kitchen and unthinkingly called for Lotty to bring him a washing cloth. His eyes closed as if in pain, and then I saw him cup his hands in the water and cover his face. I was stirred to the depths of my being.

'Dad,' I said gently in Welsh, 'there is no shame in tears.'

We did not touch and yet we were closer then than any father and son could hope to be.

'Grief is a hard, bitter thing, Davy,' he said, 'but you make it easier to bear.'

I wished then, with an intensity that hurt me, that I'd grown up with this man, sat on his knee, been his beloved son from babyhood. It was too late for that now, but if the cholera spared us I would not try and deny our mutual love any longer.

But the cholera had not finished with us yet. A week after we had buried Lotty in her tiny grave, Caroline fell sick of fever, shivering violently, sweat beading the darkness of her skin that had been tanned by the summer sun.

'We must not despair,' my mother said, busily pouring vinegar into a pot for heating. 'The sickness does not always strike with the same force; sometimes, as in Kate's case, it can be overcome.'

Her words cheered us, as they were meant to, and we all set to with good heart, cutting up squares of flannel and mixing mustard poultices.

In the middle of all the activity, there was a knock on the door.

'I'll go,' I said. 'Perhaps it's a customer for the shop, wondering why we haven't yet opened up the doors.'

Rhian stood on the step, her long hair loose on her shoulders, her eyes hostile as they rested on me, and I wondered if she knew how the manner of her son's death had come about.

'Come inside,' I held the door open for her, 'but I think I should warn you there is sickness here.'

She shrugged. 'It is everywhere, there's no getting away from it. When it marks you out, there's no running away from it.'

'Mam,' I called up the stairs, 'can you come down for a minute? It's Huw's wife come to see you.'

My mother, her sleeves rolled above her elbows, her face flushed from her exertions, came down the stairs as fast as her long skirts would allow.

'What's wrong, Rhian?' she said anxiously. 'Is our Huw sick with the fever?'

Rhian shook her head. 'No, not Huw. It's Mamgu. She's in her bed and asking for you. Huw's with her now until you come, but I have to get back to the farm.'

'*Duw!*' My mother looked at me in anguish. 'What can I do, Davy? I can't leave Caroline, not yet, when I think I'm beating the old sickness.'

Elizabeth put down the flannel she was cutting and put her hand on my mother's shoulder.

'I'll go down to Tip Row, Catrin. I'll look after Mamgu until you are able to follow me.'

'I'll go with you,' I said quickly. 'I think I know enough of the treatment methods to be of good use.'

My mother nodded. 'Yes, that's the best we can do for the moment, but tell Mamgu I won't be long; explain how it is up here.'

'Catrin!' Dylan called from the bedroom. 'Will you come up here a minute, *cariad*?'

'Go on, Mam,' I said. 'I know what I've got to take to Mamgu, and don't worry, she'll be well looked after. You can't be everywhere now, can you?'

Rhian got to her feet. 'Well, I'm sorry, Catrin, that I can't do more, but I've got my own family to worry about.' She went to the door. 'Two of my cousins are staying up at the farm with me and that makes it worse, but if it's fresh food you want, you can have any amount from the farm.'

'Thank you for coming, anyway,' my mother said. 'I'll be getting back to Caroline now.'

It was awkward with just Rhian and Elizabeth and me standing in silence in the kitchen.

'Shall I give you a ride on the cart to Tip Row?' Rhian said, and I knew the offer had cost her some effort.

'Thank you,' I smiled at her, 'but I'll just take one of the horses from the stable. Elizabeth and I can ride together.'

Elizabeth was already packing a bag with the things we needed to take, and it was left to me to see Rhian safely on her way. She looked down at me from the seat of the cart and it was hard to read the expression on her face.

'I can't forgive you for your enmity towards my son,' she said slowly, 'but that does not blind me to the fact that he was wrong. We will never be friends, David Richards, but I do give you respect. I believe you are a just man.' She turned away from me then and clucked to the horse, urging him forward, and somehow I felt she had absolved me from any blame in respect of William's death.

'I'm ready, then,' Elizabeth said at my side, and I turned to her, grateful for her very presence. 'I've told Catrin we're going.' She smiled reassuringly. 'Together we'll look after Mamgu so well that she's bound to get better.'

It was good to sit behind her on the horse, my arm encircling her, the scent of her hair in my nostrils. I almost forgot that these were the days of the cholera and that sickness walked the streets and courts we were passing through.

Huw was sitting at Mamgu's side when I opened the door of the little house in Tip Row. He smiled his relief when he saw Elizabeth behind me.

'Thank God you've come.' His words were meant for both of us. 'She's sleeping now, and I don't think she seems quite so bad as she was when I sent for Catrin.'

Elizabeth put a hand gently on Mamgu's forehead. 'It's quite cool to the touch,' she said. 'Please God it's not the cholera at all.'

'My mother will be coming down later,' I said to Huw. 'She's got her hands full looking after Caroline.' I sighed. 'If my mother doesn't get some rest soon, she'll go down with some sickness or other herself.'

Huw nodded. 'She could never stand to see other people suffering; she always had to be in there giving what help she could. She was like that even as a girl.'

He pulled on his coat. 'I'd better get back to the farm now, but I asked the doctor who lives near me to come down and look at Mamgu; he should be here any time, he's a good man, better than most doctors.' He paused for a moment at the door. 'If she gets any worse, send Elizabeth up for me and I'll come straightaway.'

I watched him walk away down the Row. The copper dust hung over his head like a cloud and he coughed a little, his big shoulders shaking. He turned the corner then and was out of sight.

'Davy,' Elizabeth said softly, 'I think Mamgu is waking up. Come and let her see you.'

We both stood beside the bed waiting for her to recognize us. She smiled like a sleepy child and held up her hand.

'There's good of you both to come, but I'm all right. I told our Huw I didn't have the old cholera, only he wouldn't listen. Stubborn, he is, like all the men in our family.'

'How are you feeling, Mamgu?' I said. 'And I want the truth, now.'

'Weak,' she said, 'but the fever is gone, see?' She smiled. 'And I'd like a cup of tea.'

She was propped up against the pillows when the doctor came. He grinned when he saw her and bent his tall thin frame over to have a better look at her.

'Your son is that concerned about you, Mrs Owen,' he said. 'He might have known an old bird like you would not be killed off that easily. You are the healthiest looking cholera victim I've ever seen!'

'Cup of tea, Doctor?' Elizabeth said, smiling. 'I'm sure you could do with a rest.'

'Aye,' he said, 'I'd like to take the weight off my feet for a few minutes, and that's the truth.'

'Well,' I sat beside him, 'we are lucky you've even bothered to come. It's hard getting a doctor, at least in this part of the town.'

377

He nodded, a wry smile on his face. 'I know, boy, but there's another side to the story, mind.'

'I'd like to hear it,' I said, and Elizabeth frowned at me warningly.

'Doctor Thomas is not here to be harassed,' she said. 'I'm sure he gets quite enough to do without you arguing with him.'

He laughed. 'Your wife is putting you in your place, which is, of course, her right; but explain I will, anyway.'

I looked quickly at Elizabeth. Her cheeks had reddened, but she said nothing.

'It's like this, boy.' The doctor went on speaking, unaware of his error. 'We have patients who pay us all the year round to look after their health. Without them we could not make a living.' He paused to make sure I'd taken his point. 'Well,' he continued, 'when there is an epidemic of this nature, they naturally expect us to care for them first. They don't like us treating the poor in case we carry the sickness with us when we leave them, and can you honestly blame them?'

'Put like that, I can see your point,' I agreed, though very reluctantly. 'Can't something be done about it?'

I pushed back my chair, unable to sit still.

'Something is being done about it,' he said, 'through people like you who want Swansea put under the Health of Towns Act. That is the right way to go about it. Condemning us doctors is unjust and fruitless.'

He got to his feet. 'I am going now, and I think I can safely say that my patient is going to make a rapid recovery.' He smiled at Mamgu. 'I will call in and see Huw and tell him my diagnosis. He will be very happy to hear it, I'm sure.' He raised his hat. 'Goodbye to you. God go with you.'

Elizabeth saw him to the door and I took Mamgu's hand in mine.

378

'I'll ride up to *Siop Fawr* and tell my mother that she need not rush over here. She will be so relieved to know you are all right.'

'Go on, you, Davy, boyo,' Mamgu said. 'I know your mam will work herself into the ground if someone doesn't stop her. Perhaps she will come and stay with me for a while when the sickness is all over. She can have a proper rest then.'

'A good idea,' I said. 'I won't be gone long. Are you sure you two women will be all right?'

'Of course!' Elizabeth smiled up at me. 'We're not little helpless children, are we, Mamgu?'

'Right, then.' I went to the door. 'Try and rest, the both of you. I want a fine welcome when I get back.'

It was cool outside and even as I rode the horse through the streets and out into the fields I felt a sense of freedom that was like a balm after all the sickness and death I had witnessed in the past months. Perhaps now, with the coming of the autumn, the fevers would come less frequently and the cholera die out naturally.

My feelings of optimism were doomed not to last. As I entered the doors of *Siop Fawr* I heard the sound of weeping. I went forward and saw Vickie sitting on the stairs, her hands covering her face, her red hair tangled on her shoulders.

I took her in my arms, rocking her gently, not needing to ask what had happened. My mother came slowly from the bedroom, her face grey with fatigue and her eyes shadowed with lost hope.

'I lost her, Davy,' she said. 'I lost Caroline. Nothing I could do was any use.' She looked up at me almost pleadingly. 'How is Mamgu?'

'She's fit and well,' I said quickly. 'She did not have cholera after all.'

'Thank God for that much, anyway.' My mother walked slowly into the kitchen as if every step was an effort, and I followed her anxiously. Dylan came down the stairs and took my mother in his arms, his cheek against her hair, and they stood wordlessly for a moment as I watched them.

'You did all that was humanly possible, my love,' he said gently. 'You need to sleep now. Let me give you some brandy; it will help to ease you.'

She nodded, completely subject to him in her despair and weariness, and she obediently drank the brandy before sinking down into a chair. Suddenly she began to cry.

'What can I do against the cholera? What can anyone do? It is ravaging the town, taking our family one by one, and soon there won't be anyone left.'

'There, there, *cariad*,' Dylan said soothingly. 'We have had a hard time of it, I'll grant you that, but we must keep our spirits up for those that are still with us.'

'I know, I know,' my mother said, 'but to lose loved ones is hard.'

I slipped out through the door without them even noticing me. I couldn't bear my mother's grief any longer. I knew how she had worked with all her strength and might in an effort to stave off the terrible sickness. It must be a bitter blow to lose Caroline as well as Lotty.

I walked away from the shop and down through the town towards the sea. The day was almost spent and the last dying rays of the sun were like blood staining the water. I was at my lowest ebb then, wondering if life was worth living.

'Self-pitying fool!' I said aloud, and I turned away from the sea, calmer in my mind, knowing that I would go back to Tip Row and be strong so long as Mamgu and Elizabeth needed me to be.

'Davy, boy!' Luther's voice called to me and I turned around to see him come plodding up the road behind me, a newspaper in his hand. 'I was just going to come to your grandmother's to see if you were there,' he said breathlessly. 'Look, boyo, there's good news in the *Cambrian*!'

'What is it?' I took the paper from him and read the part he was pointing to. 'The Public Health Act shall apply and be in force within the borough.' I looked at him. 'Does that mean we've won, Luther?'

'Well, boyo,' he said, chuckling, 'I think the Paving Commissioners are beaten, even though they're still raising a few squawks. See what it says, that there will be proper sewerage and water supplies for each home?'

He took the paper from me and looked down at it in satisfaction. 'Oh, yes, I think we will have cause to be proud, Davy, boyo, and to remember Friday, November the twenty-third, eighteen forty-nine as the date when the big truth was faced in Swansea that the poor parts of the town have got to be cleaned up.'

I sighed, feeling warmer. 'We have done something worthwhile, then, Luther. They won't go back on it, will they?'

'Oh, they'll twist and turn,' he said, 'and will still cling to their bit of power, but nothing can stop the Health Act now. It has got to come.' He grinned and punched my arm. 'And if there's any reminding to be done, I'm sure I can count on you to help me do it.'

As I left him and walked up the hill to Tip Row, I lifted up my face and looked at the gleaming particles of copper dust. My coming here had been providential because I had been able to help in some way to initiate improvements and benefits for the people I'd come to love.

As I reached the corner of the Row, I saw Elizabeth come towards me out of the shadows.

'I've been waiting for you to come home, Davy,' she said gently. Beneath her words was a wealth of meaning, almost a promise, and with a rush of love for her I took her hand and led her into the house and closed the door on Tip Row.

THE END

AUTHOR'S NOTE

By the efforts of the citizens of Swansea, a local Board of Health was brought into being in 1850 to deal with the water supplies and the sewerage of the town.

THE SHOEMAKER'S DAUGHTER
by Iris Gower

When Hari Morgan's father died, he left her nothing but an ailing mother and the tools of his shoemaking business. But what he also passed on to his daughter was a rare and unusual gift – that of designing and making shoes that were stylish and different. One of the first to realise this was Emily Grenfell, spoilt, pettish daughter of Thomas Grenfell, one of the richest men in Swansea. Emily, who resented the beauty and courage of Hari Morgan, nonetheless was delighted with the dancing slippers she made for her debut at the Race Ball, one of the grandest events of the year. It was to be the beginning of a lifetime of friendship, hatred and rivalry between the two girls for, as Hari's business and fame began to grow, so Emily's fortune began to decline.

And between the two girls lay an even deeper tension, for Emily was about to be betrothed to her cousin, Craig Grenfell, a man whom Hari could not help loving and wanting for herself, a man who finally betrayed her. From then on, Hari was determined that nothing and no-one would prevent her rise to a triumphant success.

The Shoemaker's Daughter is the first book in Iris Gower's enthralling new series, *The Cordwainers*.

0 552 13686 7

A SELECTED LIST OF FINE NOVELS
AVAILABLE FROM CORGI BOOKS

THE PRICES SHOWN BELOW WERE CORRECT AT THE TIME OF GOING
TO PRESS. HOWEVER TRANSWORLD PUBLISHERS RESERVE THE
RIGHT TO SHOW NEW RETAIL PRICES ON COVERS WHICH MAY DIFFER
FROM THOSE PREVIOUSLY ADVERTISED IN THE TEXT OR
ELSEWHERE.